The Stones of Souls

Amara Bea Glavin

ISBN: 978-1-7372455-8-2

For information address Kindle Direct Publishing.

Prologue:

May 10th, 2018

Summer was always the worst time of year for Enrique and Marcus, and it wasn't even officially summer yet. Their parents owned three food trucks that had the most popular fried ice cream in all of Miami. The lines to get these treats were always at least a few yards long, but they weren't opening for another week.

Now was the time for preparation; the trucks needed to be cleaned and repaired, the shelves needed to be filled, and the ingredients needed to be ordered. Enrique didn't hate this part as much as Marcus did. Enrique was an introvert. Talking to people was socially draining for him. On the other hand, Marcus, the elder of the two, was a social butterfly. Although, his laziness didn't serve him well in the food business.

Every year, Marcus's first complaint was, "I'm tired." Followed by, "I want my bed." And every year, Enrique came close to punching him in the face, but their parents had a special talent for calming them both down and making the job a little less painful. Usually, it involved their parents bribing Marcus to get him to do work. Buying him new basketballs and jerseys usually worked.

Their mom, Carla, always played their favorite music, and their dad, Roberto, always let them eat as much fried ice cream as they wanted to, even if it was during a shift. He would get mad only when they would take their breaks for more than one minute at a time.

It was Thursday, and Monday was the first day of opening for the Mendez Family Ice Cream Truck. Marcus and Enrique were stationed at truck number one, which was stored at their grandmother's house. Carla was at number two, and Roberto at truck three, which were both at their own house. The two brothers were given orders to make the truck spotless inside and out. It was the perfect day for it; not too hot or cold. A rare, but nice, breeze blew through the palm trees as they got out their cleaning supplies from the lower cabinets of the truck.

"Wanna take this for a spin later?" Marcus asked his little brother.

"Seriously, dude?" Enrique responded. "Abuela is literally right inside. She would know and then get us strangled later."

"She wouldn't strangle us."

Enrique cocked his head forward, smirked, and said, "I didn't say it would be Abuela. I meant it would be Mom."

"Oh yeah, she would do that."

Enrique wiped off a thin layer of sweat from his forehead with a rag and then proceeded to use the same rag to wipe off the dusty stove.

"We should at least take a break at some point," said Marcus. "I can't stand the stench around Abuela's house anyways."

Whenever Marcus had something to complain about, which was too often in Enrique's opinion, it was usually about something that Enrique could fix but didn't want to. Solely to annoy his brother more. Enrique usually wasn't up for working and talking to strangers, but he almost never complained, and if he did complain, it wasn't in front of other people.

"Okay, fine!" Enrique exclaimed. "But can we please just finish this up first? It's just gonna give me anxiety, and I don't wanna get yelled at because of you for the millionth time."

His tone shook Marcus and squeezed the ego out of him like a tube of toothpaste.

"Why are you trying to boss around your big brother?" Marcus asked, freezing so he no longer had to clean the counter.

"I'm not bossing you around. I'm just fed up, and I'm tired too, but you don't hear me whining about it every two seconds, especially when we just started!"

Marcus was significantly taller than Enrique and more muscular, but Enrique could never be afraid of his brother. Marcus only enjoyed acting tough. He had his moments, but everyone who knew him knew that he flinched at violence. But that didn't stop him from clenching his jaw and scrubbing the counter so hard the paint almost scraped off.

"What's going on out there?" they heard Abuela yell from inside the house.

"Nada Abuela! Lo siento!" Enrique shouted back. Abuela and Enrique had a special connection that always made Marcus squirm with jealousy, but he never wanted to admit it. "Can we just get back to work? I'm sorry."

"Yeah…Yeah me too," Marcus softly replied. Every apology he ever made in his life was accompanied by no eye contact and hunched shoulders. He wasn't good at apologizing, but he usually tried and usually meant it.

They proceeded to return to their duties, but moments later, the awkward silence was sliced down the middle when the back of the truck opened to reveal Abuela standing there with one hip cocked to the side and glaring eyes with a dropped chin.

"Please don't tell me you two are having a stupid fight again," she said.

"Sorry," said Enrique. "We're just tired. I think we need more of your famous iced coffee."

Marcus rolled his eyes but turned around and nodded his head at his grandmother.

"I wouldn't hate that," he said.

"Boys, it's almost dinner time," said Abuela.

"What's your point?" Enrique asked, popping his eyebrows.

Abuela laughed, brushed her long gray hair back, and said, "Oh, you boys keep me young. Fine, but just—"

She snapped her head around so fast, she almost fell over. There was something in the woods. She couldn't hear anything. In fact, the afternoon was still and calm. Not even the trees rustled in the absent wind, but she could smell something.

"What is it?" Marcus asked.

"I smell it too," said Enrique.

"Marcus," said Abuela. "Wait here. Close the doors. Enrique, come with me. I don't think we're alone."

Without any more questions, Enrique and Abuela raced out of the truck, and before Marcus could touch the doors, Enrique slammed them shut. Marcus stood there in bemusement. He wasn't shocked, but once again, the jealousy in the pit of his stomach weighed him down.

Abuela and Enrique didn't run towards the grove behind the house, but rather quickly walked while scanning their surroundings with their noses in the air.

"I can smell someone," said Abuela. There were a few palm trees behind her house that led to the beach. It was a dreary day, and it was hard to see. They passed through the grove and onto the beach, but they didn't take many steps out in the open.

"I don't think...I don't think they're alone," said Enrique. He could smell a man and a woman, and they were getting closer.

SNAP!

They whipped their heads back around to face the palm trees, but there was nothing there. Not a soul was in sight until they smelled something coming from behind them.

"There's nobody over there," said a man's voice coming from the sand. All of the breath was sucked from Enrique's lungs as he and Abuela turned to see a young man, no older than thirty, standing a few yards away from them. He had fire-orange-red hair down to his shoulders and wore a brown leather jacket, but it was his thick muscles that grabbed most of their attention.

"How would you know?" Abuela asked.

"I've been waiting for a few minutes. I had a look around. Just to make sure I wasn't about to...disrupt anyone." He took a few steps towards them. Naturally, Enrique took a few steps back, but Abuela confidently kept her feet planted.

"What do you want?" she asked.

"I'm sorry. I was told I'm not allowed to answer too many questions," the man responded.

"Who else is here? I know there's someone else here." Abuela hid her hands behind her back, hoping no one would see them shaking.

The man took a few more steps forward, but this time they were small and uneasy.

"You're afraid, aren't you?" Abuela asked. "You're new to this? Who exactly was it that sent you? Or were you the last hope?"

The man didn't deny it, but he didn't let her comments shake him. He stood with a purpose that was branded on his chest.

"It's really just...simple isn't it?" he asked. "I just need to know where it is. That's it. Nothing else will happen. Nothing else *has* to happen. Don't you see? That's just what we are trying to do."

"What makes you so cocky?" Enrique snarled. Abuela slapped his arm.

"Listen, you've got the wrong people," said Abuela.

"Oh, so you're new to this too?" the man asked. "Or else you would have said that like three minutes—"

And without any warning, Abuela lunged at him so viciously, he didn't have time to blink, but the moment she reached towards him, her arms were no longer made of skin and bone, but rather *fur* and bone, and it wasn't just her arms. It was her whole body. Suddenly, she was launching through the air not as a human, but as a large, black jaguar.

It was moments before the man or Enrique could fully process what was happening. Enrique snapped out of his amazement and ran two steps forward to join his grandmother before he felt a harsh and painful hand slap against his chest.

"Ah—ah—ah," said a woman's voice. "I'd leave this to them if I were you."

Enrique saw a young woman stand before him with pale skin and curly brown hair. The shadows under her jaw and cheekbones were darker than most women her age. But what grabbed Enrique's attention was the unusual scar across her face. It looked as if she had been burned diagonally across her forehead, over her right eye, and past her neck. But it was odd. The scar looked like it had healed better than most burn scars.

Enrique took one look at her hand grabbing onto his shirt, and instead of letting this woman see any fear, he let his eyes turn a shade of bright gold as he too took his jaguar form.

The woman's fists tightened, and beads of sweat materialized on the back of her neck. Enrique used every ounce of blood that his heart was pumping to tackle her to the ground. His paws slammed against her shoulders as they rolled against the sand.

"AHH!" the woman hollered as she felt thick claws stabbing into her skin. But in the blink of an eye, she used all of her strength to kick him off her.

The woman's strength was astounding and inhuman. Enrique was large and heavy as a jaguar, but he went flying into the air, with his claws leading him, and ungracefully landed a few yards away from her.

Enrique stood back up on all four paws as the woman stood up too. He could see his plan of attack before him, but before he could execute it, something caught the corner of his eye.

Enrique turned to see the red-haired man and Abuela carefully circling each other, but at the speed of sound, Abuela once again pounced on him and aimed directly toward his chest. This time she wasn't as lucky. With one arm, the man blocked Abuela's attack and, using her momentum, threw her twenty feet behind himself, across the beach, and into a palm tree. The moment her head smacked against the tree trunk, she transformed back into a human.

"NO!" Enrique roared. But before he could run to her rescue, the woman pulled a gleaming silver dagger out of nowhere and stabbed Enrique in his furry back. He fell to his knees, and his fur quickly returned to skin. He lay there across the beach still conscious as the pain continued to seep in.

The man took two steps towards Abuela's unconscious body, prepared to finish her off, before the woman stopped him.

"Clement, no!" she said. He stopped in his tracks, almost disappointed. "That's not what we're here for. Just leave them. They'll bleed out." She dropped her dagger and beckoned him to follow her.

While Enrique lay there, suffering and fighting his way to his unconscious grandmother, Clement and the woman quickly made their way over to the food truck. It was unlocked, but the woman dramatically ripped both doors wide open. There lay Marcus, squirming with his hands tied behind his back and duct tape over his mouth. Standing next to him was a dark-skinned man with long dreadlocks and glowing eyes. Strapped on his back was what looked like a bow, but only a few arrows.

"You said to keep him here, Kali," he said.

"Yes, thank you, Reymid," said Kali. She pulled herself up into the back of the truck, squatted down to the floor, and slowly ripped the duct tape from Marcus's cracked lips.

"Where's my family?" he shouted.

"Oh, don't be so dramatic. They're fine. And they will stay that way if you tell me where it is. And I would do it quickly if I were you. Reymid here...he gets quite eager."

Reymid gripped his bow tighter and exhaled deep from his gut.

"And what about you?" Marcus asked, without blinking.

"Marcus, look at where I am now."

Marcus hesitated for a moment, struggling to keep his focus steady. "Where's what?" he finally asked. The words tugged at his throat, but he hoped Kali wouldn't notice.

"Marcus...dear...I know you don't carry the family gene. Or at least that's what I was told, but your grandmother must have told you something. Did she really resent you that much to not show you?"

Marcus suddenly jolted his body, trying to attack her with his hands still behind his back, but with a single flick of her wrist and a small silver beam of light, Kali made another perfectly polished dagger appear before his eyes.

"As I said," Kali began, slowly and softly with the dagger pointed between his eyes, almost scraping the surface of his soft skin. "Your grandmother and brother will be fine if you just tell me where it is."

Marcus took a few more short breaths while feeling his heart pounding through his chest before he looked her in the eyes and said, "The manhole under the truck. It will lead you there, but it's pointless."

"And why should we believe that?" Clement asked.

"You'll just have to see."

Marcus could see the impatience and anger rumbling and expanding in Kali's throat and eyes.

"Clement, move the truck. Reymid, prepare your bow and arrow. You're going down there."

Clement did as he was told. He quickly jumped out of the back, and moved the food truck forward with only one arm and with the other three still in it. The wheels didn't need to turn. They scraped across the driveway instead. The rubber burned against the pavement. Marcus had never seen such strength before. He'd only ever heard about it from his grandmother.

Clement kept pushing until the manhole was completely uncovered.

"Of course," Kali laughed, as she jumped out of the truck. "Why would a manhole be in someone's driveway? How daft can you be?"

Reymid removed his bow and one of his golden arrows from his back as Clement removed the manhole cover for him. He leaned down over Marcus and cut the tip of the arrow across Marcus's arm.

"Ah!" Marcus squirmed.

Reymid brought the tip of his arrow right in front of Marcus's eyes to show him the fresh blood dripping from it. He sharply nodded his head to Kali, and with aggressive intent, Reymid dug his palms onto each side of the manhole and slid his wide legs through the small opening. He still couldn't see how deep it was, but he took the chance anyway and vigorously landed a few yards down on the rocky floor.

It was dark, but it didn't disable him from almost immediately finding the second entrance to what Abuela was hiding. As he focused his eyes on a circular, metal door, he carefully walked towards it and held the bloody arrow out in front of himself. When the arrow was held only a few feet away from the door, Reymid heard a small click and an even smaller sizzle of light before it slowly swung open.

He cracked a relieved, yet cocky smile as he continued his way forward before he stopped in his tracks and dropped his jaw and arrow as the cave smothered in ice revealed the last thing that he wanted to see.

"Can I please call an ambulance now?" Marcus begged, back in the truck.

Kali rolled her eyes and said, "Just a few more—"

"Kali!" Reymid exclaimed as he pulled himself back up through the hole.

"What?" she snapped.

He was almost hesitant to respond, but after a deep breath, he said, "There's nothing there. It's all been removed."

Kali stood there, frozen with rage. Her fingertips trembled as she fought with everything she had to not let the anger make a home in her blood.

She turned towards Marcus who was now smirking and laughing on the floor.

"Well," she said. "A deal's a deal."

Kali saw a phone lying on the counter and snatched it up before she dialed 9-1-1.

"Hello?" Kali cried as she performed. "There are two people on Point Pleasant Beach. One is bleeding and the other is unconscious. An older woman and a teenage boy. Please hurry!" She removed her dramatic and fake crying face as she hung up the phone and slammed it back down on the counter.

"What shall we do with him?" Clement asked.

"Just leave him here. He'll figure out how to get out, but not in time to follow us."

1:

"Lexi, I told you, the door is always unlocked."

Asher Rodriguez was getting tired of seeing stars while drifting off. The doctor said that it was normal, but he didn't believe them. The abstract art that stood as the wallpaper of his mind looked like it was about to suck him into a black hole. The stars were growing brighter yet the night was growing darker, or more so, it was losing color.

"H...H..."

At this point in his dreams, he couldn't talk, but he knew he would be able to at some point. Whether it was sooner or later, he never knew.

The room spun. Was it a room? Sometimes he could see figures or locations or whatever it was his subconscious was trying to tell him. Something white materialized as his gaze spun along with the room. It reminded him of a milk frother. Maybe it was another star, but if it was, it would be an awfully large star, and one that was growing at a rapid speed.

"K..."

His eyes finally remained still and locked on this white light, but soon it was no light at all. Its essence burst into dust that scattered across the space and wrapped around Asher's body.

The Sandman is coming for me, Asher thought.

His eyes were forced shut as he was swept up, but when he reopened them, he was somewhere else. And it was cold.

"Shani?" he called out for his best friend. The visuals were flawless. He stood in the cold, glowing ice cave. The same ice cave that he was trapped in eight months prior, but it was colder than he remembered. The ice was also stickier. He couldn't move his feet, or maybe that was due to his dream.

"Shani?" he called out again. Only this time, it worked.

Before him stood Shani, Brex, Logan, and Lexi. He remembered this event. All too well. All five of them had entered the cave just moments before, and in this cave was a toxic essence that was about to explode, forcing magic upon them. This was how Asher was able to fly, how Shani was able to stop a river, how Logan was able to electrify an entire bus, how Brex could torch the White House (only if she wanted to), and how Lexi could create a tropical rainforest in her living room. This was their life. They were alchelarcenists. The ones who accidentally stole the abilities of the Greek Gods.

"Guys?" Asher asked. Something was wrong. They were like zombies, even Asher. Their movement was minimal, and their breathing was slow. It was almost a perfect reenactment of the previous year. Only with less color.

"Wait!"

Three...two...one...*BOOM!*

Out of nowhere, a green explosion blinded Asher, burying him in a dark hole. But by the time he reopened his eyes, he was somewhere new.

"Ow, Brex!" he said without realizing it.

The scars that were burned into the rough skin on their left palms glowed as they grabbed each other's hands. Asher was flown into the air before his wings crashed into the crumbling ceiling.

Pieces of the flaky, white ceiling fell like snow. One by one, they slowly descended until another whirlwind pulled Asher into a different memory.

Whatever vehicle was racing against the speed of light, it was hard to see, but it didn't take long for Asher to realize which vehicle it was.

"Lexi!"

Lexi and Shani lay there on a gurney inside a stuffy, yet open-doored ambulance. Moments before Lexi and Shani had fallen off a bridge after an attack. Someone was trying to steal their magic. But due to witnesses, ambulances were immediately called, and they had some questions.

"Asher!" he heard Shani call. He had to remind himself that it was only a dream and that being crushed between the door and the outside of the ambulance wasn't inflicting real pain; he was only remembering it.

Lexi was only hurt for a few moments after they fell. That's how their magic worked. Pain was only in the eyes of whoever gave them these unique abilities. But getting her and Shani out of the ambulance to protect their identity was harder than they had thought. Asher questioned his strength. Was he strong enough to save them? A few small muscles were pulled by the time Lexi and Shani grabbed onto Asher before they jumped out, but it was nothing compared to the endless rolling along the jagged pavement on the Boston highway.

His white wings covered his face and theirs, but the bright, white color soon morphed into a void that carried him to the mountains of New Hampshire, where Lexi was captured. Only this time, she was in real danger.

"Lexi?" Shani said, hoping Lexi would wake up from the enchanted coma.

Asher could remember it all too well. Lexi's skin had a faint, green tint to her skin from floating in the magic-draining liquid for so long. Asher's wings were sore from fighting against another attack on their drive over there. But he had to get Lexi out of there. She was drowning, and losing her powers.

"I got her!"

Asher flew above Lexi's unconscious body to pull her out while Shani pushed as much of the liquid away as she could. The memory of Shani's red cheeks illuminating her dark skin was tattooed on Asher's mind.

One last tornado of an image sucked Asher into a mysterious vortex. Only this time, he knew what was coming. The unmistakable feeling of purity and clarity announced its presence. This was no memory. This was a recurring dream that probably wasn't a dream at all, but Asher had yet to figure that out.

The small room was covered in a shade of glistening blue as Asher Rodriguez stood in front of his floor-length mirror. The walls, his bed, the floors, all had a blue pigmentation to them; all but the mirror. The image in the rectangular mirror was lined with clouds, or at least what looked like clouds. It was foggy, metaphorically and literally. That was because Asher was dreaming. He knew this wasn't real. He knew he wasn't awake.

This wasn't the first dream that he had that was like this. No. The first one was back in September. Now, in the middle of May, his dream count was up to eleven. He kept a detailed diary of everything he could remember, but this dream didn't have a lot of details for him to record.

A tall, lean woman, with pale, aging skin and long dark hair with gray streaks sat in a dark corner, crouching down in her blue satin dress. She was shivering, but Asher had to take a few steps closer to the mirror to see why. She held her right arm between her knees and kept her right fingertips in a clenched fist. Asher could see blood dripping from her forearm. If he squinted his eyes, he could see cuts and old scars that seemed to go from her elbow to her wrist. Someone had been piercing and slicing her skin for a long time, and it probably wasn't her.

Asher couldn't see anybody else in the mirror. Just the woman crouching in pain, trying to mend herself with the occasional green smoke that surrounded her. He had yet to find out where that was coming from. But the first time he saw this woman in his dreams, he learned three things; 1) What she looked like, 2) Someone was keeping her hostage, and 3) She had another identity, as a snake. A white, red-eyed snake who had fangs that somehow grew three times their normal size whenever she opened her mouth.

Over time, Asher's dreams became more clear and more controllable. At first, like any normal dream, it was hard for him to move throughout the space in his room and be able to speak out loud. Now, he could feel and control his body. Every inch of his room and the mirror was in high definition. The only difference was speaking. Nobody could hear what he was saying through the mirror, and there was never anybody else in the room with him.

After a few minutes of waiting for something else to happen, nothing else happened. The poor woman stayed there, aching in pain. She wasn't dying, just hurt, and there were no bandages on her to heal her wounds. Every time he saw this woman, she was in trouble, and Asher was desperate to help. But after a few times, he came to the conclusion that there was nothing he could do. Especially since he would see her again. Even if it was an unfortunate event, she always came back, and most of Asher's dreams consisted of her.

Enough of this, he thought. He didn't enjoy seeing her in pain, and nothing else was going to happen. He was hoping to see somebody else walk through this dream, and maybe it would give him a clue as to where she was or why he was having these dreams, but he hadn't worked that out yet.

He closed his eyes and reopened them to see his ceiling and feel the soft, fuzzy sheets between his legs and fingertips. He hoped one day that he would be able to control when he had the dreams. So far, all he'd learned was how to control himself and how to get out of the dreams, but that was it. If he wanted to see someone specific through the mirror, he couldn't.

With a deep breath, he reached his hands over his head and stretched like a panther while lying between his messy sheets. He had forgotten to close his blinds the night before, and the sun shone exceptionally bright. He rubbed his eyes, hoping they would adjust, and reached for his dream journal. He always kept it underneath his bed.

"It was the woman in the blue dress again," he read aloud as he was writing. "She has more cuts on her arms this time. And the other ones haven't healed yet, and it's been a while. I'm thinking that she's being tortured for information. Though I should add, I'm still not sure if these are currently happening or if they're memories."

Knock, knock, knock, he heard on his bedroom door as he tucked the journal under his pillow.

He knew it was his roommate and best friend, Shani Simons, but he thought it would be funny to say, "Who is it?"

"Not your best joke," said Shani as she opened the door, entered the room, and walked to his bed. Her hair was freshly cornrowed with new beads that reflected beautifully against her dark hair and dark skin. Tomorrow was a big day for them.

"Ready for graduation?" Asher asked her.

"Um, yeah! You?"

Before he could answer, he noticed that she was holding her hands behind her back, or holding something *in* her hands behind her back.

"What are you hiding?" Asher asked.

"Well..." She whipped out what looked like a wrapped gift from behind her and held it out in front of her.

"Oh, no. Shani, we said we weren't going to do presents, and I didn't get you anything—"

"No, no, no! Listen to me!" She wagged her finger in his face. "I might have wrapped it like a present, but it's not. It's just something that you need." She slammed the gift down on his lap.

"So, it looks like a present, and acts like a present, but it isn't a present?"

"Correct." Shani stood by his bedside like a drill sergeant. Her shoulders were back, her chin was lifted, and her feet were glued together. She sometimes stood that way when she grew impatient.

"Okay," said Asher as he took the non-present and unwrapped it. It had sparkly red paper that Shani probably took from the leftover Christmas wrapping paper.

"Oh...wow!" Asher laughed and gasped simultaneously as he unfolded the black, leathery, but athletic, long-sleeved t-shirt that had two velcroed slits in the upper back. He guessed that they were for his pearly white wings that sprouted when he wanted to fly, even though he hadn't in months.

"Have I ever told you how brilliant and awesome you are?" Asher asked her.

"You know for almost two decades of friendship, you'd think you would say that more often."

They both laughed as Asher hugged her and gave her a kiss on the cheek.

"You know what?" said Asher. "I'm going to get you something that you need too. I don't know what it is yet, but I'm going to. You deserve it, Miss Top Twenty Students."

Shani blushed, pondered for a moment, and cracked a proud smile.

"Yeah, I do, don't I?" she said. "Hey, wait! Don't you have that interview today?"

"Yeah, it's tonight." Asher immediately started nervously fiddling with his fingers. "Hopefully, it goes better than the last one."

The last interview Asher had was a month before when he accidentally jabbed his hand into the interviewer's crotch while going for a handshake. Instead of ignoring it, or apologizing normally, Asher tried to lighten the tension by saying, "Sorry, you know us gay men." The man was nice enough to let him finish the interview, but after the uncomfortable joke, Asher would have preferred the man to be rude, so at least he could have some of the attention drawn away from him.

"Just move slowly, okay?" Shani joked.

"You sure you wanna take a gap year before grad school?" Asher asked. "You know who you are, right? You could multitask with a job, school, and adventures with no problem."

Shani dramatically exhaled and said, "Asher we've talked about this. I just don't feel like it's the right thing to do right now. I can't help but sense that something is going to happen, and it'll just be the wrong time for everything. I just...I don't know."

Asher defensively put his hands in the air. He was used to stressing Shani out, but he always tried to apologize for doing it.

"I'm sorry," he said. "I don't mean to keep bugging you about it. And besides, it's not like you're ever going to have to worry about academics. You'll probably get into every grad school you apply to when you do."

"God, I hope you're right. But for the next thirty-six hours, I just wanna have a good graduation and enjoy my time left in college."

Asher smiled and nodded in agreement.

"Breakfast?" he asked. "I know we are definitely going to be drinking tonight, so we should probably fill our tum tums as much as we can."

"Already way ahead of you," Shani laughed. "I have pancakes and fresh fruit with mimosas on the coffee table. Also, I have our favorite episode of *Friends* waiting for you to play."

All of a sudden, Asher felt a rush of sadness. He could see Shani was happy, but a touch of blue shimmered within her eyes. They'd been friends for so long and lived together all throughout college. Now their college careers were coming to an end, and they were both moving back in with their parents on Sunday. The end was right in front of them.

"Hey," he said, grabbing her hand. "Thank you. I love you, you know that? I'm gonna miss living with you too."

Tears swelled in Shani's eyes, but she didn't let them fall. She knew she had to wait until tomorrow.

"I love you too," she said. "I'm sorry. It's not even our last night here, and I'm already getting sentimental."

"Yeah, come on," said Asher as he stood up and dragged Shani by her hand out of his room. "Let's save the tears for tomorrow and go eat some pancakes that you probably burnt." Shani didn't correct him. "Have you talked to Logan recently? I know he was...well, you know...not doing so hot."

"Not in a few days, but I know. He's been depressed ever since football ended, and he's certainly not ready to say goodbye to the fraternity. He also misses using his powers. I mean, can you imagine how much adrenaline that kid must have had with that much electricity running through him?"

Before Asher could answer, he stood before a thick stack of mostly dark brown pancakes with strawberries, blueberries, and blackberries on top. And right next to the plate was a cup of his favorite iced coffee from the shop down the street.

"Okay, now you're just trying to outdo me," Asher joked.

"Oh, honey. I'm always going to outdo you." They eagerly sat down to eat.

"You know, we should have the rest of the gang over tomorrow tonight," said Asher, stuffing his face.

"Yeah! We can invite Jenna and Adam too. You know, if you want. Logan is having something at the frat house, but maybe it'll be nice to have a small group here."

Asher looked down at his plate of food and mumbled, "Yeah, yeah."

"Are those the only friends we have now?" Shani laughed before sipping her iced coffee.

"Uhh...well, yeah. Maybe graduating will be a good thing."

*****

A few miles away, in the town of Somerville, there was a professional photography studio. It was also a one-bedroom apartment, with the name, "Eversee Photography." It was a play on the owner's name, Brex Everly. Over the past few months, she had developed a small but successful business. Most of her clients were young actors wanting professional headshots, but today, she had a couple with a newborn baby.

Brex wasn't a big fan of babies, but Greyson was a cute one. His parents, Mr. and Mrs. Veroni, dressed him up in both blue and pink just in case he grew up to be a fan of both colors.

"Smile big, Greyson," said Brex in her highest-pitched voice. "This one's definitely going to be shown the first time you bring a date home."

The couple laughed, but Greyson started crying. Brex couldn't help but giggle at his reaction.

"Oh, come on," his mother said. "You were doing so good." She picked him up and rocked him back and forth.

"Sorry," said Brex. "Not everyone thinks I'm funny."

"Oh, it's okay," Mr. Veroni laughed. "He usually only cries for a minute or two at a time."

"No rush at all. You guys are my last appointment for the day."

After a few moments, he abruptly stopped crying. Brex snapped a few candids with his mouth open and drooling before he started to cry again.

"You three are going to love the pictures from outside," said Brex. "The clouds and lighting were perfect today."

"Hopefully, we got a few without Ryan's face all scrunched up," Mrs. Veroni teased.

"Oh, I doubt it," Brex responded.

Knock, knock, knock, Brex heard.

"It's open!" she shouted, and in walked an exhausted and stressed-out Logan Kwan.

"Hey! Mr. and Mrs. Veroni, this is my graphic designer, Logan. If you ever need anything advertised for your antique shop, Logan is your guy."

"Oh, perfect," said Mrs. Veroni. "We probably will. Do you have a card?"

"Oh, yes," said Logan, searching his pockets. "Um, I should...somewhere." Besides his keys, wallet, and phone, his pockets were empty.

He checked in his wallet to see if there were any there, but before he could find anything, Brex chimed in.

"Here, I have a few," she said. Brex opened the drawer to her desk and handed Mrs. Veroni two of his business cards.

"Amazing. Thank you so much. Brex, you have my check, right?" Mrs. Veroni asked as she prepared Greyson's stroller.

"Yes! You should be getting those photos in two weeks."

"Great," said Mr. Veroni. "Thanks again, Brex. And nice to meet you." He turned to Logan and shook his hand as the family walked out the door.

"Did you just wake up?" Brex asked.

"Kind of. How'd you know?" said Logan with his airy voice.

"Your hair isn't done yet. You usually put clay in it, right?"

"Yeah, yeah, yeah. Do you have those photos ready for the museum?"

"Yup. You wanna just use my computer?"

Logan nodded and walked over to behind her desk where her large Apple desktop was.

"When do you start working for your dad?" Brex asked.

"Tonight."

Brex snapped her head in amazement. She hadn't realized he would be working at a job he was going to hate before he even graduated. "Well, today is only the orientation," Logan added, "but of course, I'm not getting paid for it."

Brex couldn't hold back from shifting the conversation. Word vomit was hard to withhold.

"Do you need help packing up the frat house?" she asked.

"Nah, Adam's parents hired a few people to help. It was his graduation present." Logan quietly laughed, even though he was being serious. It was the first time Brex saw him smile since he had arrived. "I like your hair. Have I told you that yet?"

The previous week, Brex impulsively decided to cut her hair to her collarbones and put blue streaks in it. For so long, Brex had long black hair, but her new vibrancy inspired her.

"You haven't yet, but thank you," she responded, smiling, looking over his shoulder to avoid making eye contact with him.

There was a moment between them that made Logan feel jubilant but envious. He was happy to see Brex strongly fighting the terror of losing her family, but his depression was getting worse, and he wasn't looking forward to his own college graduation the next day. But ever since he'd known Brex, the feeling of latching onto something, anything, was worth the effort. He had something to fight for.

"Hey," he said as he turned his chair to face her. Brex could see that an intense moment was about to transpire. "I'm proud of everything you've done in the past couple of months. The growth of this place has been insane, and I know studio photography wasn't your first choice, and you'd rather be back in the mountains, but I'm really happy that you're happy. And just...thank you for putting up with me, I guess. I don't ever want you to think that I'm ever trying to make this all about me 'cause it's not. But...yeah, I'm sorry if you feel like I'm ever a burden on you. I know it's a lot of work dealing with such low energy all the time. It can't always be fun having me as a business partner."

Brex took a moment before she responded. Vulnerability was still foreign to her in a way, and she knew Logan was no different.

"You could never, ever be a burden on me. Everyone is kinda worried about you, ya know?" she said. "Especially me. You have every reason to feel low right now, and I'm never gonna give you grief for it."

Logan was used to her compassion, but at the same time, it never grew old. He smiled and gave her a gentle, "Thank you."

Before either of them could say anything else, they both heard a loud *Knock, Knock* on the front door, while someone simultaneously said the words, "Knock, knock." They both knew who it was.

"Lexi, I told you, the door is always unlocked," Brex yelled.

A short, blonde, curly-haired girl slowly opened the front door and walked through before she said, "I know, but it's your apartment too. I feel weird." As she saw Brex and Logan facing each other, she couldn't help but wonder what she interrupted. "What are you guys up to?"

"Logan's working on your new poster," said Brex.

"Yeah, but it's gonna take me a while," Logan added, with his face locked on the screen. "I just started. You should have it by sometime tomorrow. I have to go work at my dad's office later."

"That's tonight?" Lexi asked. "Already?" She knew how much Logan was dreading working for his dad. She couldn't tell if he didn't want to talk about it or if he wanted to start ranting about it.

"Yeah." He barely took his eyes off the screen. His voice tugged at his throat, and it didn't go unnoticed by Lexi or Brex. Lexi had her answer. Suddenly, Logan felt a vibration in his pocket and pulled out his phone. "Ah, speak of the devil." He shook his phone in front of Brex and Lexi, showing that it read, "Dad."

"Hey, Dad," said Logan, answering the phone, trying to not sound annoyed.

"Hey, Son," Mr. Kwan said on the other side. "Are you busy right now?"

"Uh, yeah. I have to finish a poster for tomorrow."

"Oh, great! Then you can work on it tomorrow. Shouldn't take you too long, right? I'm actually going to need you at the office a little earlier tonight. As in about a half an hour."

The carefree tone in Mr. Kwan's voice annoyed Logan more.

"Are you kidding me?" Logan snapped. "It takes me a half an hour to get to your office from Brex's."

"Oh. Well...sorry," said Mr. Kwan, quietly and defensively. He wasn't used to Logan being this moody. "I really need some help though, so just get here as soon as you can. Okay? Bye." And without letting Logan bid his father adieu, Mr. Kwan hung up.

"Unbelievable." Logan bolted up from his chair and ran his hands over his face. "Lexi, I'm sorry. I don't know when the hell I'm gonna get this done. I might just have to half-ass it."

"That's totally fine," said Lexi, shaking her head. "Your half-assed designs are still better than anyone else's in Boston. And I'll still pay you guys in full. Don't worry."

"Yeah," Logan mumbled and lethargically stood up from his chair. "I'll see you guys later." Logan grabbed his phone and keys and walked out the door.

"Has Mr. Kwan ever heard of the words 'boundaries' or 'overbearing'?" Lexi asked.

"He probably just thinks those words don't apply to him," Brex responded. "I think we just gotta let Logan be sad and let him adjust. His dad's firm will be fine in a couple of months. Logan won't need to be there forever."

*****

Logan blasted his headphones at top volume the second he stepped foot on the train. It was his method of blocking out the noise of the city. It was also the only way he could put his brain into a neutral mood before he went to his dad's office. He didn't try to stay positive; he tried to stay numb.

He slowly stepped off the train, trying to take his time as he made his way to his first day of training. He wasn't getting paid for the training, and it was his dad who was leading him throughout the summer. If he was late, he did not care.

As he pulled the door open to the staircase that led to the office, he noticed an unpleasant smell that had worsened since the last time he was there. It made sense. They had to let their porter go a few months prior for budgeting reasons. Nonetheless, he kept his mind neutral from any tension or external distractions.

"Hey, Logan!" said Gina the moment he opened the office door. Gina was Mr. Kwan's assistant. She was short, no older than thirty years old, and wore a small red bindi on her forehead that complimented her dark eyebrows. She had a voice that was louder and brighter than the average human's. It made Logan jump every time he heard it.

"Hey," Logan politely replied. "Where's my dad?"

"He's in a meeting! He should be out in just a few minutes."

Without saying anything, he nodded his head and slowly walked over to the chair he always impatiently sat in whenever he needed to wait for his father.

A few minutes went by, and Mr. Kwan was still in his meeting. Logan didn't mind. If part of his job for the day was waiting and sitting, he wasn't about to argue.

"Well, we will be in touch. Won't we?" Logan heard an unfamiliar voice say. He peered around the corner to see a tall, thin man shaking his father's hand.

"Yes, yes, we will," said Mr. Kwan. Logan could see in his father's eyes that he was clutched and distressed as the thin man walked past Logan and out the door.

Logan stood up from his chair to make his presence clear to his father. Without saying anything, Mr. Kwan smiled at his son with trouble tucked in his eyes.

"Hey, Dad." Logan slowly and cautiously walked closer to his father. "What, um...What was that about?"

Mr. Kwan took a long, staggered breath while looking at the floor before he finally spoke. "Oh, it's just my accountant," he said. "We were just talking about the um...the second mortgage...on the office space."

Logan knew next to nothing about money or banks, but he knew enough to know the term "second mortgage" was never good.

"Should I ask what it's about?" Logan asked while awkwardly scratching the back of his neck. "Wait," he suddenly stopped and briefly closed his eyes. "You don't....you don't have to answer that, Dad. I don't wanna be nosy."

Mr. Kwan felt a sliver of relief sprout within him as he heard those words. He pulled his shoulders down and away from his ears and lifted his cheekbones to his eyes. The last thing that he wanted to discuss was his financial troubles, especially with the one person he had to take care of.

"Thank you, Logan," he said as he relished a long exhale.

"Dad, I'm sorry if you've felt like I was being a brat, but I'm going to help you. I promise. Everything is going to be fine. You will always have me."

*****

Asher walked as fast as he could to his interview, even though he was going to be a half an hour early at the rate he was walking. He wore the only suit that he felt confident in. It was navy blue and didn't have any buttons, which in his mind, made it dapper, and just the right amount of casual.

As he kept walking, he started to feel self-conscious about everything he was doing. He noticed that his feet were scuffing across the ground as he walked, so he stiffly and gracelessly picked up his feet higher as if he were stepping over puddle after puddle.

"Stop being ridiculous," he whispered to himself. Then all of a sudden, the worst hypothetical scenario crossed his mind. "Oh, shit." What if the makeup over his hand were to come off during the interview? What if it was already off?

Without hesitation, he whipped his left hand to his face. The makeup was perfect, but he couldn't help but picture what the interviewers would think if they saw his black, circular scar under the prosthetic skin. This was something that he did often. Full-length feature films would play in his head of scenarios that never happened, and most likely never would. But the pause button was broken, and he didn't know how to fix it.

Finally, he reached the building. Before entering, he quadruple-checked that he had the correct address. He did. Then he went through the rest of his list that he had memorized. "Shirt tucked? Phone off?....And uh...Oh yeah, resume. Got it."

With a lifted chest and a partially-plastered smile, he walked up the stairs and into the building. The moment he opened the door, he could smell the strong scent of floor cleaner. He turned his attention to the left to see a small hallway with a short and skinny janitor in the shadows.

"And can you switch my appointment with Karev to twelve tomorrow?" Asher heard a voice coming from the stairs. He could also hear footsteps walking down the staircase.

"Of course, Mr. Peters," another voice said.

Mr. Peters.

He was the one who would be interviewing Asher. This was it. He had to make the perfect first impression. Out of all the jobs for which he had applied for in the past few months, this was the one he wanted the most. It was a convenient and ideal location in Southie with great opportunities to grow in the company, and he would be helping people with their mental health. It was perfect.

After checking his casual suit, he stood up straight and pulled his shoulders down, trying to make his neck look longer and more established. Asher waited for Mr. Peters to notice him first before he said anything. When that time came, the look on Mr. Peters' face wasn't exactly what Asher was expecting.

"Hello?" Mr. Peters said. "Can I help you with anything?"

Asher tried not to overthink Mr. Peters' confusion. He was probably just a busy man with a busy schedule and a busy mind.

"Oh, hello," Asher's voice cracked slightly, but he pushed to continue anyway. "I'm Asher Rodriguez. I'm here for the interview. I think I'm a little early, my apologies." He let out a subtle, yet unconfident laugh, but he couldn't stop overthinking the lame phrase 'my apologies' that he had just blurted out.

"Oh, my goodness, Asher. Yes!" said Mr. Peters with welcoming elation. He reached out and firmly shook Asher's hand. "Asher, oh no. I'm so embarrassed. I'm so sorry to tell you the position has already been filled."

Without recognizing it, Asher accidentally left a long, awkward pause between them before he said, "Oh. Um...I'm so sorry. I didn't know. Did someone send me an email?"

"Oh, no, no, no. I don't believe we did. This is my fault—"

Mr. Peters continued to talk, but Asher was too embarrassed and disappointed to listen to what he had to say. His voice faded out and blurred into the background.

2:

"Enough time to find Logan?"

Every hotel in Boston was booked for graduation day. Not only was it a special day for Boston University, but Sussex and Boston College were also celebrating their graduations. People were considering taking out loans; the hotels were so expensive.

Brex lay on her studio apartment bed, trying to get at least a few hours of sleep before she would go to see her closest friends graduate.

"Ahhhhrr," she whimpered to herself while scraping her fingertips across her face. Over the past few months, her mental health had almost exceeded her standards. She was doing well. More importantly, she was growing, but she couldn't stop pondering the idea of what could have happened if she had graduated. Would her business be stronger? Would she have better opportunities in the future? But the worst thought that refused to escape her mind: Would her parents, and her little brother, be proud of her if they were here and survived the shooting?

"Dude, shut up," she whispered to herself. The time was twelve minutes to eight in the morning. The ceremony would begin at eleven, and she promised Shani, Logan, Asher, Adam, and Jenna that she would take pictures of them beforehand, so their families wouldn't make a fuss about it afterward.

After a long, closed-eyed inhale of the warm spring air, Brex threw the sheets off her body and clumsily stood up.

Her two batteries were charged, her lenses were clean, and her SD card had a clear memory. After she put on the only dress that she owned, she looked in the mirror, not knowing what she expected to see, shrugged her shoulders, and headed out the door.

On the other side of town, Logan paced around his room, unable to sleep the previous night. Instead, he continued to frantically pack his room at the frat house. Everything was already, for the most part, packed, but he wasn't sure how else to pass the time. Therefore, he proceeded to repeatedly scrub each corner of the room and windows of any spec of dust.

"Logan!" Logan heard his frat brother, Kerry, shout as he knocked on the door.

"Yep? Come in!"

Kerry slowly opened the door, wondering at what point he was going to regret it.

"Bro," Kerry started, "Did you sleep at all last night?"

Before he could answer, he had an odd sort of flashback to the evening before during the dispute with his father. All of the yelling filled him with anxiety and caused his chest and fingertips to stiffen.

"Honestly, I don't even know," Logan answered. His voice felt scratchy and low. Not because of any illness, but because it struggled to be heard.

"Okay, well the rest of us are going to leave in an hour or so. And we're gonna take pictures here first." Kerry wasn't sure if he was supposed to wait for a response or just leave after notifying Logan of the plan. He stood still for a moment before he started to silently and slowly close Logan's door.

"A'ight," Logan mumbled when there was only a sliver of Kerry left to be seen through the crack of his door.

This feeling was all too recognizable. He knew that when he arrived at the ceremony, he would feel better, but for now, his body wasn't responding positively. He felt as though even if he did want to get up, his limbs wouldn't let him. But after he pulled his shoulders away from his neck and took a few deep breaths, he looked out the window and absorbed some sunlight onto his face, he managed to slowly pull his body up to a standing position. He kicked the anxiety behind him along with the dust on his floor, but just like the dust, his anxiety floated about him.

Logan wasn't sure his father was still coming to his graduation. Maybe he was overreacting, but he rarely ever had an impatient attitude in front of his father.

After he dragged himself into the shower and put on his suit and gown, he stared at himself in the mirror. He noticed the flaws in his skin and the circles under his eyes, but instead of letting the dreadful light of day push him back to bed, he forced a fake smile, threw on his cap, and headed out the door.

Shani and Asher were some of the few students in the senior class who genuinely wanted to graduate, but for different reasons. Shani was ready to work full-time instead of being in class all day long, but Asher was just ready to not be in class all day long.

"Almost ready!" Shani yelled from inside the bathroom.

"You've said that three times in the past half hour," said Asher, leaning up against the doorway with his arms crossed.

"Hey, did you ever figure out if your mom is coming?" Shani asked.

"She is, but I think she's only coming because Pablo begged her. You know where your dads are sitting? They'll probably wanna sit with my dad."

"Yeah, I think they're—," but before Shani could finish her sentence, they both heard their front door slam open.

"Sorry! That was a little aggressive," Lexi hollered. She was more dressed up than usual. Her curly blonde hair was half up, half down, and she wore her classiest, flowy white shirt. Along with her fancy apparel, she carried in a few bags full of what looked like Christmas presents for an entire orphanage.

"Hey! Whatcha got there?" Asher asked.

"Well, they were supposed to be surprise presents, but I've been behind ever since I picked up more shifts at the cafe. So, my bad." Lexi scrambled to put all of her bags on top of the futon.

"Lex, this is a lot. You really didn't need to do all of this."

"What did she do now?" Shani yelled as she walked out of the bathroom. "Whoa." The moment she stepped into the living room, a few of the bags rolled off the futon, but Lexi picked them up before the other bags followed.

"Geez, how big of a raise did you get?" Shani asked.

"Well, you know, I'm really persuasive. How you guys feeling? You ready?"

Both Asher and Shani nodded their heads, but with pensive eyebrows that looked like they had already made a home.

"What?" Lexi asked. "What's up with the awkward poses?"

Asher and Shani looked at each other, surprised that they reflected one another.

"I don't know," said Shani. "I mean, you guys know I've been waiting for this, but something feels off. You know? I kinda feel like we're just missing something that's right in front of us, but I can't point out what it is. But it might be dangerous."

"That's kinda how I've been feeling too," Asher added. "It's just.. .weird."

"Well, don't let anything ruin your special day," said Lexi, pulling out her phone. "Whatever is off, we can deal with it afterwards. But now is picture time. Get your caps and gowns!"

Asher laughed and said, "Isn't that supposed to be Brex's job?"

"Well, Brex is not here, and come on. I just wanted to capture a moment with just us three."

Asher and Shani awkwardly fumbled to get their caps and gowns. Lexi tried her best to be patient with them, but she couldn't stop herself from saying, "You got it?" three times before they finally came out with their caps and gowns on, as ready as they'd ever be to get their picture taken.

Shani didn't have shoes on, but she didn't care. They were inside. It didn't matter. Asher didn't have the glasses that he was going to use for the ceremony, but it also didn't matter. His round brown pair looked presentable.

"Say 'cheese'!" said Lexi.

"No," Asher and Shani said simultaneously. Lexi frowned but took the picture anyway.

Lexi admired the finished product while Shani and Asher broke from their pose and continued to get ready. They figured the picture was fine. They were going to have to do it all again with Brex when they got to the ceremony anyway.

"Hey, um. Asher, how did that interview go?" Lexi asked.

Shani's eyes privately widened as she waited for Asher to answer the question.

"They already filled the spot when I got there," Asher uncomfortably laughed. Shani could feel the tension in his tone, swinging around, pulling in different directions, but she was grateful he fully answered the question instead of shoving it off like he did the day before.

"What?" Lexi exclaimed. "And they didn't call you before to let you know?"

"No," Asher shrugged.

"Well did you tell them off? That's so rude."

Asher started to get an uncomfortable twitch in his neck, but he shook it off. He didn't want to let this bother him anymore. It truly was no big deal. He did have other interviews lined up.

"No. I would have felt kinda bad if I did that. They were nice about it and hella apologetic."

Both Shani and Asher could see a striking shift in Lexi's attitude. Maybe she overreacted a little, but only because she knew how much Asher wanted that job.

"Well...I mean that's alright," she said, nodding her head.

"Yeah, but it makes me even more irritated. If they were mean, I could have been like, 'screw them, they suck anyways,' but now I can't because of how nice they were. It just makes me want to work for them even more, even though I basically humiliated myself."

"You didn't humiliate yourself," Shani insisted. "If anything, they should be embarrassed. I'm sure they are. They were the ones that messed up."

Asher forced a smile on his face, dropped his chin, and mumbled, "Yeah."

While trying desperately to increase the positivity in the room, Lexi exclaimed, "Hey! It's a big day for the two of you! And we have to cheer up Logan when we get there, so let's not make more work for ourselves." And without the other two, Lexi walked out the front door.

"Alright, Alright," Shani and Asher shouted from behind her. They grabbed everything they needed. Shani triple-checked that she had her keys, and checked her makeup in the mirror before Asher grabbed her by the waist and ribs and gently brushed her out the door.

*****

It wasn't long before Shani regretted not ordering an Uber for the ceremony. She figured there wouldn't be any available, but her new heels didn't agree with her decision.

"Geez," she said, limping across the sidewalk.

"What? Forgot to bring Band-Aids?" Asher teased. "That's not like you at all to forget something."

"I know, I know. I'm fine though. I swear."

"Keep up! Keep up!" Lexi shouted from a few yards in front. She repeatedly turned around to walk backwards and take pictures of them walking in their gowns. A few feet in front of them was a pair of trees on the sidewalk. It was the perfect background, or so she thought. Photography wasn't her area of expertise, she was just an amateur Instagrammer.

"Smile!" she said, turning around to take the picture. But instead, she saw a short, black-haired woman with blue streaks walking towards them with a camera hanging over her jean jacket. "Hey! Brex! Come on!"

They all stopped to turn around and let Brex catch up with them.

"Hey. Almost thought I was gonna be late. Couldn't find the right lens."

"Nah, we still got plenty of time," said Asher, shrugging it off.

"Enough time to find Logan?" The rest shot a few glances at each other for a brief moment to see who was going to answer.

"Yeah, yeah. He'll be fine, we'll find him," said Shani.

The rest of the walk, which couldn't have been more than five minutes, took them through a parking lot. The smell of gas, popcorn, and freshly-cut grass smacked them all in the face as they passed by the football field and into the parking garage for their lineup. But the smell quickly changed to garbage and stale beer.

The rest of the class piled in with their phones and nips ready, although some people were already clearly drunk. Brex and Lexi had to get to their seats soon, but they wanted at least one photo of the three graduates in their black gowns, and Logan still hadn't arrived.

"Should we call him?" Asher asked.

"No, no," Shani answered. "He lives in a frat house. They definitely woke him up."

"Well, maybe we should just—"

"Hey! Look!" Lexi happily interrupted. Logan was walking with his head up and a borderline smile on his face. His graduating frat brothers walked along beside him with their baggie jeans on and gowns unironed. But they looked happier than anyone who was about to walk up on stage and shake the president's hand.

"Sorry, I know I'm a little late." Logan barely finished his sentence before Lexi threw her arms around him. He laughed and pulled her in tightly with her blonde, curly hair flopping over his forearms.

"Okay, sorry, sorry, sorry. I know we gotta get to our seats. Pictures!"

Brex took at least fifty pictures before she and Lexi made their way to their seats in the bleachers. The sun had the perfect arrangement of clouds covering it for stunning images; not too bright, just the perfect balance of dullness and vibrancy.

Lexi and Brex sat down next to each other in the large audience as Lexi pulled out all of the snacks that she had stuffed in her bag. She never enjoyed eating snacks from a stand. Besides, she always had grapes and iced tea at noon.

"Damn, they're gonna look like ants from here," said Lexi.

"Not with this shit," Brex replied, pulling out a long lens that she snapped onto the front of her camera.

"Sweet. I mean, I'll take it." Lexi and Brex glued their heads and torsos up against each other as they watched most of the ceremony through the screen. When it came time for Logan to go up on stage, Brex's hands were getting so sweaty that she almost dropped the camera between her fingers. Luckily, Lexi had stronger reflexes than Brex.

"Oh, Jesus!" Brex yelled under her breath. "That was quick, Lex." But something was off about Lexi. Her fingers were twitching as if her knuckles were in pain, and her eyes didn't tear away from the camera.

They stayed drawn down, below the horizon. Her heart felt as if it were about to fly out of her chest, and her shoulders tightened to the point she was unable to pull them away from her ears. Although, her head was too foggy for her to notice what was happening.

"Lexi?" Brex loudly whispered into her ear. "Lexi?"

Lexi shot straight up in her seat. Her eyes drifted back to normal, but the shock lingered for moments afterwards.

"What—"

"I'm fine," Lexi abruptly interrupted Brex. "Just a headache, I guess." Her lack of ability to cover up such an obvious lie was painful for Brex to watch, but she trusted Lexi enough to know when something was deadly serious or not.

"Okay," Brex mumbled as she slowly lifted her camera back up to her line of sight. It was almost time for Shani to walk onto the stage and shake the president's hand, which, fortunately, meant the ceremony was almost over because the School of Science always celebrated last. Brex was secretly hoping Lexi would at least mention the odd incident to Shani, but in the meantime, she didn't want the attention to be taken away from such a significant and powerful day.

*****

Back at the frat house, Logan ripped off his cap and gown. Brex wanted to take more pictures when they all got inside, but even Shani thought Brex was going overboard when her camera said her memory card was almost full after completely being blank that morning.

The frat brothers, their friends, and significant others trickled in after having graduation dinners with their families. Everybody pitched in to order pizza and beer that wasn't Bud Light, for a change. Logan made sure of that. But Asher, Shani, Brex, and Lexi didn't stop there. They brought in Lexi's favorite bong that Logan always smoked whenever Lexi would let him as a 'thank you' for hosting. It was a glass elephant that had puffy legs and rosy cheeks that Logan liked to pretend to pinch.

The night was perfect. The day was stressful, but the night was everything every student had hoped for. The music, the crappy gas station food, the sexy outfits, all a flawless fit. After five hours of watching numerous students walk across a stage, the new alumni enjoyed their last night together without thinking about having to start paying their student loans in six months.

Logan managed to manifest some perkiness from himself, but he felt most at ease when Brex was showcasing her favorite pictures that she had taken.

"You look a little stoned in this one," Brex laughed, trying to talk over the loud music.

"Maybe I am..." Logan said, cracking a small laugh.

"So, have you packed everything?" Brex immediately regretted asking such a question. There was almost no possibility of his wanting to discuss anything related to leaving school. Luckily, the expression on his face remained unchanged.

"Yeah, pretty much. It was painful to put all of my trophies into a box. They don't deserve such cruelty. I'll make it up to them...somehow."

"Are you gonna take them out to dinner?" Brex asked.

"They'll love Arby's, and a new polish."

A warm spark tapped Brex lightly on the chest.

"Yeah?" Brex mumbled with a giggle that had a slight scratch to it.

It was a common reaction from Brex. One of Logan's favorite things about her. "Yeah," he responded, nearly copying her and matching her energy level. The lights hit her eyes perfectly. He couldn't look away from them. They were nothing short of extravagant.

"Hey guys!" yelled a slightly intoxicated Shani from across the kitchen. "How are we doing? Are we just gonna look at pictures all night?" Shani's breath reeked of rum, but she still looked more put together than anyone in the house. "You should make a speech," she said clumsily turning to Logan.

"We don't really do speeches in this frat house, contrary to popular stereotypes."

Asher and Lexi popped into the circle out of nowhere and started loudly chanting, "SPEECH! SPEECH! SPEECH!"

After a few seconds, Asher accidentally started yelling, "CHEAP! CHEAP! CHEAP!"

Logan looked to the ceiling and shrugged his shoulders. "You guys are going to cringe about this tomorrow, but fine. How about I just make a mini-speech for you four?"

Not one of them gave a verbal answer. They all simply leaned in closer, curious as to how awkward he was going to make this.

"Forget about the circumstances, I am so unbelievably happy that we were able to have this little group." Logan pulled his four friends in close, hoping his frat brothers were out of earshot. "I know I kick absolute ass on the football field, but you guys are my real team, and I know this has been one hell of a weird year, but I can't imagine senior year without you guys. I seriously wouldn't have it any other way."

Shani, Brex, Lexi, and Asher all stood there in awe. Nothing about Logan's behavior over the past few months suggested he was capable of producing such a heartfelt sentiment. They were expecting an unrefined, corny speech, but the lack of refinement and corniness came from the rest of the group instead.

"Well....damn," said Shani, finally adding dialogue back into the interaction.

"What's going on?" asked a familiar voice from behind Brex. Jenna, Brex's old friend, hopped into the miniature circle.

"Logan is just making us cry over here," Lexi answered, resting her head against Jenna's shoulder.

"Logan!" Jenna teased, consoling Lexi.

"Hey! Happy tears over here, happy tears!" Logan defended himself. "I only make people cry for real on the field. And maybe a few teachers, but that I am less proud of."

"Yeah, like that guy from that Florida college?" Brex added. "You almost threw that kid like ten yards."

"What can I say? I'm doing well in the gym."

Brex wasn't usually the superficial, body-admiring type. But in that moment, when Logan flexed his bicep, she almost didn't notice that Jenna was poking her and calling out her name.

"Brex, babe," said Jenna.

"What?" Brex snapped back into reality.

"I just asked if I could see some of your pics from this afternoon."

"Oh, yeah. Come here. I had some really good lighting when you went up."

Her voice faded as they slithered into the corner. Shani was about to comment on Brex's distraction when she got a notification on her phone.

Teen and Grandmother attacked in Miami, Florida. Both miraculously survived! No suspects.

It was from the BBC. Shani's favorite channel. Something about this story drew Shani to want to read more, but not now. Now was the time for celebration.

The rest of the night was a blur for the five of them, not because of the alcohol, but because of how long they stayed up. It wasn't until the morning that most people left. By 6:15 a.m., Logan, Shani, Brex, Lexi, Asher, Adam, and Kerry were all sitting around the T.V., still somehow managing to stuff more food into themselves.

"Lexi is passing out hard," Brex giggled as Lexi fell asleep on her lap.

"Should we go?" Shani asked.

"Just a little bit longer," Asher answered.

"You know we're all still planning on living close by, right?" Brex asked. "You guys getting your new apartment with Lexi at some point, Logan moving back in with his dad."

"Yes, definitely something to look forward to," Logan joked.

"I'm just saying, not much is gonna change. I mean, I've been out of school for months now. Maybe I shouldn't be the one to talk."

Shani didn't want to be negative, but she had the strangest feeling that that wasn't going to be true. She didn't know why, but she couldn't shake it. Not that it mattered. It was just a hunch.

Feeling tired, Shani pulled out her phone and scrolled through whatever popped up first. Nothing was interesting on Instagram or Twitter, but when she hopped onto Facebook, she noticed the same news story from before, except this one read, *Two People Miraculously Survived Severe Stabbing in Miami.* This time, she clicked on it.

It wasn't the best-written article, but something still drew her to it, as if there was important information in it that was crucial for her to know. Almost like it was written for her.

"The police believe that there were multiple assailants, and one of them used a bow and arrow," one section read.

A bow and arrow? Shani thought. *Who uses a bow and arrow?* But after pondering that unusual detail for a few moments, she remembered that it was Florida.

Shani skimmed the next few sentences until she came across a picture from the article.

Well, what do you know? They did use a bow and arrow.

The arrow in the picture was snapped in two, and only the top half with the sharpened stone showed in the overexposed police photo.

Shani squinted her eyes and took a closer look. She wasn't sure what she was looking for yet, but it was something. The stone arrowhead had some sort of inscription on it. Shani zoomed in to take a closer look. She'd had deja vu before, and all of those times, it was as if a ball of energy slowly passed through her body, but this was different. A sharp blade of energy sliced through her soul. She knew she'd seen this inscription before. It had a small dagger-looking shape on it with gold lining. Like a Queen's sword, surging with might.

Of course. Maya's office.

Back in September, the girls had broken into Maya's office, not knowing it was the office of someone trying to save them. On Maya's shelf was a vase that had this exact drawing on it. But what did that mean?

"Oh no," said Shani, not realizing she was now talking out loud. Whoever hurt this grandmother and her grandson had to be working for Moloch. There was no way they could be admirers of Maya, but they were definitely involved with the gods.

"Hey guys," Shani whispered. "Look at this."

3:

"So, what do we know about these new alchelarcenists?"

"Alright, so how do I get his attention?" Lexi asked on FaceTime with Shani and the others listening in the background.

"You don't have to do anything," said Shani. "Just leave me on speaker, and just make sure nobody else is around. I can call out his name."

"Alright, alright." Lexi's breath was beginning to shorten. Her heart had been racing all day, but after speed-walking all the way to the aquarium, she had trouble holding up her phone.

Lexi had been to the aquarium only a few times before, and one of those times was to bring Shani her lunch before she had gotten fired for punching one of the staff in the face. She only hoped no one knew who she was.

"Alright, I'm walking in," said Lexi, discreetly, holding her phone by her side to not look conspicuous. After giving the usher her ticket, she looked up to immediately see the Giant Tank. How she was going to catch the attention of one, three-foot eel was beyond her.

As she got closer, she could see the unique and extravagant colors within the cylindrical tank. The pink and orange coral, the small, yellow fish, it all made her eyes widen and her forehead scrunch. The cluster of artificial lighting snapped her attention into focus and pulled it in with a fishhook.

Luckily for Lexi, it was a quiet day at the aquarium, but she wasn't sure how long it was going to stay that way. It would take one person to notice she was trying to talk to an eel and report her to the front desk.

"Okay, I'm at the tank," Lexi whispered into her phone.

"Alright, just let me know when someone comes, and I'll shut up, alright?" Shani asked.

"Yeah. Yeah okay," Lexi mumbled as she reached out and held her phone up to the tank.

"Um...okay. Ilisa? Ilisa? Can you hear me? It's Shani." Shani's voice was unsteady and timid. Lexi could tell the eel would never be able to hear her through such thick glass.

"Shani," Lexi tried not to shout. "You gotta speak louder."

"Hold on, I can also turn up my volume." Shani took a moment before she said, "IS THIS GOOD?" Significantly louder than she intended to. Brex, Logan, and Asher, who were sitting right next to her all jerked backwards and held their foreheads, trying to soothe their partial hangovers.

"Geez, Shani. Either louder voice or more volume. Pick one." Only one woman stared at Lexi, holding her phone to her chest for a moment a few yards away until her small child began screaming after getting her red lollipop stuck in her hair.

"Did you say 'Shani'?" Shani heard a familiar voice say over the phone.

"What was that?" Shani asked.

"What was what?" Lexi asked, looking at her phone, confused.

"Are you looking at the tank? Look at the tank! Is there a crabby-looking eel staring at you?"

Perplexed as to why there would be, Lexi softly moved her head to look at a shriveled-up, elderly-looking eel staring at her.

"Ehhh, I think I got him," Lexi whispered. She held up one finger, telling Ilisa to wait while she flipped her camera. Shani somehow recognized him immediately, but it took a moment for Ilisa to notice Shani through Lexi's screen. His yellow eyes inquisitively squinted.

"Shani, what are you doing?" Ilisa asked.

"I need to talk to you, but remember I'm banned?" she responded.

"Ah yes, that glorious encounter." He struggled to hide his delighted laughter. The memory of Shani punching her misogynistic co-worker, Seamus, the year before wasn't an unforgettable moment. He still remembered the amount of spit that flew out of the boy's mouth.

"I need you to tell me what this is." She held up a picture of the arrow from the newspaper.

"What am I looking at?" He pressed his nose up to the glass and squinted.

"It's an arrow from a news article we saw from Florida. A family was attacked. I've seen these arrows before, in Maya's old office."

"Why don't you ask her about it?"

Lexi stood there perfectly relaxed while trying to hide her phone with her sweater. A few people took nervous, perplexed glances at her, but what were they going to do? People talked to animals all the time. Lexi couldn't understand their confusion, but she was too distracted to care. Shani was speaking perfect English, yet Ilisa was speaking nothing short of perfect bubble noises.

"We don't know how. We don't know where she is. She gave us no way of reaching out to her. It was something about not giving Moloch or Kali any ideas."

"As much as I disagree with that nonsense, I'm not sure where she is," said Ilisa. "But I do know if she's not at the sanctuary in the mountains or here, you're not going to be able to find her even if she's still close. When she wants to be found, she'll come searching for you."

Brex, Logan, Asher, and Lexi could tell by Shani's facial expressions and sluggish posture that the conversation wasn't going the way she hoped.

"Well, can you at least give us a clue as to what this could be? On the arrow?"

Ilisa squinted his dark, aging eyes into the screen, but his face didn't suggest any recognition of the image.

"Sorry," he said. "I'm not entirely sure what it is, but it probably has something to do with Ares."

Shani had thought of the possibility it was the symbol or inscription of a god, but why?

"You think somebody is using the weapons of Ares? But—"

The look on Shani's muddled face almost forced him into scornful laughter.

"You think there could be more alchelarcenists out there other than Kali and us?" Shani asked. "And one of them has stolen the powers of Ares, the god of war. Why haven't we heard about them?"

"Well," Ilisa began. "Why do you think it's taken this long for Moloch to develop a strategy and steal your powers back?"

Something in Shani's stomach twitched as a fire lit up in her throat. She didn't want to answer or even think about that question. But there was no avoiding it.

"He's training them."

*****

The five of them paced around Brex's apartment. Shani had her laptop propped up on the kitchen table, searching for any sign of where Maya could be or how to get in touch with her, but they were coming up blank.

"So, what do we know about these new alchelarcenists?" Brex asked.

"Well, we don't know how many new people there are, but the news did say there were probably three," Shani responded with her face still buried in her computer screen.

"Does that include Kali?" Asher asked.

"It must," said Brex. "She wouldn't trust anyone unsupervised."

"Right," Shani agreed. "And we don't know where they got their powers from, but I'm sure Maya would know."

Lexi draped her upper body over the loveseat to try to get some blood pumping to her head, but before she fully embraced her awkward meditative state, a question arose.

"Why would Maya know?" Lexi asked.

"Because...well she has to have some map of where all of the sanctuaries are."

"But, I don't think she does. Remember?"

Shani was taken aback at the thought of Maya not knowing where other members of the Alliance were. She took out Maya's journal that was still in her possession and aggressively flipped through the pages, determined to find any information regarding the sanctuaries that weren't just Maya's.

"Shani," Lexi mumbled, standing up and trying to get her attention. "Remember when she said something about how they keep their locations confidential, so if one of them is tortured and killed, or something like that, they won't reveal where the others are?"

After a few seconds of Shani scrunching her forehead, she dragged her eyes to the ceiling, dreading the fact that Lexi was right.

"But," Lexi continued, trying to bring optimism back to the conversation, "she probably knows where a few of them are. I mean she knew where the White Mountains sanctuary was. Even Ilisa knew that."

"Yeah, but that's probably it," Logan chimed in. "And we know those powers were relocated. If the magic that these people stole wasn't here or in the mountains, we, including Maya, are at a dead end."

All they could hear was the droning sound of each other's breathing and the continuous murmur of the construction workers outside. Eventually, Shani stood up to put some popcorn into the microwave, and Asher turned on the T.V. in hopes Anderson Cooper would be on.

Shani and Brex kept scrolling through different articles about the attack in hopes some new information would be revealed. Brex thought her thumb was going to fall off before her eyebrows shot to her forehead lines. In the *New York Times*, they listed information about the victims that no other article had; their names.

"Guys, look at this," she said, springing up from her chair and beckoning everyone over. "How did they get this?"

"Jesus," Asher exasperated, "Because it's the *New York Times,* and they can get away with anything. There's no way they were supposed to reveal that information without permission."

"Assdicks," Logan commented.

"Creative," said Lexi, hearing that word for the first time.

"It says their names are Enrique Mendez and his grandmother, Maria Mendez," Shani read, looking over Brex's shoulder. "They were the ones who were almost stabbed to death, but Enrique's brother was tied up and locked in their family's food truck."

"That's gotta be a sanctuary," said Brex.

"Yeah, but whoever these people are, they didn't get their powers from this sanctuary," Lexi added. "They must have had their magic before going into this. There's no way anybody would go up against a member of the Alliance without an advantage. You know what I mean? Whoever wanted to steal the alchelesters is doing it to bring them to Moloch. Not because they want them for themselves. We just don't know where they got their powers from."

"Right, right, right," said Shani, breaking away from the circle and poking her nail in between her teeth.

Asher pulled out his phone and typed a few different phrases into Google before getting a useful result. *Mendez Family Food Truck Named Best Fried Ice Cream in the State of Florida!* This had to be it. He clicked on the article and skimmed for any information that Shani could deem relevant.

"The Mendez family," he exhaled, "The teenage boys are apparently the most well-liked workers. They moved to Miami in the year 2000 from Mexico, and they make their own chocolate sauce, which they sell in bottles."

"So which one do we think is actually a member of the Alliance?" Logan asked.

"Probably one of the parents, but—"

Shani cut him off and noted, "But the parents weren't attacked."

The five of them slowly slipped into one of their mumbled arguments where every one of them lost their trail of thought. Shani's head started to hurt, which was exceedingly rare for her, but the information they had was like a calculus class; a lot of nonsense that was leading them nowhere.

"Okay, guys can we all just—" But Shani was interrupted by a ping from her computer that echoed louder than usual. "Geez." She stormed over to slam her laptop shut, but before she could, the distracting notification caught her eye.

The email was sent from someone by the name of Shara Winters. She knew she'd seen that name before, but if there was anything that Shani hated, it was spam mail. Whenever a store asked for her email, she either ignored the question or snapped, "No," in their face. Who could this person be? But before she could finish asking herself that question, she remembered where she saw that name; Maya's journal. Maya was finally reaching out to them.

"No way," she mumbled to herself, while the others were still mindlessly talking over each other. "Guys look at this!"

The four of them trickled back into focus. Lexi was the first one to eagerly walk around the chair to see what Shani was referring to.

"What are we looking at?" Lexi asked.

"It's an email from Maya. This is one of her aliases."

"What?" Brex exclaimed. "How did she find your email?"

"Maybe it's on a list of felonies," Asher joked. Nobody laughed along with him, but he still kept a sense of pride within his introverted laughter.

"No, she probably just found it on Facebook, or the school's database or something. She *is* shockingly skilled at using technology," Brex reminded them.

"What does it say?" Logan asked.

"It's a...what?" Shani's eyes were inches away from the screen. "It's a bank account. She sent us the password and everything."

"She wants to send us money?"

Asher bit his crooked lip and asked, "Why would she want to do that? I don't have to start paying off my crippling debt for another six months."

"Um..." Shani ignored his sarcasm, but once she saw the most recent transaction, she had no choice but to say, "Well, it's a lot."

The five of them indiscreetly leaned into the small screen to see the number, "$453,658" in the checking account, and the number, "$695,022" in the savings account.

"What does she expect us to do with this?" Lexi asked.

"But wait," Shani tapped her nail on the screen. "Look, it says it's still a pending transaction. The money hasn't even gone through yet. It still could be denied."

"It's a code, but why are...wait." Lexi pulled back her hair. "Six numbers each. Sick."

"What?" Asher waited impatiently, yet still distracted by the amount of money that dangled before him.

"They're coordinates."

Logan ran his fingers through his hair and gave Lexi a five-star high-five without looking.

Lexi pulled out her phone and typed in the coordinates before she said, "Askwith. It's a ghost town in Maine. It's not even on the maps anymore, but the coordinates are still there. Wherever she's staying, it must be in the middle of nowhere."

"Do you think she has shelter?" Asher asked.

"I hope so. But...she must, right? The best place to hide is in plain sight. Maya is strategic that way."

Shani kept the bland, unanimated smile on her face, and shook her head. "Clever, Maya."

Bang, bang, bang, they heard coming from the front door.

The five of them jolted at least an inch into the air, and if Brex hadn't seen Adam through the front door, Asher would have run for his baseball bat.

"Wasssup?" Adam shouted out as Brex slowly opened the door for him. Adam clearly had just played football by the way his white shirt had grass and dirt stains on the back.

"You rang?" she asked.

"Sorry. Was I loud?"

"You don't know your own strength, do you?" said Lexi, shaking her head.

"Tell that to my coach."

Adam shook off his shoes while Shani frantically put everything away, including Maya's journal, so he wouldn't ask any questions.

"What are you guys up to?" he asked, looking at them hovered around Brex's computer shoulder to shoulder.

Too late, Shani thought.

"Just organizing some cameras," Logan chimed in before realizing they were nowhere near any of the equipment.

"Awesome. Can I help?"

"Really? You want to?"

"Oh please," Logan laughed. "Did you ever see Adam's room in the frat house? He loves the Olympic sport known as organization."

Shani shut her eyes and said, "I knew we always had a special connection."

*****

Over the next hour and a half, the six of them helped Brex clean her equipment. Then they ate Chinese food and binge-watched *Criminal Minds* on Netflix. Adam spent most of his time reorganizing Brex's equipment shelf and put the lenses in alphabetical order by brand name. He also spent some time telling Shani how crooked some of the lights were before adjusting them, but her arms started hurting after the second hanging, so she assertively told Adam to sit down and get Logan to do it.

"How's the job hunting going?" Adam asked Asher as they found themselves alone in the tiny kitchen area.

"Eh, I still have another interview coming up next week, but I don't have high hopes for this one. And it's not one that I'm too excited about anyway. How's your job going?"

Adam nodded his head while trying not to smile too extravagantly. "Oh, it doesn't start 'til next week," he said," but I'm pretty excited for it. The company seems good, the boss seems nice. Decent starting rate."

There were few things that Asher felt more appreciative of than Adam trying to be subtle about how good his career was starting out. For the past few weeks, Asher kept telling him how nervous he was about job offers, and Adam did nothing but encourage him with his soft smile and high-pitched laugh.

"That's awesome," Asher smiled. "Proud o' you." They clinked their ice-cold beers together and talked the night away.

After getting a bit tipsy and getting a minor stomach ache, Asher rolled out of the kitchen and said, "Damn guys, I should head out. Sorry if I overstayed."

"Never," Logan responded, nearly tackling him into an aggressive bro hug.

"Asher should walk you home," Shani suggested. Asher had already changed into his pajama pants and ripped-up tank top.

"I mean, yeah," said Asher. "Somebody at least should." Adam held his head down, but Asher could see a subtle lift in the corner of his mouth. "I should just, ya know, put something else on." Asher ran to the bathroom, which was only about five feet away from where he was standing, and threw on some dirty pants and a hoodie.

Adam stood outside Brex's doorway and started doing a stiff, step 'n touch dance while softly singing, "Let's go, let's go, let's go!"

"Oh, come on. You didn't have *that* many drinks."

"I know, this is just me in the kinda mood that no one can handle."

"Who says I can't handle it?"

Without saying a word, Adam stopped performing his little dance, stiffly stood up, then let out a tight-lipped laugh.

"Alright, lightweight," Asher laughed with him. "Let's go."

The color in the sky had already faded a little past twilight; navy blue with a hint of pink. Adam and Asher walked along the park before taking the turn to Adam's new apartment.

"You know we can order an Uber or a taxi," said Asher.

"Nah, that's no fun. And besides, I wanna enjoy the outdoors before it gets blistering hot outside. Unpopular opinion, but I hate summer." Not knowing how to respond to that statement, Asher kept walking and smiling with his gaze on his feet. "You know what makes me just so happy for some reason?"

"What makes you just so happy for some reason?" Asher asked.

"The fact that you, Logan, Lexi, Shani, and Brex all formed a band."

"A band?" Asher couldn't help but blush. He appreciated the strange choice of analogy.

"You know what I mean. I'm just really happy you became friends with Logan, because it basically got like...you and I closer."

Once again, Asher wasn't sure how to reply, but he noticed a slight twist in his stomach. Not a tightness one feels when seeing a bad grade on a test. It was a feeling that resembled seeing a steady snowfall for the first time, or standing on top of a mountain with nothing but blue and green valleys untouched by mankind.

"Hey," Adam mumbled. Before Asher could meet his eyes, Adam gently hooked his first few fingers to Adam's wrist and slowly pulled him closer. After a quick smile and a small chuckle, Adam planted a soft kiss on Asher's lips.

"Really?" Asher asked as he opened his eyes and looked at Adam's flawless chiseled face.

"That's what your reaction is? 'Really'?" Adam teased. They both burst into laughter for what felt like a moment that could last forever. Then without any warning, Adam's eyes spread as wide as they could reach before he screamed, "Asher look out!"

It was like a foggy dream. Asher couldn't move his eyes as Adam pulled him out of the way only to be slammed into the ground, ripping his jeans and scraping his knee. He felt and heard a loud bang, but couldn't identify the cause of the noise, which seemed far away. A shadowy figure passed over them, holding what Asher could only guess was a gun, but he didn't have time to process what was happening or what was about to happen. Asher used what little control he had over his arms and pushed himself off the ground.

The dream-like fog almost evaporated as Asher leaped toward whatever was in front of him. He didn't have time to think about what or who it was, but as his legs ferociously and tensely kicked behind him, he felt something stir in his upper back. Something he hadn't felt in a while.

There was no time to acknowledge it. He tackled the attacker to the ground and, without realizing it, knocked the gun out of their hand. Asher's anger took over. He could barely see from the lack of light, but all empathy escaped his body as he grabbed onto the dark-clothed man's arm and leg. There was something in Asher that convinced him he could pick this man up and throw him across the sidewalk. He didn't know what it was, but he was certain of his strength. Without any pause or any breath, Asher effortlessly wound up his body and watched the hooded figure shoot through the air, only to violently crash into the pavement.

Asher couldn't see this man's face. He wasn't even sure it was a man, but he didn't care, and he didn't care what he had just done. After he watched the failed thief pull himself to standing and run away, Asher turned to Adam to see if he was okay. He didn't care about the thief until a frightening thought exploded in his head.

What if he works for Moloch? Asher thought. *Shani's going to kill me.*

But he would deal with that later. Adam needed him.

"Adam!" Asher exclaimed as he saw Adam still on the floor, rubbing his head and holding his bloody knee. "Are you okay?"

Stunned, Adam shook his head to refocus his vision, but didn't answer Asher.

"Wha—what?" That's all that came out of his mouth.

"What? What's wrong."

Adam slowly lifted his index finger and pointed directly behind Asher. At first, he thought the thief had returned, but when Asher turned around, all he saw was his bright, beautiful, white wings.

"Oh, shit."

4:

"Could Maya even do something like that?"

"What in the hell was that?" Adam screeched, shaking, but sitting frozen still at the same time. "And what—are those wings?"

Asher thought of the time he first got caught with alcohol when he was sixteen. His dad caught him with a beer in his hand, and he still tried to convince his dad that he hadn't been drinking. The idiotic explanations haunted him ever since.

"Yeah," said Asher, realizing he could put his wings away now. He gracefully pushed them back, but still almost gave himself whiplash.

"How...what? How did you even...? How can you...?"

"Adam, Adam," Asher slowly walked back to whatever they were to each other now, trying not to scare him. "I swear there is a logical explanation for this. I just don't know how to explain it to you yet, because I'm really not sure how much you're going to fully understand. It took me a long time to wrap my head around it too."

There was no questioning what he had seen. Adam wasn't stupid, but that didn't help the fact that he couldn't push the fear away. It wouldn't stop crawling all over him.

"Just—" Adam started, but took a moment to finish. "Can we just get out of here? And you can explain all of this to me somewhere else?"

Asher's throat clenched at the accusatory tone in Adam's voice. But he kept his voice soft. "Yeah," he said. "Sorry, let's get that knee cleaned up too."

Asher wasn't ready to tell the others that someone else knew about their powers. He needed another hour to figure out how he was going to make Shani stop yelling, so they went to Adam's apartment where

Asher wrapped Adam's knee with small Band-Aids and paper towels since that was the extent of Adam's first aid kit.

"Ow, geez," said Adam the moment Asher ran water over the scraped-up knee. Asher could picture Lexi standing beside them and commenting on the weakness of men as she laughed at Adam's whining about water pouring over his leg.

"Don't worry," said Asher, managing to stay calm. "It'll stop hurting in a minute."

Adam still couldn't look Asher in the eye. It was different now. Their strong, electric connection shifted in a direction that was foreign to him.

"So, are you going to start talking, or what?" Adam asked. He wasn't sure how else to put it, but he didn't care. At this point, he had little desire to hold his tongue from any thought passing through his mind.

"I'm not entirely sure where to start, and I'm not sure how many secrets are mine to tell."

"What's that supposed to mean?"

I should not have said that, Asher thought. Now he was stuck. What trainwreck road could this possibly lead him down? But before he could think of an answer, Adam interrupted his catastrophic train of thought for him.

"Are there other people like you?" Adam practically whispered as if Asher was a criminal.

"No." Technically he wasn't wrong. After all, he was the only one who could sprout giant white wings and fly with them. He finished patching up Adam's bloody knee and said, "Just hear me out, okay?"

Asher proceeded to tell Adam a vague version of what had happened back in September, but he purposefully left out the scars, the dangerous people who were trying to come after him, and the fact that Shani, Lexi, Brex, and Logan also had supernatural abilities. All of the words coming out of his mouth seemed to jumble and melt together. He felt numb reciting such twisted versions of the truth. More than anything, he wanted to tell Adam the *whole* truth.

"Well...what?" Adam exclaimed, making Asher briefly believe that he wasn't paying attention the entire time.

"What do you not understand?" Asher asked, not caring how his tone came off.

"How did this cave even disappear? It couldn't have just vanished. Are you just saying that to me, so I won't go looking for it?"

The raspy timbre in Adam's voice closed the door to Asher's vulnerability while the accusation smacked him right in the face. Was he incensed with Asher for getting these abilities that he, in no way, had asked for?

"Why would I do that?" Asher asked. "And if you distrust me so easily now, then why did you kiss me?"

There was a look on Adam's face that suggested that he had almost forgotten about kissing Adam, but Asher felt no remorse. It surprisingly gave him comfort.

"Because I really wanted to," said Adam in his softest tone. A little twitch in the corner of his mouth almost lifted to a smile. "I'm sorry. I like you, Asher, but I'm not sure how to handle all of this. I believe you about everything. Don't get me wrong, but I...I can't explain it."

Asher's gut wrenched throughout that entire apology, but the worst part about it was when Adam reassured him he believed everything that Asher said. The lies might never stop. If Adam was to find out about everything, especially Logan's involvement, Adam's best friend, he would never forgive Asher.

*****

It was almost daybreak when Asher walked back to Brex's apartment. He almost ordered an Uber, but decided to take a walk instead to think everything over, even though there was almost nothing to think about, and he had been almost killed on the dark street. After a few moments of pointless thinking, he decided to practice going over what he was going to say to Shani.

"Don't kill me," he mumbled. Without question, he knew he needed to start with that. "Adam saw me with wings, but don't worry. Everything's okay!" Straight to the point. Perfect. "No way she's gonna buy that everything's okay, idiot." After rubbing his eyes underneath his glasses for most of the walk home, he figured winging it would be the best bet. Memorizing lines wasn't his strongest skill.

The front door creaked open in a horror-movie way. It was slow and loud with pristine audio quality that masked the background noise, but it didn't scare him as much as it usually would. He was just attacked while simultaneously revealing his secret, and now had to tell Shani. There was no way a creaking door was going to make him jump in terror.

The lights were still on while all four of them were passed out. Logan and Brex were on the tiny couch while Shani and Lexi were under blankets on the rug. Some documentary about England was playing on the T.V. If Asher were to turn it off, Shani would surely wake up, so he kept walking past the living room and into the bathroom to change. He even made the effort to take off his shoes to tip-toe as quietly as a mouse, but before he even touched the doorknob, he was stopped by a weary, but stern voice.

"Hold it!" Shani sounded like she yelled into her pillow with her eyes still closed shut. "Get your ass back here."

Asher still had his hand up to reach for the bathroom door in hopes she wasn't talking to him, but after no one else responded, he slowly pivoted his feet back towards the living room and casually walked back to the four people who were no longer asleep.

"Yes?" Asher asked as if he had nothing to hide.

"That took way too long. What happened?"

Asher didn't answer right away, but there was no point in lying. He wasn't sure what the next step should be in this situation. Telling Shani and the others was the only way to address the catastrophic events of the night.

"I really didn't mean to but—"

"Oh my God, what?" Shani would have figured that out if she let him finish, but proceeded to cut him off anyway.

"Adam saw me with wings."

"What?" they heard from Logan's section of the couch. It almost startled Asher until he saw Lexi and Brex sit up from their messy sleeping positions. Everybody was now listening to the story of how their secret was now out.

"Adam saw my wings fly out. I didn't mean for it to happen. We were mugged, and they just kinda flew out."

"WHAT?" Lexi screamed.

Asher had to stop himself from saying, "The next person that yells 'What?' is going to get kicked in the face."

"Guys, everything is fine," he said instead. "I'm going to figure it out, but I need you to tell me how to do that first."

Shani stood up and started pacing around the room with her fingers plastered on her forehead. "Oh my God, oh my God. We have to wipe his memory."

Brex and Logan seemed to agree, with the endless bouncing of their heads.

"Why would we have to do that?" Lexi asked, also standing up. "It's Adam."

"Asher, why don't you answer that?" Shani stood with her arms crossed, curious if Asher could come up with a counterargument.

There was nothing more that he wanted than to have Adam's discovery and this confrontation cut from the universe. But if he had to wipe Adam's memory, there wasn't a chance of preserving the tender moment they shared. But it would still stab Asher in the chest repeatedly and there wouldn't be enough blue blood in the world to heal those wounds.

"I'm okay by the way," Asher stated, wiping his sweaty head. "In case anyone was concerned."

"Hey!" Lexi put her finger in his face. "I practically screamed a few seconds ago. Don't say I don't care."

"I know, I know. I'm sorry." He wrapped his arms around her, but only felt a little bad about unraveling a portion of his anger. No matter what was going to happen, he was going to overthink every second of this night and feel like a helpless little piglet with needles stabbing into the back of his head.

"Why don't we ask Maya what to do?" Brex suggested.

"Yeah, but we gotta do it in some sort of code," Logan added.

"But hang on," Lexi interrupted. "Could Maya even do something like that? She doesn't actually have any magical abilities."

It was too early in the morning and also too late in the night for noise and conversation. Not just this noise and conversation, noise and conversation period. Asher was having none of it and a panic attack was right around the corner, waiting for its moment to pounce. Maybe it was just the fatigue, but the minor chaos needed to be paused for the next twelve hours.

"Guys," Asher recited, dragging his voice. "I'm sorry for everything and you can yell at me more in the morning, but I'm going to bed right now. Good night."

The others knew Asher could be confidently militant when he felt the need to be, but they were still disappointed to see what their attitudes had brought upon him.

"Good night," the rest all mumbled together.

Asher didn't sleep a wink that night. He kept reliving the kiss, the attack, and Adam's face on repeat. Nobody had ever looked at him the way Adam did when his wings were sprouting from his back. It was almost disgust that oozed from his face. Then again, no pedestrian had ever known about Asher's powers, but he knew that feeling.

What was going to happen? Would they actually be able to erase Adam's memory? And if they couldn't, would Adam be trustworthy in keeping their life-altering secret?

Back in the living room, Shani lay awake with her hands over her heart as if she were in a coffin. Asher was going to hate her for what needed to be done, but without waking their passed-out friends, she tiptoed into the bathroom and opened her laptop.

In the subject line of her email, she wrote, "In need of assistance" and typed in Maya's secret email address. She didn't find her caution to be necessary, but there was no such thing as being too cautious in the owner's manual of her life. Mirroring Maya's security precautions, Shani typed out the words, "SECRET'S OUT! Adam, Asher's friend is having a birthday party, but unfortunately, he knows everything...and I mean everything! BOOOO!"

With only a few seconds of turbulence and hesitation, she finally hit send. For what felt like an hour, Shani clasped her sweaty hands to her face and ran through all of the times Asher had rambled onto her about how badly he wanted to tell Adam everything. Shani was usually at least half paying attention. He often caught her at bad times like watching John Oliver or tightening her braids. But now, she couldn't get Asher's whining out of her head.

The likelihood of Adam being trustworthy was dominant, but if Maya found out that a commoner knew their secret, or even just a fraction of it, she would lose trust and even hope in them. That was something they couldn't risk, and Shani resented the idea anyway.

Instead of going back into the living room, or just brushing off her fatigue for a handful of seconds, she lay on the bathroom rug, crossed her arms, and fell into a deep, yet discomforting sleep.

•••••

Asher slept for about an hour and almost prayed in gratitude that he didn't have one of his unwelcome dreams that required an exhausting amount of attention. The sun had already said a gentle, "Hello" to him when he went to sleep, and an even more aggressive, "HELLO" when he woke up shortly after.

A few eyelash bats and a stretch or two later, Asher rolled over to see a text on his phone that he certainly wasn't expecting.

"Hey, can we talk?" Adam texted him. What was he supposed to say back? Yes, of course, they could talk. Why wouldn't they? But what did Adam want to say?

"Yeah. Of course." And before he was prepared with an emotional speech, Adam's name popped up on the screen. His legs caught up with his brain as he ran out of Brex's apartment and into the hallway, carefully closing the door behind him. After his mind stopped racing, Asher swiped his thumb across the phone, answering Adam's FaceTime.

"Hey," Adam blurted out before Asher could say his hello. "How are you?"

"Me?" Asher chuckled. "I'm fine. I've been worrying about you all night." The words fell out of his mouth, scrambling across the floor. He was barely conscious of what he was saying. Instead, he listed every possibility of what Adam would want to discuss. In usual Asher fashion, his mind bounced back and forth between every negative outcome and some hope.

Oh my God, he never wants to see me again, or he's moving to the other side of the world...

"Figured you would be, but I don't want you to worry about me."

There stood a hint of resignation in his voice that didn't sit well with Asher. "What does that mean? I mean...crap...what do you mean by that?" The harsh tone in his voice wasn't intentional, but it wouldn't leave.

"I mean that I don't want you to worry." Adam couldn't help but laugh. Asher's skepticism in their conversation was a mixture of amusing and concerning.

"Are you sure?"

The pause between Asher's and Adam's voices made Asher's fingertips shake with sweat, but Adam quickly took him by surprise. "Asher, I can keep a secret. Seriously, I don't even have to tell Logan that I know."

Asher would have burst into laughter if it wasn't for the severity of the situation. "Well...he already knows about...everything." The struggle to talk in his normal cadence was irritating him almost as much as everything else was, but it was his frozen eyes that told Adam everything he needed to know.

"Oh my God," Adam whispered under his breath. "That's why you guys have been hanging out together so much."

A twitch in Asher's shoulder sent a twisting tension throughout his chest and gut.

"Yeah," he responded.

"And to think," Adam carried on, finally able to laugh. "I thought it was kind of weird how you were always hanging out."

"Why?" Asher's instinct to hold back had fallen weak. "Because I'm not an athlete? Or because I shouldn't have straight friends?"

"What? No?" Adam scoffed. His voice dripped with suspicion, but Asher ignored it. Asher waited for Adam to elaborate on his bewildered statement, but instead, he said, "So Logan's got wings too?"

"Okay, the answer is no, but I really shouldn't be telling you anymore, alright?"

The silence returned, and this time it slapped Adam upside the head. Adam couldn't wipe the disappointment off his face. Yet Asher couldn't pinpoint the origin of his guilt.

"I'm sorry," Adam blurted out, but quietly and subtly.

"For what?"

"I don't know." Adam couldn't stop the defensive tone from slipping out. He didn't mean to, but he couldn't stop. A wave of frustration crashed into him. "I guess pissing you off? I don't want to make you angry for whatever reason." Adam remained lost in the conversation.

"For whatever reason?" Asher leaned his head back on the wall in distress.

"What do you want me to say?"

It suddenly dawned on Asher that maybe he viewed the situation the same way that Adam did. He didn't want to upset Adam, and he didn't want to fight, but he couldn't simply let his turbulence go. Besides, the suppressed effort remaining compacted in Adam's voice gave Asher the impression Adam wanted the conversation, or any conversation with Asher to be over.

"Why don't we just talk later?" Asher suggested. "I'm exhausted and I can calm down now that I know you're okay."

The way Asher's exhausted, yet caring voice sunk into his gut told Adam everything he needed to know at the moment; there probably wasn't going to be a "later," and it made both of them feel lost and lonely.

"Okay," Adam responded. The words, "Talk to you later," almost escaped his lips, but he stopped himself before they let slip. "Bye."

"Bye," Asher mumbled. He slowly hung up the phone, walked back into the apartment, and gave his pillow a single punch before he closed his eyes and eventually fell asleep.

5:

"That might be a better question to ask when we're on the road."

Halfway through the trip to Maine, the five of them realized they overpacked snacks. Lexi's small legs couldn't move behind the front passenger's seat, and Shani was losing feeling in her thighs from holding a giant bottle of Coke on her lap.

Logan kept getting lost after driving into the towns made of just fields. There were few signs that led them to where they were headed, but Asher withheld his skepticism about being led until they finally arrived at a small, sand-colored trailer.

It looked abandoned. But maybe it was supposed to look that way. Unlike the residency that Maya was used to. Most of the trailer was covered in trees. Hidden enough for suspicious eyes to not look twice.

"This is where she is?" Asher asked. "How do we know for sure?"

"The transaction memo that she sent included, 'Don't worry. Only you all will have access. Just use your special codes.' I'm guessing that means it's a real house. This is the only house for miles.

"Only us?" Brex whispered to herself. "Alright."

The five of them walked up to the house, and as they got closer, they could see the number "26" nailed onto the door in gold lettering. But as Brex was about to say, "Hey, Shani. You were right," she felt a sudden rush of wind, heat, and pressure in her head all at the same time. After gasping for a deep, audible breath, Brex looked up to see that the rest of them felt it too. Logan was clutching his chest, Lexi was looking around, wondering where the odd feeling came from, and both Shani and Asher scratched themselves continuously, hoping that bugs weren't crawling all over them.

Unsure why, Brex looked at her left palm and peeled back her faux skin, hiding it under her jean jacket. The normally reddish, blue scar beamed the color orange then slowly faded back to its original color after a few brief seconds.

"Clever," Brex chuckled. "Only alchelarcenists can pass."

"What?" said Shani with a raging fire in her eyes. "What about that crazy bitch, Kali? As an alchelarcenist, she can get into Maya's house! Did Maya even think about that?"

"Don't ask me." Brex knew she was going to have to brace herself again for Shani's short temper and bossiness, but she felt worse for what Asher went through daily.

Logan wanted to be the first one to step on the small, old porch and knock on the door, but as he lifted his fist, the door swung open before he could make a single noise.

Maya was in a baseball cap that was tilted downwards, covering most of her face. She was a petite woman who always wore her hair in a bun. The baseball cap clashed with her floral outfit, but hiding behind the door, she wasn't showing much of that either. Just a sliver of her dark skin was showing.

"Well, don't just stand there," she loudly whispered. "Come in! Now!"

They all scurried in with Lexi being the last one to walk through the door, but before she did, she took a quick glance around the vacant land. Something about this place gave her an uneasy feeling, and she knew in the back of her head that the feeling wasn't going anywhere.

"Sit down, sit down." Maya flicked her wrist towards the chairs and couch, frantically beckoning. "Oh, silly me, wait." She jogged over to the kitchen impressively fast. The kitchen was in the same room and only about six feet away, but the small shred of youthfulness she had still clung onto her.

She came back into the living room with a bowl of grapes and a pitcher of lemonade. "I bet you are all hungry from the drive up here. Eat up. I made the lemonade myself." The pride and excitement on her face made the five of them feel bad about having overstuffed their stomachs in the car, but Lexi encouraged everyone to dig in regardless by eagerly reaching for the glass of lemonade that Maya was pouring.

"Thank you. We really appreciate it. You practically read our minds." Lexi took a big sip of her lemonade, not expecting to drink such a sweet, bubbly drink. For half a second, she expected to be brought into a magical forest with rainbows and unicorns.

"You like it?" Maya asked, almost jumping out of her seat.

"I love it!"

Maya came closer to jumping out of her seat. The thought that Maya probably hadn't seen or talked to many people in the last seven months scarcely crossed Lexi's mind. She was grateful to be there.

Lexi noticed nobody else had taken a sip yet. She was unable to stop herself from whacking Asher on the upper arm, and instead of violently flinching, he immediately caught onto her vibe and chugged his drink. Maya was delighted to see the rest have the same reaction as Lexi.

"Delicious!" Shani and Brex said together, but Asher and Logan kept on chugging and eventually poured everyone another glass without anyone asking.

"I'm delighted to see that you're all safe, and I'm so happy you are all here. There's much to discuss." Suddenly Maya's tone and face shifted. Her frown tightened as she bit her cheeks.

"You heard about the attacks in Miami?" Logan asked.

"Of course, Maria is a member of the Alliance. I didn't know her family was guarding the Miami sanctuary, but I'm guessing they've been there for quite some time."

"Can I ask you something?" Asher asked. "Why did they both survive? I don't even think we would have survived."

Maya gently shook her head. "I wouldn't be too certain of that, but they survived because they are Naguals. Very powerful beings. They are all Aztecs from Mexico."

"Naguals?" Lexi questioned.

"Shapeshifters. They have the power to turn into jaguars. I'm certain you wouldn't guess that by looking at Maria. But Enrique. There's powerful potential in that young man. He's an apprentice for the Alliance. He will likely become a guard himself quite soon. His poor brother didn't inherit the gift, but it might be for the best." Maya poured everyone, including herself, more lemonade.

"Why would you say that?" Lexi asked.

"I don't think he understands the dangers of this organization, but never mind that. I believe there's more to this story than you all realize."

The five of them leaned in an inch or two, and adjusted their seats, ready for the answers they'd been waiting months for.

"Do you remember what I said about the gods being put to rest?"

The others shrugged their shoulders and nodded their heads.

"All of those years ago, when we took their magic, we didn't *just* take their magic. The only way to revive them, when the time came, was to take their souls as well."

Without meaning to, Brex flinched in her seat, but she quickly sat on her hands.

"We divided their souls into two stones that two Alliance members wear at all times. Unfortunately, they take years to make. We only had two."

"The best place to hide is in plain sight," Logan commented.

"Precisely. Back in 1937, when Kali almost found my sanctuary, she did manage to take my necklace with the stone on it. But eight months ago, when she returned and Moloch carelessly burned the skin on her face, I took it back. I imagine she was under the delusion that they could find both of the stones, but even I don't know where the other one is. I never know. It was a miracle they found the sanctuaries that they did. One of the sanctuaries just happened to be one where the guard had the stone. Well, I'll say, I doubt there will be another miracle for them. Especially because I took the necklace back."

Shani admired the way Maya held her back straight and her voice calm. Her red cheeks stirred with stress, but she kept her breathing at a steady rhythm.

"And these are the two necklaces they need to stop time or whatever it is they want to do?" Shani asked.

"Correct, but that's not all they need. And this is not their first attack. Did you hear about the robberies in Vancouver?"

"Robberies?" Shani asked. "With guns? In Canada?"

"The media is talented in portraying stories however they want to, but it doesn't matter. It was a lie. It was a murder. They killed one of our best. Manash. He apparently was guarding the Staff of Moses. Another ingredient they need. Zara was the only one who knew his whereabouts. She spent time training with him too during the beginning of her apprenticeship. That's when I knew."

"Knew what?"

Something in Logan's subconscious plummeted with stress. If they needed more ingredients, it would take more time, but if these demented lunatics got to these objects, or whatever they could be, before them, everything would be over.

"We will get to that, but first, they will also need a few more things: one, Poseidon's trident, which they clearly are already in possession of; two, water from the underworld. Although I am sure they already have plenty of that as well; three, a petal from the Flowers of Persephone."

"Right, the woman who started seasons or something like that, right?" Asher asked.

Maya smiled and nodded her head. "A contribution to time will assist to end it."

"What do you mean?" Logan asked.

"Persephone was captured by Hades long ago. She's the daughter of Demeter. She created a cycle when they made their agreement. Persephone would spend spring with her mother, and that's why the flowers bloom, but when winter arrives, that's when Persephone returns to Hades. Demeter couldn't live without her, and the bitterness in her heart manifested through the fields of the North and South Pole. Demeter was so depressed that Persephone was stuck in the underworld for four months that she didn't allow anything to grow, which caused winter. When Persephone returned to her, Demeter allowed the seasons to turn to spring. Although the flowers grown from Persephone's garden would grow in the underworld and start to wilt when spring was coming, knowing she would leave soon. All they need is a single petal. It will break the natural cycle."

"Interesting," Asher mumbled.

"And of course, they will need two other things," Maya added.

"The souls and the magic of the gods," said Lexi.

"That's all correct. Of course, there will be other circumstances. I believe they will have to be at a fairly high altitude and will need specific weather. And—" Maya calmly paused, but she had yet to stop twisting her heel against the wooden floor.

"What else?" Shani asked.

"I'm not quite sure. I believe there is more to the puzzle. I've gleaned this information from journals, books, and other research, but I only know so much. Although something about it seems...simple."

Brex put her now-empty glass of lemonade onto the shaky coffee table and casually intertwined all of her fingers. "What is it that you need us to do?"

"The other ingredients," said Maya, deeply inhaling and sitting up straight. "I know it's a lot to ask, but I know the five of you are strong enough to endure this task."

"You want us to go on this great big mission and find these things?" Logan asked.

"Oh no," Asher mumbled.

"But you don't want them to be found," Logan continued. "If they're already hidden, shouldn't they stay that way? It's not like we need them, right?"

"You're right, Logan," said Maya, reaching for his hand. "But it's not only that. Zara and I have spoken. We believe that it would be of great use if you were to find out where they are and relocate them. More so, have the guard of each sanctuary relocate them. Only, of course, if they are guarding anything when you find them. We can't risk it. This has been a secret of mine, but I cannot ignore it any longer. Someone is leaking our information. I know it. There has to be a mole."

"A mole?" Brex asked, swallowing. "And you have no clues as to who?"

"I don't. As you may remember we did think of Ilisa, but I've been monitoring him. He's had no communication with anyone but Shani and Lexi."

"So, that's why you sent us that email?" Shani asked. "You hacked into the aquarium's security cameras. You saw Lexi there. You knew we were anxious."

"Anxious and ready. Anyway, Moloch will come nowhere near you. You are all aware of this, and now that you are all getting stronger, you can protect yourselves from Kali if that's ever needed. You are all more powerful than any of the members of the Alliance. I will have to keep relocating in order to protect this stone that is around my neck, but I am certain if I had protectors like you five, it would be safe."

For Lexi, Shani, and Asher, this potential adventure would be a pathway out of their bubble of stagnation. Asher hadn't found a job yet, Lexi was still part-time at her coffee shop, and Shani was taking a year off.

"I really don't want to put my business on hold," Brex told everyone, "But if this is our only choice, it's our only choice. And it's not like there's anyone else better for the job."

The others laughed and agreed, but Logan still sat there, frozen as a spider. His hair fell over his tired eyes.

"Oh, God," he whispered to himself.

"Is there something wrong?" Maya asked. Maya was not under the delusion this job would be easy for them, but Logan's reaction caused her hands to clench together.

"I'm just—" Logan couldn't find the words. He wanted to find them, but they didn't want to find him. "I'm sorry. Everything is fine, but I guess I just need to walk for a second."

Logan stood straight up without looking anyone in the eye and looked around for a back door. It wasn't far away, only a few feet to the right of the refrigerator.

The rest of them watched him hold his face in his palm as he swung open the screen door.

"Was it something I said?" Maya asked.

"Maybe we should just give him a second," Brex suggested. "He's had a rough couple of months, and he's probably just worried about his dad. Shani always knows what to say."

It was true. Usually, Shani was the right person to reach out to when struggling with anything. Except when one needed to know how to break the news that would make Shani's head blow through the roof. That was Lexi's job. But Shani seemed hesitant and shook her hunched-over head as she second-guessed the suggestion.

"I think this is actually a job for Asher," she said.

Asher leaned back in his seat and waited a few seconds before he realized she was being serious.

"Me? Really?"

Shani pointed her index finger and said, "You will never hear me say this ever again, but I think he needs a guy right now, and someone who's had the most experience dealing with a difficult parent."

For half a second, Asher felt a sense of pride and a sense of worth even though his mother could never see it. Asher was too surprised to flaunt his toxic masculinity.

"Alright." Asher shook back his shoulders and trotted out the door.

A few feet away from the house was a rock that Logan sat on with his head plastered into his lap. Asher thought it looked like a dramatic movie scene in a tragic love story. Logan snapped up when he heard footsteps coming his way.

"I'm sorry," he said, almost defensively.

"For what?" Asher asked. "For going through shitty changes at the end of an important time in your life?"

"I..." Logan looked to the sky, unsure of how to answer that. "Yeah, I mean...yeah."

Asher quietly laughed, and soon after, Logan cracked a silent smile.

"What exactly is going on?" Asher asked. He sat down on the ground next to the rock.

"It's my dad. There have basically been no improvements in my dad's firm for the past seven months, and I promised that I would be there for him. I've done nothing but disappoint him, and I will have no chance at redemption if I leave."

Asher didn't know the first thing about law firms, or what Logan did for his dad's company, so he sat there in silence, staring at the sun before he could come up with a helpful response.

"You think he'll have to sell the firm if you leave?" Asher finally asked.

"Probably."

Asher knew this was clearly the wrong thing to ask after Logan shoved his eyes into the heels of his palms and audibly inhaled through his mouth.

"I know that this is stupid." Logan threw his hands down and shook his shoulder and arms, trying to let loose. "I'm an idiot. We were just talking about saving the freedom and humanity of the human race, and I'm complaining about...well basically just money. Like the stupid privileged kid that I've always been."

Asher shook his head, this time knowing exactly what to say.

"We all know it's way more than that. It's about your dad too. I know he's pretty much the only biological family that you have right? Or at least that you're close to?"

Logan shrugged and nodded his head.

"Then you know it's not just about money and the firm. Your dad relies on you emotionally too. He must. Watching your mom leave for Afghanistan couldn't have been easy for him, especially when she didn't come back. He didn't have a choice in losing her either. You have every reason and right to be stressed and upset about this."

Logan knew he was right, but it took him a moment to come to terms with the fact that he wasn't going to come up with a better solution than leaving his father behind after he gave his father his word.

"I am definitely going to need to have a few drinks tonight," he said. "I think that's the only way I'll be able to mentally prepare myself.

Asher held his stomach as he laughed. "Well, good thing I packed a few extra glasses of wine and beer." He winked and silently put his index finger to his mouth.

"You thought Shani would yell at you and say, 'What do you think this is? Your mom's basement?!'"

"Yeah, but I imagine Lexi would say something along the lines of... 'sick.'"

The two young men felt only a single drop of relief lift from their necks and shoulders, but it was something. Asher reached out his hand to help pull Logan to standing, and as Logan took it, Asher overdramatically and jokingly grunted as if Logan were two hundred pounds heavier than he actually was.

Down in the basement of the cottage, Maya already had beds made up for the five of them. They were more like nests because they were made up solely of many blankets, ratty pillows, and old duvets that were probably from the seventies, but the second Lexi stepped down and saw the basement with the ugly yellow fluorescent light, she was at ease. It was just like home.

"This reminds me of my grandma's house. It was basically our summer house, except we paid absolutely nothing for it."

"Thank you, Alexandra," said Maya. "That's very kind." Maya went around, refolding a few blankets to make them appear tidier, but it was no illusion for any of them. "Is there anything I can do for you before I tuck in for the night?"

The five of them aimlessly looked around at each other before Shani chimed in and said, "I think we're all set."

Maya headed back upstairs before telling them where the light switch was, so Asher made it his mission to find it. It took him four minutes to find it under the painting of a boat that was next to the door.

"So, who wants to sleep where?" Logan asked before he realized Lexi was crawling around, sniffing all of the blankets.

"The best way for me to sleep is to have a blanket that's as close as possible to the one I have at home," said Lexi. "Fluffy, with the scent of wet wool." The last blanket that she tried seemed to be up to par as she took three deep breaths in through her nose. "Sick. Definitely closer than I thought I was gonna get." The rest looked at her, patiently wondering if there was an end to Lexi's quirks. "What? You know that I don't adapt to change well... or at all. I need to at least somewhat follow a routine in the middle of the woods."

They all joined in laughter together as they snuggled into their beds. Logan didn't necessarily aim for picking a spot right next to Brex, but he didn't resist a smile when he realized that he had done so.

"How are we all...feeling, I guess?" Brex asked with a chain pulling back her voice.

"That might be a better question to ask when we're on the road," Lexi answered.

"Yeah, that's true." Logan saw the corner of her mouth curve as she exhaled a small chuckle. Logan was worried about Lexi. He couldn't help it. "You sure you're okay, Lex?"

"I just don't like to see change actually happening, so I can ignore it," Lexi laughed. "I mean, guys, I made it through going to college. That was the biggest change of my life. It went against every step of my routine."

"Yeahhh," Shani commented, "but, honey, I don't think you can bring your guitar on this little vaca of ours."

Lexi immediately stopped laughing and instead made a small squeaking noise in her nose.

Brex was hesitant to add to her pain, but she pushed through it. "And you're probably gonna wanna wear some pants instead of your hippie skirts, dude," Brex laughed.

"BUT WHY?" The rest of them propped themselves up from their beds to calm her down.

"Lexi," said Logan, holding out his hands. "You weren't there when we were attacked in the truck. It's gonna be hard to defend yourself in a long skirt."

"Mulan wore a skirt."

"Did she?" Asher asked before pulling out his phone to google it.

"That was a movie, dude," said Brex, trying to resist laughing into a pillow. "No, no, no. Correction; it was a *cartoon*."

"Exactly!" Shani was sure Lexi was going to jump up from her bed in excitement. "Also, lady cops wear heels all the time, which I've honestly always found weird."

"Lex, I promise we will get you new pants that are basically just like your hippie skirts. I've seen you wear something like that before. I believe in you."

There were no tears. No shaking. Just a dropped jaw weighted by fear and wide eyes to complement it.

Shani took her hand. "Like Brex said," Shani softly spoke, "we believe in you."

"Oh, I said that I believed in her. I honestly wasn't sure 'bout you guys," Brex said.

Lexi whacked her in the arm and finally laughed once again. She wasn't sure which relieved her the most, the whack or the laughter.

"Hey, guys," said Logan as the laughter died down. He continued when he noticed everyone's attention was on him. "We should promise each other something." The mood in the room suddenly vibrated earnestness through the air, but it was conclusive and absolute. "No matter what happens, even if we need to split up at any point, which will most likely happen, we won't give up on each other, and we won't leave anyone behind. We will always be honest and not hide anything."

The others knew exactly what he meant. He didn't need to say anymore. This was what he had to do to his father tomorrow. Logan couldn't trust himself, but he needed his friends to. They didn't have any other choice.

"Logan," said Asher, "We're basically indestructible. We're not going anywhere."

6:

"Typical American. Always forgetting that other countries exist."

Compared to Boston, everything was still and quiet. No horns beeping. No fire trucks racing in the middle of the night. It was refreshing for Asher to sense that the entire earth was frozen in time. He looked around to see the others comfortable in their homemade beds. He was the only one awake. For some reason, he knew if he fell asleep, he would have another dream. It was almost becoming an instinct, and for another unknown and odd reason, he had a bad feeling about this one.

Nevertheless, he flattened out his entire body and let his eyes linger towards the dark, wooden ceiling. The beating in his chest slowed down so softly, his heart felt like it was made of feathers. His entire body was at peace, but in the back of his mind, he couldn't shake that nagging feeling.

The birds outside started to chirp. At first, it was just one, maybe two. Then the bright, wakening sounds layered on top of each other.

Is it almost morning? Asher thought.

Maybe he wasn't about to fall asleep, but he knew he needed to, and if anybody in the dream was going to tell him something, or at least try to tell him something, he needed to know what it was.

While scrutinizing the darkness surrounding him, he drifted off into what could have been mistaken as a deep slumber in a dark, blank void until he reopened his eyes and was relocated to a building he had yet to visit.

It was more decorated than the building he usually visited. The building with the woman in blue, huddling in the corner was more dreary and less colorful. Even though he hadn't seen much of it. This decor had a dark vibe that rode along with it, but the pigmentation varied more. The top edges of the wall were lined with floral patterns that centered around a small cross and gold lining that covered the crease of the ceiling and wall. He had yet to witness this much detail.

Something about this place prevented Asher from taking a single step forward for a brief moment. But after he heard a few floor creaks come from down the hall, he managed to pull himself forward, one foot at a time.

He knew he was getting closer. Another noise layered on top of the floor creaks. A voice, or maybe more. At least one of them sounded feminine and firm. Maybe an argument was on the rise.

The hallways were wide, but Asher's fatigue made them feel closed in. He could still smell every plant in Maya's house which were all smaller than a grapefruit. Maybe their petite aesthetic matched the knick-knacks Maya had scattered around the living room, or maybe they were easier to move the next time Maya had to abruptly change her sanctuary's location. But their smells helped him push through the anxiety. His breaths were soft and silent, not because they were listening, but because he needed a precise location as to where those voices were coming from. Asher approached a four-way intersection in the halls, but instead of the voices, he followed the vibrations. His feet instinctively followed them. Whoever was stomping around their corridors was most likely tall, but more likely angry.

"Whe' ha' he 'en?" said the mysterious voice.

What did they say? Asher thought. Without second-guessing, he changed from a saunter to a stride.

After taking a sharp right, Asher could see the light coming from an open door. The light. It was delicate. Appropriate for a night's work in the office. The voice was becoming clearer, but for some reason, whoever this person was, they were starting to whisper.

"No, I'm sorry. I'm so sorry. This will never happen again," said the unidentified voice.

It was Asher's natural instinct to want to peer into the office from around the door. His confidence in these people not being able to see him in these dreams was beginning to decline.

The room was filled with antiques. Some of them looked like they were from Ancient China. Others looked like they were stolen dinosaur bones from an overpriced New York City museum. The walls were probably painted red, but there were too many decorations for Asher to be sure.

With little movement, Asher pushed himself to see more of the room, but the second he saw a tall blonde woman with dark skin and a gold dress, he froze. Barely breathing.

"Well, that's not my fault," she said. "I really just can't make myself care. We will have to figure something else out."

She whipped around so quickly that her long, bronze hair flew in a beautiful, rippled circle. She held an old phone to her ear. Maybe from the 1950s. Or maybe...*was* this the fifties?

Asher wasn't sure what it was called that old phones with a cord cling onto when the call was finished, but she carried the base in her non-dominant hand and dragged the cord behind her.

"Fine, I can get it done," the woman said as she dropped the phone onto her desk, not caring if she broke it or not.

She stood there for a breath, maybe two, staring down at the phone. Her head turned to almost face Asher. She looked solemn as if her husband had just left for war. But Asher tried not to concern himself with what she was thinking. He had to remember her face. An aching feeling reached from his gut and into his throat. He *needed* to remember that face.

There were only a few more seconds left. He could sense it. Frantically, Asher looked around to try to find anything else that would be useful. Any paintings that were significant and not just decorations, or anything that would give away who this woman was and how she was relevant to the people in Asher's other dreams.

Everything started to fade, but slowly. He was waking up, and there was nothing he could do about it.

*****

Brex, Shani, Logan, Lexi, and Maya were already up and eating. Brex and Logan were by the window, munching on cinnamon sugar and butter with a little bit of toast underneath, while Lexi and Maya were chatting at Maya's homemade, unsanded kitchen table, and Shani was already on her third cup of coffee. From Asher's point of view, it looked like they were plotting a bank robbery with all of the papers in front of them, but they were probably just going over the next step in the plan.

"Morning, Sunshine," said Lexi.

"You feeling okay?" Brex asked, looking at him with concern which was unusual for Brex.

For some reason, Asher grew annoyed by the way everyone was looking at him. What was the big deal? Everyone probably thought it was just a normal nightmare, right? And it wasn't like it was Asher's first time sleeping in late.

"Yeah, why?" Asher asked, reaching for the orange juice on the kitchen table.

"I just tried to wake you a few times," Shani answered. "And you wouldn't."

"Did you at least check my pulse?"

Shani grinned wide enough for Asher to see all of her teeth. "No," she said, "but you were breathing, and I figured that was enough."

Asher laughed with her, but he was still confused. What time was it? He didn't think he was in his wherever dream for that long. The clock on the microwave, from the year 2003, said it was almost eleven in the morning. The usual time for a wake-up call, but Shani was undoubtedly just being impatient.

"What are we working on?" Asher asked, trying to change the subject. He looked over Lexi's shoulder to see a small map of the world.

"Well, Maya knows where another sanctuary is," Lexi responded.

"Really?"

Maya rocked her head from side to side with her eyebrows clinging to her hairline. "Maybe," she said. "I knew it was there a while ago, just from conversation, but I'm not sure who guards it now."

"Great. Where is it?"

"Aruba."

"Damn. You mean they're not all in America?" Asher could feel all ten eyes shooting straight to him in both disgust and amazement.

"Typical American. Always forgetting that other countries exist."

Maya refused to even look at him, but that made Asher feel better because of how much he was blushing.

"Sorry, that was stupid. I mean my parents are from Puerto Rico—"

"Still part of the U.S., honey," Brex said, patting his shoulder.

Asher opened his mouth to respond.

Shani cut him off by shaking her head and slicing her fingers across her neck to get him to stop talking. Besides standing there with his arms awkwardly down by his side, Asher slid into a plastered smile, pretending that he didn't feel like an idiot.

"Alright, everybody come around now," said Maya, beckoning Brex and Logan from the window. "Let's go over the details of the sanctuary. It won't be easy to find."

"Why is that?" Shani interrupted.

"I've never been there, and no one has told me exactly where it is. We never release details that meticulous to one another."

"Makes sense."

"Plus, I think it's underwater, and certainly on the side of the island where they lure the sharks away from the tourist's beaches. Stronger security that way. There aren't many beaches, mainly just rocks."

No more discussion was needed. Silence fell as they all turned their heads to Shani.

"Yeah, yeah. I know," she responded.

"Another is somewhere in the United Kingdom or the Republic of Ireland. A young apprentice named Jethro, a rather handsome, young, blonde boy was stationed there not too long ago. Although, I know he just recently changed locations. There may be something in Italy, but I haven't heard anything about that location in at least two decades." She sat for a moment, concentrating on her breath and the activity that surrounded her.

"Is there anything else you know? Anything that would help us?" Brex asked with her anxious fingers twiddling.

"The only person that I know that definitely isn't currently guarding anything is Zara. She used to be in the White Mountains, remember?"

"Right. Where is she now?"

"It's better if I don't say. The more people I can protect, the better. But I'll tell you this. In the twenties, when they killed the guard, Yari, in South Africa, it was too much of a coincidence. They just so happened to fall upon a sanctuary that protected one of the stones? No. Someone leaked information to them. But now two within a month? They're gaining on us. Something has shifted."

No shivers shook anyone's spine. This came as no surprise to anyone. It only reminded them how little trust they had in anyone else but themselves.

"Wait," Logan said. "Moloch had both of the stones for decades? Before you took the other one back?"

"Yes, but I understand what you're inferring. They are useless without the alchelesters. But rest assured, they hold great power."

Lexi scratched her head before she said, "And you're sure Aruba is the best place to go to first?"

"The last guard that I knew there was Shiva. He's quiet and kind. He'll never forget anything you tell him, and people trust him. Confide in him. If he is still there, he'll direct you on the right path."

"How do you know he's not the mole?" Shani asked.

"Anything is possible, Shani, but Shiva is a unique leader of his people. He's unparalleled. His teachings aren't like what you see in other religions. His intentions are pure, and it would be hard to believe he could break his vows. There are better candidates. I promise you."

"How much time do you think we have, Maya?" Logan asked.

"I'm not sure, maybe a few weeks. Whoever is leaking information probably doesn't know much themselves. Just like the rest of us. But as I said, it must be some sort of business transaction. It's taking them a while to gain trust, but they're getting closer."

"Then we should leave as soon as we can," Shani stated.

"Yes, but before you do, rest up a little longer. We won't know when the next time is that you'll be able to sleep. We'll have you leave in the middle of the night. You'll be harder to detect in case they have access to any street security, and we should change your license plates."

"Alright," said Shani.

"Here," said Maya, standing up and adjusting her jacket. "We'll start by packing up a few things before I forget. Shani, I trust you'll keep these safe."

"Sure," Shani said, following her into the kitchen.

"I'm sure I still have a few useful things somewhere. When the fire destroyed my building last year, I was prepared. I could only assume something was going to happen eventually. I kept these safe."

Maya scrambled through the kitchen cabinets. Clinking glasses together. Lexi leaned forward in her seat to see Maya opening every cabinet door and not closing a single one. The only flaw in Maya's passionate, clean patterns that Lexi could point out. But something quickly stole her attention.

"What are those glass bottle things on the left?" Lexi asked.

In a cabinet that was so high Maya almost couldn't reach it was a rack of neatly labeled glass bottles that had too many colors to be a spice rack.

"Oh, it's just a few potions," Maya answered. "Some of them have expired I'm sure. I didn't make any of them. Most of them were gifts. Zara has a talent for potions. She spent more time with the Salem Witches than I did."

"What do they all do?" Lexi asked, keeping her curious eyes on the rainbow-filled cabinet.

"It's been a while. I'm sure I can't remember each one. Most of the labels are in Latin. But I do remember this twilight shade right here with the starry texture. That's how you know it's a potion to alter memory in one way or another. Or this." She pointed to a smaller bottle on the other side of the cabinet. "These thick, red, mucky, cloudy ones. The texture and color. That's how you know it's an antidote to something. It must be taken orally. I'll go through them. Maybe something will be useful."

"Sick," Lexi mumbled.

"Ah, here it is." Maya crouched down to pull a dusty, wooden box that was no larger than an elementary school student's lunch box out of the lower cabinet.

"Come." Maya beckoned the rest to the kitchen. Lexi popped up eager to see what the box was for. Brex and Logan patiently followed, but Asher stayed on the couch for a few more seconds. Curiosity didn't lure him the way it did the rest. The eager energy that put a spotlight on everything Maya presented to them didn't put a stop sign in front of Asher, but certainly a yield sign.

"I haven't opened this in decades," said Maya, gently wiping off streaks of dust. "It was also a gift."

"What is it?" Shani asked.

"Take a look." Maya grabbed a kitchen knife from her creaking drawer and gently placed it in the box before she closed it and locked it. "Always wait a moment, and make sure you lock it before opening it back up." She didn't take her eyes off the box until she opened it back up to reveal nothing but the dusty wooden lining.

"Sick," said Lexi.

"But it's not just a magic trick." Maya reversed her steps to take the knife back out of the box and held it up to them. "Whatever you put inside, it will not be detected. One of your cell phones could be in there. No GPS tracker will find it. And no weapons will be seen through an airport security system."

Maya gave one last brush off the top of the box before handing it to Shani.

"Thank you, Maya," said Shani, failing to hold back her over appreciative smile.

"Anything else you got for us?" Lexi asked.

"Oh, I'm sure." Maya clasped her hands together and pressed her fingers together. "Let's divide and conquer to get everything ready. Maybe I can make you something to fall asleep sooner. Then, you can all leave when the time is right."

"Alright," said Shani. "Let's get to work."

*****

The rest of the afternoon was a blur. The five of them napped when they could, but everyone had a job to do. Logan was checking Zazu Junior, the jeep to make sure it was ready for whatever the trip was going to bring them. He enjoyed spoiling Zazu Junior after what happened to Zazu Senior the year before when they had to rescue Lexi and Zazu was totaled during a violent battle with driverless, demonic cars.

Shani was in charge of the food. Lexi was in charge of mapping out their quest with Maya. Asher was in charge of taking everyone's phone and texting the people closest to them, saying they were going on a 'screen cleanse' and they were not to be disturbed. While Brex was in charge of packing extra supplies, she seemed to find distraction in playing target practice outside on the back lawn with her fire.

The door to the back porch almost didn't open, it was so old. The wood was rotting and cracked, but it was a style nonetheless. Brex pushed it open to be greeted by a ball of fur running towards her.

"Baymour," she laughed. The oversized hellhound drooled all over her forearm the moment she reached to scratch his neck, but she wouldn't have it any other way. He was the size of a Sprinter Van. The spots that covered his thick fur would look similar to a Dalmatian's if the color wasn't so dark. He had fangs the length of a household butter knife, and his eyes could light up a football field if given the chance.

Brex played catch with him for a while. She found a stick that was so big she needed two hands to throw it. That was until he refused to give it back to her and changed it into a chew toy. Brex had yet to see his grin so wide.

It was a lovely yet dreary day. Clouds covered the sky, but Brex's eye-melting fire lit up the small field, and the small target she had made out of recycled cardboard which she pinned to the closest tree. Asher couldn't help but peek out the window to spy on her workout.

"Brex!" Asher called out, stepping onto the creaking porch. "You ready?"

"Yeah, I think so," Brex called back with half the enthusiasm. By the way Brex punched her flames into the air rather than aiming them at the target, Asher figured she might need some sort of assistance.

"Hey, Baymour," Brex reached to give him a good scratch under the chin, but Baymour had a different idea.

"Ruff!" Baymour bit down on Asher's shirt and flipped him over his head to carry him and race around the yard.

"Whoa!"

Brex did nothing to help. She enjoyed watching Asher almost slip off Baymour's shiny fur.

"Brex!"

"Use your wings, dumbass!" He did as he was told, but the height of the bumpy ride made his landing less than graceful.

"Smooth," Brex laughed.

"Thanks. What's on your mind?" Asher took slow steps approaching her. He had lasted this long without getting hit by Brex's fire. He planned on keeping it that way.

"I can't tell. It's kind of all blurred together."

"If it's money you're worried about, I'm sure Maya will help us figure it out. I promise your apartment will still be there when we get back."

Brex took a moment to wrap her head around what he was saying. Her gaze dropped to the bright green grass. "Yeah, maybe that's it," she mumbled.

Asher wasn't buying it, but what good would nagging her do? Brex had an open soul, but sometimes it was open by only a little crack.

"Time will tell," said Asher standing there trying to be supportive, but Brex was too busy aggressively scratching her left palm.

"Damn it, the fake skin is making me itchy after I use my fire."

"Let's get something else for you. It's supposed to be sunny tomorrow. We shouldn't risk it."

Before Brex could say anything else, Maya burst through the door with something in her hand.

"Say no more, say no more." She waved a piece of cloth that looked like a wrist wrap in the air. "I knew you were going to need it eventually, so I made this. It's fireproof." Brex almost dropped it as Maya tossed it to her. She slipped on the rough material, and coincidentally, it fit like a glove.

"You've been a lot more prepared than we have, Maya. I'm sorry."

Maya's satisfied smile suddenly sank into concern. "What do you have to be sorry about?"

The lilt in Brex's chin and the tension in her eyes caused her focus to fall again. "Nevermind," she said. "I have a weird need to apologize for everything. How did you even make this? What do ya got back there?"

"Too much magic for even me to handle, but my dear Brex, you're more powerful than you think. Don't let anything or anyone from your past tell you otherwise."

The half-cracked smile on Brex's face shook with hesitation, but she mumbled, "Thank you, Maya," and sat down on the porch.

"I'm going to start making dinner. The sun will be down in about an hour." Maya took her time walking back into the house while Asher took his time sitting down next to a now non-flaming Brex.

"Is that what you're worried about?" Asher asked. "That we're not prepared?"

"Not exactly. I think my anxiety is more aimed at the fact that we're as prepared as we can be. What else do we know? Who else can we trust? Maya has to stay here to guard the sanctuary, but what if we need her?"

Asher shook his head. "We're not going to need her. We know everything that she does now, and in case she's lying to us, we have her journal. We'll figure it out."

Brex ran the rough material on her wrist through her hair and said, "I hope you're right."

7:

"Please don't ask anymore questions."

The five of them got comfortable in their seats as they watched Maya's small hut shrink in the back window. It was just past two in the morning. Logan sat in the driver's seat, dreading the five-hour drive to the airport in Boston, but Brex handed him doughnuts that she was hiding earlier, so they weren't eaten all at once. He quickly loosened up.

"So what's next, Shani and Lex?" Brex asked. Shani and Lexi shifted in their seats and cocked their heads back. "You guys are good at direction a.k.a. you always get mad if I don't ask you first or let you take the lead before anybody else gets a chance."

"Correction," Logan commented from the driver's seat. "They just come up with something first while the rest of us forget to pay attention."

"That's not completely wrong," Asher whispered with his hand over his mouth.

"Well," Lexi started, holding her scrunched-up skirt in both of her hands. "I think a Walmart or something is our best bet. I gotta get a new pair of pants, and we're gonna need some supplies that Maya didn't have, and more snacks to hold us over before we get to our next stop. Maybe just some random tools, like pocket knives, and some Band-Aids for our scars and first aid."

"Sounds good," said Logan. "Let's stop at a Walmart right outside of Boston. We should all get our backpacks too, right?"

"I don't think it's a good idea to have too much to carry," Shani added. "Maybe just two backpacks. We'll just have to pack a few t-shirts to sleep, some underwear, and a toothbrush. We're probably going to be doing a lot of walking and just traveling in general. We'll take turns carrying them."

Brex shrugged her arms and threw her palms in the air. "You just proved my point," she exclaimed.

Being the designated driver, Logan kept repeating lists and locations out loud. "Right. So Walmart, then back to our places to get some backpacks."

"We can drop off your car at Jenna's," Brex proposed. "She's maybe twenty minutes away from...wait no that's not a good idea. Kali will know to look there when she finds out what we're doing. What if we need the car again?"

"You think?" Logan asked, surprised.

"Just in case," Shani added.

"Why don't we park it at Adam's mom's house?" Logan suggested. "He rarely goes there." Asher looked out the window, hoping not to be involved in this part of the conversation.

"Yeah, yeah...good thinking," Lexi commented, while still looking at her phone. "It looks like flights to Aruba are a little more expensive than I thought. Are we sure we can afford it?"

"Unless Asher wants to carry all of us, I don't think we have another option," Shani joked. "But maybe there's a boat."

"Hey." Asher held his finger up, ready to give a lecture. "Don't underestimate me. I'd be way more fun than a boat."

"If we end up having to go to Europe, which it looks like we definitely are, we can save our money there, but we have to get to Aruba fast."

Lexi shivered, looking at the expense of the trip, but she held her breath as she put Logan's credit card information in and pressed the button that said, "BUY TICKETS!"

"Okay," said Lexi. "We're good to go."

"Don't worry, Lexi," Logan assured her. "My dad won't even notice. He doesn't handle his credit cards. His business manager does, and she loves me."

"I can't even imagine how much the rest of the trip is gonna cost," Brex added.

"Well, think of it as just that; a trip. It'll be great to get away."

For a fraction of a second, Brex felt a spark of relief. It was a dangerous mission they were pursuing, but Logan needed a change. He gained his determination back. Something meaningful that he was longing for.

"Anything to keep us calm throughout this whole thing." Brex patted his shoulder, holding her hand there longer than she usually did.

"Speaking of calm," Logan laughed. "I gotta stop at my dad's and tell him the good news. I won't be working for him this summer after all. Yay..." Logan shifted his tight jaw, preparing for another joke, but the anxiety overpowered him.

"Could you just leave without telling him?" Shani suggested, instantly regretting it.

"I can't." Logan had to remind himself to not get distracted by stress. The roads in the middle of Nowhere, Maine were surprisingly curvy. "I owe him. I might not be able to make it up to him now, but I owe him. We've done so well these past few months. He doesn't deserve that." The insecurity rained upon him. Logan hated the unintentional bitterness in his voice. "But that would be pretty funny."

"You're ridiculous," Brex mumbled as laughter returned to the vehicle once more.

After about four hours of driving, they made their stop at Walmart to stock up on more supplies as the store was opening. Lexi was primarily concerned with buying new, solid pants, even though they were her least favorite thing to wear. The only pair she had a shred of fascination for was a harem cargo style that had more zippers than she could count. They were tight on the legs but loose on the butt. Comfortable enough for Lexi to convince herself she was wearing a loose skirt if she didn't look down.

"At least Walmart sells cheap, stretchy pants that won't shove up my vagina," Lexi commented as they walked through the parking lot.

They spent about fifteen minutes in the store before noticing the manager's lingering eyes were getting too close for comfort. Asher stuffed a few pocket knives in his new backpack that he was buying as well before he and Shani got into an argument about whether or not they were going to be able to fit all of the knives into the hexed container that Maya gave them. Asher ultimately won the argument, but that didn't stop Shani from reminding everyone (not just Asher) that they might need to put something else in there. But Asher put the container in his backpack before Shani could threaten him further.

The rest of the backpacks were stuffed with snacks, first aid supplies, and a few of Brex's inhalers. Shani had made a point a few weeks prior that Brex needed not one, but two backup inhalers in case anything happened to the first two. Brex listened only to make her shut up, but the more she thought about it, the more paranoid Brex got. But she would never admit to Shani that she was right.

The only other thing that they needed was cash. The only place they could get that was Shane Kwan's house. Shani also made a point of reminding Logan that he needed to get the cash out of the safe *before* he told his father that he was leaving.

This is going to be a long trip, Logan thought as Shani finally calmed down in the backseat.

Logan pulled up in his driveway, secretly hoping his father was still asleep, so he would have a legitimate excuse to leave a simple and short, yet thoughtful note. But alas, the lights were already on. It wasn't even half past six in the morning, but Logan took his time preparing himself for what was to come.

"It'll be fine," said Lexi, reaching forward to pat him on the arm. "You'll just walk in there, get it all out, and then you'll just come right back in here with us. We're not going anywhere."

"I hope not, 'cause I'd be really pissed if you stole my car."

Brex playfully pushed him as he got out of his car. He took a deep breath, threw his empty backpack over his shoulder, smelled the dying roses that his father had forgotten to water, and took one step at a time as he headed for the basement door.

It reminded him of last year when he had to steal his old Hummer, Zazu, in order to save Lexi, even though he totaled his car on the way. He wasn't sure which would be worse; last year's catastrophe or the one he was about to step into.

Shane Kwan was probably talking on his phone as usual, and Logan didn't see him through any of the open windows. Even if he walked through the front door with an airhorn covered in disco balls, his father probably still wouldn't notice. But he didn't have the time or effort to test that theory.

The door to the basement was a creaky one, but Logan chose to rip the Band-Aid off and get it over with. The safe was just down the stairs and on the left behind a picture frame. A few years prior, Logan tried to explain to his father that if a burglar came in and tried to find the safe, the first place that they would look was behind a random, lonesome picture that was hanging up with no other decorations in the unfinished part of the basement. But as always, Shane Kwan wanted to hear none of it.

Logan quickly lowered the picture, typed in the code, and slowly opened up the metal door to see hundreds, maybe thousands, of Benjamin Franklins neatly stacked in the safe.

"Shit, Dad," Logan whispered to himself. He wasn't sure what he was expecting, but seeing this much money tucked away was definitely not it. Was this supposed to worsen his guilt? Should he only take half of what was in there?

"Half. Half, yeah that's good." He neatly stacked them in his backpack, knowing the piles would get messed up later, closed the safe, zipped up his backpack, threw it over his shoulder, and walked back to the staircase to see his father standing at the top of the doorway.

"JESUS, DAD!" Logan jumped and clenched his fist to his chest. He almost collapsed against the wall but managed to collect himself before doing so. "What's wrong with you? You know I don't like the dark."

"How was I supposed to know it was you?"

"I don't know, but right now, I'm really glad we don't own a gun."

"What's in the backpack?"

Logan froze. His original plan was to leave the backpack outside before he went and spoke with his father, but now, he was trapped.

"Nothing. I was just getting a few things, but I...can't find them." The backpack was zipped. Nothing was visible, but that didn't stop Logan from pinching his elbows and shoulder blades together so the bag was as hidden as possible.

"What can't you find?" his father asked, stiffly putting his hands in his suit pockets since he was already dressed for work.

"Nothing. It doesn't matter."

"Well...where are you going?"

Logan prepared a short and sweet speech that he was going to give to his father, but in that instant, his memory was wiped clean, and it dawned on him that there was a chance he may never see his father again, and if he did, everything would be different. His hard work building the current relationship he had with his father was all about to go down the drain, and he was never going to be able to repair it. No matter how hard he tried.

"Dad, I have to go away for a while."

To Shane, he sounded like a seven-year-old telling his parents he was about to run away. He couldn't help but chuckle. "What do you mean?" Shane asked. "Where are you going?"

"I can't tell you."

"Why not?"

"Please don't ask any more questions. I can't—I just can't."

Shane's face drained of any amusement. Instead, his cheeks were immobilized with fear. Logan rarely confided in him, and he never made a big deal out of anything.

"Logan, what's wrong?"

"What did I just say, Dad?!" The exclamatory vibration in Logan's voice shocked his father. Something in his stomach jumped and twirled, only to land ungracefully. "I can't tell you. I can't tell you anything. I have to go away, and I'm sorry that I'm letting you down again."

Shane suddenly knew what he was implying. "So," he said with his chin to the floor. "You're not going to be at the firm for the summer?"

"No, but I can help you find someone—"

"Logan, enough." He shook his head and still refused to make eye contact with his son. "Whatever it is you're doing, I hope it goes well, but I wish you would just tell me what it is."

"But I—"

"I know! I know! You can't." Shane threw his hands in the air, unable to control them. "We've worked so hard to get where we are, and now you're abandoning me when I ask you to do only one thing. One thing, Logan!"

Logan rarely saw his father genuinely angry. He was more of an "I'm not angry; I'm just disappointed," kind of parent. Logan knew his father was rarely thrilled with Logan's choices, but now he looked like he didn't even know Logan more.

"I don't have a choice, and that's all I can say."

Shane twiddled his fingers and left his stare lingering into Logan's eyes. "Why can't you just talk to me?"

"Believe me, you don't want me to talk to you. There are things that I never want you to know about. Why can't you just accept that? You've never been interested in hearing what I have to say anyway."

"Since when? And how do you know it's just me? You haven't been the most available in this relationship either."

"Dad, I'm sorry. I know I'm not perfect. Will you stop giving me grief about it? And that's not even what I'm trying to say here. I'm just trying to protect you."

Shane scoffed so hard, his throat almost tied in a knot. "Protect me? Logan, that's not your job."

"Fine, then can you just trust me?"

"Trust you? Right...okay." His feet sank into the floor, and his mouth quickly dried from persistently rubbing it. "You're seriously just going to leave me here alone? Alone? Will you at least not do anything stupid?"

"When do I do anything stupid?"

"That's not what I meant. I just want you to be safe."

"Dad, I have to go."

"Logan..." Shane tried to reach for his son's arm, but he was already out of reach.

"No, Dad. I'm sorry." Logan couldn't look back. He wanted to, but he couldn't. The pages were now turned and ripped from the book. What came from the conversation was not what he was expecting. Logan was so fixed on trying to not let his father's law firm down. Shane barely even mentioned the company. He just wanted his son to be safe. It turned out Shane could read his son better than he thought. But the one thing Logan wouldn't be able to stop thinking about throughout this journey was the fact that his father was now alone. No one was there to take care of him. Logan's mother had been gone for a while, yes, but Shane always had Logan. He never had to think that he was about to lose his only son.

Logan almost tripped on the curb on his way out. The grass was extra sticky, and the friction slowed him down.

"Ahhhhh!" Something popped in his throat, but there was a bigger pop in his knuckle when he punched the birdhouse that was hanging on the side of the porch until it shattered into pieces.

"Jesus, fuck." It didn't hurt, but the intensity of the blow almost took his fist off. Luckily, no birds were in the house, but the nests were in crumbles. He didn't remember the last time he paid any attention to this birdhouse that had been there since before they moved in, but he still couldn't block the guilt from searing his soul.

"Shit, Logan." If he had the chance, he would fix it if his world didn't come to an end, but for now, he would calmly walk back to his Jeep, and keep his resting heart rate steady for as long as he could.

"Ow." A few bloody scrapes painted over his knuckles, but the blood quickly slid back into his skin. He hadn't seen his magical healing abilities do this in a while. He almost forgot how much it stung and tickled at the same time. He was about to let it go and wipe the blood off on his shirt, but something caught his eye first.

"No...no, shit!" His left palm was completely barren, minus the deep, dark scar embedded in his skin that shone under the breaking dawn. He wasn't sure how quickly or how long his scar needed to be in the sunlight before Kali and Moloch could track his location, but he couldn't take any chances.

Logan shoved his fist under his shirt and ripped open his car door. The rest sat there, calm and silent. Brex kept her head down. She was the only one who was expecting his anger to overpower the rest of his emotions. She knew that feeling all too well.

As Logan turned the key in his car, his instincts were telling him to look up. Next to the house, under the night light, stood his father standing, still staring at him for as long as he could, lost and alone.

"There's nothing I can do," Logan softly spoke. "We have to go."

"Logan..." Brex whispered, wanting to reach for him, but resisting.

"It's okay...I'm okay." Logan wasn't a good liar, but that wasn't what disclosed the feeling in the pit of his stomach.

"Can I drive?" Brex asked. "I genuinely want to. I'm not as bad as Shani, I promise."

The laughter was postponed, but Logan finally allowed it. Just a huff exhaled from his nose, but it was there.

"Okay."

He hopped in the passenger's seat before he reached for his phone in his pocket and texted his dad, "Also please stay at the beach house for the next few weeks. Please, just one last request, I promise. And I'll be back soon. I love you."

8:

“I need to talk to Kali alone."

The new hideout was a lonely one, but that’s what made Moloch see its value. They’d had it for years, but they had only just returned with their new staff. The walls were tight in most rooms. The clutter was overwhelming, but it was Moloch’s favorite hideout. Between the city noise, the dark corners and alleys, and the thick walls, no one from the Alliance would ever guess such an obvious answer. At least that’s what Moloch believed, and Kali agreed with him. The only thing that she had trouble tolerating was the smell. The piles of dust everywhere didn’t complement the design of the room, and the last thing they needed was someone to bang on the door, complain, and bring along unwanted attention to them. But so far, Kali sensed the isolation the moment they stepped foot in there, and nothing could distract her. If anything had even a chance at stealing her attention away, it would be the thick, red and black scar that ran diagonally across her face and over her nose.

She stood in front of a dirty mirror that had minor cracks in it. Her small stature fit perfectly in the small frame, but the bright yellow light in the room emphasized the unseemliness of her scar. The longer she looked, the more energy drained from her, but perhaps that was because she hadn’t taken any iron pills that day.

She searched for her stash of iron pill bottles in the room, but the clutter made her wonder if it was worth looking for the bottle or not. Usually, her daily dose was about one bottle a day, making it a total of two hundred pills throughout the morning, afternoon, and evening. Some days were worse than others, but if she added a large steak to her evening meal, she would act a bit nicer to Clement and Reymid the next day.

The headaches were always unbearable. She could handle the dizziness, but the more she used her powers, the less iron remained in her bloodstream. After Kali half-heartedly looked for a bottle, one appeared underneath a chair that probably hadn't moved since the last century. She opened it to see that only eight iron pills remained in the bottle. Thirty pills wouldn't have been enough to eat with her first meal of the day, but she threw the pills to the back of her throat anyway before she tossed the bottle over her shoulder.

"How many of those do you have to take a day?" asked a voice that came from the doorway. Kali turned around to see Clement standing motionless like a lifeless doll. His eyes were drooping as they always did, and his pale skin was greener than it usually was.

"Why do you want to know?" Kali asked.

"Just curious."

"I would call it being nosy."

"Fair enough." He barged into the room. His feet moved too slowly for Kali's liking. She also hated the way he wore his hair. He looked like a ginger Thor, and the only thing missing was his hammer. She wasn't sure if it made her feel threatened, but she avoided making eye contact with him nonetheless.

"What do you want?"

Clement kept his stiff composure as Kali kept her stiff tone. The firmness in a feminine voice wasn't familiar to him, but he continued to stand his ground. With caution that he was hoping to hide, he handed her a ripped-up news article.

"What is this?"

"Just read it."

The headline read, "GRANDSON AND GRANDMOTHER SURVIVE ATTACK IN MIAMI!"

Kali didn't need to read the rest, and she didn't want to. Moloch's instructions were clear. They weren't supposed to live.

"We had to get out of there quickly," said Clement. "You thought they were just going to bleed out."

"Yes, I'm aware. Thank you." Kali crumpled up the paper and threw it on the floor. Her pessimistic anger led her to pace around the room randomly.

"What's the plan now?"

"I don't know, Clement. Why does it even matter? They're two nobodies in the Alliance. That's why there were no alchelesters down there. They're not useful enough to guard any of the gods' magic."

"There were no alchelesters when we *got* there. There could have been alchelesters an hour before we arrived. You're the one always kindly reminding us to not underestimate anyone in the Alliance."

Without missing a beat, Kali leaped into focus and twisted her wrist, releasing a sharp blade of iron steel into Clement's jacket and the wall right behind him.

Clement was able to open his eyes again after the blade stopped rattling.

"How many more times are you going to do that?" he asked as he pulled the blade out of his punctured sleeve.

"Funny," Kali said with a blank expression. "But I've got over a hundred years on you. I wouldn't be worrying about your nineties leather. Besides, I ruin a lot more of Reymid's jacket's than yours."

Clement scuffed the floor as he took a small step towards her. "You don't usually underestimate people, Kali. You don't want to start now, do you?"

Kali's broad, black shoes were planted into the ground. The rage spiraled out of control as she pulled the smooth iron out of Clement's hand and into her grasp. Without touching Clement, Kali reached out to point the tip of the blade less than an inch away from his bold chin.

"What makes you think that I'm underestimating anyone, including you?" Kali held her stance as Clement didn't blink. "Remember, I am the teacher here. You are learning from me, which means I understand how those protein shake-addicted brain cells of yours rub together. I see your strategies from miles away, and if I don't, which will never happen, I'll know exactly what to do. It's part of the job. Maybe one day you'll learn that, and I am begging for that to be soon."

Kali could tell Clement wanted to flinch. He needed to, especially after the disquieting silence that followed, but the only disturbance that made Kali lower her weapon was the sound of Reymid's footsteps running down the hall.

"Kali," Reymid said out of breath.

"What?" she impatiently snapped.

"We found something."

*****

The basement in the hideout was only secure because of Moloch's ability to melt most of the broken locks together. It looked like no one had been down there in decades. Then again, it was an abandoned building in the middle of Astoria. Decades was a possibility.

Kali hated the crunching, textured sound the stone stairs made when she stepped on them. The bottoms of her boots were more than an inch thick, but that still wasn't enough to stop her from cringing every time her foot felt like it was stepping on glass. She didn't care much for the smell either. The rest of the house didn't have a mold problem. If it did, Kali would know. For the past seventy or so years, her senses heightened to the point she needed to plug her ears when walking anywhere to prevent sensory overload. Therefore, stepping into Moloch's section of the house was pure torture. Just the way Moloch liked it.

"What is it?" Kali asked. Moloch stood there with wide eyes, saggier than usual. He was thousands of years old, but on a typical day, his eyes were at least a bit more lively. His leather jacket was dirtier than usual, and his shoes had a bit more mud on them, but his determination dripped from the sweat on his neck.

"Come look at this," he spoke, with a dehydrated yet firm voice. On his chipped, antique desk, mountains of papers lay under the pale, yellow light hanging from the ceiling. Most were wrinkled and ripped, but they were carefully organized in a way that only Moloch could understand.

"What am I supposed to be looking at?" Kali asked.

"One of the guards from the Alliance might have been spotted in Berlin. It's just like she said." Moloch pointed to a few pictures that were sent to him by an anonymous source. The rest glanced at the picture quickly without recognizing anyone in it.

"Which one are you talking about?" Clement asked.

"The one in the middle."

"Her?" Kali interrupted. "And what did she tell you exactly?"

"She used to be the guard for the Berlin location, and after she left, she wasn't sure if someone took over for it or not."

"We've looked in Berlin. Remember?" Kali threw the picture to the side.

"No, *you* looked in Berlin."

"What's that supposed to mean? You were too weak then, and I looked exactly where she said it was. Nothing was there."

"So, they probably didn't move it too far."

Reymid picked the picture back up and said, "That's probably just going to be a waste of time, but we can't rule it out."

"Oh, shut up," Kali snapped.

"That's enough, Kali." It wasn't the first time he had said these words to her, but the two other men in the room were new, and they needed to trust her. The lack of authority she was given by Moloch was insulting, unhelpful, and not the point of her presence. How was her input ever going to be of use?

"Do we have any other leads?" Clement asked.

"We might soon. Our source has been able to gain the Alliance's trust again," Moloch kept his eyes staring at the messy table, trying desperately to connect more dots, but he struggled to see the lines diagrammed in his head.

"Therefore, we can't trust her," Kali added, as always.

"It's a foolish thing to not trust the only lead we have."

"I didn't say she wasn't trustworthy. I'm saying she's an idiot." Kali grabbed the picture out of Reymid's hand and crumpled it up.

"Okay, now you're just being rude," Clement commented.

"Would the lot of you shut up already?" Moloch demanded with his dark eyes bulging out of his bald skull. "I need to talk to Kali alone."

Clement and Reymid despised the tension. Their constant dismissal was defeating. Their status crumbled beneath them as Moloch flicked them away like a still-lit cigarette butt. Nonetheless, they co-operated. They eventually made their way out of the room.

"Why did it have to be men?" Kali asked, leaning back with her arms crossed.

"Why did I have to pick a woman?" Moloch asked, keeping his stance strong.

"Please, I'd love to see who else you would have picked. They would have been dead on the side of the road by now."

"Is that what you think of them?" Moloch asked.

"No. Unless they all of a sudden decide to claim their dominance that doesn't exist."

"So, you don't trust them?"

"They've done nothing to deserve my trust. And it's not trust that's needed here. Are you just now realizing that?"

"That's a joke, correct?" Moloch walked away, almost feeling too exhausted to continue. "You say you respect what I am doing. Trust comes with respect."

"You think any of you respect *me*?" Kali asked, uncrossing her arms.

"I really don't have time to explain to you what that means."

"No, you don't have time to explain what that means to *you*."

Kali expressed no offense. The corners of her scarred mouth popped out of place, and her eyebrows lifted with curiosity.

"What are you saying?" Kali softly asked.

"I'm saying we're running out of time. We can't find Maya. Therefore, she has an advantage. Until we receive more information, we have no leads, and we don't have time for that. We can't let them beat us to it."

"What makes you think they're going to do that?"

"There!" Moloch towered over her as he looked down on her with locked eye contact. "How many times do I have to tell you to stop endlessly questioning them? That is the most probable way that we will fail. That's how anyone fails anything. It's a waste of time."

Kali didn't drop her eye contact, yet her vulnerability surged. Something surprising, but equally unexpectedly powerful.

"Fine," she admitted. "You're right. They're smart."

"Always assume that they're smarter than you think they are."

"I know. So, what do you want me to do?"

Finally recognizing their compatibility, Moloch straightened his jacket and shifted his agenda. "They're going to think we're after them, but the likelihood of them knowing anything is small. Maya knows better than that."

"So, we go after Maya?"

"No, she's stronger than that. She would never tell us anything. But..." His voice drifted off, but his chest inflated with pressure strong enough to hold him still.

"Moloch?" Kali whispered, but he didn't hear. He couldn't see her either. Instead, he saw the image of a young, handsome man covering up a circular scar that was tattooed on his left palm with his hand under his shirt. He quickly looked around. The image could evaporate at any minute. A sign close to him said, 'Gilman Street' and the stunning cream-colored exterior of the boy's house wasn't to be missed either.

"FUUUUHH!"

He gasped for a hot, fiery deep breath. His chest was cold for a moment before he could see his surroundings once more. It was only recently that he had managed to control these abilities. His strength wasn't always loyal to him, but for the past thirty or so years, it was faithful, and now, it was finally paying off.

"What did you see?" Kali asked.

"It's that boy, Logan. I can see him. At his father's house in Boston. Or...it must be his father's house."

"I can—"

"No!" The verve in his voice had vanished, the hope was starting to make its overdue return.

"What?"

"They've only begun their journey. They'll lead us there. Let's wait for this opportunity until they know something. They're smart. It won't be long."

*****

One of Lexi's least favorite places in the world was the airport. Not the air*plane,* the air*port.* Statistically, the safest way to travel was no problem for her, but the place where hundreds of people were screaming, crying, running, and yelling at customers was not her idea of fun. It was unnatural to her. Everything was always out of order and nothing ever went according to plan. This time wasn't going to be any different.

Logan parked the car at Adam's mother's house, without telling her anything about it, and the five of them double-checked that their bags had everything they needed and walked the rest of the way to the airport, but before they could leave the car. Lexi couldn't help but try to stall.

"I can't find my hair ties," she said, scrambling through her backpack.

"You don't need a ton of hair elastics," Asher commented, rolling his eyes.

"And besides," said Shani, "they're right here." She tossed the small packets of blonde hair ties to Lexi who stood there frozen with her eyes closed.

"Lexi," said Logan, "we'll make sure everything follows our plan as much as we can. We don't have to talk to anyone, and we have everything we need. It'll be fine."

"Okay, okay," she mumbled, clearing her throat. "And thank you, Logan, for being the only one with a bit of sympathy."

Brex didn't hesitate to glare at Shani and Asher, but they only returned the favor with a squinted look that said, "Hey Brex, Lexi is talking about you too." But they didn't speak of it again the rest of the way. They hoisted their backpacks on and hiked to the airport.

Lexi made a point of announcing her disapproval of the airport's smell, but she surprised herself when passing a Dunkin' Donuts in the building. She was able to calm down, but only a bit.

The time was eight o'clock in the morning, but Asher insisted on using military time as a better way to communicate. "They use it for a reason, come on our flight is 0945 hours." But so far, he was the only one participating. They had some time to kill, but in usual Shani fashion, she felt the need to remind everyone that they couldn't be seen or draw attention in any way shape or form. Blending in was their best hope to get where they needed to go.

"Is anyone hungry?" Brex asked. "This might be one of the few chances we can sit down and eat a decent meal."

"I love how you consider fast food a decent meal," Logan laughed.

"You're not just learning that about me now, are you?" She nudged him with her elbow and continued to walk by his side until they approached Lexi's worst nightmare; airport security.

"Lexi," Asher asked, "out of curiosity when was the last time you flew?

"A few years ago. That's why it feels so weird. I don't recognize this sensory overload."

"Don't worry. It'll be okay. It'll be over before you know it." The second the words escaped his lips, Asher leaned behind Lexi and stuck his tongue out at Logan.

"Okay, how old are you, asshole?" Logan whispered.

Brex and Shani followed in line behind them, sluggishly dragging their feet behind them. Shani looked over at Brex and mumbled, "This might end up being a four-person trip soon."

"And whose life will you be ending?" Brex asked. "Yours or someone else's?"

"Yes."

The line went by faster than they expected it to. Lexi kept her head down for most of the time standing there, but when it came to sending off her belongings through the conveyor belt, she was able to push through her anxieties.

"Shoes and electronics in one bin, everything else in another!" one TSA agent hollered.

Lexi was quick and efficient as she always liked to be with everything. After all her stuff was neatly stacked as it was supposed to be, she strode over to the full-body metal detector and stood with her hands up.

"You're all set, miss," another agent said to her. Lexi's chest was almost fully deflated until she heard a small beeping noise coming from behind her.

"You see that?" said one agent with a mustache, pointing to the screen. Lexi's shoulders immediately started to tingle again. After jumping off the small platform, she quickly scanned the conveyor belt.

"Where is it? Where is it?" she whispered repeatedly. But her bag was nowhere to be found. It was currently being scanned.

"Miss?" A tall, bald man approached her, softly speaking down to her. "Is that your bag right there?"

"Mhmm," Lexi gulped.

"We just have to have a quick search through it."

After Asher was finished being scanned, he ran up to Lexi and whispered in her ear, "It's fine. We didn't bring anything on board. They're probably just doing a random search."

"That's not what it looks like."

Lexi stood there with a smile plastered on her face. How could the TSA agents suspect her of anything after seeing the innocence radiating from her?

"They're just trying to scare you, Lex," said Shani, also running up behind her. "That's what they always do."

"What on Earth could they possibly gain from that?" The anger in Lexi's voice began to tighten and rise at the same time. Something that didn't happen often.

"Oh please, they're men!"

"Miss!" The bald TSA agent beckoned her to come closer. The drop in his chin while he eyeballed her made Lexi's gut drop even farther.

"Yes?" Lexi squeaked.

"Did you know knives aren't allowed on the plane?" The agent held up one of the pocket knives that they had bought from Walmart in his hand. It was supposed to be in the hexed box.

"Ohhh, fuuuuck," Asher whispered with his jaw shut tight.

"Sir, that was supposed to be...uh...in another bag with the rest," said Logan until Brex stomped on his foot to make him shut up.

"What?" the agent exclaimed.

"Nothing, sir, nothing. Just throw it out, please," said Lexi, gaining her voice back.

"Miss, you might have to come with me." He stood up out of his stool and beckoned a few more agents to join in Lexi's torture.

"For a knife that she forgot was in there?" Brex asked.

"She hasn't been on a plane in a while," Logan added. "She just spaced."

"And you're all with her, yes?" the agent asked, trying to tower over them, except for Shani.

"Yes!" the five of them all said in unison.

"Excuse me," Shani said, lifting her chin, preparing to sneeze. "I think I have to—ACHOO!" The violence of the sneeze ruptured the silence of the room, causing every head to turn her way.

A few "Bless you" wishes scattered about for a brief moment, but luckily that moment died when Shani looked the agent dead in the eyes and began speaking in a soft, yet firm voice that could calm a hurricane.

"You're going to let us pass. There's nothing more to be done here, and you're definitely going to forget the name, Alexandra Flannagan, aren't you? You've never seen this woman's face before. So, now, we're going to leave."

Brex, Lexi, Logan, and Asher all looked at her as if she was reciting a Shakespeare play drunk, with a dildo stuck to her forehead. But then, they smelled it. They didn't know what it was, or if they liked the smell or not, but it was old and unique. Something magical.

"Okay," the agent mumbled with numb eyes.

The five of them slowly backed away and returned to their normal stride once they were out of sight.

"What the f—" Asher started until Shani poked him with something.

"Satori blood powder from Japan. Maya gave it to me just in case, but only for emergencies. She's low on supply."

"That was blood turned into powder?" Brex asked. "Ew."

"Why didn't we know about this earlier?" Asher aggressively asked, trying to get in front of the still-walking group.

"Because she's in short supply! I don't like to be wasteful. You do. You take like four showers a day."

"That was one time!"

The plane was only about three-quarters full. Lexi was always appreciative of her small stature when crowded into tight spaces. On the other hand, Shani liked to make a scene from a soap opera about her long legs when squished in a tight spot.

"How are my knees supposed to stretch out after this?" she asked everyone individually, with about three minutes in between.

"Your dads usually fly you first class, don't they?" Brex asked.

"Oh, don't get her started," Asher mumbled while slowly flipping through the Vogue magazine that was from 2010.

"They don't have *that* much money, but at least economy plus."

Brex rolled her eyes and grabbed her eye mask from her bag.

"Also," Asher continued, still not looking up from his magazine, "in case you haven't noticed, Shani is the type of person that likes to make fun of everyone that points out how tall she is and then repeatedly does it herself."

"I don't do it that much!" Shani defended herself. "I only point it out when I feel it's appropriate. Like now, do you see how—" But before she finished Asher and Brex gave her the side eye that said, "Dude."

"Are you guys going to do this the entire flight?" Logan asked, already half asleep, from the row behind them. "Just tell me now, so I can kick you when needed."

"I'll join you," said Lexi, sitting next to him.

"Guys, we should all try and get some sleep," Shani intervened.

"Already ahead of you, Shani," said Brex, sliding her mask on.

"Okay, well, goodnight."

The five of them made themselves as comfortable as they could after a long night of traveling, packing, preparing, and worst of all; waiting. Lexi couldn't keep her mind off the fact that every second they were waiting and not moving, they were wasting time. If only there was a way to move faster, Logan wouldn't bother her every time he was worried about her.

"Hey," he said, poking her. "You good?"

"What?" Lexi asked. "Yeah, I'm good, why?"

"You sure? You just seemed on edge in the airport."

Lexi didn't bother to try to hide her sigh. "It's like I told you; airplanes are fine. Safest way to travel. But airports?"

"Right, right, right. Everything is out of order and unpredictable. That's so soothing, such a good business model."

"I know. What about you? How are you doing? Okay?"

"I think so. Just as long as I keep my mind off my dad, which is damn near impossible, I'll be fine and dandy."

The tenderness in his eyes sank into Lexi. She could never imagine her life without her father. What would Logan's world be like if his father was in it all alone, or if things went wrong, not at all?

"Between the five of us, we're going to make sure everything's gonna be okay? We are going to make it happen. We've done it before."

"Yeah." Logan could feel a small spark of happiness mixed with relief fighting its way through the darkness.

"What about everything else?" Lexi asked with her eyebrows to her hairline.

"What do you mean?"

Without saying a word, Lexi nudged her head to Brex, who was sitting directly in front of her. Logan could only look at her for a moment before the tornado in his stomach became too much. "It's that obvious, huh?"

"It was that obvious eight months ago."

Logan pressed his lips together and silently laughed before he said, "It's nothing. At least not now."

"She feels the same way," Lexi whispered. "Sorry, I kind of just blurted that out, but I know she does. I can see it."

"You can?"

"Look." Lexi scooted herself to face Logan. "After I heard about everything that Brex went through, I understood why there was so much fear behind her eyes all the time. It looked like a permanent scar that was never going to heal, but when she looks at you, it's like she's pushing all of that fear away. Like it can't control her anymore, and maybe, just maybe, her scars slowly heal, and they turn into wonderful memories instead that smother the pain."

Logan didn't know what to say. There were too many scenarios, and too many anxieties rushing through his head that he couldn't focus on just one.

"Telling her would be wonderful," said Logan, "but that would be way too much to deal with right now. The last thing I want to do is overwhelm her…or both of us."

"Isn't that what you said last year? You've been having these feelings for her for that long, right? I mean, it wasn't that hard to figure out."

"Yeah but—"

"What if you never get the chance to tell her?"

"I will, just not now. I promise you I won't wait too long." Logan held out his pinky finger. Lexi silently laughed and shook her head. "But it's just not the right time. She doesn't need to hear that right now."

"But what if it's exactly what she needs to hear right now?"

What if she's right? Logan thought. He turned his head to the window, knowing it was exactly what Adam Sandler would do in a rom-com moment. It didn't take long, maybe half a heartbeat for Logan to realize how much of a relief it would be for him to tell Brex exactly how he felt. Even if the conversation didn't go well, or as planned, the tension would spring from his shoulders. The less he was holding back, the stronger he would feel. What if that was the same for Brex? She was one of the strongest people he knew. Did she need to feel that way?

"I'll have to think about it. I—" But when he turned his head back to Lexi, something was wrong. "Lex?"

"I…ow!" The sweat dripped from her left hand. Her right hand was gripping her left wrist so tightly Logan could see her hand start to turn blue.

"Okay, okay, let it go. You need to get circulation."

"Okay," Lexi slowly let her grip loosen. "It won't stop shaking, and it just kind of hurts. I don't know what's going on."

"Shake your wrist out." Lexi listened. After a few seconds, the pain was slowly dripping away, and the color was returning to normal. "You okay? Drink some water."

"I'm okay." Lexi chugged the rest of the tap water that the stewardess had given her and pulled out her potato chips.

"Has that ever happened before? Has it shaken like that before?"

"No. Well, not exactly."

"What do you mean?"

Lexi sullenly looked up. Her hope that the issue was nothing to worry about was now gone. "Last week at graduation, my hand wouldn't stop twitching. Just twitching, and it only lasted for about the same amount of time."

"So it's escalating?"

Lexi shrugged and nodded at the same time.

"And you don't know why?"

Lexi shook her head with her eyes glassy and eyebrows scrunched together. "We gotta find those amulets."

9:

"So, you do know something?"

Aruba looked larger than Shani had pictured it being from the plane window. The tropical island was only twenty-one miles long, but the amount of shoreline overwhelmed her with the thought that she might not ever find the sanctuary, or she would get eaten by a shark first.

"Asher," Shani started, "do you think a shark would still eat me after telling him not to?"

"Probably," Asher responded with no hesitation and a little more amusement than he meant to. "Blood, it's like heroin to them. Or like popcorn to you."

"Great, this is gonna go so well."

"Good, 'cause that's exactly what I was going for."

The seatbelt sign finally turned off after they pulled up to their gate. The five of them rushed out of the plane as quickly as they could without drawing attention.

"Excuse me..."

"Pardon me..."

"Coming through..."

Due to the fact that he had just woken up, Logan almost tripped over a young toddler who immediately burst into tears after running into him.

"Mommy!" she cried, until Logan ran back over to her, threw her a candy bar that he had in his bag, mumbled his apologies, and ran back to the group.

Logan could have sworn he heard the mother say something along the lines of, "The what?" He proceeded to move along anyway. Their time crunch didn't have room for bends and bruises anymore.

"How are we going to get to the other side of the island?" Asher asked.

"They accept dollars here. We'll just have a taxi take us as far as we can go."

Shani called the taxi company that was on the card she had taken from the airport. The taxi driver knitted his eyebrows when they requested to be dropped off at the end of the island where swimming was banned, but he didn't have the energy to ask any questions.

The sun was to set soon, but the clear Caribbean waters were already beginning to darken. Their pink shade hid behind the clouds, ready to tuck in for the night. On this side of the island, the beach was made up of rocks and small cliffs instead of smooth sand.

"So, are we just going to walk along the coast until you find something?" Brex asked.

"I guess that's the only thing we can do," Shani replied.

"Shit, we're actually doing this aren't we?" Logan asked in disbelief. "Nothing's felt too risky yet, but shit just got real."

"Come on," Shani said, recentering everyone. "Walking along nothing but steep rocks will be fun."

The five of them began their journey across the seashore. Lexi stepped first, feeling the most confidence in her balance due to her being the closest to the ground. Shani proceeded close behind, hoping her connection with the water would help her, and everyone else if needed.

The waves crashed in a beautiful, catastrophic symphony. No two notes were alike. The cathartic visuals and sound loosened Logan's tensions, but when he came close to the surface of the water and witnessed a small octopus slapping and suctioning one of its tentacles to a rock above the water, his calm vanished along with Shani's patience.

"It's just a pygmy octopus, Logan," Shani calmly said. "It's not gonna hurt you. Come on."

With a shaken and snappy tone, Logan replied, "Well...could you tell it not to, just to make sure?"

"Just get over here before I make you, please."

Logan had no problem with moving away from the doll-sized octopus. His legs stretched as far as they could as he leaped from one rock to the next, but Lexi wasn't as lucky.

"That's a little far for me to jump," said Lexi.

"Here, I'll help." Asher reached out his hand after he took off his jacket and let his wings sprout and stretch as far as they could.

"Okay." Lexi cautiously took a step forward, grabbed Asher's hand, and jumped. But even before her toes left the ground, she had an instinct that something was wrong, and in a split second, she realized that she was right.

"Ah!" Asher felt his wet hand slip through Lexi's. To his body, the moment was instantaneous, but to his mind, the moment of watching himself almost drop what he was supposed to be protecting was endless.

"Lex!" Shani screamed as her reflexes kicked in. She didn't need to think about it. The water splashed under Lexi's feet. The whirlpool whipped in a tunneled circle. In a flash, Shani could almost see the liquid transforming into a cushioned, solid lifeboat as it slowly brought Lexi to the ground. Lexi's feet sunk into the foamy water, but the foam felt more like bubble gum than water. Her knees shook as she tried to stand tall. The sound of the swirling water spraying away from her, fighting to conjure up the magical lifeboat calmed her, but she didn't stop shaking until she was back to standing on the solid boulder.

"Shit," Lexi whispered.

"Lexi, I'm so sorry!" Asher shouted through his fingers that grasped his face.

"It's okay, it's okay. Just grab me by the waist this time."

Lexi's shaking didn't bother her. Not even when Asher scooped her back up and gently brought her back up to the rock. Lexi wouldn't let it. This was no way to start their journey. How would she screw the cap back on if it kept popping off too quickly?

"You good?" Brex asked, rushing to her.

"I'm fine. Let's just keep looking."

Lexi spat out all of the seawater from her mouth and pulled herself back to lead the rest. "Well, come on." She beckoned them all to follow her, hoping nothing would get worse.

The clouds in the sky suggested impending rain, but Logan was confident he could handle anything that came their way in that department. Shani's eyes quickly grew tired due to searching and examining every inch of that beach. What was she looking for? The deeper she focused, the less she could concentrate. How was this progress?

"Anyone need a break?" Brex asked.

"Is that Brex for 'Can we take a break?'" Logan asked, teasing her.

"No," she coldly responded. Logan quickly pulled the smug look from his face. He wanted to clarify the intention, but couldn't form the sentence to do it.

"Is anyone at least hungry?" Asher asked. "I could eat."

"Wait!" Shani exclaimed.

"What?" Lexi asked.

"I don't know."

The other four stood still, not wanting to move a muscle. Shani was now more lost than before. She knew something was there. Something that she might not be able to see, but what if she could, and she just wasn't looking at it yet?

"Something's here...I just...don't know what it is," Shani muttered.

"Okay," Brex said quietly, but loudly enough for her to hear her over the waves. "Just take your time."

Shani knew to keep her eye on the water. She didn't know why, but where else would she look? She couldn't remember the last time her connection to the sea was this strong. All she had to do was to trust the ocean.

"The fish," she whispered. What about the fish? She still wasn't sure, but it didn't take long for her to notice. "They're swimming in circles. Come, look!"

The rest of them gathered around to see the multi-colored creatures flapping their scales from side to side. No two fish looked alike, but the harmonious choreography they swam was hypnotizing. "They're basically making a perfect circle around this one rock," Asher observed.

"I think..." Lexi began. "I think they're guarding something. God, it looks deep."

"You gotta go down there," Brex added.

"What? I don't have my diving gear or anything."

"You're not serious are you?" Asher asked. "You think you still need those things? We knew this was gonna be underwater."

"I mean..." Shani stared at the water as if she'd never seen it before. "I just don't know what I'm doing."

"Shani." Lexi consolingly tilted her head, trying to be empathetic and understanding. "You'll figure it out. You'll be fine."

With Shani's anxiety prickling her in the back of the head, she didn't believe Lexi right away. But her alpha personality overruled. She took off her short-sleeve shirt and shoes, leaving her in her camisole, and soccer shorts. "I'll be as fast as I can," she said, scanning her friends.

"Take your time," Asher responded. "We're not going anywhere."

The water couldn't wait for her any longer. As it usually did, the ocean called to her, but this time, she was calling back.

Shani dove in, fingertips first. The water inhaled her as the cold ocean slid across her skin. The last time she breathed underwater, she didn't try at all. It was an accident. What if she did it wrong this time? She wasn't going to have much of a choice soon. Her feet thought faster than her lungs. She was already a hundred feet deep at least. It felt natural, but not yet comfortable. She needed to breathe. The ocean would save her.

"Huuuuuuuuuh!" She could hear herself perfectly underwater. Every sound that passed, every echo in the distance, she knew exactly what it was. Her vision was blurry, but the more she blinked, the clearer she could see.

"Shit." She almost forgot what she was doing. Still, she didn't know what she was looking for. All she could do was keep swimming.

The light shined in patches. The floor of the ocean looked like a checkerboard that was chewed by the family dog. She was gaining speed, but still, there was nothing. Nothing peculiar caught her eye until she inched just a little bit closer to the floor and finally noticed it; the bubbles.

"Gotcha."

To her left, a boulder the size of a car was surrounded by a circle of bubbles that floated like seaweed. The air from the bubbles had to be coming from somewhere. For the first time during the cold swim, Shani smiled and swam as fast as she could to the mysterious contraption.

Naturally, the bottom was the darkest part of the ocean. At least from what Shani could see, she was hidden in the shadows of the water, but if she looked closer at the bubbling rock, an outline of light, less than a millimeter thick, was slicing across the middle of the boulder, parallel to the ocean floor. Something had to be in there. It had to be hollow. It had to be an *opening*.

"Okay." That was the only word of encouragement she could give herself. The boulder was massive. Yes, it was hollow, but how hollow? Hollow enough for Shani's skinny arms to tip it over? Or however she was supposed to remove it.

"One...no just fucking do it, Shani." Again, the only words of encouragement she could muster. The rock didn't move an inch, or a half an inch, or a quarter of an inch. It showed no sign of potential movement. Shani didn't bother with continuing to try. In order to open it, there would have to be a different way.

"Ohhhh, shiiiit." So many bubbles came out of her mouth, she couldn't see what was in front of her until they disappeared. The memory instantly came back to her. The previous year, Maya had informed the rest that payment was to be made when they were trying to save Lexi. The only problem was the payment. She would have to release some of her powers, and her meter would go down. The thought of losing some of her magic made her stomach flip upside down and then flip back over again. How much was it going to take? Last time they divided the payment between Logan, Brex, Asher, and herself. The nagging pain in her head repeated, "You have no choice." If there was no stone, trident, staff, or anything down there, it would all be for nothing. Shani wanted to take all her anger out on this voice in her head, but they were right. And without thinking about it, she placed her left hand on the boulder, and the force of it ripped the energy from her skin.

"Ahhh!" She didn't remember the payment hurting this much last time. Then again, she had more magic in her system back in September.

The cries of the ocean whistled in her ear as the cylindrical entrance rose above her head, giving a shimmering silhouette from the daylight above. A small, yet prominent, metal door materialized inches away from Shani. She reached to open it before it did the job for her. Whether it was a welcoming gesture or not, she wasn't sure, but she proceeded to accept the invitation anyway.

Her slender body slid through the opening before the door slammed behind her. The chilling darkness wasn't what she thought it was going to be. Calm, for sure, but besides the ocean water, what else could be disturbing her presence?

An abrupt thud came from above Shani's head, only inches away. Even as she heard the water initiating its drain, there was still no light to be seen. Once the air surrounded her eyes, nose, and mouth once again, she was expecting a cold rush to drip down her skin. But it never came. Instead, there was a mucky heat wave that brushed through her hair the moment the crate underneath her feet began to lower.

"The f—?" Shani rarely ever felt faint, but something in the air was making her head pound and her knees weak. Was this because of her payment? Or worse; could it be a *warning*? But suddenly another, bigger door opened to a dry, open, and sandy room.

"Hello?" Shani hollered with a few droplets of ocean water still stuck in her throat. The room was dark, but her eyes hadn't adjusted yet to any light. She had to rub them a few times before she could make out the antique furniture that hadn't been aging well. Most of the artifacts were covered in dust or chipped beyond repair. Nonetheless, it felt like a home. A sense of security and comfort rushed against Shani, eager to get through to her. Her guard wasn't about to lower anytime soon. Not until she found what she was looking for and got herself out of there.

"Hello?" Shani called out one more time.

"Maya, is that you?" said a voice from behind a wall.

"No, it's—"

"How did you find my new location? I could have sworn I—" The old man standing before her wasn't surprised, yet. But he remained calm as his suspicious eyes moved closer, wondering if there was any danger before him.

"I'm not Maya, but she did send me," said Shani, holding her stance firm and tight.

"Yes, yes, she did."

He was recalling a nostalgic memory as he let down his guard and stepped closer to her, or at least that's what it looked like from Shani's point of view. His aging chin held so much white hair, Shani was scared to think about what might be under there, but just below the beard was a half-moon pendant that hung around his neck. The sandals that were strapped to his shaky feet slid across the concrete floor, making a noise that forced Shani to tighten her jaw, that was until she noticed the gentle, yet striking eyes that belonged to the snake around the old man's shoulders. A bomb might as well have exploded in her stomach.

"Did she contact you?" Shani asked.

"No, but I can see the truth manifesting from you," the old man said. "Forgive me, I am Shiva."

"I hoped you were," Shani muttered, trying to laugh it off. "I wasn't expecting to see anyone else down here. I'm Shani."

"You need something from me, don't you, Shani?"

"I'm hoping. I'm not sure if you have what I need, but for now, could I have a towel?"

Shani almost mistook Shiva's laugh for a hiccup.

"I could," said Shiva, "but I have the strangest feeling you could dry yourself off without such assistance."

It didn't matter how soothing his voice was or how twinkly and comforting his eyes were, Shani couldn't stop staring at the snake that brazenly stared back at her. Her vulnerabilities never felt so defenseless.

"Don't worry about him," Shiva said, noticing Shani's trepidation. "He won't harm you. He doesn't harm anyone."

"Okay, thank you. I...um...I haven't learned how to dry things yet, let alone my whole body."

"Well, then. Let's change that. Shall we?"

Shiva held out his hand, and although the knots in her gut told her to swim back up to her friends, Shani took his hand, hoping the tension would release. But she was just grateful that it didn't worsen.

"Alrighty, then," she said before following him.

As she left the ordinary room, she noticed a shift in the smell. Where was the overwhelming scent of the ocean escaping to? Instead, the air was filled with grass...and roses...and anything else that brought peace wherever it was needed.

"Where are we headed?" Shani asked.

"Where do you need to go?" Shiva responded.

Shani hated games, but whatever needed to be done, she was going to have to go along with it. What was the point of fighting?

"Like I said, I need to get dry, but—"

"Why do you wish to dry off? If you're just going to get wet again when you leave?"

Hmmm...I don't like feeling wet? Shani thought. *Even though a towel wouldn't help much, but at least I know I tried.* But she didn't need to say that. He already knew what she was thinking.

"I don't know," Shani said.

"Right there in that room." Shiva nodded his head toward the small opening in the wall. Shani peaked her head around the corner to see a proper bathroom.

"You have a real bathroom?" Shani asked, reaching for the closest towel.

"I have a real body. I'm not imaginary, you know?"

Shani stepped into the small bathroom without any more questions. She grabbed a surprisingly soft towel and squeezed as much water as she could get out of her hair. "Sorry. I don't know too much about spirituality. I don't really know how it works."

"You don't need to know. That's why there are people like me. My teachings, just like anyone else's, are for the people who want to learn them."

"Okay...but a bathroom?" Shani finished drying herself off as much as she could and folded the towel before neatly placing it back on the rack.

There was that hiccup-laugh again. It was soft, and trusting. "Let me put it to you this way, Shani. I have a real body, but a different soul from yours. Perhaps the similarity between the two has grown since your...incident."

"How did you know about my powers?" Shani laughed and shook her head. "You could tell right away, couldn't you?"

"Well, it was a curious thing. Watching a human breaking through such powerful security. But I also know what that scar means."

Shani didn't mean to look at her scar. She didn't want to. Thinking about the power that she lost due to breaking in did nothing but put great stress on her and squeezed her chest like a boa.

"I need your help."

"Anything for Maya. That means anything for you."

Shani nodded, but she didn't know where to start. She hung up the towel on a metal hook that looked like it was about to fall out of the wall, walked back into the hallway, and said, "Um...I need to know what you know about the Alliance. Any last locations that you know of? Which of them have alchelesters hidden in the sanctuaries? Everyone needs to relocate. Everyone. Moloch. He's building an army, and there's a mole. Someone that's been feeding him information for years. We need to help guard anyone that we can. And we need to warn anyone that we can. And I know you don't know me, but I need to know if you have any of the alchelesters yourself."

Shiva's center stood still as a rock.

"Your troubling adventure is just beginning, isn't it?" Shiva asked, walking over to the small table in the kitchen and sitting down.

"You're the first stop," Shani responded, still standing.

"I see, good choice. I wouldn't want you to waste time."

Shani's heart sank. "What do you mean?"

"I'm afraid I don't quite have the knowledge that you're looking for. I sense you were assuming I would divulge more information than I have."

"So, you do know something?" Shani eagerly sat down across from him.

"Shani, forgive me for saying such a thing, but I don't think that's your most troubling dilemma."

"I know people are after me," said Shani, keeping her eyes forward, and her chin up. "That's why my friends and I have to move now. We have to warn everyone. Before any more information is leaked. They're moving fast."

"They are," said Shiva with absolute certainty. "But that's not it either."

"What do you mean?" Shani's fingers clenched the red and green cloth lying across the table in front of her.

"Shani." He leaned in closer to her, not wanting anyone else to hear, forgetting no one else was there. "Peace isn't what you have to worry about. You'll find your way. It's trust. Not everything that you will hear is the truth. For better or for worse."

"Do you mean, I shouldn't trust the people I want to trust? You think they're lying to me?"

"There will never be a perfect balance in this world. You should never expect that."

"I don't. I don't trust a lot of people."

"That's because you have the soul of a warrior. Keep it that way, betrayal won't be your friend. But it won't be your enemy either. You have too much intelligence and restraint for that to control you."

Shani didn't say anything. His peaceful voice hummed with protective concern. What if he was referring to one of her friends? She needed to trust those people more than anything.

"How do I know if someone is lying to me, or not?"

"I have faith you'll know. Maybe not now, but when the time comes." He stood up, looking down at her. "I apologize, Shani. Have I frightened you? I can assure you I didn't mean to do so."

"I'm not scared," said Shani, with a quiver in her voice.

"My dear, you will soon come to learn that fear is not a weakness. It's an instinct that will draw you in the right direction. I'd be concerned if you weren't afraid. Use that. It'll only benefit you. However you are feeling, use it."

Shani understood, but she sat still.

"When was the last time you were above the surface?" Shani asked.

"This morning."

"What?" Shani almost coughed out ocean water. "Do people ever see you?"

"Not if I don't want them to."

"Sir, any other information you have, I could really use."

"Let me see your list."

Shani was certain she had not mentioned anything about a list, but she pulled it out of her pocket anyway and took it out of the sealed plastic.

Shiva only needed a moment before he said, "Ireland."

"Ireland?"

"Young Jethro. Smart boy. Recently became an official member of the Alliance. Maya told me he was a brilliant apprentice. I know he's in Ireland, but I don't know the whereabouts of his sanctuary."

"Oh," Shani mumbled, disappointed.

"But I know where he is employed."

"Where he works?" Shani's spine perked. "Yes, anything. That'll help."

"Well, I don't know of the name, but I do recall him mentioning a statue that he always admired on his way to the pub. He tends to the bar. If I'm not mistaken, it's in the shape of a fox with an arrow in its mouth and a half-moon necklace around its neck. I'm sure you can see why it would remind him of me," he said, holding his half-moon pendant. "Anyway, it's in downtown Dublin. That's all I know."

"Thank you." She wasn't sure if she should shake his hand or bow. "That's all I need. You've been a great help. But what about your sanctuary? You don't guard anything?"

"Oh, don't worry about that. I've already moved it. No one will ever find it."

Shani opened her mouth to ask for more details, but she didn't want to know, or she couldn't. The less she knew, the better.

He reciprocated her gentle smile before Shani said, "I should go."

Shani turned around to leave, but Shiva quickly and gently stopped her. "Shani..." She turned back around with her chest tight and her knuckles clenched. "Please, do retain what I said. Implement it into every decision that you make, but please don't let that stop you from listening. You have a special place in your army, but your friends have value, too. You were each given unique abilities to reflect your unique qualities."

Shani's chest expanded once again. As much as it pained her to hear her weaknesses being repeated to her, she knew she needed to hear it.

"Thank you, Shiva. I know I need to be reminded of that all the time."

"Be careful. Always."

Shani smiled, and before any more hesitation, she returned to the cylindrical exit.

The opening seemed smaller than a few minutes before, but maybe that was just because her eyes had finally adjusted to the dark. She wasn't sure if she needed another payment to leave, but before she had to look for an ATM, the gate began to rise back to the water. She couldn't ignore the suffocating feeling no matter how many times her subconscious reminded her she would be fine. It was like watching a bathtub filling up, but only if the bathtub was a moldy black and with faucets shooting out water from all different directions.

"Oh boy," Shani mumbled to herself. She didn't like the way the mucky darkness made her toes tingle. The faster the exit went, the less of a chance she had of throwing up. Water was never an issue for her, but dark, small spaces made her spine twist and crack. Especially when she needed to be in them more than once.

"Okay...okay...okay." She repeated this to herself over and over again when the water started to pour back in. It smelled worse than usual, but she didn't think anything of it. Once the water filled up the tank, and the small door slid open, any tingling in her body vanished, but she didn't trust it. Not for a moment.

Everything at the bottom of the ocean was a shade brighter. Not happier, but it glowed with more passion. More strength and fire in its soul.

Shani pushed her way through the last part of the exit. She felt exposed. As if everything was looking at her, but calmly.

"Come on, come on, come on." A thought was poking at the back of her head, but watching the bubbles float to the surface as she talked to herself kept her distracted. Although, it didn't last for long.

Woooosh...

Shani almost gave herself whiplash. She turned around, but nothing was there. Still, she felt the rush of the water push against her.

Woooooosh...

She felt it again, but this time it was coming from the opposite direction. The glow faded, and it was replaced with darkness, a darkness that made Shani's tingling return.

"Stop it," Shani said to herself, or so she thought.

Her head slowly drifted back towards the surface, but there was something in the way. Something that caught the corner of her eye before she fully caught sight of it. But the image didn't fully process until she was eye to eye with it. And when Shani saw the flowing dark green hair before her, she realized it wasn't an *it* at all.

"AHHHHHH!" Shani screamed. The woman's face was so sunken in, her cheeks almost touched. The moss-like skin was rough, scaly, and dark, but didn't radiate any beauty like most marine life. Before Shani could swim away, or move at all, the mermaid's slimy hand grabbed her by the wrist and pulled her down. Her strength was overwhelming. There was no advantage Shani had that she could use. The speed of her strokes was nowhere near as fast as this creature's. Did all merpeople have this strength and speed?

"N—" Shani tried to scream for the mermaid to stop, but there was no use. The cold ocean water rushed against her, and the pressure was too much. Her fingernails were too short to dig into the creature's skin. Even if they had been sharp and long, they probably wouldn't have made a difference. The density of her green scales was closer to a rock than human skin. Even the moss-like patches were strong. She couldn't resist the mermaid dragging her to the ocean floor.

No matter how fast Shani's aching heart was pumping, her legs weren't taking in any of the adrenaline. The fatigue quickly sank in, along with her eyes. Her sight was slowly fading. She had no idea where she was. The bottom of the ocean was getting closer. Shani could sense it. The pressure was rising, but it didn't bother her. Her wrist and lungs were in too much pain.

Their speed was increasing. The mermaid had only been ripping Shani away for a few seconds, but those seconds were increasingly growing longer. She could feel her friends getting farther away from her. They had no idea what was happening.

Shani tried one last time to pull herself away, but she was still too stunned to say anything. The knuckles cramped the more they grasped. She tried to put her legs on the mermaid's hips, or whatever they were called, to use as leverage, but before her long legs could fumble their way through the water, a sudden shift in the mermaid's balance took Shani by surprise. They stopped.

"Ah!" The abrupt halt cracked Shani's back, but the mermaid loosened up on her tight grip, and Shani could take a deep breath of mucky ocean water once again. "Let me go!"

The mermaid understood her perfectly, but she didn't say anything in return. Instead, the mermaid pointed her dirty, green, bony finger towards a giant boulder that Shani's squinting eyes could hardly see.

"What?! What do you want?! Let me go!"

The mermaid didn't listen. Her grip tightened once more, but this time, Shani saw comfort and concern in the creature's eyes replacing the anger and fear. The mermaid pulled Shani over to the rock and smoothly drifted behind it to see another mermaid injured and lying across the sandy ocean floor.

Shani's heart filled with stabbing pain. The blood was slowly seeping out of the wound. The bloody water was fogging up her vision and making the surroundings darker than they were before.

"Oh..." What was Shani supposed to do? Why did they think she could help this poor creature?

Other merpeople surrounded her. Not too close, but close enough for them to worry. One small mermaid, who looked no older than a ten-year-old girl, hid her face behind a large merman that stood taller than most human men. Was this her mother? A sister? It didn't matter. Shani needed to try.

"I don't know if I can help," Shani's tired voice lethargically mumbled the words, hoping they would get across. "But I'll try."

Shani shook out her aching wrist before she swam over to the injured mermaid. Her eyes were slowly adjusting to the dark once again. For better or for worse, she could see that the injury was much more crippling than she thought. Multiple bite marks ran along her stomach, and they were deep.

"Can you hear me?" Shani asked. The mermaid nodded. She hoped that meant the same thing in mer-language that it did in the human world. "Does this hurt?" Shani pointed to the girl's stomach. Her face squirmed in pain. She took that as a *yes*.

Shani held her hands there, hoping the pressure would help. She knew that was the proper procedure for a bullet wound. Why wouldn't bite marks be the same?

"Just breathe, okay?" Shani asked. "But gently."

The mermaid did as she was told, but the more Shani's skin connected with hers, the more the deep calming sensation rippled throughout Shani's body. And from the glowing veins repairing the mermaid's body, Shani guessed the mermaid felt the same.

"What's happening?" Shani asked. "Are you okay?" The mermaid didn't answer, but the sudden increased movement in her tail gave her the answer she needed.

"Whoa..." Shani whispered to herself. The mermaid sat up straight. Her hair was longer than Shani had expected. It blew in the gentle, rushing water. The small mermaid swam over to her mother. Their foreheads lovingly touched before they wrapped each other in an embrace.

Shani stood there, floating a few inches above the sea floor while the entire group of merpeople swam to float in front of her. Their glowing eyes were their most beautiful feature. The glow could light an entire aquarium. One by one, each pair of eyes momentarily disappeared as they each bowed their heads to Shani. She was sure most of them were smiling, but their faces were surprisingly stiff, and it was still terrifyingly dark.

"I should go," said Shani. "Thank you...I mean you're welcome...I...yeah." And before she could keep babbling on, she swam back up to the surface faster than before.

The bright light almost burned her eyes, but slowly. Air never tasted so fresh and cool. Shani tried to search for her friends, but she was almost a mile away from shore.

"Shani!" she heard Lexi scream. "Shani!" Lexi was waving in the distance on a tall rock.

She swam back toward the island and her friends. She could hear them cheering for her the closer she got. It was tempting to splash them when she finally returned to them, but she didn't want to scare her friends with such an abrupt shift in personality.

"You okay?" Asher asked.

"What'd you find out?" Logan asked before Asher could get an answer. "Did you find Shiva?"

"I'm fine." Shani was still out of breath, but she was able to stop shivering once she was wrapped in a warm towel. "Yes. I didn't find out much, but we're going to Ireland."

10:

"We gotta get these cameras away from us."

It was already dark out by the time they ran back to the airport. No taxis were in sight, so they had to speedwalk the whole way there. Lexi begged her phone to load, so they could look for plane tickets, even though she knew her phone wouldn't listen. Siri repeatedly said, "I didn't quite catch that, could you—"

Although, every time, Lexi would interrupt and say, "BITCH, SHUT UP!" And then Siri would say it again.

"Are we almost there?" Asher asked.

"Yes, you will get your fried plantains," Shani answered.

"How did you know that's what I wanted?"

"You've been talking about wanting to try them since we were fourteen."

"Aww, you remembered."

"Can everyone please stop talking until I have food in my stomach?" Brex asked. "I need some Caribbean spice."

"Guys," Lexi called attention. "I can't get the tickets. We'll just have to get them there, and wait in line."

"That could take hours," Logan added.

"The population in Aruba is about a hundred thousand people. I highly doubt that."

"Okay," Asher stopped in his tracks and held up both of his index fingers. "We are all obviously hangry, so I agree with Brex. We should just stop talking to each other until we get our tickets and food."

The rest nodded silently in agreement without eye contact, and they kept their agreement until they stepped foot in the quiet airport.

Once they arrived, Lexi insisted on doing all of the talking to get the tickets while the rest paid no attention, standing in line with her.

"Do you see any good places to eat?" Shani asked.

"Whatever nice sit-down place is good with me," Asher answered. "We need to fill up. The next flight is gonna be a long one."

"Guys," Lexi loudly whispered. "Pay attention!" Her small arms could have powered a windmill with how impatient her beckoning was.

"What? What?" Brex asked.

"They don't have any flights to Ireland for another three days."

"We can't wait that long," Logan insisted.

"She's already told me that, sir," the tall, thin woman said, standing behind the customer service counter.

"There's another option," Lexi continued, "and I think you're gonna like it."

The woman handed them a small map of Western Europe with microprint directions on it. "You can take a plane to Paris that leaves in five hours and then take a ferry from France to Ireland."

"A boat?" Logan asked. "I get soooo seasick."

"We'll take it," said Shani. "Logan, we will buy you Dramamine."

The five of them chowed down as much food as they could at a halfway decent Caribbean restaurant, restocked on snacks and drinks, and waited around for their next flight, but Asher couldn't sit still.

"Asher, stop doing that," Shani bossed him around.

"Doing what?"

"Looking over your shoulder and staring at other people. People are going to complain. Just stay calm. We'll be on the plane soon."

Asher compulsively scratched his thighs and didn't listen to anything Shani said. He couldn't shake the feeling that he was someone's prey.

"Does anyone else feel...kinda weird?" Asher asked the rest.

"You gotta be a lot more specific than that," Lexi declared.

"It's hard to describe because I don't feel like someone is watching us now, but I feel like they're going to pop out any second."

"You're probably right?" Brex commented, with confusion buried in her voice. "That's why we're trying not to draw attention."

"Right, but I feel like...I don't know. Like they're coming soon. Maybe they already know where we are and where we're going."

The rest were tempted to ignore his claims, but they weren't baseless. If this was a message of warning, Asher would be the first one to sense it.

"It's inevitable at this point," Brex mumbled as she audibly exhaled. "We just have to be prepared for it."

The flight number was finally called before the five of them stood up and walked to their gate.

"How you feeling, Lex?" Shani asked.

"Fine now that we're about to board. Just as long as my passport still works and my ticket isn't crumpled too much."

"You sound like my mother," said Asher.

*****

The five of them got some decent rest as they all slept for seven hours straight. The plane was roughly half full. Therefore Shani shifted her complaints from how *cramped* her legs were to how *sore* her legs were from the previous flight, but Asher quickly shut her down by pretending to snore and then actually falling asleep.

The next sunrise, the five of them stood by the large, crowded dock, waiting for the white boat to open its doors to them. Lexi had already purchased their tickets, but Shani couldn't help but worry that something was going to go wrong. The dock looked overcrowded.

"What time is the boat leaving again?" Shani asked.

"In a few hours. The only boat that leaves today. It's gonna take eighteen hours from dock to dock."

"Oh, okay." It wasn't the last time that Shani asked, but once they were on the boat, in their rooms, and after Shani waited to make sure no one intruded to claim there was a screw-up and the room was actually theirs, Shani finally stopped talking.

"Sooo..." Logan groaned. "What do we do now?"

The room wasn't filled with much. A few water bottles, shampoo, and soap bars filled the only drawer that sat in between the two bunks.

"I don't know," said Lexi, "but there are only four beds, who's gonna squish?"

"Please," Brex chuckled. "You know that you and I are the only ones that *can* squish."

"We're not just gonna sit here though, are we?" Logan asked. "Why don't we go get some food?"

"We just ate," Shani mumbled.

"We ate like ten hours ago."

"We did?...Oh, shit."

"Come on." Logan pulled everyone up by their hands except for Brex. She smacked his hand away before he even reached.

The five of them made their way to the docks. Lexi led the way until she got them all lost, and Asher insisted on taking over. That was until he got them even more lost and led them to the toilets which were surprisingly dirty, compared to the rest of the boat. Brex took over after that and finally brought them to the kitchen area.

"Damn it," Shani whispered.

"What?" Asher nudged his way to her.

"I can't believe I'm saying this, but I feel kind of seasick."

Asher maniacally laughed. Shani always used to tease him for getting seasick when she never would. That was until one time in Maine, when he threw up all over her favorite sweater. She never laughed again after that.

"It's not funny. I swear those mermaids did something to me," said Shani.

"No shit, dude," Asher scoffed. "We knew something like that would happen, and our powers are fading. What did you expect?"

"I'm not answering that."

Asher laughed as they both strolled toward the smell of fried eggs, even though Asher was secretly hoping that Shani would move faster. It was indeed a fresh smell.

"Shani..." Asher started. "You're mainly just scared. It's like PTSD. The last time you breathed underwater, you thought Lexi was hurt. These are just your protective instincts. Remember what you said about the water telling you something bad was going to happen, and it was right? It's basically the same thing now, only your mind is playing tricks on you."

"But what if it's not?" Shani asked, fighting to keep her voice calm.

"I seriously doubt that, but if it's true...which it's not...the rest of us are here this time. And there's nothing you can do now. That's the other problem. We are on the fastest route to Ireland. We have our next plan. All we can do right now is relax. There's nothing that you can control right now...just...chill."

The itch to slap Asher across the face whenever he told her to relax was currently throbbing in her palms, but he was right.

"Come on," said Lexi. "Let's get a seat along the edge of the dock before they're all taken."

The boat was so steady they didn't notice it leaving the dock. Everyone except for Shani. The sound of dolphins and sharks scurrying to find food while avoiding being hit by a big clump of metal smothered the white noise around her, but only if she paid attention.

The rest of the afternoon was a windy one. Lexi hated the sound of the whistling noise and the numbness of her face, but by sunset, it had calmed down. The sky never looked so pink, and Shani was getting surprisingly used to the seasickness.

"Anybody want a drink?" Logan asked.

"I've *been* drinking," said Lexi, holding up what everyone originally thought was just orange juice. "Catch up, dude!"

"Oh, right. I forgot that the Irish girl was headed to Ireland."

"Irish-*American.* Don't go saying that in front of Irish people now. Come on! Let's get this thing going!"

The music played a little louder in the middle of the deck where no one but the five stood. Lexi was the best dancer out of all of them. At least that's what Logan thought. Lexi was loose, but simultaneously bold. Shani tried to reach Lexi's level, but even after three shots, she still looked like she had bricks in her boots.

A few patrons joined them as the night went on, but those patrons mainly included toddlers who were bugging their parents to stay at the dinner table.

"Shhhhh!" one little boy said after Asher hollered too loudly.

"You shhhhhh!" Asher said in return before Lexi had to pull him away.

"More drinks?" Shani asked before almost tripping over Brex's foot.

"I don't know. We should probably head in for the night soon," Brex responded, trying to catch her.

"Why don't we—?" But before Asher could finish, there was a slight pinch in the air. A whistle that sounded closer to a scream.

"Please, no," Brex whispered under her breath.

"Ahhhhh!" They heard it again, only this time, the sound was crisp. Not as if it were coming closer, but there was more behind the voice that it belonged to.

"Look," said Brex. "No one else is reacting."

She was right. The music was still blaring. No one was paying any attention. Smiles were still bright, and no heads were turning. Only theirs.

"Are we the only ones that can hear that?" Asher asked. But no one had to answer. One more scream shook the night before the rest of the patrons finally noticed a shift in the air.

"Is that the ship's whistle?" Asher asked. "Damn, our senses have heightened."

"No, it can't be. That has to be someone's voice," said Lexi. "I can sense the pain."

"Come on," said Shani. "Let's go."

The rest followed Shani, unsure how discreet they were supposed to be. A few of the other patrons trickled behind them, but most of the guests ignored the sound.

"Does anyone still hear it?" Logan asked.

"No, but—" Shani spoke too soon. She had to stop running. If she hadn't, she probably would have run into something. A vision took over.

"Shani," said Brex. "What do you see?"

She was no longer in the same room. She could see someone in her mind. She was no longer on the dock, but inches away from the water on the side of the boat where a young boy was crouching in one of the ship's rocky lifeboats, and one of his legs stuck out of the bottom of the lifeboat.

"Please, no," said Shani, trying to lock eyes with the boy. "He's this way." Shani let the emotional wave of water in her lead the way.

"Help!" the voice screamed, scratching its vocal cords. The harsh wind's attempt to drown out the cry for help immediately failed when Shani reached the front port side of the ship. Asher knew what to do the moment he knew the voice wasn't coming from inside the ship, but that plan was compromised for two reasons. First, crowds of people came swarming in with their cell phones recording and their eyes wide open. Second, the boy probably couldn't get out himself.

"Hey, kid," Asher hollered over the whistling wind. "What's your name? I'm coming down to help you!" It was securely attached to the side of the boat, hung by a crane, but it was at least twenty feet down, and there was only rope and chains to hang on to.

"What?" Shani whispered. "Asher you can't use your—"

"Just trust me." Asher reached one foot over the rail and began his slippery descent. He could already feel the ocean water striking against his bare forearms. Maybe it was all in his head, but the closer he got to the water the faster the boat seemed to go. "Kid, what's your name?" Asher asked to distract himself. The rope was wet, but his grip was firm. His legs squeezed together as they slowly slid down to the lifeboat. Asher looked up to see how far down he'd gone. Getting down was the easy part, but he was going to need a stronger sense of creativity to get back up.

"Sam."

"Hi, Sam. I'm Asher. Can you tell me what's going on with your leg?"

"I don't know, but it hurts. It's stuck in the wood."

Hurts? Asher thought. *Oh no.*

He couldn't see any blood yet, but he didn't like the slimy feeling it gave him in his gut.

"Just hang on, okay?" Asher articulated. He was only a few feet away from the boy, but the rocky waves shook his confidence and the grip below his feet.

"Hurry!" Sam hollered.

If Asher fell, he could heal. He was a few feet above the lifeboat. He didn't have any more time to waste. He released his grip. His ankles stung before he collapsed onto his shoulder. The wood on the bottom of the lifeboat could have been cement for all he knew, but the stinging soon faded. His eyes met with the boy's small and limp body. Terror filled his lungs while the air seeped in. Blood dripped down the boy's small leg, which was still sticking out the bottom of the lifeboat. The hungry hole that entrapped the bleeding leg prickled it along the edges. His leg must have busted through the floor when he fell into the boat. Little light shone on the rough wood that poked through his skin, but Asher could see a loose floorboard that he could potentially pull up to free the boy's leg. But he would need to be careful. Almost half of the boy's small body was tucked under a bench. Asher wasn't sure how on Earth that was possible. But it didn't matter. The boy needed to get out and fast.

"Just stay still, okay?" Asher tried to hide his shaky hand, but there was no stopping it.

"Asher?" Shani shouted from above. More people with their cell phones stacked behind her. Every inch of Asher's body was covered with eyes not even fifteen feet away from him.

"He'll be okay," said Asher. "Just get everybody back!"

"Everybody, back up!" Shani shouted to the crowd.

"But there's a little kid down there!" said a man only a few inches taller than Shani.

"I said back up." Her voice didn't crack. She didn't shout, but the man obeyed her every command.

"Okayyy..."

Asher struggled to find something sharp. He had to be cautious around the boy's throbbing injury, but those were the only loose floorboards he could see.

"Sam," Asher said, employing a consoling tone in his voice. "I'm going to need you to look the other way, okay?"

"Why?" Sam asked.

"Just trust me, okay?"

The whimpering softened. His small head turned away, and his eyes shut tight.

"Guys?" Asher hollered above as he took off his jacket.

"You're good," Lexi loudly whispered. "Hurry up!"

Asher sprouted his wings and ripped the small, yet sharp blade of wood from the boat into his wing. The cut wasn't too deep, but the skin under his nails dug into the squishy wound before he got enough blood to—

Wait, Asher thought. *There's no way this kid is gonna eat this. I have to put it on his leg. Will it work? I have to try.*

"Deep breath, okay? This is gonna feel weird."

Asher rubbed the blue blood, dripping from his wing over the kid's leg. The reaction was delayed, but after Sam's breath returned to normal, the movement in his leg revived.

"Ow...ahhh!" Sam screamed. It still wasn't there yet, but it was getting closer.

"Come on, bud. You can do it."

"Asher!" he heard from above. Shani didn't have to continue to shout his name. He knew what the warning was implying.

"Shit," he whispered to himself. He closed his wings so rapidly, it almost hurt. He could hear more voices pouring over the edge of the boat. Although Shani's voice overpowered all of them put together.

"Back up! Back up!"

Lexi, Logan, and Brex's voices trickled among the chaos, but Asher didn't have time to roll his eyes. Sam wiggled his leg free from the hole in the floor, scratching his vocal cords, even though the tears continued to pulse.

"Ah!" Sam screamed, but he pulled back the tears, biting his bottom lip.

"Are you alright?" Asher asked.

"I think so. Thank you," Sam muttered.

"Don't thank me just yet." Asher grabbed the kid by the waist. "Close your eyes, for me one more time, okay, Sam?"

Once again, he kept his eyes closed as Asher checked once more to see if anyone was watching. He spared no time once he knew he was in the clear. The tickling feathers brushed against his skin once again before he flew to grab onto the edge of the boat's railing. His wings were already tucked away before his palms slammed on the metal.

"Ahhh!" screamed Asher.

Shani rolled her eyes. Asher may have been overdoing it.

"Oh my..."

"Is the boy..."

"Give him CPR..."

An endless parade of worried, drunk adults stumbled upon Asher and Sam. Sam was no longer bleeding, but that didn't stop his mother from pushing her way between two bulky men and through the crowd.

"Sammy?" she slurred her words.

"Mom? Where were you?" Sam asked.

Jesus, Asher thought. He needed to get out of there as fast as he could. Or more so, *they* could.

"Come on," he whispered to the others. "Let's go."

"Sir!" One woman came rushing toward them with her phone reaching toward his face. "What happened down there?"

"I don't know," Asher spat. "Ask his mom."

"Hey!" the mom defensively shouted. Asher assumed she was going to continue, but instead, she was too focused on trying to walk normally to continue her accusations.

"Come on, Mom," said Sam. "I'm sorry I was just playing. Let's leave."

"Should we let them leave?" Lexi asked.

"We'll tell the captain or whoever later," said Brex. "But for now, we need to leave. We gotta get these cameras away from us."

•••••

Kali's nails were so bitten down, they almost didn't exist anymore. This wasn't a new reaction to anxiety. She was always given grief for it.

Clement stood in the middle of the room, preparing to break the four-foot-wide, deep, tall block of cement. He wore a black glove that was ready to strike at any moment. Reymid impatiently leaned against the wall farthest away from Clement. Although he did find Clement's dramatic, unbreakable focus amusing.

"Are you waiting for permission?" Kali asked.

"HAH!" Clement obliterated the square rock. The force was so damaging, no pieces lingered in its place. The scattered cement rolled away continuously as Kali patiently yet intentionally walked over to Clement's black glove.

The meter read, "27" knots of force.

"You're not increasing as fast as I'd hoped," she said.

"What can I do?" Clement asked.

"Age a hundred years."

"Is that a joke? I can't tell with you. You're not good with jokes."

"I should have gotten women." Kali walked away with the black glove and put it away before she reached for her pills and downed half a bottle.

"Don't worry, Clement," Reymid chuckled. "This is all just because she's finally reaching her peak."

"Peak of what?"

"Your fear."

Kali dropped the bottle of pills. "What about this experience tells you that I'm afraid?" she asked.

"Just because you're not backing down...and just because you're angry...it doesn't mean you aren't afraid."

Kali let the corner of her mouth meet her sweaty cheek. There was a respect there that she wasn't expecting. She didn't flinch. Her anger wasn't currently bubbling inside her.

"I'm well aware that fear isn't a weakness," she softly spoke.

"Good."

"Guys..." said Clement. He held his phone in his hand, and his chin dropped to his chest.

"What?" Kali snapped.

"You should see this." Clement held his phone up with a crooked smile and wide eyes. On the screen was a viral video on YouTube of a boy being pulled up off a lifeboat and back onto the main ship. They recognized a few faces.

"Where are they?" Kali asked.

"The comments said the ship is heading to Dublin," said Clement.

"Convenient."

11:

"What makes you think there's something else?"

Downtown Dublin wasn't what most people would call "walkable" from the ferry dock, but the five of them walked anyway. Every cab was taken at the dock, and none passed by. Therefore, Uber or Lyft were their only options, except they weren't because turning on their GPS could give away their location, and Asher forgot to fix his phone plan to international even though Shani had reminded him of it right before the plane took off. Walking it was.

The streets of Dublin reminded Asher of Boston. The brick pavements, the antique street lights, the audible pub culture, but the rest couldn't see it. Shani reminded him again that Ireland and the U.K. were too similar to America for her taste, and there were plenty of other countries in Europe that Americans hadn't explored enough. "There are many other cultures that we are going to be exploring. Different from ours. Rich in culture," she said, in various ways, over a period of less than an hour.

"Hey!" Lexi responded. "My people have plenty of rich culture. Just don't have such a woke touristy outlook on it. I promise you there is so much more to see."

The blue sky was now fading to a pink-gray, but the streets were illuminated with a soft yellow light that stretched all along the city. The evening mist faded in and out the farther they walked down the road.

"This is a pub we're going to, right?" Asher asked. "'Cause I could go for some Guinness."

"We just drank a shit ton after everyone bought you shots," Brex reminded him.

"That was yesterday." Asher threw his hands up in the air and ricocheted his hips from side to side as he walked. "It's a new day, and the night is young, bitches!"

"He's still drunk, isn't he?" Lexi quietly asked herself.

The five of them continued for another half an hour before Logan spotted something. "Guys," he quietly hollered. "Isn't that the road Shiva was talking about? See the statue?" It was dark, but the closer they got, the better they could see the fox statue that stood a good two feet taller than Shani.

"Come on, let's keep moving," she said.

"Guys," Lexi loudly whispered. "It's over there. I see it." She beckoned her head to the end of the road ahead. Before them, a small and bright, purple sign beamed. It read, "Oliver's Pub."

"Finally something that isn't green," Logan laughed.

"You are so stereotypical," Lexi flipped her hair and urged everyone to walk faster per usual.

The pub was larger than they had expected and more crowded. The lights stayed at a muted orange with a low ceiling that Shani could almost touch. The walls were covered in a smooth, rounded wood to make it look like a cabin by the lake. The bar had a colorful, wide collection of liquor that covered an entire wall. Surprisingly, the bar was the least crowded spot in the whole room. Men and women of every age were scattered about, occupying themselves with pool and darts, with a target that had too many holes in it and needed replacing. The perfect timing to find an employee. If only the bartenders weren't all young, blonde, white men.

"Wow," Shani mumbled. "Talk about some great diversity."

"I'd say it's Europe, but Europe at least has women," Brex commented. And without anyone eyeballing them for their obvious tourist attire, they made their way to the bar.

"Maya did tell us that he was cute," Asher whispered to the others, trying to be helpful.

"They're all cute. They all kinda look like blonde Colin Farrells."

Lexi leaned up against Brex and said, "Thank you so much for putting that image in my head." They giggled as they continued to try to blend in and sat down at the bar.

"Hey," Logan tapped on Shani's side. "What about that guy over there?" Logan pointed to a waiter that looked exactly like the others except for the fact that he had a soccer tattoo on his arm.

"No." Shani subtly shook her head. "I think Maya said he was pretty tall. He's probably the shortest one out of all of them.

"Do you think it would really be that big of a deal if we just ask which one he is?"

"Yes. He definitely doesn't go by that name, and we'll just scare him off. What if he runs?"

"Okay, okay. Fine. Just keep...observing."

A few more people waltzed into the pub, most of them already drunk. Brex couldn't bear the stillness around them any longer.

"Okay, we look really American over here, so I'm gonna order us some drinks."

No one argued. She squeezed her way through the growing crowd to find a bartender who wasn't engaged in conversation. One, who happened to be the tallest one in the group, stood there bouncing to the music as he was washing a few glasses.

"Hey, can I get five glasses of Guinness?" she asked.

Immediately recognizing her accent, the bartender smiled and said, "First time trying?"

"Yeah, for me anyway."

"Daniel?" He beckoned to another bartender a few feet away. "Can you get some Guinness for this lovely lady?"

"Sorry, how many did you say?" Daniel responded in a perfect American accent.

Brex's heart skipped a beat, and her chest made that clear. It was Jethro. Brex knew it. She couldn't release her stare, and neither could he, but she walked closer to him anyway while he started on the drinks.

"So, Daniel? Do you have a middle name to go along with that...or is Daniel your middle name?"

"Wow," he nervously laughed. "How inquisitive of you."

Brex leaned in closer and intertwined her fingers. Her palms had yet to break a sweat. "Let me ask you this instead...why'd you keep your American accent?"

The eye contact remained, but he forced a small chuckle, not knowing what else to do. "Maybe it's because I'm American. And how do you know I'm not Canadian? You're American, right? Shouldn't you be better at being able to tell?"

"Not necessarily," Brex muttered with tight lips.

"Hmm."

Finally, after the foam settled, one glass of Guinness was placed on the table. Brex took a quick gulp and said, "But also...I know where you grew up, Jethro."

Jethro didn't move, but the world seemed to slow down. For both of them, not just Jethro, but it was his body that stiffened with fear.

"I don't know what you're talking about," he mumbled through a tight jaw. No matter what he did, nothing would loosen. His disguise, his only form of protection, was now failing him.

"Yes, you do, and it's okay. I need your help," said Brex, keeping her voice low.

"Again, I don't know what you're talking about."

"Does this clear things up?" Brex slid two fingers under her wrap to subtly show him a dark, itching scar on her left palm.

Her eyes never left his. She left them soft, not wanting to scare him. She couldn't spoil the illusion that she was building trust between them. Jethro, on the other hand, couldn't help drawing attention to himself as his cheeks bellowed with every breath he exhaled.

"What do you want?" he asked as his face slowly came closer to hers.

"I told you." Brex continued to decrease the volume in her voice. "I need help. I'm a friend, and I really need you to trust me."

"How can you be a friend? We don't know each other," Jethro muttered.

A switch flipped for Jethro. His eyebrows and ears pulled back as he violently swallowed.

"You're her..." he whispered.

"What?" Brex said a little louder.

"You're Kali. Why are you here? How did you find me? I can't do anything for you. I know nothing!"

"No, no..." Brex wasn't sure how to de-escalate the situation, but as people so often told her, the best thing for her to do was to be nice and to tame her intimidating eyes. "I'm not Kali. I'm trying to stop her."

"Then, how did you get that scar?"

"How long have you got?"

Maybe Jethro was seeing things, but he could have sworn a few other bartenders stepped a foot or two closer to him. Were they suspicious? What did they already know?

"How am I supposed to know you're not working for Kali?"

"Because I'm working with Maya."

"That doesn't help."

Maybe Brex was seeing things, but within just a fraction of a second, a sudden shift transformed Jethro into a different person. Now there was anger with a hint of frustration, but his sense of hopelessness remained.

"Maybe we should talk about this somewhere else," Brex suggested.

"I need to finish my shift," he responded.

"Seriously?"

"It ends in twenty minutes. Relax."

"He's telling you to relax?!" Asher mumbled a few feet away.

Brex defensively put her hands in the air and backed away when all of a sudden, a tense silence tickled her ear. Shani stood there, crossing her arms, hovering in front of Logan, Lexi, and Asher.

"What?" Brex asked, still defensive.

"What was that?" Asher asked.

"What do you mean?"

Shani needlessly pulled her back, trying to get away from the people at the bar, only to get closer to the people playing darts.

"What if people are listening?" Shani quietly asked, keeping her back to the street in case anyone walked by. "And why did you tell him that he can trust you? We don't even know if we can trust him."

"Because we *need* him to trust us. We need any information we can get out of him. We need to find those stones. I'm not tip-toeing around him, and you're not in charge here."

"So I've heard, but I thought we agreed to ease him into it. You just ripped the Band-Aid right off."

"I did rip the Band-Aid right off. I just smoked a little weed first to make it easier."

"Jesus Christ, let's go."

*****

The five of them waited outside for almost an hour. Jethro told them to wait in the back, but between the squeaking rats running around and the drunken men walking past, they didn't feel it was safe, but Brex said she would light anything that crossed their paths on fire after she told everyone to quit whining.

The sky was now pitch black. The only guidance they sensed was from the North Star and the full moon.

"Where is he?" Asher asked.

"Probably counting his tips," Logan commented.

"I don't think they tip bartenders in Ireland, or anywhere else," Lexi snapped.

"Oh," Logan squeaked in a cracked voice. "Then...he probably left without us."

"I believe it," Brex snapped.

"Look." Asher clapped his hands together with impatience. "He doesn't trust Maya. That's gotta be it. If we said that literally any other guard sent us, he would be here right now."

"Would you shut up about the whole Maya thing?" Shani begged and whimpered.

"Fine, fine." Asher returned to his pacing and mindlessly kicked around rocks to pass the time.

"Just wait a little longer. He'll be here," said Brex.

"Why are you so sure?" Logan asked impatiently. Brex didn't appreciate the tone in his voice, whether he knew it was there or not.

"I don't know. He seemed...lost."

"Lost?" A voice came from the shadows. "Why do you say lost?" Jethro appeared out of the darkness with his bag, jacket, and crooked eyebrows.

"Nevermind," Brex muttered under her breath. "Let's all take a walk."

The atmosphere of the night fooled them into thinking it was still young. Maybe it was the over-exhaustion, or maybe their determination was kicking in.

"What do you need to know?" Jethro asked as the six of them aimlessly walked in the moonlight.

"We need to know if you have one of the stones or any of the other items Moloch is looking for," Logan stated, not liking the smirk Jethro had smeared across his face.

"And why would I tell you if I did?"

"Because we need to relocate and protect it. Whatever leads Kali and the others have, they need to be steered off course."

"Why?"

Jethro's lack of knowledge and genuine confusion didn't sit well with Shani. Her teeth clenched together and she dug her nails into her palms. Why was he so out of the circle?

"Because there's a mole," Shani didn't leave a drop of disdain or frustration out of her voice.

"We think there is," Lexi corrected her. "It would be the best explanation. Has no one told you this?"

"Nope." Jethro took no more pleasure in discovering what he didn't know than the rest did.

"Who was your mentor?" Brex asked.

"It was Dimitria, but she relocated to Greece. Plus she hadn't had anything in her sanctuary for over a year."

Brex almost laughed at the plausibility of the scenario. "And she didn't take you with her? I'm confused."

"They wanted me to have a different mentor anyways. Makes it easier for me to be untraceable."

"So, does Maya have plans for you?" Asher asked. Shani knew what he was trying to do. She didn't hesitate for a moment to give him a side-eye glare.

"Maya hasn't tried to get in contact with me for almost two years, but it's alright. I figured she would at least try and do her job eventually."

"Can I ask a question?" Brex asked, flapping her wrist in the air, desperate to change the subject.

"Okay," Jethro subtly chuckled.

"How old are you?"

Jethro nodded his head as a smile began to slither onto his face. "I honestly don't know. My adoptive mother never told me, and I don't think the rest of my family knows. But for what it's worth, I think I'm a bit over a hundred."

Brex's shoulders and chest twitched as she tried to hide her contorted face.

"Wow," Logan loudly spoke with a straight face. "Old." Brex gave him a nudge with her elbow, but he only smiled to himself, recognizing his boldness.

"So." Shani shoved her shoulders down and lengthened her stiff neck. "What do we have to do in order for you to tell us if you have one of the stones or not?"

"I haven't decided yet, but tell me more about Maya. What do you know about her?"

Asher was about to list off everything he wanted to express until Shani physically shoved him aside and answered for him.

"She's the reason why we are what we are, but she's the only person we can trust, and we want to help. We're choosing to. No one is forcing us."

"She's the reason you are what you are?" Jethro let his eyebrows drop closer to his nose. "Elaborate."

Shani, once again, stepped on Asher's feet before he could answer. "She was trying to help everyone around her and protect her sanctuary. Making us alchelarcenists was the only way Moloch wouldn't get a hold of them. Just as long as we stayed hidden and protected."

Jethro didn't respond. He stayed silent to ponder what that could mean, but he didn't have to for long. This type of behavior was familiar to Jethro, coming from Maya.

"Alright," he nodded his head. "That sounds about right. What else can you tell me?"

"She has her big dog," Lexi added.

"What's his name again?" Jethro asked. His cheeks lifted while his jaw relaxed. Shani knew this was a rhetorical question.

"It's Baymour. He's a hellhound."

"And what other breed?"

Oh no, Shani thought. Was he a mix? Did they know this already? Did Maya ever tell them?

"It's okay," Jethro admitted. Shani took longer to think than she realized. "I don't remember either."

Brex chuckled with her mouth and eyes closed. Jethro returned the favor.

"Why don't you tell us more about you?" Logan impatiently asked.

"Why?" Jethro asked, confused. "You want to know if I'm the mole?"

"It wouldn't hurt to know." Logan couldn't help that suspicion was leaking from his mouth and eyes.

"I'll show you why I'm not the mole." Jethro leaned his head towards Brex with his eyes only slightly open. "Come with me."

The only one who wanted to resist was Logan, but the rest ignored him as he dragged himself along.

The six walked until everything started to look alike. All of the buildings blended together, and time was an endless circle that was measured by how many street lamps they walked by.

"Are we actually going somewhere? We could get an Uber, you know?" Logan asked.

"It takes a second, and I don't have the app," Jethro shouted as he turned around to give Logan a sideways smile.

Brex walked next to Jethro. Logan didn't like the way Jethro looked at her. It wasn't a dangerous look. Logan hated to admit it, but he did think that Jethro was a good lead. He simply didn't like watching Brex walk next to him.

"Almost there," Jethro shouted once more. Only this time, he didn't speak as much to the crowd as he did to Brex, and before Jethro could turn his head back to the front, Logan caught a glimpse of a popped smile meant for Brex's eyes only.

"Dude." Lexi looked at Logan as if he just asked her how long to put a turkey in the microwave. "You good?"

"Me?" Logan asked. "Swell."

"You absolutely can't pull that word off."

Logan didn't have the energy to reciprocate a sarcastic comment. He only slouched a little more than he already was and kept his dead eyes on the increasingly chatty pair that walked in front of them.

"You're not seriously jealous, are you?"

"There's nothing to be jealous of. If they were gonna like...make out and be all cutesy and shit then, yeah I'd be jealous. But they're just talking, and he's painfully handsome. Why should I be jealous?"

"Why would you not be?"

"That's not helpful!"

Lexi crossed her arms and let her head tilt back so far, she could almost see who was walking behind her. "I was just validating your feelings."

"Well, my feeeeelings are stupid."

Logan muttered a few more reasons why he wasn't jealous, but Lexi stopped paying attention, and even if she wanted to chime back in, they had finally reached their destination.

"Here we are," said Jethro, making a grand gesture towards an abandoned building.

"You live here?" Shani asked in disgust.

"No," Jethro laughed. "That would be too obvious. It's right next door."

The building next door was average. Clean, red paint on the front door, and bricks with a few chips in them. They still weren't sure what he was trying to show them, but they followed him through the front door anyway.

A long hallway extended in front of them. Small chandeliers hung every foot along the clean, white ceilings, and to the right and front of the main door was a staircase with a wrought-iron railing that led to the second floor.

"What is this place?" Brex cautiously asked, starting to walk up the stairs until Jethro stopped her.

"Don't worry," Jethro laughed again. "It's just through this wall."

Wall? Logan thought. *Which wall?*

Logan looked around to see which wall had door handles or hinges, but they were all the same. Every wall standing to their right, left, or to their front was a smooth, beige color.

"This wall," Jethro answered as if he were reading Logan's mind. The wall to their right, before the beginning of the staircase, slowly creaked open. All Jethro had to do was press a small button under the golden picture frame that hung on the moving white wall which contained an old photograph of Achilles in front of an apartment building that looked like it needed a deep cleaning and a new roof.

Jethro walked through the open gap and everyone followed. One by one, they noticed the cold winter air jumping about them and making them shiver. They walked down a small, but steep spiral staircase that led to an open room that was covered in nothing but white, shiny ice.

"Ah," Shani said with a heavy breath as if she were the first person to notice. "This is your sanctuary."

"You got it," Jethro smiled. "And you know what's not here?"

"The alchelesters?" Logan sarcastically asked.

"Bingo."

It was true. The empty pool in the center of the room shined with the absence of the green liquid of Hell. Not a drop remained. The alchelesters couldn't have been there recently.

"This doesn't tell us anything," said Logan.

"Logan," Brex whispered, embarrassed, pressing her lips together.

"What? Think about it. He would be the perfect person to guard one of the stones. If Moloch or Kali found him, they would only get a stone, and not a stone with some alchelesters and other shit thrown in the bundle."

Jethro straightened his spine and batted his eyelashes, impressed by Logan's caution and suspicion.

"Take a look around, Logan. All you want."

Logan didn't hesitate to obey orders, but there was nothing to look around for. The ice cave didn't involve luxuries such as drawers or closets. It didn't take long for Logan to complete the task.

"You need help?" Jethro asked as Logan scratched his back and whipped his head from side to side and in circles.

"Well, of course, you're not going to put anything else in here. Like you said, too obvious, right? You could have put the stones, or anything else in the kitchen or something."

Jethro let Logan mellow in his frustration before asking, "Kali and Moloch would have been here long ago don't you think? They would detect it."

"Well..." Logan coughed and scratched his forehead.

"Are you done?"

"Yup," said Logan with little confidence.

"I don't have anything." For the first time that night, Jethro seemed genuine. Not nervous, not cocky, just genuine. Everyone but Logan believed him. "But I might be able to help you."

"That's all we want," said Shani, looking around for agreement.

"There's a river in China, the Yellow River. My mother spent a lot of time there. Plus, I know someone that's probably still there. But maybe not. I can't promise anything."

"What else?" Brex asked.

"What makes you think there's something else?" Jethro cracked a half smile.

Brex didn't answer. She didn't move a muscle.

"Fine. The National Historical Museum. It'll lead you to Dimitria's sanctuary. I was there recently. She hasn't moved."

"How will we know—"

"You'll know it when you see it." Jethro crossed his arms and poked out his strapping chin. "Any other questions?" His smug face searched around the room, but the rest remained quiet. "Good." The room fell silent. Jethro could sense their eagerness. He adjusted his collar and said, "Follow me."

"More walking?" Asher moaned. "Are you kidding me?"

Logan turned to Brex suspiciously. Without saying a word, Brex grabbed him by the hand, shared a firm, yet affectionate glance and shook her head. That was enough for Logan to shut his mouth and keep it that way.

"Where are we going?" Shani asked.

"My apartment. I have a few things there that at least might help you find Persephone's Flower."

"Thank you, Jethro." Shani sincerely appreciated his efforts, but that didn't stop her from impatiently making her way to the front of the group before they stepped back onto the spiral staircase, including Jethro.

"Hope you guys like cats," Jethro laughed. "'Cause I got a few of them."

"I like cats," Brex admitted, "but I'm pretty sure everyone else hates them."

"That's alright. I promise we won't stay there for too long."

Logan silently scoffed as Jethro closed the wall behind them. He made sure nobody saw him, but he secretly hoped Jethro would see him in the reflection of the window.

They made their way down the front steps and to the gate before Jethro asked, "Is anyone hungry? Everything is still open. We can find something if you want."

But no one answered. The rest were too fixated on a small yet significant distraction that stood in the middle of the brick road.

"Hello?" Jethro hollered when he finally noticed what they were all staring at.

The young brunette woman didn't need to say anything in order for them to know what she wanted. The burn mark smeared across her face said it all.

"Hello," she softly projected. "We haven't met. I'm Kali."

12:

"What was that? You can still practice magic?"

Kali wore a brown, tight, suede jacket with black sleeves and boots that could break down a storm door. She wasn't the tallest person in the crowd, but her stature and demeanor proved that was not limiting for her. She wore light makeup even though no plastic surgery could remove the bright red scar across her face. She didn't move. Not a single finger, but her solid stance was prepared for any threat.

"What do you want?" Shani asked her. All six of them remained calm, but not as collected as they would have liked to be. They weren't expecting Kali to find them this soon. The plan had officially shifted.

"That was rude," Kali smiled with one corner of her mouth pushing up her scarred cheek.

"So?" Jethro snapped.

"I'm going to give you a choice." She finally broke her frozen posture. Her arms stuck to her side as she slowly walked to the group. She wasn't surprised when they didn't back away from her in intimidated unison.

Lexi didn't hesitate to shift forward and ask, "And what makes you think you're in any position to make threats or bargains?"

"Damn," Kali silently laughed. "I was really hoping to stump you on that one. But in all honesty, I do have over a hundred years on you. Your magic is not to be underestimated, but I'm stronger, faster, and more skilled. And if I'm not mistaken, I understand your abilities better than you do mine."

"So?" Jethro asked, again.

"Is that seriously the only grunt you can muster?"

"What's the choice you want us to make?" Brex snapped. She was almost caught off guard by her own booming voice.

"Thank you for asking." Kali's stiff yet smooth vocals harmonized with the quiet night. "Simple really. You can probably already guess what I need. You are well aware by now that I can't actually harm you. That would be disruptive, but I can stop you. I can capture you, all on my own. So here's the deal; you can either go on your merry way and eventually be captured one way or the other. Or if you help me, I will make sure you are immune to this change. I know stopping time will be a big adjustment for you."

The six held their stance and dignity as they pretended to be interested in her offer.

"And why would we do that?" Shani asked.

"If you refuse my offer, I could kill you eventually when I don't need you anymore. But if you accept, your lives could stay on the exact path you always dreamed of. Maybe I'll even make some of your friends immune. Nothing will change for you. Unless, of course, you want it to. That's the whole idea anyway. I know it's hard to understand my reasoning. You're not the only one."

"So you're admitting that nobody else wants this change but you?" Lexi scoffed.

"They don't know what's happening. They don't know how much they need this yet."

"That's too bad, Kali," said Brex, keeping her voice monotone. "We outnumber you. So when we refuse your offer, it might take you a little longer than expected to hold us down."

"Tell that to the arrow that's pointing at your head."

At first, Brex didn't believe her. That was until she felt the tip of the arrowhead poking the lower part of her skull.

The rest moved their heads to see Reymid standing less than two feet behind Brex. Otherwise, they didn't move a muscle, and Reymid wasn't blinking. He was at Kali's beck and call. Her wish was his command. But Brex never took her eyes off Kali. She wasn't afraid. She didn't have a plan yet, but Kali knew Brex would momentarily.

"Reymid, I'm guessing? Powers of Artemis? Nice to meet you. Where's the other one? Clement, is it? Powers of Ares?"

"I would be more worried about the arrow that's nearly impaling your neck, Brex." Reymid's voice was raspier than she expected.

"You can't kill me," Brex whispered, knowing Kali heard every syllable.

"Oh no, darling that arrow won't kill you," Kali responded. "You know that dust that Maya gave you to influence uncooperative people?" They didn't answer, but Kali understood what they were saying. "She didn't think she was the only one in possession of it, did she?"

Brex took a breath, starting to develop an idea, but she needed to keep stalling. "What's your point?"

"If you make one wrong move, the toxins will release, and you will no longer be in control. I don't think Shani would like that very much, would you?"

"Normally, I would say no," said Shani, "but it's not you who's in control right now anyway."

Kali didn't see it coming. Literally and figuratively. The flames didn't start anywhere. They simply appeared. Reymid had to blink and shiver a few times before his body agreed with his eyes that his arrow was engulfed in flames, while Brex didn't flinch.

"What? Shit?!"

Logan couldn't wait any longer. His reflexes surprised even him. Nothing else mattered. If Kali reacted before him, so be it. Gathering his lightning took longer than Brex to light her flames, but the jolt of electricity shattered through Reymid's body. Reymid fought to keep standing, but after stumbling back with legs stiff as a rock, he collapsed and hit the back of his head on the brick pavement.

Lexi heard a small flutter coming from Kali, which she could only assume was the sound of Kali morphing the iron from her blood into a shiny, smooth, and sharp weapon. The shine was unmistakable, before Lexi turned around, she could see the reflection shining in the window of the building next to them. Kali snapped the dagger into the air. Lexi prepared to duck, but instead, a rush of wind brushed across her cheek and shoulder. To the left of her stood Jethro with arms up like he was preparing to climb a mountain. The veins in his forearms popped out, and only inches away from his face was Kali's dagger, smooth as skin, and the size of a ruler that floated in mid-air.

Clunk!

A smooth, transparent sphere sucked Kali's blade into Jethro's force field. The bubble vanished as the blade dropped to the ground. The threat of the weapon vanished with the breeze the moment the metal tumbled onto the pavement.

"What?" Asher mumbled.

"Oh damn, I forgot you're a witch," said Logan, louder than Asher.

Jethro didn't have time to make a sarcastic comment. He pulled everyone together and sucked them into a small space that ripped away the night sky and replaced it with a bottomless black hole.

"N—" Brex heard Kali holler before Kali vanished out of sight.

Woooooosh! That was all they could hear, but only for half a second before they heard the sounds of birds chirping and trees blowing in the wind once again. They weren't in the city anymore. They could see only trees, mountains, and stars for miles.

"Whoa!" Shani fell to the ground which was now covered in dirt and grass.

"What the fuck just happened?" Brex asked with her feet spread wide and bent knees. "Where are we?"

"Did we just teleport?" Logan asked, already pacing, looking for danger in their new barren location.

"I need to shit," Asher said before he collapsed.

"We'll find a bathroom for you," said Jethro, "but we need to move...now."

The six of them gathered up the little energy they had left and followed Jethro in a direction that could have been the opposite direction that they needed to go in for all they knew.

"Jethro," Shani asked. "What was that? You can still practice magic?"

"Of course," he said. "How do you think I finished up my apprenticeship? You think just because I was raised with witches that I'm somehow extraordinary, but I can't use magic?"

"I don't know." Shani picked up the pace and blatantly ignored him.

"Where are we going?" Brex asked. "We must be miles away from your apartment."

"The closest airport is this way," said Jethro.

"How do you know that?"

"Don't worry about it," Jethro smiled. The shift in his attitude made Brex's chest flutter, but made Logan's eyes roll.

We get it, you're a witch...very funny, Logan thought. *He's not seriously that cute, is he?*

The night sky took up most of the space. The twinkling lights beaming from the stars, and the glowing moon were the only sources of light they had. Lexi almost started to doze off while tripping over her own feet. Or maybe they were Shani's. She was too out of it to ask.

"How much longer?" Logan asked after about ten minutes of walking.

"A few more miles," said Jethro, "but I should leave you guys here."

"What, why?" Brex asked.

"I should get back to the sanctuary."

"No," Brex's voice shook with fear. "You said there's nothing there."

"Yes, but what if they find something that will lead them to the rest of the sanctuaries? They could have already found something."

"What would they find?" Logan asked. "You didn't make a list, did you?"

"What?" Jethro's voice dropped a full octave. "It could be anything. Besides, for me, it's not that hard to turn invisible." He winked at Brex without any hesitation. She dropped her chin, not surging with admiration, but not pushing it away either.

"What do you suggest we do?" Shani asked.

"Start south of the river in China. Near the Great Wall. Go north. Even if you pass the river. I know the sanctuary is near there, so you'll eventually get there. Asher, you sure you can't carry everyone?" Jethro joked.

"I'm sure," Asher said with tight lips.

"What was it that you wanted to show us in your apartment?" Brex asked.

"Oh." Jethro scratched his chin, keeping his gaze low. "Just something from an old friend. Don't worry about it."

"What do you expect us to do about food?" Lexi asked with her arms crossed and shoulders hunched over.

Instead of answering, Jethro held out his hand with multiple different types of seeds.

"Lexi, you can use these to grow in the ground. Trust me—"

"It's Ireland. I know, there's grass everywhere."

Jethro didn't seem bothered by the interruption. He didn't seem bothered by anything. Brex stood there with her exhausted, baggy eyes and asked, "Do you need anything from us?"

"Just stay safe, and whatever you do, don't tell anybody anything. You've already told me too much."

A light flashed with minimal dust and smoke, and then he was gone. No other trace of him was to be found.

"I guess we should keep these," Lexi said as she tucked away the seeds.

"Why don't we walk for a few hours and then take a rest?" Shani suggested.

"It would have been really nice if he told us how much longer it was going to take to get there," Logan snapped.

"What if he didn't know?" Brex snapped back.

"Oh, please. Of course, he knew. Maybe he just didn't want to tell us."

"What do you mean? Do you not trust him?"

Logan ran his fingers through his hair and scoffed in the back of his throat just enough so Brex wouldn't hear it.

"He literally just told us not to trust him," said Logan.

"Guys," said Shani. Her voice remained soft. Anger wasn't cutting at her. Fatigue overwhelmed her too much to bother with that. "Just shut up. You're bickering more than Asher and I right now."

Logan bit his tongue. "Sorry," he mumbled. "I didn't mean to get jealous."

"What?" Brex cocked her head back.

"Nothing."

From then, there was nothing but silence. Even the sound of nature stirring in the background didn't calm them. Hours went by before another syllable broke through.

"I need food," said Brex.

"Okay," said Lexi, nonchalantly. The seeds were all the way in the back of her backpack. She unintentionally groaned as the strap almost ripped out some of her hair as it slid down her arm.

"Got any strawberries?" Asher asked.

"As you wish." Lexi kept her eyes focused on the grass that she could only guess was still there. The seeds blew in the gentle wind before they all scattered across the field. Lexi's stomach started to rumble when the thought of berries filled her. Luckily, it didn't take too long for them to grow.

"Ireland's got good agriculture," Logan commented.

The smooth, ripe, fuchsia berries sprouted randomly in a small patch of dirt. The deep, rich colors could be seen through the dark night.

"Okay," said Shani, wishing her fatigue would evaporate so she could be more impressed. "Let's eat."

Peace fell upon them once more. Maybe the fresh juice pacified them, or maybe the silence seduced them.

"Do you hear something?" Shani asked.

"Uhhh..." Brex mumbled with a mouthful of blueberries. "I don't think I do. What do you hear?"

"What?" Shani's forehead crinkled, and she couldn't keep her eyes open. "I don't hear anything, I just...something's off. Something's not right."

"What do you mean?" Lexi asked.

"I can't explain it, but it's making my chest hurt. It's not me."

The unrecognizable feeling swirled around her. Not in her, around the air. Something was coming for them.

"We should go," Shani grabbed the backpack that she wasn't carrying earlier and whipped it over her shoulder, she noticed another odd feeling. The shaking earth threatened to attack by boiling in a wave of destruction.

"Oh, no," Brex mumbled.

"Asher," Shani said as loudly as she could without her voice cracking. "Grab the backpacks and fly. The rest of us need to run as fast as we can."

Asher grabbed the backpacks while the rest stomped across the field of now-squashed berries. They didn't have time to gather the food they desperately needed. The earthquake was for them, and it wasn't going to stop without them in it.

The air gradually rose in temperature. Not just because of the friction igniting in their jeans and sneakers, but because the core temperature of their surroundings spiked to an uncomfortable level.

What? Shani thought, fighting to exert any distractions. *Heat, why heat?* But the warm aroma aroused quickly. Shani couldn't help it, she had to look back.

The steam spiraled above the cracking ground. She couldn't see the boiling, orange and red mixture. It was too far down the opening, but she could smell it.

"LAVA!" Shani screamed.

"Lava?" Asher screamed back. He turned around and flapped his fatiguing wings high enough to see a sliver of lava boiling against the rocky earth.

"What the—? How?" Asher asked himself, but the heat was pulling him into a daze, and he was falling behind. He flipped back over and flew against the racing wind.

"IT'S GETTING CLOSER!" Brex screamed. Her voice cracked from fatigue. Adrenaline was in reach, but nobody could catch it. Brex started to fall behind, but only by a few inches. The fear of watching the rest running ahead without her punched at her chest. She picked up the pace, throwing that fear behind her.

The plangent echo of the tumbling waves chased after them.

"Don't look back, you'll move—" But they didn't run fast enough. The rumbling earth ruptured in front of them and swept them off their feet. The hungry lava cried louder the closer their sweaty skin got to it. The grass disappeared into the boiling soil. But the quaking earth made a mistake. Instead of swallowing the five of them, each of them latched onto the edges of the cliff by the widening chasm. They staggered, hoping the sweat wouldn't let them slip. But it wasn't the sweat that Shani had to worry about. It was the lack of rocks for her feet to step on.

"No, no, no." Shani slipped before she could scream, but the boulder that caught her and knocked her unconscious was only a few feet below.

"Shani!" Brex screamed, but she had herself to worry about. The rocks holding her up broke away from the edge before she could reach for safety. "Ahhhh!" Brex couldn't hear herself scream, the rumbling lava was so loud. Brex rolled on her back, landing on the edge of another boulder only a few feet away from Shani. The scathing, hot, jagged surface didn't catch her fall. Brex had to do that herself. The sharp edges scraped along her jeans as her legs dropped over the cliff. She tightened her stomach muscles to flip over onto her front. Her bony hips dug into the dirt, but her nails dug deeper as she fought to pull herself up. She couldn't help but notice the radiating heat invading the insides of her body. Brex managed to stand up, but the air squeezed her lungs so tightly, they almost felt like they were going to pop.

Oh no, Brex thought. *Please, not an asthma attack. Not now.* But it didn't take long for her asthma to become her second priority. In the process of pulling herself up to safety, the platform that kept her from falling to her death had broken away from the edge of where her friends stood. She was trapped. And the moment she looked down, the heat that was rising from below her grew ten degrees hotter, as the boiling hot lava covered the bottom surface of the cracked earth.

Don't...look...down...

Shani's loose but long and unconscious body lay across the bumpy and sharp rocks that held her where she was. Her eyes opened slightly to see nothing but the dawn about to break. The cliff wasn't in sight because she was right on the edge of it, inches away from rolling off. Her eyes were glossy, but she could find boulders to latch onto. Her hazy gaze looked away from the boiling lava and back onto her path to safety. There was a way up. She just had to climb.

"Okay." Her long legs jumped up so she could grab onto the sandy rocks that created a safe ladder. It was a long ladder that somehow stretched time like an elastic, but after kicking down a few loose rocks, she reached the dewy grass. Her long legs kicked over to the top, but it wasn't until she looked back that she realized she hadn't rolled over far enough.

"Ah!" The orange and red smothering her view didn't look real, but it still zapped her body awake. Shani's knees and feet dug into the dry earth and pushed her body away from the cliff, but she couldn't go far. Her sharp vision returned to her, but the more it focused, the more her heart raced. She quickly caught the image of Logan and Lexi hanging on the edges of the cliff.

"NO!" Shani screamed. Lexi's entire body, except for her fingertips and knuckles, hung over the side of the earth. She might have been able to pull herself up if it hadn't been for Logan hanging onto her other wrist.

"Lexi!" Logan shouted with his chin to the dark night sky. "Are you okay?!"

"Shut up, Logan! I can hold you! SHANI!" Lexi screamed with a tight throat. Shani crawled over to them, digging her elbows into solid rock.

Shani reached for Lexi's forearm before she realized there was an easier way to do this. "Wait," she said. "Where's Asher?"

"I don't know," Lexi coughed up the dirt spiraling past her tongue. "We'll find him. Just pull us up."

Shani's increasing adrenaline wasn't enough. She needed to adopt a fear. A fear only she knew that could bolster her heightened strength. That wasn't hard to find the moment she noticed that Brex was about to fall off the platform that stood two feet in diameter.

"No, BREX!"

Lexi finally got a grip on the grass once more. Her bicep cramped as her other shoulder stretched to its maximum length. Logan caught his foot on the lip of a small niche, allowing him to push himself farther up without ripping his shoulder off.

"Brex," Logan lost every ounce of breath he had left trying to say her name. "Where's Brex?" His ribcage crashed into the ground before he could get up and look, but all he needed to do was follow the path Shani's tired eyes aimed towards.

"ASHER!" Shani called out, but he was nowhere to be seen. He was the only one who could fly. What was trapping him?

"Shani!" they all distantly heard. It was Asher. The voice was lower with straining scratches, but it was Asher.

The three survivors tripped over themselves trying to look for where the voice was coming from.

"ASHER!" Shani called out once again. It wasn't until the sound of a landslide stumbled down the cracked earth that they could catch a glimpse of Asher's bright white wing beaming off the red and orange lava.

"He's over there!" Lexi pointed out. Only a few feet away, Asher was trapped. A rock the size of a grown tortoise was crushing Asher's right wing. The more he tried to squirm his way to freedom, the more he strained the already-weakening muscles in his wings. Regardless of his torturous situation, he kept his eyes on one thing.

"I'm fine!" Asher screamed. "Lexi, get Brex!"

Lexi didn't have to be told twice, but her powers did. Her knuckles cramped from tightening. No soul of the earth was listening to her. The unresponsive souls froze and ignored her desperate call.

"It's not working!" Lexi cried. "No one's listening to me! Why is no one listening to me?!"

Asher could use one arm to try to free himself, but Asher's right wing was still stuck. Shani reached as far down as she could, but the tip of her middle finger seemed miles away from where Asher was being held hostage.

"Asher!" Brex thought she whispered, but she was screaming. The sound spiraled into a blur. The heat burned away her vision. She couldn't feel the legs that were her only source of safety.

"Brex!" Asher screamed. "You have to sit down! I'm coming!"

"Brex," Logan cried. "Please!"

But Brex didn't hear a word. Even if she did, there was no more connection between her senses and her actions. Her head boiled at a sizzling, dangerous heat, but the pain soon passed. The numbing sensation crippled her ability to fight back. She couldn't sit. She couldn't move. Brex stayed balancing on the island no more than twenty feet away from the solid land.

"BREX!" they all screamed together. But it wasn't enough. The catapulted sound slowly passed by Brex. She wanted to hold on. She wanted to catch onto their words, hoping they would keep her steady. But they weren't strong enough. The string that held her to her friends was frail and close to snapping. Her knees loosened, and her boots felt like they weren't touching anything. The sparkling flames raced by her, but she floated in slow motion, with the air swirling in circles around her until it finally released her.

Logan sat, not twenty feet away from her. He couldn't rip his eyes away from her, and somehow, he knew Brex couldn't either. Her soft, tired eyes looked at him almost apologetically. And the acceptance that came along with that made Logan's stomach stir with nausea.

Brex exhaled one last breath before the heat punched her in the stomach, and her feet stumbled back. Her eyes rolled to the back of her head as she fell backwards, quickly diving into the boiling lava.

"NOOOOOOOO!" Asher screamed. That was all he needed to free himself. He didn't care about the pain. He didn't even know if it was there or not. And he certainly didn't care about the boiling wind that struck against his face as he raced towards Brex's tumbling body. He had never flown so fast before, and his wings could feel it. This he couldn't ignore.

What if his wings gave out? What if they cramped? Was that possible? The heat was becoming unbearable. The boiling lava bubbled in the distance. She was already unconscious. Was the lava going to hurt Brex? He couldn't take that chance. Asher picked up speed.

Come on, Asher thought. *Almost there.*

Asher was fixed on the image of Brex's tumbling body. The wind pushed against the skin on his arms so immensely, he almost couldn't lift them, but his heart raced a beat faster. A beat that would be lifesaving if he kept up his speed. The lava boiled more intensely the closer they got, almost as if it was waiting for them.

Come on....COME ON!

Inches away from her, Asher slogged through molasses of frustrating time, but the second his arms snapped against her back, time sped up again.

"Got you!" he croaked. The metal buttons on her jacket already left burn marks on Asher's skin. He didn't care. He didn't notice. He almost hit a few falling boulders, his eyes were so foggy. He could already hear the cries of Shani's scratchy voice. "You're okay, Brex. You're okay."

She wasn't conscious, but her eyes twitched as if she were dreaming. Asher's adrenaline remained steady as he raced Brex to the surface. His eyes stayed locked on the starry sky, but the moment his gaze leveled with the horizon, he dove toward his friends, gripping Brex tightly.

"Back up!" Asher exclaimed. "We need to let the opening close!"

"Okay, okay! Bring her over here!" Shani demanded as she beckoned them to the only soft part of the ground that was close to them. Brex needed space to get her breath back, but they couldn't resist holding her, just for a moment.

"Okay, okay," said Lexi. "Give her room." Lexi checked her pulse. It was faint, but it was there. Her breathing, on the other hand, was questionable. Lexi plugged Brex's nose and gave her CPR three times before Brex slowly pulled in a deep breath.

There were no wails. No swearing. Only more holding, and this time, they weren't letting go.

"I need my inhaler," Brex whispered in a dry voice.

"You need water too," said Lexi.

Shani searched for her inhaler in the backpack, but couldn't find it. Even after completely emptying the entire thing.

"Logan, give me the other backpack!" Shani quickly muttered.

"Shani," said Brex, but her voice was raspy. Shani didn't hear her. "Shani," she said again. "Front pocket."

"Oh," Shani's voice surged with urgency. She reached for the inhaler and tried to shove it into Brex's mouth, but Brex stopped her before any teeth were knocked out.

"Here," Lexi said, calmly. "Drink this." She handed her a small bottle of water after Brex took two shots from her inhaler. But the water wasn't going to be enough. They needed to refill their bottles, and soon.

The five of them didn't notice that the crack was still open, until they heard and felt a jolt in the ground that made the earth a giant trampoline. It finally closed. Even the night stars jumped. The soft grass and the patches of Cornish Oak trees were still. The peace returned. As long as they didn't step over it again, they would be safe.

"We need to move," said Shani. "Now."

Logan helped Brex up, but she didn't need much assistance. Her legs jiggled, and her hands shook, but she kept her head up straight. She wanted to listen to Shani for once.

Asher went to reach for her forehead to see if she was overheated until he remembered that her fire powers would make that concern redundant, but she took his hand in hers instead.

"Asher," Brex's soft voice, was a little clearer now, but her throat still hurt. "Thank you. I love you, you know that?"

"I love you too." He squeezed her hand, not wanting to let go, and fought back tears. "I love all of you. And none of us are going anywhere. Nothing is going to happen to us, okay?"

They all nodded and quickly hugged each other one more time before they started their journey again.

"I think I'm okay, Logan. Thank you," said Brex, letting go of his shoulder, but not going far. "I think I just need more food."

"We'll get you some, okay?" Lexi said, hoping there were enough seeds left. "Let's just walk a little more."

13:

"It's only happened a few times."

Brex woke up the next morning with the rest surrounding her. They must have been half a mile from where the earth had split open, but it was hard to tell. The trees, bushes, and flowers all looked the same. Lexi had a bottle of water in her hand, and Shani was cuddling the inhaler. Brex sat up with an aching back, but after cracking it a few times, she felt a small amount of relief. The grass smelled like it always did. Just like in New England; fresh and wet. She was surprisingly warm for having a sweater for a blanket and another sweater for a pathetic little pillow. Maybe she was too desperate for sleep and rest.

"Brex?" Shani asked while shooting herself upward, ready with the inhaler.

"Shani, I'm fine," Brex responded. "We should get going though. I think it's midday."

"What?" Logan mumbled as he rubbed his eyes. "Really?" The rest slowly groaned and pushed themselves to a sitting position. Lexi's jaw almost locked from yawning too widely, while Asher's vision nearly went black from sitting up too quickly.

"Everyone sleep okay?" Shani asked, rubbing her back.

"Sort of, but we don't have a plan yet," Lexi pointed out.

"We still haven't decided where we're going next," said Shani, pulling out the list that Maya made for them. "Next place is Greece."

"Greece?" Asher asked. "Geez..."

"But," Lexi muttered, "what about China?"

"We have more of a lead with Greece," said Shani, vigorously rubbing her forehead.

"Didn't he say something about the Yellow River?" Brex asked. "That's something."

"It sounds like a long walk," said Lexi, squinting her eyes. "We're kind of running out of time. Don't you think?"

"We'll figure it out when we get there. Come on. The airport is less than a mile away."

"But wait," Asher stopped everyone. "Where are we going first?"

The tense shoulders and foreheads said everything, but someone had to say it.

"I think it's time we split up," Shani suggested.

"Now?" Asher asked. "No, we're not ready. We don't have enough information. We should wait until our next stop."

"We're running out of time, Asher," said Brex. "Kali probably already knows where we're headed next."

"Okay," Logan breathlessly said. "Who's going where?"

Lexi cleared her throat before she said, "Logan and Brex should go together, and then I'll go with Shani and Asher."

"What made you decide that?" Logan asked, scratching his head.

"You and Brex work together really well, and same with Shani and me. Asher's obviously going to want to follow Shani around like a puppy dog."

Asher bit his smile before he said, "I'm so glad you're coming with me."

Lexi mimicked his smile before she nudged his shoulder and said, "Obviously. Would you like me to follow you around like a puppy dog to make you feel better?"

"Are we sure this is a good idea?" Logan interrupted. "I don't have a good feeling about this. Plus, we haven't been apart since Christmas."

"We'll be okay," said Brex. "Like Asher said, we're not going anywhere. It'll all be okay."

"How are we going to communicate?" Lexi asked.

"We won't." Brex ran her fingers through her dirty hair. "We'll know when we're in trouble. Why don't we just meet at our next location?"

"Good idea," said Shani, surprising herself after not having something insightful to say.

"Where is the next location?" Asher asked.

"Florence, Italy." Shani mentally checked it off.

"Okay," said Logan. "Let's go. We'll figure out the details when we get to the airport. We need to figure out our flights."

*****

The rest of the walk to the airport dragged on, but by the time they were inside, scuffing their dirty shoes all over the polished floors, Shani finally pulled her shoulders away from her ears and stretched her legs. Brex wasn't planning on saying anything nice if she heard Shani say, "Bitch, OW!" one more time.

"We need to organize the passports and everything," said Asher, pulling off one of the backpacks. Brex and Logan walked up to buy their tickets while Shani squeezed her way through Lexi and Asher to do the talking. Asher pulled out the prepaid Visa from the backpack with burn marks on the bottom. He didn't notice what the lava had done until Shani's eyebrow bled with sarcasm, hoping the travel agent would stop judging their dirty appearances.

"When do you guys leave?" Lexi asked Brex after they bought their tickets and while Shani was continuing to slightly raise her voice to the woman holding one of their few sources of money.

"An hour," Brex responded. "You?"

"Hour and a half."

"Okay. We'll do more planning."

The airport was surprisingly busy for the size and population of the surrounding area. They found a small space in a corner near Logan and Brex's gate. In front of them were at least twenty different water bottles that they had chugged, and Shani put most of them in front of Brex.

"How are you guys feeling?" Brex asked, trying to draw the attention away from her.

"I'm feeling okay," Asher said, looking around and hoping everyone else agreed.

"We need to sleep more when we're on our planes," said Shani.

"Believe me, I will," said Logan. "Brex whacked me in the face in the middle of the night and woke me up."

"I did?" Brex laughed while taking a sip of water. "Did you deserve it?"

"Always."

"Alright. Do we need tickets to this museum?" Lexi asked.

"Probably," said Asher, taking charge. "I'll look them up, but we should use a prepaid card, right? Do you think they'll take it?"

"Yeah, it doesn't have our name on it, right?" said Logan.

"No," Asher said sharply, surprising the rest.

"Whose name is on it?" Shani asked.

"Jenna's."

Brex leaned back against the wall, biting the sarcasm off her lips. "Seriously? You don't think that's traceable, Asher?"

"Sorry." His eyes stayed big, and his chest remained tall.

"Whatever," said Brex. "We'll see if we can find anything in China before our knees crumble to bits."

Asher twiddled his thumbs and scratched his nose uncontrollably. "What if we're waiting in Italy for days, and you guys just...never show up? Or vice versa?"

"Then, we'll just have to wait," said Lexi.

"If we're really in trouble we'll know," Shani added. "And if we really, desperately need each other, we'll figure out how we're tracked from the sun and go from there, okay?"

"I don't like this," Brex commented, biting her lips. "I can already feel the separation anxiety...the difference. What if it affects our powers?"

"I doubt it will," Lexi shook her head.

"Is there anything that we need to exchange or need more of?" Logan asked.

Asher's face relaxed. An idea sunk into him. "I'm gonna go to the bathroom," he said. "I'll be right back."

"Group A can now board," he heard over the intercom. They weren't until group C. He had some time, but he still dreaded what he knew he had to do.

The men's bathroom was empty, but Asher wasn't taking any chances. He went to the handicapped stall, which he always hated doing due to anxiety mixed with guilt, and locked the door.

"Okay, okay." He pulled off his shirt and threw it on the floor. The initial sweat was already layered on top of his skin. He could smell it. He pulled out the knife that was hidden in the hexed box. Finally, a use for it.

"Three, two, one." His wings ruptured and before letting any more time to think about it, he took the knife and cut a small, yet deep incision on his wing. "Owwww." It only hurt for a moment. He needed to squeeze out as much blue blood as he could into his purple, reusable water bottle.

"Now boarding Group C."

What?! Asher thought. *What happened to B?*

He put away his wings, put his shirt back on, put the rest away, and ran out the door, double-checking if he left anything behind on his way out.

"Asher?" he heard Lexi call out.

"I'm coming, sorry!" He ran up to Logan and Brex, waiting in their line. "This is for you." Asher held out the tightly capped water bottle in front of them.

"What's this?" Brex asked.

"The blue blood," Asher responded. "Or...the ichor. In case you need it. I just have a bad feeling that you will."

Brex hugged him without another beat. Then before they knew it, the five of them embraced one another, suffocating everyone involved.

"It'll be okay, guys," Lexi whispered. "We'll be okay."

"Last call!" the air stewardess barked. "Last call for flight 293."

"Be safe," Logan mumbled, grabbing onto his backpack and slowly walking away with increasing resistance.

"Come on, let's go," said Brex. She turned around to say to the others, "Don't be late for your flight."

The other three nodded, smiling, and within a few long seconds, Brex and Logan were out of sight.

"Come on," said Shani. "Let's get something to eat for the plane."

*****

"How long did you say the flight was?" Logan asked.

"Seventeen hours, I think," said Brex. "That's why we got KFC, McDonald's, and Domino's. I learned not to trust airplane food a long time ago."

"Yeah?" Logan asked, finally getting comfortable in his seat on the plane. "What happened during that lesson?"

"I'll just tell you, they had to close one of the bathrooms on a nine-hour flight to Scotland. Poor eleven-year-old Brex never stood a chance."

Logan laughed as he tried to shove their backpack under the seat.

"Where did you fly to? Five-star hotels, right?" Brex whispered through her teeth.

"Not always, thank you very much, and lots of places in Europe, but mainly London. My mom's parents were from there. My dad always loved it. So did my mom."

Brex shook her head. "Rich kids crack me up." Logan squirmed in his seat, trying to laugh. "I'm not trying to give you grief."

"Yeah, you are," Logan laughed.

"Yeah, I know."

Logan finally relaxed over the chair in front of him. "That's not why I'm squirming though."

"What's wrong?"

"There's something stabbing my ass."

Brex wanted to be helpful, but what was there to do?

"What is it?" she asked.

"I don't know, but I think I'm almost there." Logan's face was already uncomfortably squished up against the seat. His eyes were so tightly shut, Brex was worried he might pop a vein. "Got it!" But before he could realize what it was, Logan pulled it out to put it right in front of his face. He wouldn't have done that if he knew it was his small pocket knife that he forgot to put back in his hexed box.

"Logan! Put that away!" Brex whispered, louder than she initially wanted to. "Can we seriously not remember where these things go?"

"Is there a problem?" an Irish stewardess asked. The hope in her accent didn't match the solemn look on her face, which looked like it hadn't smiled its entire life.

"No," said Logan. "Nothing at all. She was just tickling me."

Brex wanted to deny what he had said, but she wanted to let her head flop back in exasperation even more.

"Americans..." the stewardess mumbled as she walked away.

Brex wanted to smack him, but as the stewardess walked away, they burst into a laughter they hadn't shared yet, and Brex's heart beat a little faster.

*****

"Did everyone get enough food?" Shani asked as she shoved the backpack under her aisle seat on the plane.

"Actually, I don't think I did," Asher answered.

"WHAT?" Shani jumped in her seat. Asher didn't have to say anything to her. He only had to lower his chin as he glared at her. "That's not funny."

"Asking us if we got enough food for the fifth time isn't funny either."

Lexi was the only one enjoying the altercation. She always did.

"How do you think Logan and Brex are doing?" Asher asked, already pulling out his food, just to make sure Shani wouldn't ask again.

"Oh...I think they are doing just fine," Lexi smiled. "Maybe we could go to Hong Kong after this."

"We should have bribed Maya into getting us anything we asked for after doing this," Asher joked before realizing that would have genuinely been a solid idea.

"Where would you want to go if we could?" Lexi asked Asher.

"Easy, Spain. I know the language. I'm a beautiful Latino man. The country is also beautiful too, I suppose. How could I resist?"

"What about you, Shani?" Lexi asked, leaning over Asher.

"Oh, I know this one," Asher laughed, shaking his head.

"What? What's so funny?"

Shani sat there, wanting to cover her face, but she resisted. She wasn't ashamed. The ambition remained in the glimmer of her smile.

"The bottom of the ocean in Antarctica," she answered.

Lexi tried hard not to laugh, but she didn't know why. "May I ask why that specifically is appealing to you?"

"You may as a matter of fact," Shani sat up straight to prepare for her speech. "Did you know that there are lakes underneath Antarctica?"

Lexi was sure Shani was going to answer her own question, but when she didn't, Lexi had to do it herself. "I did not, Shani."

"It's fascinating. I personally have a feeling that that's where most undiscovered sea life is. You know how people always say ninety-five percent of the ocean is unexplored?"

Lexi figured she needed to answer like before, but this time she was wrong. "Well, I—"

"I know! It's crazy. There's so much wildlife that can survive those temperatures and the density of those waters. I'm going to be the one to discover them. I'm telling you."

"I'm gonna be the first one to buy your book, you know that, right?" Lexi asked.

Asher thrust his chin back before saying, "Maybe we could buy it at the same time, but I'll probably deceive you and throw down my credit card first."

"Let's shake on it anyway." And so, they did. But before Lexi could let go, Asher noticed something he couldn't ignore.

"Lexi," Asher whispered, unsure of who he was trying to hide this from. "What's wrong with your hand?"

Maybe Lexi was in denial, or maybe she didn't notice her recurring twitch uncontrollably shaking in her fingertips and wrist.

"I...um," she mumbled, pulling her hand away. "I think it's fine. It's only happened a few times."

"What? A few times?" Shani, again, said more loudly than she intended. "How many times has this happened?"

"I don't know, Shani." Lexi's stern voice couldn't be controlled. The expansion in her diaphragm was unexpected, but she needed that fresh air. "This is literally the last thing I am concerned about. I don't need sympathy, and I don't need any concerning eyes staring at me."

She leaned back in her seat, ready to get yelled at by an attendant to put it back up.

"Lexi," Shani whispered, knowing yelling wasn't going to help. "It's just because we need you. We can't afford to have you be weak. I'm not trying to be bossy. But I'm sorry. I know it's coming off that way."

"I know," said Lexi. "But I don't wanna talk about it, I just wanna eat some food and sleep, okay?"

"Yeah," said Asher before Shani could say anything else. "Let's all get some sleep." Asher also leaned back in his chair, trying to get as comfortable as he could, sitting in between the tension that he knew would dissipate soon, but that he couldn't forget about.

"Ladies and gentlemen," said the Irish, saggy-faced flight attendant. "Please fasten your seatbelts as we begin our take-off to Athens."

14:

"Are you Logan?"

Reymid wasn't used to being alone in a room with Moloch, but Moloch remained calm whenever he could hear the steady rhythm of Reymid sharpening his arrows. The only thing that would sharpen them was a single, small blade of Kali's steel. Small sparks would blind him like fireworks that were too close to him, but it reminded Moloch of the Underworld. He could sense the warmth of the friction radiating off the colliding metal. But after an hour or so of the audible meditation, Moloch needed a change.

"Go tell Kali that no amount of pacing is going to make anything go faster. Tell her to check if Clement is back," said Moloch, keeping his eyes on his table of stacked drawings, papers, books, and maps.

Reymid didn't answer. He did as he was told, but silently. The only noise he made was wiping his long, black dreadlocks out of his face.

Outside the basement door, Kali stepped one foot in front of the other, pacing back and forth. Moloch wasn't to be disturbed. He wasn't fond of being awakened if the news wasn't important enough for him.

"Is he ready? Does he have anything?" Kali asked Reymid as he walked through the door.

"No," Reymid responded, without blinking. He threw himself into a red chair far enough from Kali to avoid her impatience as much as he could.

"Why?" Kali stopped pacing and held her feet firmly in the ground.

"He doesn't have the energy."

"That's not an excuse." Kali grabbed the open bottle of whiskey that rested on the edge of the uneven countertop. She chugged it before she realized there wasn't enough left for her liking, but that's not what poked and tugged at her chest.

Her wrist ached as if there were an absence of blood. She turned her palm over to see the needle on her scar now closer to her thumb. Her magic was over halfway gone. But before she could ponder any longer, Clement's tall and broad shadow appeared from around the hallway corner.

"Yes?" Kali asked impatiently.

"I've got him," Clement responded with only half of his teeth showing through his slim smile. His red hair was a mess, and the buttons on his white shirt were torn off, but his eyes said he wasn't done.

"Well, where is he?" Kali asked, with less patience than before.

"He's been a little slow. He whined about not having the energy to continue the entire journey."

"Men..." Kali whispered with tight lips. "If he doesn't want to cooperate, he doesn't have to. No one's forcing him to be involved. He has a choice."

"I don't think he's seeing it that way," said Clement.

"And I was so hoping he would see this as an opportunity. Oh well, bring him down anyway. Reymid, help him."

Reymid pulled himself up from the comfort of the red chair and quietly joined Clement around the dark corner.

Kali couldn't help but pick at her scar while she had the chance. Her sense of security shook with every second that her eyes met with the dying scar. Something she hadn't felt in a long time, but it was a familiar feeling.

"Come on," Reymid grunted as he pulled a pale, long arm behind him, but it wasn't Clement's arm he pulled, it was a handsome, blonde man who still wore his bartender uniform.

"Jethro," Kali shouted louder than usual. "It's good to finally meet you. Sorry about earlier. You're a lot faster than I imagined. Then again, you are pretty old. My mistake. I should know better, considering my age."

Two giant cuffs, the size of cantaloupes wrapped around Jethro's wrists. They connected to one another by a single chain that glowed every time his strong, resisting forearms pulled against them.

"Oh," Kali laughed. "I'm sure you've figured out by now that your magic is suppressed with these on. Moloch made them years ago. And don't even try to pry them off and put them on one of us. They only work for witches. You didn't think we would come completely unprepared to visit you, did you?"

Jethro kept his mouth shut, but Kali continued to calmly pace around him. Beads of sweat dripped from his forehead the more he shook. Clement and Reymid aggressively pulled him to the chair that sat near piles of messy papers. Kali kept her eyes on him. He didn't resist, even when she gently touched his shoulders and thick blades of steel swirled around his arms and the chair. The embrace of his shackles didn't leave any wiggle room for Jethro to resist.

"Is this comfortable?" Kali asked. "I hope you know my intentions are pure. I genuinely want you to be comfortable. We're going to be here for a while."

Jethro's eyes hadn't left her since the moment he stumbled into the room. His eyes were quickly drying out, he had yet to blink. "Why am I here?" he asked without flinching.

"There's that handsome voice." Kali smiled.

"If you were really paying attention, you would know that I don't have anything. My sanctuary is empty. It's been empty for a while. And you know that we don't tell each other anything. I don't know where my alchelesters went. So we can protect one another if we're tortured."

"Why do Americans still think torture works?" Kali rubbed her face, mumbling to herself. "I know how strong you are, Jethro." She gently brushed her hand across his bicep and over his chest. "I'm just trying to get you to trust me."

"Trust you?" Jethro laughed. "Remind me of your name again."

Clement scoffed with minimal laughter into his fist before Kali rolled her eyes.

"Sorry. I forgot," Kali stretched the corners of her lips to her cheekbones in a stretchy smile. "I'm Kali, and I know that your sanctuary is empty. It was pretty obvious when we broke into your flat before you returned. I need something else from you."

"And what is that?"

Sitting inches away from him, Kali slowly rubbed her hands together before she intertwined them and placed them gently on Jethro's knee.

"The Salem Witches aren't trustworthy. You should know that. Your own mother abandoned you after all. But anyway...they know things we don't, and I need you to tell me what they are."

For the first time since he sat down, Jethro briefly closed his eyes.

"I'm sorry, what? Could you be more specific? What do you not know?"

"I'm not sure." Kali kept the blank expression firmly on her face.

"That's helpful." Jethro scoffed and let his cheeks loosen.

"Don't laugh. I'll get it out of you eventually. It'll just take a moment."

Kali's pacing slowed down, and her shoulders relaxed against the rest of her body. Her breathing naturally inflated her skinny face and limbs. She could wait for a while.

"Why don't you leave us?" Kali asked Clement and Reymid. They did as they were told, but not without exuding an air of supremacy, leaving gazes lingering. The door echoed behind them, but Jethro didn't flinch.

"What makes you think kicking them out will make me talk?" Jethro asked. His voice grew raspier with every syllable.

"I don't like it when men are in my head. I think better with their absence. I figured you were the same. Most people are."

Jethro couldn't disagree. Kali leaned in closer to him with her sweaty arms crossed.

"I know that there's something these witches told you. A secret that you promised to keep. Or maybe gossip that you overheard."

"Is this a theory or just a hypothesis?"

Kali laughed. His amusing smile was unexpected. "It would be an explanation. That's all. It just doesn't add up."

"I guess you have a point, but I don't know anything." His chin dropped to his chest, but that only drew her closer to him.

"I don't believe you." She whipped her hair around to sit a few feet away from him on a pile of messy boxes.

"If your method isn't torture, what is it?" Jethro asked.

"Exchange. I have information that you want, or at least I think you want. I don't know you that well after all."

"And how did you plan on doing that? What did you have? Or...I guess...how do I know that I can trust you'll hold up your end? I don't know you well either. Whatever this is, how do I know that you will be truthful and give me what I want after I give you what you want? Which again...I have no idea what that is."

"I know where your mother is."

Jethro's jaw slowly numbed after the small muscles jumped around in a dance. "No, you don't."

"You're right, sorry. I should clarify. I have *information* as to where she is."

Jethro's body sliced against the thick steel as he slammed his chair in place. "HOW?"

The anger took Kali by surprise, but her flinch slowly shook off her. "So, you do care?" Kali asked. "That's good to know."

"Answer my question!"

"Okay, this is why I said men get in my head too much—"

"I SAID ANSWER IT!"

Kali slapped her hands on his knees and brought her nose inches from his. "Because Moloch was there that night. Don't you remember? He took her as collateral. He still remembers her squeals when he ripped her away from you. He described it to me in perfect detail. I knew that sound all too well. Believe me, I know how much you would love to see her again. How much you *need* to see her again. Who wouldn't want that? But here's the thing. It was all too easy. I didn't believe for a second that the witches didn't have some sort of collateral either. Maybe even a simple lie that he would believe. Those witches and Moloch are the same, really. They'll make anyone believe them. So tell me what you know, and I promise you I will help you find your adopted mother. The only mother you ever knew. I will tell you what I know. I have no reason to lie. You seeing your mother again won't hinder my plan at all."

Jethro's breath raced no matter how hard he tried to slow it down. His tense jaw wouldn't move, but he needed to give his answer.

"Well..." Jethro stuttered. "There was one thing, but I don't even know if it's true. It could be a lie, but it would make your plan obtainable. If I tell you everything will change. I swear."

"Tell me."

*****

Brex's and Logan's legs almost collapsed the second they boarded the train in China. If they had to take one more step, their knees would never forgive them.

"I can take the backpack when we need to move again," said Brex.

"I don't believe that for a second," Logan yawned as he mumbled, "and I ain't moving until my feet apologize to me for being the wusses that they are."

Brex threw her hands up, but her arms were too tired to lift them high enough to match her attitude. "Those wusses scored you more touchdowns than most athletes dream of. I don't think you should be talking to them like that."

Logan didn't have the energy to answer. He couldn't even think of mustering enough energy to move his little finger to scratch his wrist.

"You hungry at all?" Brex asked. "I think they'll have a food cart."

"Only if you give them the money. I can't reach for it." The volume in Logan's voice steadily declined like a feather floating through a canyon. Brex didn't handle her exhaustion in the same way.

"Ow!" Logan loudly cracked his voice when he felt a jacket with a sharp zipper hit his head.

"You're such a baby." Brex held her finger close to his face. "I can't nurture you whenever you are in pain and sore. Haven't you ever gone on a hike before? You grew up in New England for God's sake."

"I loved hiking. When I slept for a living."

Brex laughed. Her cheeks felt unexpectedly hot, but only until she cracked open the window.

"I'm sorry. I'm stressed. I don't mean to take it out on you. You're just such a boy. An annoying little boy."

Logan took her hand. "Sorry. This is just how I deal with stress too."

The heat returned, or maybe it had never left. She wasn't sure.

"But seriously, you want food?" Brex asked, quickly pulling her hand away. "I'm curious to see if American Chinese food is authentic in any way, shape, or form."

"Depends on who you ask. If you ask Shane Kwan, no. If you ask me, also no, but that's only because my dad wouldn't take yes for an answer."

"Did he ever cook at all for you? Like real Chinese meals?"

"No, but my mom did. I don't remember her cooking, but my dad said her cooking was halfway decent except for her dumplings. He couldn't get enough of them. Apparently, that was the moment he fell in love with her. The first time she ever made him her famous dumplings. He got pretty good at making them too. So, that's the only thing he's ever made me."

Brex lay down across the empty seats and put her jacket under her head. "I miss my mom," she said.

Logan hated feeling at a loss for words, but this wasn't one of those situations.

"I've never heard you say that before," he gently spoke.

"I guess it took me a while to say that, but it took me a hell of a lot longer to say that I missed the rest of them too. It makes absolutely no sense, I know. But that's how my brain works. I guess it was just a defense mechanism."

"I get it," Logan said with a cracked voice. "I don't like it when people think I need them. It makes me feel weak. And I don't like getting all sappy either."

Brex shifted in her seat and gently twiddled her thumbs, unable to stop looking at them. "But I need you guys. I...I need you."

Logan's already stiff body tightened, but he lay there motionless. His lips and nose felt as if they were about to fall off; they were so numb, but he didn't notice. He didn't want to look away from her.

"I know. I don't know what I would do without you here." Brex looked into his eyes waiting for him to continue. She desperately longed for him to keep talking. About anything. She didn't know why, but she needed to keep listening to the sound of his soft, yet strong voice, but all he said was, "We should get some sleep. I think it's going to be a few hours."

Her heart sank, but it still beat. A painful beat that wasn't slowing down.

"Okay," she whispered with a jaw that wouldn't open normally. "Yeah, you're right. Good night."

"I think it's three in the afternoon," Logan responded, "but good-night, Brex."

Her one-syllable, solid name never sounded so delicate. She wanted him to say it again, but she was just going to have to wait. He had already fallen into a deep sleep.

*****

The Great Wall of China stood taller than they expected. The closer they got the shorter they felt, but the sensation was nothing compared to the breathtaking sight of the mountains that carried the stone wall and shimmered in the sunlight. The Great Wall was thousands of years old, yet it looked like it could have been built the day before. The luminous mountains were overwhelming. They didn't know where to look first. Although, they took in the view with a grain of salt. Their feet and thighs were already aching, and they only made it up their first mountain.

"That's okay," said Logan after staring at their future journey. "I wasn't married to the idea of playing football again."

"For some reason, I think I'll lose my birthing abilities after this trip," Brex commented before they locked eyes and burst into laughter. "Come on. Let's go."

Hours later, the night sky quickly painted over the blue one. The stars and moon reflected more light than they had expected. Besides, Brex didn't want to pull out a flashlight yet. The chilling darkness never failed to calm her.

"You know what we should do after this?" Logan asked.

"Sleep?"

"Yes, but I was going to say we should take a real vacation. Somewhere that we aren't visiting now."

Brex's smile tingled. "I don't know. I kind of like the idea of returning to these places, knowing that our lives are not at stake. What do ya think?"

Logan shook his head and bit his smile. Something minor in his chest was ticking and waiting for an explosion. "That sounds pretty great. Not gonna lie. Besides, I think Shani would kill to see China. Especially here. It would be nice to have us all together."

"What? Am I not good enough company?"

"I don't know. Do you always snore like a pregnant tigress?"

The laugh burst out of her, but she had to admit, "I've been told I do on occasion."

They walked for a few more hours before Logan suggested a break. Brex had wanted one at least an hour before he asked, but she was tempted to see if Logan would break first. Her competitive tendencies were right.

They stopped at one of the highest peaks there. Brex noticed the river that stretched beyond the horizon. It was the shimmering centerpiece of the canvas. She'd never seen such a complete image that had so much to say with such little light and color.

"Look, right there." She pointed to the river. Somehow it sparkled with a brighter light the more she looked at it. "We're close. Wherever the sanctuary is, we can't be too far away. It can't be too far away from the river."

"Good. I'll keep watch if you want to sleep," said Logan.

"No, it's okay. We shouldn't stay here for too long. You need any food?"

"Why are you asking me, ya goof? I have the backpack. I should be asking you."

"Why? Am I incapable of serving myself?"

Logan's face froze, but not before he bit down on both his lips. "Alright...you got me." He laughed and sat down across the dewy grass.

"Do you think we're going to need a break from each other after this?" Brex asked, lying down next to him.

"Oh please, we're not going to be capable of that. But maybe we'll need to re-evaluate in like ten years or so."

"Yeah, probably."

The crickets took over for a while, filling the air with peaceful white noise that neither one of them wanted to break. Even the silence between them drew them together. They couldn't explain it. Logan sank into the earth. The soil held him and molded to his body. He didn't want to leave. Just as long as she was there.

"Hey, Brex—"

"Do you smell that?" Brex interrupted.

"Smell what?" Logan couldn't smell a thing. Or maybe he did. He quickly sniffed. The dark night clouded his other senses.

"I smell...fur. Geez. These heightened senses are getting weird."

"Fur has a smell?"

"Yeah. It has all kinds of smells."

"Like different animals?"

"I don't know. I don't think our powers have heightened our senses that much just yet. Come on." Brex pulled Logan to his feet. She held his wrist for longer than he expected, but he was also surprised by how quickly she let go.

"Okay," Logan mumbled. "You think it's a wild animal or something."

"You think someone lost a house cat with all the tourism in this area?"

"Not your best joke."

"Maybe something died over there," said Brex running down the small hill.

"Brex, wait hold on. I can't see you." Logan followed her, but Brex made the footwork look too easy.

"Ow!" Logan caught his foot on a rock, or maybe it was a tree branch, but his other foot couldn't steady him. Brex had to do that instead.

"Jesus." She pushed his shoulders up to meet hers. Her impressive reflexes were even more so when she realized he would have head-butted her if she hadn't caught him.

"Thanks," said Logan, trying to stop himself from smiling too much after seeing how amused she was. The two were about to squeeze out a joyful laughter, but they didn't get the chance. Their breath was ripped away instead.

"RAAAAAAEEEERRR!"

They didn't have to look, even if they did, the darkness would smother whatever it was that sharpened its claws inches away from them. Brex couldn't hear anything. Her body was moving, but she was in a dream. Nothing was real, and the moment seemed rewindable, but no matter how hard she tried to wake up, she couldn't. The danger was running after them.

"LOGAN!" Brex screamed. "COME ON!" But it was too late.

The moment swam through water. A leopard that stretched longer than a pick-up truck leaped onto Logan's back. Its claws plunged into his shoulders before it pulled him down and threw him against the cold grass. It wasn't the bloody scratches that caused his voice to fly with the wind. It wasn't even the giant cat that hovered over him. Instead, it was the excruciating pain that ignited in his shoulder and flashed all the way down his back. His shoulder dislocated the second it slammed against the ground, and Brex wasted no time in throwing every spark of flame her arms could ignite into the leopard's furry, yet suspicious face.

"RAAAAAAEEERR!" it screamed again.

"GET OFF HIM!" But it didn't matter. No matter how many thick flames she threw at the beast, the leopard wouldn't move.

"Enough!" the cat screamed, at least Brex thought it did. Logan was still occupied cradling his aching shoulder.

"Wha—?" It wasn't the first time Brex had seen a talking animal, but she couldn't help but convince herself that she was hallucinating.

"Are you Logan?" the cat spoke again. Only this time, Brex knew what she was witnessing. "The one everyone is talking about?"

"Yes, yeah...that's him," Brex stuttered. "What...what are you? Who...GET OFF HIM!"

Logan's breath quickly caught up to him, but he wasn't letting go of his shoulder anytime soon. Brex pulled him up, once again, but he almost didn't make it. Even his grumpy feet sympathized with the pain of his shoulder injury.

"I'm sorry. I didn't mean to pounce," said the leopard, who sat on the back of her hind legs.

"Yeah, okay." Brex blotted the small ounce of blood off Logan's forehead, trying not to look at the green-eyed beast.

"Then I heard your name. I figured it wasn't a coincidence."

"Okay, first of all," Brex held up her finger and clasped onto Logan's forearm harsher than she had intended to, "I screamed his name before you pounced; therefore you have no excuse. Second of all, what do you mean 'the one everyone's been talking about?' No one knows we're here."

The leopard's ears perked, almost as if she was amused.

"You think in a world where you can send millions of watts of electricity through your body without frying yourself, you can keep a secret that you're going around to all of the sanctuaries, trying to relocate them? Please. Spare me the amusement."

"Who else knows?" Logan finally spoke, cracking his gentle voice. "How many other people have been warned?"

"I don't know," said the leopard. "But I doubt many. I worked closely with Jethro. We find ways to communicate when we can."

"You know Jethro?"

15:

"I told you, it's in the Wall."

"I used to not too long ago. We were both apprentices in the Alliance together."

"You..." Brex's jaw dropped and her eyebrow popped. "You were an apprentice?"

The leopard silently rounded the corners of her furry, wide mouth. Slowly, her shoulders rounded forward, and her head tucked into her chest, but her chest wasn't the furry, rounded form that it once was. Instead, it was bare, smooth, and pale. And her round head that had sculpted every inch of fur at a matched and perfect length wasn't there. It morphed into a round sphere of thick hair that flashed in the moonlight like a high beam on the freeway. There stood a beautiful young woman with hair whiter than cotton, wearing a dark green, skintight suit that stretched from neck to toe. The only thing that stayed the same was her bright, green eyes.

"I'm sorry, who are you?" Brex asked. Her confusion quickly kicked her anger out of the way.

"My name is Krina."

"And you're a—" Logan didn't know what to ask. His hands flew from side to side as his head stiffly followed.

"I think people call it a shapeshifter."

"So..." Brex began. "You're not a cat?"

"I'm not an anything. This feminine figure is just my preferred form. The one I am most content with. When I heard there might be strangers crossing my path, I took caution."

"What animal even is that?" Logan asked, trying to finally move his shoulder.

"A North China Leopard. A rare species, but smart and quick. I thought it would be a better choice than a panda bear."

"That would be a little stereotypical, wouldn't you think?" Brex asked. Krina only shrugged her shoulders, but Brex's judgment lingered along with her tilting chin.

"A panda bear wouldn't almost break my arm in half though," Logan muttered. He squeezed his arm as he tried to move it forward, but he could take only so much before cradling it again. "Brex, where's the blue blood?"

"Blue blood?" Krina asked. "Do you mean ichor? How much do you have? Please, don't bother wasting it."

Brex brushed her long, sweaty hair out of her face and snapped, "Did you have something else in mind?"

"Come on. I'm sorry, yes. Come with me. I can heal it."

Krina turned around and started down the hill without them. Brex finally released her grip on Logan before realizing she had no idea how to hold him and assist him down the mountain.

"Brex, my legs are fine."

"Oh, right," Brex mumbled.

"Don't worry. Just keep your eyes open, okay?"

"I know." Brex brushed his cheek and followed Krina along the dark path of nothing but uneven grass and trees.

The walk wasn't long, but Brex remembered the backpack and went back for it, and even though Logan was only standing there waiting, the stinging pain made the seconds drag by, taking one small step at a time.

Krina impatiently guided them, stopping every few seconds to wait for them to catch up.

"Here we are," said Krina, walking up to nothing but more grass.

"Let me guess," said Logan, "underground sanctuary?"

"Even better," said Krina. The skin on her fingers reddened, but they hadn't yet moved. Nothing ruptured from her skin, but Krina held her stance as if she were asking permission. The starry night sky morphed into a glassy portrait that waved in ripples. The grass and trees remained still, but it was almost as if the stars pulled an invisible blanket off something much bigger than a tree. It reminded Logan of the one time he had taken acid and couldn't see where his bed was when he wanted to lie down and collapsed on the floor instead. Brex couldn't stop blinking. It was becoming a reflex. Even after the blank slate of grass suddenly had formed a hut made of trees and vines the size of a trailer, Brex's eyelashes felt like they were about to fall off.

"Blood passage?" Brex whispered. "Except her house was invisible. Cool."

"Come on," said Krina, gesturing for Logan and Brex to walk in through the small hole in the tree trunk. "In here."

Brex and Logan nodded their heads instead of giving thanks, but once they were in the tiny home, they couldn't stay silent.

"Oh wow," Brex gasped after picking up her jaw. The house had grown twenty times larger than how it had appeared on the outside. "How did that happen?"

"Oh, it's just an optical illusion. If I explained it more, I'm afraid you might turn into a flat-earther."

"This is your sanctuary?" Logan asked, already touching too many things.

"No, this is my home. The sanctuary is hidden in the Great Wall."

"So, what made you want it to be invisible?"

"It's a distraction, I suppose. If someone finds this house, they'll think they've found the sanctuary. There's an ice cave in the basement. Therefore, they'll think this one is empty and move on. And trust me, they would find this one first. Kali is smart."

Brex's ears went numb at the lack of white noise in the background. She had never been in a sound booth before, but she couldn't imagine it being any worse. It was too quiet, dead air, tomb-like, and claustrophobic.

"I feel like my head is going to explode," said Brex, squeezing her head and hunching over.

"Oh, you'll be fine," said Krina, walking through what Brex guessed was a pantry and waving Brex off. "You get used to it. It's just the insulation."

"What kind of insulation...you know what? Nevermind." Brex threw herself next to Logan on the couch, which was so broken that they almost sank into the floor.

"How long have you been here again? Ow!" Logan couldn't hold still as Brex uselessly examined his shoulder.

"A few years. Before, I was in Athens."

Athens? Brex thought.

"Really?" Logan asked. "That's where our friends are right now. They're searching for alchelesters there. Do you know if there are any at that sanctuary?"

"Sorry, I don't." Krina pulled out a mason jar the size of a basketball. "We switch completely randomly. Dimitria once only had alchelesters in her sanctuary for ten days."

"Dimitria? Dimitria was your mentor? And guard?" Brex asked.

"Yes, Jethro's too. She might have moved her location by now, but who knows?"

The giant mason jar shook the table that Krina dropped it on. Whatever was in it sat thicker than blood, and darker than a boiling, polluted swamp.

"Oh, God!" Logan pulled his long, dirty sleeve over his mouth to protect himself from the smell. "What is that stuff?"

"Trust me," Krina said, smiling through gritted teeth. "You don't want to know." Logan took his shirt off and Krina scooped out a large spoonful of the substance and smeared it all over Logan's shivering, bruised shoulder.

"Where did you learn how to do this?" Brex asked, wiping away the tears that spilled from her watering eyes.

"My apprenticeship. Dimitria. She's a demigod, kind of. She spent a lot of time with Asclepius. God of healing. She taught me everything I know."

"How often do you have to use this stuff, or...any of it? Oh, shiiii-iiit." The medicine was slow to kick in, but it had a peculiar way of greeting Logan and making its presence known. It wasn't ointment that was rubbed all over his shoulders; it was a pile of needles that stabbed into him all at once. But not a doctor's needle, needles that were on steroids themselves and twice the size they needed to be and didn't know how to slide in properly, so they took their time doing their job.

"You'll get used to it. You'd be surprised at how often I've had to use these. Once I'm injured in one form, the injury could look completely different in another. If I injure my shoulder and I morph into a cheetah, or a bear, or whatever, the injury could be in my heart. I can't take any risks. But the one that I use most is the one for skin rashes. You have no idea how many things I am allergic to out here."

Logan squeezed Brex's hand so tightly, the color of her skin almost turned as dark as the medicine, but as his pain lightened up, so did the color of her fingers. Logan's back arched against the couch. For once, his hair wasn't perky and waving in the wind. It pulled against the beads of sweat on his forehead and smelled almost as bad as his shoulder.

"Thank you, Krina," said Logan as he caught his breath.

"Of course, it's my job." Krina took a sip of her drink which looked like it had been sitting on the dusty coffee table for days. "So, why are you here?"

Brex pursed her lips together and knitted her eyebrows. "What do you mean? We need to help you relocate your sanctuary. I thought you said you knew what was going on."

"Yeah, I can't do that. You can't know what's in my sanctuary."

"What?" Logan asked. "Krina, there's a mole in the Alliance."

"No, you *think* there's a mole in the Alliance. And besides, how do I know it's not you two? I don't know you."

Brex slapped her hands against her lap so vigorously, it could have been mistaken for a clap of thunder. "You're kidding, right? We aren't a part of the Alliance. We don't know shit. What could we have done?"

"You're human. You have no idea of the advantages that it gives you. People will trust you with anything."

Logan wiped the sweat away from his forehead and took a sip of whatever Krina was drinking. "Yeah, that doesn't seem to be my experience so far."

"Oh, yeah?" Krina asked.

"Yes," Brex and Logan said simultaneously.

"Then why did Maya tell you to travel to all these places to find the sanctuaries when not a single one of us is supposed to know where any of the locations are besides our own?"

The answer floated about them somewhere, they just couldn't find it, and it was going to either land soon, or float away and be lost forever, but Brex's gaze dropped to her lap while Logan smashed the back of his head against the couch once again.

"It was the best idea that she could come up with," said Brex.

"And why couldn't she have done this herself?" Krina asked.

"She has no special abilities besides her reincarnation. How was she a better choice?" Logan shrugged.

"Look," said Krina, leaning forward. "I know Maya, and she is one of the smartest beings to ever live. Just a trail of her knowledge puts her in a position of power that you will never understand. Don't underestimate her."

"I believe you," said Brex, trying to keep her impatient voice soft. "But I'm asking you to do the same for us. Please, don't underestimate us. We don't need to know where the items are going. We shouldn't. That's what I'm saying, we can't leave any traces. When was the last time it was moved?"

Krina's still, relaxed chest fluttered as it pumped out. "A year ago," she said, matching Brex's vitality.

"Exactly. Trust me, there's a good chance Kali and Moloch know or will know where it is. We have to move fast."

For the first time that night, Krina let the attitude slide off her cheekbones and down her arms. She confidently locked eyes with Brex. "You make a good point," she said, "but I can't show you the sanctuary. Trust me, I can't."

Brex unclenched her jaw. "Just tell me why."

"Because I don't have access to get into the sanctuary."

Brex couldn't tell if Krina was joking or not, but she was too impatient to think about it before she started to scream.

"What? How? Why? Whose bullshit idea was that? What's the point of you being here?"

"Like I said before. It's just a different way of hiding in plain sight. A different tactic to use to conceal what we carry. I'm a *distraction*. Any repetitive method we use won't help us."

The pain in Logan's shoulder was still fading, but the pain he had left quickly morphed into impatience.

"Do you know where it is?" Logan asked.

"Yes," Krina nodded. "Of course, I know *that.*"

"Do you know what you guard?"

Krina bit her lip and stiffened her chest. "The flower of Persephone."

"Krina," Brex whispered, "it needs to be relocated. Somewhere buried. Somewhere random. We have no other choice."

"It won't be easy."

"Then," said Brex, rubbing her thighs, "we better get going. We'll just have to figure it out when we get there."

*****

The walk wasn't far, but Brex quickly grew sick of Logan's panting and scratching even though his shoulders were healed.

"Where is this place?" Brex asked.

"I told you, it's in the Wall," Krina answered, holding up a small flashlight that needed its batteries changed.

"I know, but how is it hidden?"

"You'll see."

Brex accepted the answer with a shake of the head and an eye roll before she moved on. Luckily, her patience didn't have to be tested.

"Here we are." Krina held up the flashlight to four discolored cement bricks that sparkled a little brighter than the rest and stacked on top of each other like a pile of encyclopedias. The only thing Brex and Logan found peculiar was the discolored cement bricks weren't infrequent in the sculpture that was the Great Wall. They were scattered everywhere and the differentiation in color wasn't drastic enough to be conspicuous.

"What are we looking at?" Logan asked.

"The entrance," Krina responded.

"Are you sure?"

"Yes." Krina cocked her head out and gently squinted. "I'm sure."

Brex reached her small hand to touch the cold cement, but nothing moved. "And you don't know how to get in?"

"No," Krina huffed, "they didn't give me access."

"Wait, so you do know how? You just can't?"

"Right." Krina hopelessly leaned against the wall, thinking the point was clear. "My blood wasn't given access to open any of the sanctuaries. Not even my own. Think of it as a fingerprint scan, only my blood doesn't actually touch the opening, it just detects it."

"Do you even have blood?" Logan asked. Brex wanted to smack herself in the face, but Krina changed the subject before she could.

"It's not like I really needed to. I just sit around and guard the gate as a fly or mouse or something."

"Well," said Brex, pulling up her sleeve. "Luckily, we do have access. We just have to pay for it with these." She tapped her scar and hovered her sweaty palm above the center crevice of the four bricks. With a bit of shifting and waiting, the four bricks shook with a gentle vibration that quickly turned into a glass-shattering jolt that split open the four bricks which shifted in all different directions.

Logan's eyes couldn't keep up. The spiraling images stabbed his skull between his eyebrows. But once the blue darkness blossomed from the interior of the wall, Logan had another problem.

"Alright," said Brex. "Let's go, Logan. You keep watch?"

"Brex, no. You hate the dark."

"Logan, it's fine."

"I guess I could keep watch?" Krina suggested, raising her hand. "But you might need me to crawl in small spaces."

"Krina's right," said Brex. "You don't know what obstacles are in there."

"We'll be fine," said Krina, gently removing Brex's hand from Logan's forearm. "Brex, wait here, okay?"

"Okay," said Brex with tight lips. "I'll be here."

Logan gestured for Krina to go first, and she gladly accepted, but not before she spiraled into the form of a dark barn owl that perched on Logan's shoulder.

"Trust me, I'll be able to see way better like this."

"I could just—" Brex began to say, holding up her arm.

"No, we have to be careful." And with one more look, Brex took a step back and watched Logan fade into the dark hole. Crickets had never made her heart pound so deeply.

The cement floor was mostly level. Every few steps, Logan tripped over a small, yet sharp bump on the floor, no matter how high Logan picked up his feet.

"Walk slower," said Krina, "and keep your hands out. I see a few dead ends coming up."

"What do you mean, dead ends?" Logan's arms stiffened as more sweat dripped down his already sweaty face.

"I mean there are a few random walls. No one's been in here in a while. The cobwebs are gonna get pretty intense."

"Okay," said Logan, swallowing painfully.

"Logan, you're doing fine. It can't be that much longer 'till we find something."

"Okay," Logan mumbled again. When she put her claw on his shoulder to console him, he was so tense that Krina thought she was perched on a rock instead of human flesh.

"Stairs. Downhill. Don't worry, there aren't many. Ready?" Krina asked.

"Mhmm," Logan lied.

"One step down, in three, two..."

The journey wasn't perfect, but they didn't fall. Logan's heart made a joyful leap that didn't thrust against his ribcage.

"How did you get into the Alliance anyway?" Logan asked. "Did they ever tell you why they didn't give you blood access?"

"I didn't ask, but it was because of Jethro. He'd known me since I was young. I was taken in by the witches. My tribe thought I was a freak. Not everyone, but still. They didn't want me."

"Why was that...you know...if I may ask."

Krina's breath was soft, but Logan could still hear it. "Because I was unnatural. Normally, we are only supposed to turn into one animal."

"Oh like—"

"If you say Jacob in *Twilight*, I will bite your nose off."

Logan stayed silent, but it didn't come easy.

"Anyway," Krina continued. "I also didn't like staying in my birth form. It was a short, young boy that had a weird nose. I always stayed as my tall, dark-skinned, white-haired self. It always felt right, but no one understood. Except the witches did."

"Well, were you happy with the witches?"

"I didn't stay for very long. I had my own life to live, but I can't think of a different path for my life. I wouldn't have it any other way."

Logan smiled. "In a way, you sound like Shani. Just wait until you meet her. She's another alchelarcenist."

"Are you scared of her too?" Krina asked. Her monotone voice didn't shake once.

Logan's mind raced to come up with a different answer, but he didn't have one.

"Yes."

"We're almost there," said Krina.

"How do you know?" Logan asked. "Can you sense something? No, you're lying." Logan stopped cold. "You've been down here before."

"No, Logan. I can see the flower right there." She flapped her feathery wing toward the center of the room, but Logan only knew that because of the feathers ruffling. "Owl eyes, remember? You don't have the powers of Hades. I can see a lot better in the dark than you can."

"Oh, okay."

Logan picked up the pace. His sudden confidence took him by surprise, but that didn't make him second guess.

"Just a little further," Krina whispered with a soft and shaky voice. "Logan, be careful."

"I am."

A blue, transparent, glass case the size of a microwave stood in their way. Logan tried to remove it, but it must have been glued or enchanted to stay put. Logan snapped his elbow through the thick glass managing to miss most of the sharp edges. If he squinted, he could almost see a reflection. The petals were smoother than he had expected. He was worried, just for a moment, that he would break the stem in half. The moment slithered past him as he gently picked up the flower, but the euphoria waited until he could see his hand tightening all of a sudden due to the flames that burst about the room, covering their pathway.

"Logan," Krina screamed. "Go! It's a trap!"

Krina flew off his shoulder. He couldn't see where she was going, but he couldn't afford to look. A nauseous pain in his stomach had already erupted. The heat was too overpowering.

Outside, Brex stood still while a sudden blast of flames quaked inside the wall, but it wasn't what caught Brex's attention. It was the intruding, unfamiliar burning smell that refused to leave.

"Logan?" Brex screamed. "LOGAN!" She didn't stop for anything. She threw the backpack off her back before she leaped into the sanctuary. The cracks in the floor didn't dare catch her off guard. The inflamed walls refused to touch her. The boiling lava preparing in her soul was too powerful.

"LOGAN! KRINA! ANSWER ME!"

There was no answer. Instead, she had to listen to the coughing that continuously poured out of their throats. A few feet away was Logan's hunched body with Krina's green reptile skin protecting him as she continued to guide him.

"LOGAN!"

Krina's white hair blew in the hot wind, but Brex's body circled the air as she ran. She leaped for the wilting bodies, but her heart almost beat her to it. Her lungs were sparkling clean, but the fire was eager to poison Logan's and Krina's lungs. Brex was running out of time.

"Follow me!" Brex hollered.

The journey was like running through water; slow and desperate. Time doubled, but the real challenge was the race.

Rrrrrrrrrrruuuuuuuuuhhhhhhh!

A new vibration ignited, but it wasn't coming from the rupturing flames. It was coming from the ceiling. The ceiling that lurched toward them boiled their blood. Each rock fell one by one, but it wasn't slow enough. They felt no patience. Brex pulled as hard as she could, but they couldn't make it. The collapsed ceiling blocked them in and knocked them off their feet.

"Nooooo!" Brex screamed.

The air wasn't scarce anymore. It was nonexistent. Logan's face was covered in soot. He only guessed his insides looked the same. Brex crawled on the floor to reach for him while Krina sprung to her feet and pushed the collapsed ceiling out of the way, brick by brick. But according to the anxious, hungry flames, that wasn't going to be fast enough.

"Brex," Logan whispered.

"Logan, I'm here." She didn't see how it happened, but his shoulder was already burnt. She wasn't a doctor or nurse, but there was no doubt about the degree of the severity. The blood said it all.

"Brex," he said once again. She didn't say anything in return. She waited, but Logan didn't need to say anything either. While her ashy hands held his shoulder and face, Logan's limp arm struck against the peak of the piled cement, or more specifically, his lightning, creating a hole that he hoped was big enough for them to fit through.

"Let's go!" Krina said, pulling the two of them to their feet and pushing them up a mountain of debris in the small pathway.

It was a foggy path ahead, but the blazing trail of melting bricks followed them, trying to win the race, but the sparkling lava underestimated the agility and stamina of the three racers.

"Come on, Logan," said Krina, approaching the opening and reaching for his hand. "Go first." Even Krina's breath was elusive, but she could see the starry night waiting for them.

Logan threw himself feet first and tumbled down the other side, but he didn't go far. He couldn't. Not until Brex was in his sight once more.

"Go, go, go," said Brex to Krina. "I'll be fine."

Krina didn't argue. She couldn't. There was no time. She slid through the opening with the flower in her hand. No scales caught onto anything, but after Brex stepped through, head first, she didn't follow in the right footsteps.

"Ah!" Brex screeched. Her foot was stuck. She could barely wiggle it after she stepped on the wrong stone and sunk in between two broken pieces of ceiling.

"Brex!" There was no hesitation. Logan's fatigue and rusty lungs faded away before he threw himself off the grass.

"Wait!" Brex screamed, holding out her hand. "Don't come any—" She didn't have to finish the sentence. The explosion that threw Brex forward and down the pile of crumbled cement gave every command Logan needed. She tumbled into his arms. Brex couldn't see anything through the dust, but she felt Logan's arms wrap around her as they rolled onto the cement floor.

"Come on!" Krina hollered picking them both up. The door was only a few feet away, but the escape wasn't as easy as they hoped it would be. The echoes in the background hovered over them, still trying to overpower them, but they couldn't. Krina transformed into her preferred skin before they rolled down the mountain. Only this time, the mountain was made of grass.

"OOF!" Brex stopped herself before she ran into a tree. Luckily, the other two didn't land far away from her.

"Okay," said Krina, standing up and brushing herself and the flower off. "Let's go, we need to get rid of this thing before someone sees us with it."

16:

"No one has brought anything to me lately."

Asher lost track of how long they were on their bikes for, but his glutes succeeded in reminding him that it had been too long. If they had butt massages in Athens, he was going to be a good-paying customer.

"Asher, keep up!" Shani shouted with the fresh breeze flowing through her curls.

"What are you talking about?" Lexi hollered from the other side of Asher. "You both keep up! I'm kicking both of your asses!"

"I'm trying!" Asher screamed at her. "Do you not see me trying?!" He would have flipped her off if he had ever learned how to ride a bike with one hand.

"Sit up straight!" Lexi hollered to Asher. "You'll be able to breathe better."

Asher did as he was told, but he was still tempted to make a point so he could keep complaining.

"Please at least tell me we're almost there!" Asher asked.

Shani showed off by leaning over her shoulder and hollered, "Maybe if you stop complaining for five minutes I'll tell you!"

"So, you're saying it's gonna be more than five minutes?!"

Shani didn't respond, but with the buttery-yellow Greek sun shining down on her glowing skin, Asher could have been sobbing for all she knew, and she wouldn't care.

A steep hill appeared in the distance. The closer they got, the steeper it looked, even to Shani.

"Alright," she breathed with a heavy sigh, and she didn't think twice about stepping off her bike. She needed to wait for Asher to catch up anyway. "Why don't we take a break and reevaluate?"

"You've been evaluating this whole time?" Asher asked, trying his hardest. Clawing to detach his water bottle from the bike, even though his hands were too sweaty.

"Come on, let's go," said Shani. "And remember, we're getting closer to the museum. Jethro said we'd know it once we see it."

The three of them pushed their aching bodies and their bicycles up the hill, and once they reached the top, their bodies didn't ache as much anymore.

"Whoa," Lexi mumbled as her jaw dropped and her eyes glossed. At the top of the hill, the bright blue, white, and green view painted over the horizon like watercolors seeping into the sun. The blue roofs floating in the sky lit up the view as if the architecture were performing for its patrons. The people of Athens strolled along the streets of the village in and out of stores, sipping on their hot coffees. It was hard to tell with all of the sun shining in Shani's eyes, but a few other bike riders were floating along the pathways. Shani couldn't see their faces, but she could tell they enjoyed their bikes more than Asher did.

"So, this is where it all started," Lexi whispered.

"I wonder if they know we're here," said Shani. "The gods, I mean."

"How so?" Asher asked.

"I don't know...just...I feel a sense of home here. Like we belong. But I think...I think we're also missing something."

Shani longed for something. The sadness in her heart tingled in her chest.

"The rest of the gods," said Lexi. "This city is missing them. Now that we're here, we're reminding the city that they're gone."

"Don't worry," Asher whispered, wiping the sweat from his forehead and neck. "We'll get them back."

"Come on," Shani shouted, suppressing her straining feelings. "Let's go. We don't have any more time to waste. This might take a while."

The three of them got back on their bikes and raced their way down the other side of the hill until Asher got too scared to ride that fast and walked after he had made it halfway.

The feel of the village shifted once they got back down. Maybe it was their anxieties finally sinking into them, or maybe it was the sun beaming a shade darker once their feet touched the dark sidewalk.

"What was the name of the museum again?" Asher asked.

"The National Historical Museum," Shani answered, pulling out a wrinkled piece of paper with scribbled directions out of her pocket. "It's coming up here on the right."

It looked like a boarding school that also happened to have a courthouse inside it. The garden's grass was healthier than anything Lexi had seen in Maine or Boston. The columns that guarded the front doors weren't what Asher was expecting. They didn't resemble the Parthenon, but the exquisite staircase that led up to them did. They were slimmer with a deeper, richer color. The angelic, smooth pigmentation nested under their feet before they made their way in.

"Did we need to get tickets?" Asher asked.

"I got them online," said Shani.

"When did you do that?"

"On the plane. Don't worry I used an alias. Like we talked about."

Lexi bit her cheek and asked, "You're sure they aren't going to ask for IDs?"

"Nope."

Shani charged up to the front desk and threw them a printout of their tickets. The guard looked as if he were about to ask Shani something, but she didn't stop walking. Lexi and Asher weren't about to stop her.

"They didn't want to check our bags or anything?" Asher asked.

"Asher, this isn't America. They have like no guns here. Why would they care?" They both nodded and continued on their way.

"Okay," said Asher. "But we should blend in for the rest of the trip."

"I am a black woman in Greece," Shani snapped. "Good luck with that." Once again, they both nodded and continued walking.

None of them had a clue as to what they were looking for, but it was already hurting Asher's head. Every few seconds, without thinking about it, his first two fingers pinched the top of his nose in between his eyebrows. The brief moment of keeping his eyes closed was all the relief he needed, but the moment Shani spoke again, he was going to need something more.

"Asher," Shani asked. "What's wrong?"

"I don't know. I think I just need some water. I'm overwhelmed."

"You're not alone," Lexi said, chiming in. "Slowly is the fastest way to find whatever we're looking for. Let's start in the archives section. We'll go from there."

Asher swallowed his anxiety, along with most of his patience, and followed close behind Lexi.

Nothing stuck out to them in the archives section. Shani spent a lot of time staring at a drawing that strikingly looked like Baymour. At least that's what she told herself until a tour guide came up to her and told her it was a drawing of a dead rodent. Asher stood there with his hand smothering his face, hoping she wouldn't notice his suppressed laughter, but she made it clear that he didn't do a good enough job when she punched his shoulder.

The library was surprisingly useless, even though Shani was convinced that was not the case and spent more time in there than she should have, but it wasn't nearly as futile as the collections section. The stunning, detailed, lively paintings had too many stories to tell for Shani to not listen to each and every one. But Asher soon slipped away when he realized she wasn't going to leave without finding the answer that probably wasn't there.

The photograph archive took him by surprise. He didn't realize how much history was in one small country. He didn't know much about Greek history. He'd been so distracted by the mythology, he had almost forgotten there was information in photographs, not just storybooks.

To his left was a photograph of an armed soldier who couldn't have been more than twenty years old. He couldn't read the title, but he supposed it was either from the Greek Civil War or World War II. He couldn't think of anything else. To his left was a picture of a little girl standing in front of the Parthenon, looking beyond the distance and into the orange sky. But in front of him was something else. Before he grasped the image, he knew it was different. He *recognized* this photo.

"Oh, Jethro."

Asher stomped his way back to Shani and Lexi who were both devoured by the same painting of an extraordinarily muscular man with minimal clothing. Shani immediately gave him grief for pulling her away, but he didn't hear a word she said.

"Remember the photograph that Jethro has hung in the front of his sanctuary?" Asher asked Shani and Lexi as they quickly walked back to the photograph.

"Yeah," said Lexi, knitting her eyebrows. "The one with the statue of Achilles on a random sidewalk in front of old apartment buildings or something?"

"Exactly," said Asher, stopping abruptly and pointing to the photograph. "It's the exact same one. He was Dimitria's apprentice, right? She must have given him a copy or something."

"Or the original photograph," said Lexi, although she wasn't sure if she was joking or not.

"Great," said Shani, "but where would the sanctuary be? Do you see any outlines of a potential wall opening?"

"No," Lexi answered, letting her chest expand and her cheekbones lift. "Because the photograph isn't hinting where the sanctuary is, it's showing us."

"Genius." Asher shook his head with his arms crossed.

"Who? Jethro or me?" Lexi asked.

"Wouldn't you like to know," said Asher, winking at her.

"Stop flirting with Lexi," Shani joked with a straight face.

"Make me."

"Okay, okay." Shani rubbed her hands together and got as close to the picture as she could without getting yelled at for doing so again. "There you are."

"What?" Asher asked.

"I can see a street sign in the reflection of that window." She pointed to something in Greek, but Asher and Lexi couldn't see any clue.

"How do you know that's a street sign?" Asher asked.

"Because I don't know what else it would be. Besides, we're running out of time." Shani took out her phone, looked around and snapped a few furtive pictures. She didn't catch anyone's eye, but Shani pulled Asher and Lexi along anyway.

*****

"Is it this building?" Asher asked for a third time in the last hour.

"No," Shani responded, keeping her eyes glued to a map that she bought in the museum. "I don't think so."

"You don't think so?!"

"Oh my God," Lexi whispered to herself, pulling her hair back.

"Why do you even have a map out right now?" Asher peeked over her shoulder, but Shani pulled it away.

"Because I'm paranoid about trying to stay on the right street."

"You mean you think we're on the wrong street?"

"I don't know!" Shani crumpled the map together and threw it in a puddle.

"Shani!" Asher took off his glasses to rub his face dry. "Why did you do that? Now how do we know where we're going? What's going on with you?"

"I thought you said the map was stupid."

"I never said that."

Lexi drew a deep breath in and ripped Shani's phone out of her pocket. "Okay," Lexi said, clearing her throat, "first of all, the map was not stupid, Asher. Was it being paranoid? Yes, but that's where we are at right now. And Shani, no you didn't lead us down the wrong street because we're here. See?"

Lexi held the phone up to her head, displaying the picture side by side with the real building. She was right. Before them was an old apartment building that must have been built in the twenties or thirties. The window frames were the same. The basketball-sized dent was still there. Even in the black and white photo, they could still absorb the rich, white color that coated the building in the center. This was it.

"The only question is, how are we going to figure out which room it is?" Lexi asked, giving Shani's phone back.

"The impatient way," said Asher, charging at the building. Waiting for no one.

"Wow," Lexi said to Shani, "you're rubbing off on him."

The front door was unlocked, to their surprise. The hallway was an elegant, shiny resemblance to a 1950s hotel that embraced the imperfections of cracked ceilings and dusty floors. In the center of the lobby stood a round, tall desk with no concierge, manager, or clerk, and fresh flowers in the center. Asher went to test if they were real or fake. He got his answer quickly when he immediately sneezed after sniffing just one of the purple flowers.

"Okay," said Lexi. "Should we just start knocking?"

"It's almost evening," said Shani. "People will probably be home, right?"

"Dimitria definitely will be. She's a guard. She's not supposed to leave the sanctuary."

"Wait," said Asher, holding out his arms. "What's down this hallway?" Something caught Asher's eye. He wasn't sure what it was yet. Was it the color? Maybe. Was it the wallpaper? Perhaps.

"Asher?" They followed him down the long hallway to see him staring at nothing. Just an empty wall. Then he realized it wasn't his first time wandering these halls.

"That floral pattern with the cross in it, the gold lining on the ceiling? That's unmistakable. I've been here before in one of my dreams, but why would it show me the hallway outside of her room? I thought it was her apartment that I saw."

"You mean these designs and patterns were in her apartment?" Shani asked.

"Yeah." Creases surrounded his eyes. "I think she owns or rents an entire floor."

"And where do people stay when they have the entire floor?" Lexi asked.

"Top floor."

Without any more fuss, the three of them chugged up the stairs until Lexi took one more look at the picture and noticed it was an eight-story building. They quickly switched to the elevator.

"What do we say when she opens the door?" Asher asked, stepping out of the elevator.

"Ask if her name is Dimitria?" Lexi suggested.

"Okay, okay, I like that," said Shani, vigorously nodding her head.

"And what if she slits our throats immediately afterwards?" Asher asked. "We don't know what this woman can do."

"We'll just have to figure it out when that happens."

"*When*? Not *if*?" Asher asked.

But Shani had already knocked on the door. It was gold with blue flowers on it. Different from the rest of the other doors. They could hear footsteps on the other side. Shani quickly wiped the sweat from her forehead before the door swung open and a tall, dark-skinned woman with bronze hair stood in the doorway. She towered over Shani, and her upside-down smile only made Shani sweat more.

"Yes?" the woman asked.

"Are you Dimitria?" Lexi asked. She could feel Asher flinching behind her. But to Lexi's surprise, the woman didn't flinch at all. Not even a blink of the eye.

"Show me your palms," the woman demanded.

"Oh, well. Um..." Shani slowly pulled up her left palm, struggling to find the right words that would hopefully stop her sweating.

"Look, kids. I know Moloch has three wannabes out and about doing his dirty work, so just prove to me that you're not them."

"That might be hard, considering we have the same scars," said Asher, ripping off his prosthetics. His hands were red and a little swollen from the heat, but the scar was as ripe as ever.

"Would it help if we told you Moloch's followers are one woman and two men while we are two women and one man?" Lexi asked. The woman didn't respond. Her dead eyes locked with Lexi's and still didn't blink.

"Ma'am," Shani coughed. "Please. We work with Maya. Jethro helped us find you."

"And yes, Jethro is safe," Asher added.

Finally, the woman rolled her eyes, audibly exhaled, and said, "Fine. Yes, I'm Dimitria. But if you are working for Moloch, I will know before you do anything foolish." She jerked her head to beckon them in, and they quickly did as they were told.

"Thank you," Shani mumbled, unsure if Dimitria could hear her or not.

"So, how is Jethro?" Dimitria asked, brushing her floor-length, silk dress back before sitting on what they guessed was her customary chair. It was red, like the color of the vibrant blush that Dimitria wore, but not as bright. And it matched the other furniture perfectly, but it wasn't part of a set. Eclectic designs seemed to be the theme of the apartment. Each section of the room was from a different decade. The abstract paintings that only had different shades of gold were from the seventies, but the collection of windchimes hanging out the window screamed for the twenties in the deep South.

For the furniture, the patterns of the decorations varied, but the colors were similar. If the colors were different, they blended into a harmonious formation that faded into one another like a rainbow, but with less extravagance. Asher couldn't help but fight to keep his jaw from dropping and search every inch of the room. It was almost as if he was back in his dreams.

"He's...he's good," Asher answered. "He's living the good life."

"Still drinking?" Dimitria asked.

"Um...he's in Ireland," Lexi answered. "So probably."

"So, what is it that I can help you with?" Dimitria crossed her legs and grabbed her glass of wine that was almost empty, as was the bottle that was right next to it.

"Well," Shani started, finally getting the courage to sit down. "We're sorry to tell you this. This may be a little overwhelming to hear."

"But that's where we come in," Lexi chimed in. Dimitria flipped back her hair and sank deeper into her seat.

"Maya believes that there is a mole in the Alliance," Shani declared. "Someone that's giving out everyone's location. We're trying to find as many sanctuaries as we can. We have to get everyone to relocate. Do you have any alchelesters?"

"Or anything else that they might be after?" Lexi added. "And do you know of any other sanctuaries that we can go to? We need to find as many as we can."

Dimitria's breath was steady, but her eyes fell to her wine glass, and her fingers twirled her hair. "I don't. I haven't really been involved with the Alliance all that much. No one has brought anything to me lately."

"Really?" Asher asked. "If I may ask, when was the last time you had anything in your possession?"

"Not since Jethro and Krina were my apprentices."

"Krina?" Shani asked.

"Yes, my other apprentice. I don't know her whereabouts, but they've been away for a few years now. Everything is at random of course, but this is the longest I've been without anything. I'll tell you, it's been quite nice."

"I believe it," Shani laughed uncomfortably.

"Shani, you good?" Lexi asked.

"Yeah," she answered, clearing her throat. "It's just hot in here."

"What were they like as apprentices?" Lexi asked. "Maybe there's something that can help us find Krina."

"Well," Dimitria twirled the stem of her wine glass and bit down on her rosy cheeks. "They seemed sweet on each other if you ask me. Both smart. Trustworthy. Jethro always seemed troubled. Always wanted to know everything Krina knew. Or maybe it was just because he was rather nosy."

"May I ask," Lexi began, "how did you join the Alliance?"

Dimitria's hands lay still and crossed over her lap. Only her eyes bounced back and forth between Lexi and Shani before she finally answered. "My father. He knew and supported many of the gods. He wanted to protect them."

"And where is your father now?" Shani asked. "Is he a member of the Alliance as well? Is he a guard?"

"I don't know. I haven't seen him in years." Dimitria's eyes fell to the floor, not in sadness, but with distaste. Her lips curled as her breathing deepened.

"Weeeell, what can you tell us?" Asher asked, unaware of how long he'd been staring at Dimitria with eager impatience.

"Keep poking and prodding, dear," she responded, finally looking at him. "I'm sure you'll come up with something."

"What can you tell us about Moloch?" Shani asked before Dimitria retracted the offer. "What else is there that we need to know?"

"Some people think he is too powerful to defeat. They're wrong. He wasn't always strong."

"Yeah," Lexi nodded. "I think Maya mentioned something like that."

"After the expansion that he is much too desperate for, he will be weak again," Dimitria explained. "Just like he was after the witches made the spell that gave you those scars. The magic took too much out of him. It wasn't in his nature to screw around with magic that didn't belong to him. That being said, it doesn't mean you can easily defeat him. A few years after the gods were laid to rest and he was still weak, but suddenly, so was the world. That's what he and every other dark leader has thrived off of. The more people die, the more substantial his power is."

"The 1918 flu pandemic?" Lexi asked. "And the war?"

"Smart girl," Dimitria replied, popping her shoulder. "We won't be immune to dying. We'll be immune to living. But I'm sure you've sorted that out by now. Still, we will all be closer to death than being alive, but it won't change the temporary damages it will surely inflict on Moloch."

"How do you know all of this?" Shani asked.

"I know too much, dear," Dimitria flipped her hair and leaned back in her chair. "You'll find you'll be the same when you've been around as long as I have."

Asher coughed uncomfortably, hoping to get a break from the awkward conversation. "May I use your bathroom?" Asher asked.

"Of course," Dimitria smiled with no teeth. "Down that hall to the left." She didn't lift a finger, only leaned back with a lift in the eyebrows, but it didn't matter. He wasn't going to the bathroom.

"Thank you. I'll be right back."

He darted out of sight. Something gnawed at his gut. There was an answer here or some sort of clue. Something he couldn't find in his dreams, but where *would* he find it?

"When you switched last, who took your alchelesters?" Lexi asked, back in the living room.

"Zara. You might know her, she's rather close with Maya." Dimitria smiled with confidence. But not the confidence that Shani was expecting.

"Right," said Shani. She could have sworn Zara just finished her apprenticeship last year. That's why she lived so close to Maya. Was she wrong? But if Dimitria was telling the truth, she would have known that her location was in the White Mountains, where the last fire was eight months before.

"Wait...Dimitria," Lexi softly spoke. "Did you say three wannabees earlier?"

"Yes," Dimitria replied.

"But Moloch had only one follower the last time anyone knew. How did you know Moloch had two new followers?"

Silence fell upon the room. Something stirred in the air. Dimitria didn't twitch until she gasped for a single, large breath.

"Oh no," Dimitria silently laughed. "I was really hoping I wouldn't have to use this. Before Shani or Lexi could react, a yellow steam ignited from Dimitria's bracelet. They didn't see how it was releasing such a thick substance before they could investigate further. They couldn't see anything at all.

Asher decided to check the bathroom since he hadn't visited it in his dream, but there was nothing that he could find. Next was the door across the hall, but it squeaked. He didn't want to be rude, but that wasn't going to stop him from checking at least one more room. The room at the end of the hall was cracked open. Probably somewhere that Dimitria visited often, but it was dark. The secrecy drew him to it and pulled him in with a slender string.

His footsteps remained quiet. And even better, so did the door when he slowly swung it open. But what wasn't quiet was the sound of his heart when he spotted a long, shiny trident that hung on the wall of the dark room.

"GUYS!" he screamed before he realized that it was probably a poor choice, yet he couldn't stop himself. His feet almost made the floor steam; he ran so fast to the living room. "SHE'S THE ONE THAT TRIED TO TRAP US IN THE EARTHQUAKES! SHE'S THE MOLE!" But Dimitria had already beaten him to it.

"Apologies, Asher," said Dimitria, standing over the unconscious bodies of Shani and Lexi who were now tied up on the floor. "I can't let you run out of here just yet."

17:

"Athens. That's all I need."

They walked for hours, but they finally found a small cave to hide in and sleep in for the night. Brex used a small fire, emanating from her fist to lead them in. It was small, dark, and cold, but not for long. First, Brex found small branches near the entrance to make a fire. But still, she refused to take her eyes off Logan. Even though looking at his burnt shoulder made her heart shudder and her eyes moisten.

"Either of you need anything?" Krina asked, unsure of what else to say to them.

"I'm okay," Logan said before Brex could answer for him. "Brex?"

"No, I'm fine."

"One of us should keep guard," Krina suggested. "We don't know what's out there."

"Good idea," Logan yawned. "I'll take first watch."

"Like that?" Krina asked. "No way. I'll go first. Get some sleep. I'll be back in a few hours. Maybe we can get moving by then. Use whatever's left of that blue blood."

Krina pointed to the cracked, leaking, purple water bottle that Brex held in her hand. It had maybe one ounce left of Asher's sparkling, blue blood.

Krina stood up, put her satchel back on, and walked around the corner. Before she disappeared into the darkness, Brex watched Krina's long, white hair transform into the feathers of a black crow. A crow with glowing, golden eyes that reflected the gentle moonlight.

"Smart," Brex laughed. "How are you feeling?"

Logan was reluctant to answer. He wasn't healing as fast as he would have hoped, but nonetheless, he was heeling.

"Fine, I suppose. The burns still tingle. They're still noticeable, but tolerable. I wish one of us had the power to heal."

"Sorry I threw the backpack and broke the water bottle. I still haven't gotten used to this strength. That tree also came out of nowhere."

Logan bit his lip and laughed. He wasn't sure why, but laughing made the stinging worse.

"It's okay," said Logan. "We should only use that if one of us is dying anyway."

"Well, the bottle is toast. We don't have anything to store it in. And that burn is taking longer than usual to heal."

Logan cleared his throat before he nodded and said, "Okay."

Brex slowly and carefully tucked her two fingers under the slimy liquid and rubbed as much as she could into Logan's deep wound.

The blue blood was colder than Logan expected, but it was the relief he needed, though it didn't last for long.

"Did it do anything?" Logan asked.

"It's a bit less red, but it's probably going to stay that way for a while," Brex answered.

"Okay, it's fine. I'll be fine. I promise. It does feel a bit better."

"Maybe I should try something," said Brex, holding out her hand. "I don't know. I might be able to do something."

"Okay," said Logan, reaching for the offered hand. He took it and placed it on the burn that somehow already stung less than before. But instead of releasing his hand from hers, he kept it there, holding her hand to his shoulder.

Brex looked at him before she could move. "I don't want to burn you even more."

"You won't."

A tether of trust connected them that didn't shake or wobble. It was indestructible. Never able to break, no matter how hard they tugged.

"Let me just try something," said Brex. She knew the feeling all too well. The fire in her blood never left her. The light within her brightened as she pulled away the pain from the burn. She opened her eyes to see the burn fading to pink. It wasn't what she had hoped for, but it healed. The swelling calmed and she removed the pain from its epicenter.

"I'm sorry," said Brex. "It looks better than before. I can keep trying."

"I don't need you to," said Logan. "It'll heal soon. Are *you* okay? I'm sorry you had to panic that much."

Brex was about to nod her head, but there wasn't enough truth in it. She couldn't find the right words to answer the question.

"I don't know. I just know I don't want to leave you now." The last few words blurted out of her. She couldn't stop herself, but she didn't regret saying them to Logan.

"I'm okay, Brex," said Logan, reaching for her hand once again, but still keeping himself a few inches away from the tips of her fingers.

"I wouldn't put it that way."

"How would you put it?"

Again, she was at a loss for words. Spontaneous, impulsive words were the only ones she could find.

"I can't lose you, and I almost did. So no, I'm not okay. I don't want you to be hurt ever, and you were almost seriously hurt on my watch. I can't let that happen again. I can't."

Logan didn't say anything. He didn't mumble anything. He only wrapped his arms around her and lay against the uncomfortable rock wall. He slid down to fit his body within hers. Her forehead was naturally warm, but her palms were twenty degrees hotter. He didn't care. He held onto her tightly.

"I'm sorry. I didn't mean to scare you. I was being reckless," Logan whispered, stroking her hair.

"No, no, no," Brex stuttered, wiping her damp face. "I'm sorry. I just needed to tell you that and freak out for a second. I'm okay."

Logan smiled and shook his head. It was contagious. Brex almost forgot she was upset when she locked eyes with him again.

"Do you want me to try again?" Brex asked, placing her hand on his burnt shoulder.

"No, save your magic. We're going to start running low soon."

Once again, he placed his hand over hers, but this time he slid her hand down his arm to clasp his hand around hers. Silence fell upon the cave. Even the sound of the fire faded away. Noise lost all its meaning except for the sound of their breathing.

"Why are you looking at me like that?" Brex asked, already knowing the answer, or at least she hoped she did.

"Like what?" Logan asked. "I've always looked at you this way."

Brex didn't need to hear anymore, but the feeling her heart gave her was addicting. The pulsing in her throat grew, and she hoped Logan couldn't hear it, or maybe she did. Logan leaned in faster the closer he got to her. Her lips were now centimeters away from his. Brex took in one last staggered breath before she wrapped her fingers around the back of his warm neck and kissed him.

She didn't realize how much she had longed for this moment until they sank into it. Logan felt both of Brex's steaming palms pull tighter around his neck. They drifted away into their own world. The fire could have gone out, or the thirteen-thousand-mile-long wall could have imploded, creating an endless echo. Nothing could rip them apart.

*****

Dimitria's long, curly, bronze hair dangled over the three motionless bodies that were tied to their respective chairs. Asher knew his glutes were going to be sore from sitting in his chair for what felt like hours. But it didn't matter. Asher and the rest must have been unconscious when Dimitria dosed them with something. No matter how much they wanted to, they couldn't fight the ropes that trapped them in their seats. Any tension they had rushed to their heads and settled there since their facial features were the only muscles they could move.

"I must admit I didn't think it would take this long," said Dimitria. "I also thought Moloch would be here by now, but my guess is he never fully regained his strength after he had given up so much power to make yours."

Lexi was slowly adjusting to being tied up and not being able to feel the enchanted ropes cutting off her circulation. If she didn't try to fight it, the discomfort wouldn't bother her.

"Is that a question?" Asher asked. His fatigued, puffy lips flapped as he spoke.

"I heard about you," said Dimitria, staring at Asher.

"I'm honored." Asher rolled his sleepy eyes as high as they would go.

"I was referring to all of you."

Lexi finally felt one of her toes wiggle before she said, "Sick, we kinda got that. Or did Asher screaming about the trident give it away?"

"Why haven't you given it to them?" Shani asked. She figured letting Dimitria ramble would give them time, but time for what? Shani had to figure that out and fast.

"Maybe you're confused," said Dimitria. "I'm not working for either side. I'm working for whichever side gives me what I want. Right now, neither of them are doing me any favors."

"What is it that you want?" Lexi asked.

"Protection. If you must know."

"Protection from what?" Asher asked, surprising himself with a sudden increase in annunciation. In the corner of his eye, he could see Dimitria glance at her reflection in the mirror. She cleared her throat and rubbed her tight chest.

"You're mortal." Lexi's teeth clenched together. *This woman betrayed the people who had trusted her the most to live longer?!*

"I'm sick. You wouldn't understand. For the past few years, Moloch has been finding ways to extract the immortal essence from the alchelesters to give to me. To make it permanent. I know nobody wants to die, but it would be a waste if I did. So, therefore, I can't be relying on him like you. You need his immortal essence to recharge. I can't have that. When he does make me immortal, that's when I'll give him the trident."

"We're not judging you," said Shani, using her lifted, judgmental eyebrows. "We don't want to die either. We won't say anything."

If Asher could have turned his head, he would have quizzically cocked his chin to her, wondering if he had heard her correctly.

"Don't patronize me," Dimitria loudly hissed.

"I'm not," said Asher. "This is what I propose. Don't give him the trident. That's all we care about. We don't need the trident. We're only doing this to prevent him from finding the ingredients he needs. We're only doing this because of you. So, don't give him the trident. When he gives you the extract, trick him. Give him something else, or don't give him anything at all. You said so yourself; you don't have a preference what happens. You'll be mortal either way. If you come back to our side, Moloch won't have a say in when you die. It'll all be on you. Don't you think that's better?"

After a beat of silence, Dimitria's long face remained still as she mumbled, "You don't know that."

"What do you mean?" Lexi asked, feeling another toe wiggle.

"We don't know exactly how this expansion of Hell will work. Too much power will be given to one man. He'll get rid of his followers. Whatever he says will happen...there's no chance it'll be the whole truth."

The three limp bodies fell silent, but Lexi needed to keep her talking.

"Then why are you working with him at all?" she asked. The numbness faded away in her left foot like a TV screen turning black at the end of a movie.

"It's not your concern," Dimitria scoffed.

"Really, now?" Shani mumbled under her breath.

"Really, Shani. Now, shut up until Moloch gets here!"

"So, we can talk again once he gets here?" Asher asked. But his humor didn't last once Dimitria struck his face with the back of her hand.

"Ah!" Asher grunted as he fell over and couldn't stop his fall against the cold cement floors.

"Asher!" Lexi and Shani hollered at the same time when they heard something crunch.

Asher was in more pain than he had expected. That only made his nerves ignite slowly, but when the tingling pain settled in his chin, he knew he would have his strength back soon.

"I'm sorry about this," said Dimitria, rubbing the back of her hand as if she were putting on lotion. "I don't know what he's going to do. I know he'd rather not kill you. Whatever it is, I hope it's quick."

Dimitria turned around, unguarded, and unprotected. Lexi spotted the back of Dimitria's head with her gloomy eyes that were slowly refocusing. Her target was simple. Asher wasn't the only one who had gained a spicy shot of energy. Lexi broke one foot away from the chair, but however fast Lexi was, Dimitria was faster. Dimitria gripped the shard of wood and whacked Lexi in the skull, leaving her bleeding on the cold floor.

*****

Brex couldn't tear her hands away from Logan's beating, warm chest. Logan brushed her hair away, behind her ears, and only a few seconds after, Brex reflected his emotions, but any ounce of happiness that perked their lips was soon ripped out of their bodies.

"AHHHH!" Brex was familiar with the pain. The excruciating pain that made her want to cut off her left hand. She hadn't felt this agony in almost a year, but she knew what it meant. No amount of pain could block her memory, but that unfortunately meant she remembered something else. If she was in pain, so was everyone else that shared the stinging scar.

"Logan?!" She somehow managed to say his name through her gritted teeth.

Logan could only grunt deep from his gut, but she couldn't see his face. He lay away from her with his knees to his chest. Brex didn't hesitate to throw her arms around him, but, her elbows and forearms only carried her so fast.

"Logan," she coughed. "Logan?!"

Krina ran into the light so fast she slid across the brown dirt. She was almost at a loss for words when she caught sight of deliberate pain, yet no threat.

"Brex! Logan!" She stumbled towards them, trying not to touch them. "What do I do? Just tell me what to do!"

"Ath—" Brex couldn't finish. The pain traveled to her throat. It pulsed with unbearable swelling.

"What?" Krina brought her ear closer to Brex. "What are you saying?"

"Athens," Brex gently hissed, pushing out every ounce of air left in her with her tight abdomen.

"Athens. That's all I need. Don't talk. I got you."

Krina only needed one arm to whip across her body and transform all ten fingers and all ten toes into clawed paws that grew to be the size of Brex's head. Krina wasted no time in using her front claws to throw the two screaming bodies onto her scaled-back. Within seconds, Krina's now ten-foot-tall body flew through the small tunnel and out of the hideout. She secretly hoped no one was watching. She knew she was never going to have the energy to explain why civilians saw a fire-breathing dragon flying in the starry night sky to the rest. But Logan and Brex didn't have time for Krina to worry.

"Okay, okay let's go," said Brex. She gently pulled Logan up to standing, hoping he had enough energy for whatever was to come. And with only Krina's scales to sit on and hold onto, Brex's and Logan's hair tossed back as Krina shot into the air like a rocket with endless jet fuel.

*****

"He'll be here soon," Dimitria mumbled without making eye contact with anyone.

"You've been saying...that for a...half an hour," Asher stuttered, while his lungs still crunched against the floor, still bound to the chair.

"It's not as if his timing concerns you."

"No, but if Lexi remains the way that she is, you might lose your leverage."

Lexi lay on the floor, bleeding from her head. She was conscious, but groaning. She had been still since Dimitria gave her yet another dose of whatever was paralyzing her.

"I highly doubt that. Moloch will figure it out. He's a big boy."

The three remained calm. Asher's breathing had slowed down, but it was still staggered.

In through the nose, out through the mouth. Concentrate, Asher thought. What was her weakness? What was in here that could put them back in power?

"How are you mortal?" Shani asked. "What if someone was lying to you? Who told you that? I thought demi-gods were immortal."

"No, they aren't. But I see where you're confused." Dimitria took a step forward and crossed her arms. "I'm the offspring of a demigod. My father was a son of Ares."

"Well, that explains a lot," Asher, once again, whispered under his breath.

"How did you end up with the trident?" Shani asked.

"You don't need to do that."

Shani scoffed. "Do what?"

"Distract me. It won't do you any good. Save your breath." Dimitria finally sat down across the room in a red, velvet chair. She crossed her long legs and her shiny green dress rippled down to the floor.

Shani used the little energy she had to look over at Asher, hoping they could communicate an escape plan, but his panicked, shaky eyes didn't relay any messages.

"Muh..." Lexi groaned. The blood was slowly drying. She pulled herself to the side, away from the rest. All Shani could see was Lexi's shiny blonde hair dripping bright red blood.

"Lex? Lexi?" Shani coughed, trying to manifest more strength than she had. "Please, help her."

Dimitria couldn't be bothered. Her eyes stuck to the floor as her impatient feet twirled in circles. But Shani didn't notice. Something else caught her attention.

Shhhhhh...

Oh no, Shani thought. *He's here.*

But nothing happened. None of the doors broke down, and no one else made any more noise. What was stealing Shani's attention?

Without looking, Dimitria dropped her head back, rolled her eyes, and asked, "What are you—" But a sharp jab at her throat cut her off. Right next to her was a tree the size of a football. The dark green leaves blended into the wall, but Shani could see the dark branch wrapping around Dimitria's throat and extending all the way to the orange pot.

"Lexi?" Shani gasped. Lexi was no longer on the floor. If Shani was dreaming before, she wouldn't have been surprised. Lexi's fatigue looked as though it had never existed, or it vanished into thin air.

"Let us go," Lexi said with clenched teeth. Her arm extended out to the front. The dirty, dark branch slithered tighter around Dimitria's neck. She couldn't make a sound.

"Lexi," Shani whispered. She didn't want Lexi to stop. She couldn't, but she silently begged Lexi to step carefully as she tip-toed closer to Dimitria.

"No?" Lexi asked with puckered lips. "Then you'll stay this way. For as long as I like. I won't kill you. I won't loosen my grip. You'll just stay choking until I say you're done." Her eyebrows didn't tighten. Her jaw was loose and soft. The only thing she needed to maintain her power was already being executed.

"I—I..." Dimitria stammered.

"Oh, my apologies," Lexi laughed without losing eye contact. "Just nod yes, or shake your head no. I thought that would be a given, but I'll let it slide."

Dimitria's head remained still, but her eyes deepened in color. Her dark skin flushed with red all over her sweaty hands. The determination in her eyes said she would never relent, but the friction heating up between the bark on the tree and the skin on her neck said otherwise.

"Dimitria!" Lexi hollered. "I need an answer."

Without any more hesitation, Dimitria nodded. Her head could bob only a few inches, but Lexi quickly loosened the trunk.

"Good choice."

Dimitria coughed and rubbed her neck before she stood up. But the weakness didn't last long.

"No chance in Hell," Dimitria scoffed before she wrapped her sweaty fingers around the cylindrical plant, preparing to hit Lexi over the head with the little energy she had left. The only problem was, Lexi had never lost control of the deadly bark. Dimitria wouldn't have been able to see it coming even if she hadn't blinked. The crackling sound snapped in mid-air and made Shani and Asher flinch, forcing them to look away. Dimitria was still hunched over when the bark struck against her throat. The force was too strong. There was no recovering from her fall, and there was no recovering from the collision when her back met the sharp tip of the Poseidon statue's trident.

"Ahh!" Lexi threw her face away from the spraying blood, but she had to look back. The smell pushed her away, inch by inch.

"She's dead," Shani said, trying to catch her breath after it was sucked away from her. "Lexi, she's dead. We have to go, find the antidote."

Shani was right. Bright red blood flowed out of Dimitria's lifeless mouth. The dripping liquid looked like crayons melting on a pale canvas.

"I—I didn't mean to," Lexi couldn't find the right words.

"We know," said Asher.

"I was just protecting us."

"Lex," Shani deepened her voice. "Moloch could be here any second, we need to leave. Untie us first."

"Okay, okay." Lexi fought to keep herself standing, but her trembling hands managed to unwind Shani's and Asher's tight knots that dug into their skin.

"In the cabinet," Asher mumbled. They could see Lexi screwing her head back on as she scrambled about the room.

"Right, right." Lexi threw open the cabinet doors. It was a jigsaw puzzle, only every piece looked the same. The potion bottles all looked like they came out of an antique shop. "Come on, come on, come on!" The labels were in multiple languages: Greek, Spanish, French, Latin, and luckily, English. But it was a mess. Lexi didn't care that bottles were being thrown everywhere and smashing all over the floor if she knew it couldn't be the antidote until something caught her eye.

The misty glass bottle on the top shelf. She recognized that color. What was it that Maya said about antidotes?

The color, Lexi thought. *Always mucky with a little red.*

"Please let me be right," Lexi mumbled as she broke the top of the glass bottle, even though it was only covered with a corkscrew, and poured half of it into Shani's mouth, and the other half into Asher's.

"Whoa!" Asher coughed. "That was a lot. So gross."

As Lexi predicted and hoped for, Shani and Asher's breathing increased.

"Come on, come on," Lexi mumbled, whipping her head from side to side, hoping they weren't too late.

Shani's arms shook like an electric massager, beating her muscles to the core. Asher could barely open his eyes to look at his own feet struggling to get a firm grip on the floor. But once they were firm, his legs might as well have been made out of concrete. The substance was kicking in, and it was doing so faster than Asher enjoyed.

"Why do I feel like I'm going to poop twenty-pound weights?" he asked, aiming the question at no one.

"Ugh, Asher, let's go." Her head felt light and normal before she stood up. It almost fell to one side and hit a wall, her head felt so heavy.

Lexi ran to the room in the back, took the trident off the wall, and the three of them began their jog, almost forgetting where they were going. Every brick hall looked exactly the same.

"Lexi," Asher spoke, louder than he expected. "Were you faking being hurt the entire time?"

"After about forty-seven seconds, yes. I needed her to let her guard down. She needed to be distracted. You didn't think a stupid head injury like that was going to genuinely hurt me, with this thick skull, did you?"

"Lex," Asher surprised himself with how well he was speaking after running for more than thirty seconds. "You lost a lot of blood back there. Are you sure you're okay?"

"I'm fine, I swear. I know it doesn't sound plausible, but it's weird. I feel way more energetic than before. Must have inhaled some of that antidote too."

They ran for what felt like hours. Maybe it was the drugs, or maybe it was the antidote for the drugs. But they were taking a euphoric toll, and reality blended with their imaginations.

"Come on," said Asher. "I think the exit is this way."

But suddenly, a short flashback ignited in his head. He wasn't searching for these flashbacks, they just came. None of them lasted longer than half a second, but he retained more information each time. Which turns he had taken in his dream, which color the wall changed to when he entered the room. The flashes kept coming, but it didn't take long for the three of them to recognize where they were.

"Look!" Lexi exclaimed. The front door and their savoring exit stood straight ahead, but before they could reach it, an unfortunate yet preventable obstacle prohibited their passage.

"Uh oh," Asher mumbled before he lost control of his speed. He veered too far to the right and ran straight through a wall covered in elegant green paint and silver flowers. He made it out to the other side but so did all of the sawdust and insulation that smothered his face and skin. He was almost blinded by the essence of the wall. It wasn't until he collapsed on the floor with small pieces of wood poking him that he finally said, "Ow."

"Lexi," said Shani, also having a hard time stopping herself from running into something. "Imma let you handle this one."

"Couldn't agree more," Lexi pulled him up and brushed him off as best as she could in the few seconds she had before something shifted in the air.

"Did you hear something?" Shani asked. Looking away from them, and toward the archway.

"What?" Asher asked, spitting out a bit of spackle.

"I thought I heard...geez." It was the antidote. Not only did it heighten their already extraordinary strength, it heightened *everything*. Either that, or they were hallucinating, which had probably already been happening.

"Wait," said Asher, ripping a tiny piece of wood out of his hair that was stabbing him in the ear. "No, you're right. I hear something too. Some beat, like footsteps. Again and again."

"It's probably just the poison shit playing tricks on us."

Lexi cocked her head to the side and tightened her lips before she asked, "Then why do I hear it too?"

They wanted to move. Every twitch, every breath was an attempt to stop them from making any noise, but they couldn't move, not yet.

"Stay close," Lexi whispered to Asher.

Besides the strength that was forced upon her, Shani didn't know what else to use to defend herself and her friends. What was Lexi going to use? Were there any houseplants that could morph into a weapon? Was Asher too concussed now to fly? Would he be able to fly in a straight line if he could? Would any of these be useful? They hadn't faced Moloch before. They didn't even know what he looked like. They had no plan.

Thump!

Shani coughed while Asher let out a small squeak. The repetitive noises were getting closer. The threat could have been right outside the open door for all they knew.

"Shani," Lexi whispered as Shani reluctantly took a few steps down the hallway and toward the door. They couldn't see much, but there was a small pool of light that shimmered across the sidewalk. They would have to be careful. It would be easy for someone to hide out there. "Shani!"

Shani didn't listen. She needed to risk it. What was out there? Who else knew that they were there? It had to be Moloch. Shani turned around to look at her friends. Her apologetic eyes sank into theirs. The corners of her lips quivered. She shook her head before she turned back around and plunged her body toward the door only to run into another body doing the same thing.

"Ahhhhhh!" Shani screamed.

"Ahhhhhh!" another voice reflectively hollered. A voice that was all too familiar.

"Brex?" Shani asked, still holding her fighting stance.

"Shani, what are you doing?" Brex asked. Her hair had more volume than it usually did. It was as if she stood in front of a giant blow drier and lost track of time.

"I—I..." Shani still hadn't dropped her stance. She was as still as a statue, standing under the doorway. "I thought you were someone else."

"What happened?" Logan asked, jumping off Krina's scaled back and running over to them.

Shani finally dropped her arms the second Krina's fiery, golden eyes pierced through the dim light.

"Are you okay?" Brex asked.

"So...so we're just going to ignore the fact that a dragon is sitting right over there?" Asher asked.

Krina shook out her fatigued head and slowly morphed back into her preferred, human form.

"Sorry about that," said Krina, cracking her neck. "Got a little winded after flying six thousand miles an hour. I forgot I could do that as a dragon to be honest."

"And you are?" Shani asked in her deep voice and with more attitude than she was expecting.

"Krina. I'm a guard for the Alliance."

"Oh...Krina. And why are you a dragon, Krina?" Asher asked with his eyes still wide open.

"I'm a shapeshifter. I met these two at one of our secure locations, and don't worry. We have what we need."

Shani lifted her cheekbones to her eyes and whispered, "Okay."

"How did you know where we were?" Lexi asked, helping Asher walk in a straight line.

"It was the scars," said Brex, holding out her hand. "We felt the pain. It was only for a few minutes, but we didn't want to risk it. We weren't sure if you were okay."

"But...how did you know where we were?" Lexi asked again.

"I...um...I don't really know. We both just told Krina where to go."

Before anything else could be said, Logan spotted the green and silver trident that stood almost as tall as Lexi and reflected the light beautifully in the dusk.

"You've got it," said Logan.

"Yeah," said Lexi, audibly exhaling. "We got what we came for. We need to—"

But before she could finish, Shani's and Asher's screams told Lexi that plans were about to change.

"LEXI!" Shani yelled.

Lexi turned around to see a bloody, pale Dimitria walking toward them with her arms out, down the hallway of the lobby, ready to destroy whatever was in her path. Her bulging, red eyes popped out of her head, about to burst. Lexi had only one idea.

"No!" Lexi screamed. Dimitria's spit sprayed onto the six of them, she had gotten so close. Lexi couldn't let her come any closer. Her rage outweighed her intellect. Lexi's reflexes told her to kill Dimitria immediately. Without looking, without wondering what would happen next, she lunged toward Dimitria, and plunged the trident deep into her heart.

"Ahhhhh!" Lexi screamed once again. Dimitria's now certainly-lifeless body was thrown up against the green wall. Blood splattered the room within a ten-foot radius. The blood resulting from the first homicidal attack was hardly a sprinkle compared to this attempt. Perhaps that was why Lexi shook with anger mixed with resentment when she observed the blotchy outcome of her rage.

"Why..." Lexi stuttered. The strike had knocked the wind out of her, and she struggled to find the right words. "Again...I didn't mean to."

"Yet, it was enjoyable both times," Asher sassed before everyone's jaws slightly dropped at his lack of restraint.

"Okay," Brex held out her hands in front of her, "regardless of whatever just happened, it sounds like we should go."

"Come on," Shani said to Lexi and Asher. "Let's go."

Buzzzzz...

It took a few vibrations for Logan to realize it was *his* pocket that was buzzing. "What?" He pulled out his bloody phone to see that his dad was calling him. "Jesus. He can't be serious."

"You should answer it," said Shani, still trying to catch her breath. "Just in case it's an emergency."

"I'll just be a second. Hold on...Dad?"

"Not exactly," said a familiar voice that didn't belong to his father. "Logan, it's Kali."

18:

“We don’t know where the rest of the ingredients are for your transition.”

“He’s not with you,” Logan slithered his tight voice through the phone. “You have no proof that he’s there.”

“No?” Kali asked.

It was only a moment of silence, but it lingered for longer than Logan was comfortable with before he heard the sudden crack of his father’s voice.

“Logan?”

It was a punch in the gut. Logan forgot how to speak.

“You...” He was so afraid of throwing up, he almost handed the phone to Shani, but he had to push through for him. “That could be a voice recording.”

“Oh, it could. But you won’t know until you give up that trident.”

“How? Why?”

“When Dimitria called, Moloch knew she wasn’t going to win going up against you. I told you, Logan. I’ll never underestimate you. But I will say, you were a bit reckless. Even when your scar only touches the sunlight for a second, I can still see exactly where you are. Finding it did take a moment, but I just needed you to find what I was looking for first. Perfect timing.”

“You’re not getting the trident,” Logan responded.

“So, your father is disposable?”

“You’re not gonna hurt him.”

“Of course, I’m not. What’s the point? But he doesn’t know that.”

Logan struggled to fight the urge to throw his phone against the ugly brick wall. But he couldn’t give up yet. He needed to stall.

“Where are you?” Logan asked.

"Meet us in Egypt. The Sphinx. You'll see why."

The click on the other end made Logan jump. He slowly brought the phone back down to his pocket. No one dared to say a word.

"She's got my dad," Logan quivered. "I can tell she's not lying. I can feel it."

"That's why Moloch didn't come," said Shani. "Of course."

"Where does she want us to meet them?" Brex asked.

"The Sphinx in Egypt." Logan could hardly stand. "This was all for nothing. This was the plan the whole time. Using us as guinea pigs. As bait. They were just planning to follow us. To find out what we know. We haven't even gotten to the rest of the sanctuaries."

"But we took down the mole," said Asher. "We don't need to."

"We don't know what they know," Shani snapped. "And it doesn't matter. We need to get Logan's dad back."

Logan rubbed his tight neck. "This was all for nothing," he said.

"We don't know that," Lexi softly said with her chin to her chest."

"Well, I'm not predicting any other outcome."

"Logan, we'll figure it out." Brex ran up to him to put her hand on his forearm. "We aren't defenseless. We have two more people than they do. We have a chance. And they don't know that we have the flower of Persephone. We just need to come up with a plan."

"And a fucking good one," Asher whispered under his breath. "We can't bring the flower with us. They can't know we have it, let alone where it is. It will just be another ingredient that they can steal."

"Definitely not. We should probably do more strategizing on the way," Krina suggested. "Don't worry, I can get us there faster than you think."

*****

The wind didn't strike against their cheeks as harshly as Shani had predicted. Although, Krina's dragon scales poked her inner thighs more than she would have guessed. But the wind was more of a meditative whistle that massaged their skin and muscles. A bubble that protected them from anything that flew against them. Asher held on tighter than the rest. He vowed to himself that if he were ever able to fly as fast as Krina could with his own wings, he wouldn't. Did she enjoy nausea? There was already enough risk to flying in general.

"How much longer?" Shani asked, even though she had asked roughly a minute and a half before.

"About twenty minutes," Krina answered. The deepness and raspiness of her voice rippled the scales on her back.

"Are you sure the flower is safe?" Lexi asked.

"Yes, and trust me. I hid it cleverly. It's better if you don't know where it is. Kali won't be able to touch me," said Krina.

"What do we think?" Shani asked the others. "This is my idea. We'll split up. But Logan will go looking for his dad if he's there. The rest will look for Kali and the others. We'll come from all different directions to corner them in, but keep the trident out of wherever they are.

"Why without the trident?" Asher asked.

"In case his father's not there. We need to maintain our power and advantage."

"Right," Logan mumbled, trying not to look down.

"Who's going to have the trident?" Asher asked.

"The one that can avoid them the easiest," Shani answered. "You."

"I was afraid of that." Asher sulked.

"Remember," Lexi said, raising her finger in agony. "They need all of our blood to get our magic. We can't be in the same room at the same time. We need to play hide and seek. We'll all split up."

"And then play tag," said Asher.

"Where do you think they are?" Logan asked.

"They must be in some sort of hideout," Krina answered. "And they're lying if they say there's only one entrance."

The rest of the ride felt longer than any of the airplanes they had taken on their journey so far. Lexi let her face go numb before the vibration made her skin melt. But before they could all uncomfortably fall asleep on Krina's scratchy back, the dust of Egypt showered their faces.

"We're almost there," Krina said, trying to go faster. "Remember, Kali doesn't know I'm with you. I have to keep myself hidden."

"We should probably land before we get to the Sphinx then, right?" Lexi asked.

"Good idea, but don't get too excited about walking in the dead of night in the desert."

The wind could have been worse, but goggles would have been useful. Shani craved water, and the thought of running through fire with no defenses caused her dry lips to crack.

"We should have brought water," she said, swallowing.

"Something tells me Kali has plenty," said Lexi.

Inches away from the Egyptian ground, Krina dipped her claw into the swirling sand before her heels plummeted into the ground and came to a screeching halt. The dry coughing abruptly broke the buzzing white noise.

"I don't see anything anywhere," said Shani, brushing the sand out of her thick hair. A hallucination tried to burst through the bubble that protected her. The quiet air seemed ready to attack her comfort zone that had respected her when she was flying in the wind.

"Where do we go?" Asher asked.

"South," said Krina, turning around and pointing to the sky. "See the North Star up there? We have to walk away from it. Follow me."

They did as they were told, but not without keeping their eyes on Krina. They couldn't afford any more surprises.

The heat seeped into their skin and throats. Thinking about soaking in the sun instead of the night heat made their stomachs bubble.

"There it is," said Krina, finally returning to her preferred form. Once her surreal transformation finished stealing their attention, their eyes followed the shimmering footlights that highlighted the assertive eyes towering above them, even from hundreds of feet away.

"That's a lot of ground to cover," said Asher.

"Kali is impatient," Shani commented. "She won't make it too difficult to find her."

Each step was its own journey, its own struggle. The endless grains of sand pulled at them until it was clockwork muscle memory. Their chins were glued to their chests while their lips were zipped together. Lexi was the first one to cover her mouth with her shirt before the others pretended they knew to do that all along. But before anyone relented to the stabbing pains of crystallized sand, they reached the leveled ground that carried the paws of the Great Sphinx that stood sixty-six feet tall, but stood submissively in front of the Pyramid of Khafre. It wasn't until then that they understood why it still existed as such a great wonder to the world. The immense size, the ravishing beauty. Their eyes were immediately arrested. The clashing emotions were almost too much to contain.

"I didn't know people lived so close to here," said Asher, looking over the small village that stood next to the ancient campus.

"Me neither, but we should keep moving. We don't want anyone from the village to see us."

"Hold on," said Krina. "I need to do something first." As one smooth motion, she inhaled deeply through her nose, closed her eyes, and softly crouched down into a ball. Her knees bent at a steady pace, but before her chest reached the ground, the fluffy fur already started to blow in the blustery wind. Her eyes reopened. Only this time, they were black, matching the night sky so perfectly, they almost blended in, but not as well as her tan fur. They almost couldn't see her as she stood on four legs above the light brown sand.

"Oh my God," said Lexi. "You are so cute."

Krina had transformed into a small Fennec fox that looked as if she needed a few more years to grow into her ears.

"Thanks, that's exactly what I was going for," Krina commented with spice dripping from her tongue.

"Would it be inappropriate to pet you?" Asher asked.

Without shifting her line of sight or head, Krina assertively and clearly said, "Yes." She walked away with her tense shoulders ready to pounce.

"Meh," said Asher mockingly.

"What? Are you annoyed by her sarcasm?" Shani asked. "God, I can't imagine what that's like."

Shani followed Krina before Asher mocked her and got in line. The rest audibly exhaled, dreading the time to come.

"What are we looking for?" Logan asked.

"I don't know," said Lexi. "A sign of some sort."

"I would describe it as more of a threat," Asher hollered from a few feet behind them. He pointed his shaky finger to something sticking out of the sandy wall. The shine was unmistakable. The blade came from her. Kali's blades were too smooth to miss. It wasn't dangerously long, but that didn't make the dagger any less lethal. It stuck out of a smooth tomb just a few yards behind the Sphinx, yet there wasn't an opening anywhere in the ground.

"Take it out?" Asher asked. "It looks like it's been in there for a while."

"No, there's gotta be something else around here." Shani began circling the tomb, looking up and down. "I could climb up there, on the tomb."

But Asher had already ignored her. She ran back around to the group the moment the rumbling almost swept her off her feet. The small pebbles bounced against the floor like tiny basketballs. Asher stood there, holding the blinding blade in his hand.

"Or we could just take it out."

It was no time for egos. Shani left her face a blank slate.

A circular whirlpool washed away the concrete that blocked the entrance which could have easily been mistaken for a black hole. The ground vibrated, but not as violently as they were used to.

"I can't even see if it's a staircase or a slide," said Logan.

Brex snapped her wrist to ignite her fire. Her deflated eyes didn't flinch. "Two of us should go this way."

"I'll come with," said Lexi. "We'll split up once we're in there. Kali can't be too far."

"We'll stay out here," Shani added. "We'll find other entrances and keep the trident away from Kali."

Brex didn't want to check how low her magic was. Logan didn't have to say anything for Brex to know how anxious he was. Brex knew that feeling. His father needed him. The angst radiated from Logan.

"Logan," Brex said before she was about to fully engulf herself in the black hole. "When you find your dad, just get him out of here. Don't wait for us. I guess...we'll just figure out a way to distract Kali. We don't know what she's up to. And...I'll look around here too. Maybe there's something else along this path."

He nodded with sincerity before he asked, “Do we have a meet-up place?”

Why not the front of the Sphinx?“ Shani suggested. “Under his chin?”

“Okay,” said Logan before returning his soft eyes to Brex.

“Be safe,” said Brex.

Logan nodded before he muttered, “Hey,” taking a hold of Brex’s non-inflamed hand. “Be careful.” He looked at Brex as if he never wanted to look away. “Both of you.” He turned to place his hand on Lexi’s shoulder. “Don’t scare me, Blondie.”

“We’ll be fine,” said Lexi. She leaned into him before she said, “Nothing will happen to her.”

Logan cracked a smile with a twinkle in his eye. The two followed the darkness slowly, but with courage and intent. Time was already taking their side, and time was fighting a nasty battle; the wrong battle.

“Come on,” said Shani. “Let’s start over here.”

*****

Brex and Lexi inched down a spiral staircase that had never seen the light of day or a broom. The air was thinning and growing colder, but they paid no attention to it. Brex didn’t want to take any chances. Her flames softly dimmed, and the sound of her footsteps was almost non-existent. Lexi tried to keep her breathing undetectable, but her heart wouldn’t let her. The pressure was like a sack of flour beating at her lungs. If they did have Logan’s dad, where could he be hiding? He didn’t feel close. Nowhere near it.

To their right, a sudden light ignited without anyone touching it. Whether it was an electric, gas, or candle-lit light, they couldn’t tell. It was a small, steady light with a slight orange shade that reminded Lexi of a basement lamp that no one had bothered to fix in years, but it wasn’t bright enough to tell how deep the hallway was, or if it led anywhere else. Lexi silently pointed to it before they followed it.

The farther they stepped, the deeper the mucky water was that covered the cement floor. Lexi gently gripped Brex’s wrist. Neither of them knew what was in that water, or what was around that corner. Maybe it was seaweed that occasionally brushed against the cold, bare skin on her ankles. She couldn't fathom how that was possible, but maybe it was. This mystery was the best way to keep her alert and keep her movement slow and steady.

The light was only inches away. To each side was a new hallway. Hallways that stretched longer than they could clearly see. Small beams of light clarified that there were indeed endings, but if there were any more answers down either of these paths, Lexi and Brex weren't sure what they would be.

"We're running out of time, we have to split up," Lexi mouthed with little noise escaping her lips.

"How are you going to see?" Brex asked, hoping Lexi could understand her.

"I'll be fine."

Brex could not risk making any more noise. She simply nodded and stepped back, still keeping her eye on Lexi. It wasn't until Lexi's long, blonde, curly hair was out of sight that Brex finally turned around and continued on her path.

Brex's faint footsteps quickly faded away, along with Lexi's patience. She couldn't see well, but she could manage. Lexi clapped her shoes against the splashing water as much as she pleased. If Kali heard her, good. Anything to maintain the distraction. But Lexi had thought out every step carefully. If her ruckus was too overwhelming, Kali would solve their messy puzzle instantly. The woman's intelligence was nothing to underestimate. But if they weren't loud enough, the darkness might swallow her whole.

A few more hallways with more electric lights finished her maze. Finally, an echo rippled far enough to reach Lexi's ear. Something clashed. Maybe metal, maybe wood, but it was a lead.

"Mr. Kwan?" Lexi muttered with a trembling jaw.

No, she thought. *Kali couldn't have made it this easy.*

"Mr. Kwan?!" She ran. If she ran into a wall, so be it. Whichever direction she looked, only inches of light bled into the hallway, coming from somewhere else. It couldn't be a dead end. Not yet.

"Sir, if you can hear me, answer me!" No answer. No sound. Nothing. But before there were no more answers, there was light; light that grew the closer she got. Only a few steps later, she could see the outline of a rectangle, but one side bled more light than the other. It was a door, an *open* door.

"Mr. Kwan?" Lexi ripped it open only to see Kali standing there...alone.

She heard her heartbeat in her throat. Sweat was dripping down her neck. But her face remained paralyzed. She wanted to tighten her fists, tighten anything, but she couldn't.

"Alexandra," said Kali. "What a surprise. How did you get here so fast?"

"Where's Mr. Kwan, Kali?"

"Oh, he isn't here."

"Where is he then?" Lexi's neck sweat had already reached her lower back.

"He was here. Don't worry I'm not a fan of lying. It doesn't usually get you anywhere. Logan's father, a kind man I must say—Logan really should be nicer to him—he wasn't of use to me anymore. He's back at home, sleeping it off. He won't even remember a thing when he wakes up. There was no point in boring him any longer. But here's his phone in case he wants it back." Kali tossed her the old, shattered iPhone, but Lexi didn't flinch and let the screen shatter on the cement floor. "Those are pretty expensive, dear," Kali smirked.

"I don't have the trident," said Lexi.

"I can see that," said Kali. "So, who has it? I'm guessing the others are trying to find another way in and catch me by surprise, correct?"

"How did you ever figure that one out?" Lexi asked, lifting her cheeks to her bulging eyes, keeping her voice monotone. "But to answer your question, I don't know. Besides, it's all we have. We don't know where the rest of the ingredients are for your transition."

"Then why are you here?" Kali asked, finally taking a step toward Lexi. Kali took a breath as the tables turned. "You knew he wasn't going to be here. What about the others? What about Logan? Are they as smart as you?"

"I'm here for answers," Lexi's voice cracked. "I need to know what you know, in case I need to stop you. You're never going to find what you need. There's no trace of the alchelesters. You can take our blood all you want, but it's not going to be enough. It'll take you another century. I killed your mole. You lost your leverage."

"Is that so?" Kali crossed her arms and gently rolled back her shoulders.

"What has Moloch told you that makes you put all of your trust in him?"

"What makes you think I trust him?"

Lexi pushed her hair out of her face. "Good question. I mean, I highly doubt he trusts you. Where even is he?"

"I don't need to trust him, and he just needs to have a small amount of faith in me. That's all. Still, I'm doing this for me, and he's doing this for him. I don't care about his reasons, and vice versa."

"Fine, let me rephrase that. Why are you listening to him? Because last time I checked, you listening to him gave you that...what are you telling people it is...a birthmark?"

Kali unexpectedly laughed, but her eyes never closed. "That's a little discriminatory, don't you think? Some people really are born with this. I can't imagine."

"Right," Lexi mumbled. "I'm sure you have so much sympathy."

Kali crossed her arms and stood an inch taller. "I must admit, you're funny, Alexandra. But what about you? Do you trust easily?"

"I trust my friends more than anyone. And not because I have to, but because I do."

"I wasn't talking about them."

Lexi stood frozen. "What?...Maya?"

"You tell me." Kali patiently kept her fingers tucked under her arms. Her chin never fell, and her feet never shuffled.

"I'm not sure. I don't know her as well. I'm not even sure I know what she is, but I suppose it's more complicated than that."

"Interesting," Kali chuckled.

The muscles in Lexi's chest twisted. "Why is that interesting?"

"There are two possibilities right in front of me. One; you could be lying to me. Two; Maya is lying to you."

The muscles added a tug-of-war. "About what?"

"What did she tell you the ingredients were?" Kali lowered her voice, settling her calm eyes.

"The alchelesters, the staff, the trident, the flower, and the two Stones of Souls. But by the superior and condescending tone in your voice, I'm guessing you were told something different? So tell me, Kali...what were you told?"

"And by your implication, you're thinking Moloch was the one who told me the ingredients."

"Who else would have told you?" Lexi's patience spiraled out of control.

"You really don't know, do you?"

Lexi didn't answer.

"You have the potential to be so independent, Alexandra. You don't need to rely on anyone."

"I know that, but you still haven't answered my question."

Kali softened her smile, gently breathing. "I'm sorry to tell you this. I really am. I know how hard you've worked."

"Tell me what?" Lexi could feel the steam swirling from the top of her head.

"Maya hasn't been honest with you. She knew this all along, trust me. No one kept this information from her."

"Tell. Me. What?" Lexi's firm voice vibrated through her fingers.

"It's not fair to y—"

"SPIT IT OUT!"

"We don't need all of the alchelesters."

Lexi waited for her to say more, even though the information was processing slowly, or maybe she was subconsciously and deliberately blocking it out. "What?" she asked.

"We only need Zeus's."

Lexi lost control of her jaw, but her head still hung on by a single, brittle string. "So...you—"

"Yes, I just need Logan. Easy lie, right? Of course, Moloch believed it. Smart witches. I'm sure Logan's around here somewhere. After all, those trapped doors won't catch themselves."

Lexi didn't scream. She didn't wait, but she did run. Her long, blonde hair struck against her neck she bolted so fast. Her powers were kicking in, she knew it. She needed them.

"LOGAN!" Lexi finally screamed. She didn't know where she was going, and she didn't care that she couldn't see. "LOGAN! LO—" She slowed down. Something was behind her. It was already pitch black, but there was another darkness that clouded the room, or wherever she was. Eyes glared at the back of her neck. She could sense them. Someone else's eyes. Someone who wasn't supposed to be there. Hopelessness and agony dawned upon her, but she didn't recognize it. Fear followed in her shadow. She needed to turn around, but not because she needed to see who was there. She knew.

"Alexandra," said the dark voice. It stood a few feet away. She knew why.

"Moloch."

19:

"I can't blame you. It's in your nature."

Brex wouldn't have heard Lexi's cries if Brex hadn't moved so slowly. But Lexi's voice was a sudden crack that almost gave Brex whiplash. Her heart bounced between her lungs. Yet Brex was still. Her body was frozen, but her mind was not. There was no room for recklessness or impulsivity. If Lexi was screaming, Kali would be walking behind her, wherever she was going. Or would she?

"No!" Kali's stern voice echoed in the distance. "Moloch has her under control, so don't mind her just yet. We only need Logan and the trident. The rest come second."

The heavy footsteps that followed her voice must have been Clement's and Reymid's, but what was it that she had said? Logan? She only needs Logan? Why?

Distant splashing grew closer. The animated water grew more viscous the more the footsteps sloshed. Whom they belonged to, Brex didn't know, but as she looked down to see the deep water almost touching her ankles, she quickly slinked into a clove that was meditative and dark and whispered harsh silence.

"Which way is it?" Brex heard Reymid ask.

"Come on, to the right," Clement answered.

"I thought you said they were near the Temple entrance?"

"Someone is."

"Well, that's this way!"

Temple entrance? Brex thought. *How do they know? Cameras. They must have cameras. I need to take them out. Would that help? Damn, fuck!*

Brex held her breath as she heard the voice of Clement inches away from her. If it wasn't for the sloshing, strident water, her covert location could have been discovered.

"No!" Clement demanded.

"Yes, it is."

"Fine, if you're so certain, you go right. I'll go to the Temple."

Reymid didn't answer, but by the echo of splashing diverging in two different directions, Brex assumed it was safe to return to her plan...whatever it was going to be.

*****

"I think I feel something," said Logan.

"Feel what?" Shani asked.

"Something metal-like...I think." He reached deep into the sandy ground. Sand dripped into the hole the more he moved, but the more he dug, the less he could find.

"Logan, there's nothing here."

He left his hand stuck in the ditch a few moments longer only to imply Shani wasn't the one to tell him what he should have already known.

"Yeah, I don't think there's anything down there." Logan finally said.

"You don't say?" Shani scoffed.

"Guys!" Asher shouted from the roof of the Temple. "I think Krina found something!"

"Asher!" Shani shouted her whisper. "You need to stay hidden, and stop waving the trident everywhere!"

"I'm not!"

"Guys," Logan whined. "Come on, what did Krina find?"

Logan and Shani stumbled over to Krina, hiding in the dark and sniffing around the empty field called Mastabas, but something caught her attention. Something that froze her small legs, and perked her large ears.

"What is it?" Shani asked.

"I smell something weird," Krina replied, keeping her chin level.

"Smell what?"

"Water..."

"It's probably how they keep their electricity going," Logan suggested. "Running water. God, how big is this place?"

"Running *ocean* water," Krina pointed out after a deep breath. "Damn."

"Are you sure?" Shani asked.

"That amount of salt is unmistakable, I promise."

"GUYS!" Asher hollered while still standing on the roof of the Temple. He didn't need to say anything else. Shani would have hollered back. Asher pointed to a black hole forming in the sand to his left, while another materialized on the back of the Sphinx's leg. He didn't know what they could mean, until he saw two armed men pop out of each of them. One had red hair and muscles that could shatter cement. The other had dreadlocks longer than his waist and a metal bow and arrow.

The sudden strain almost froze them, but the few seconds that they did have led them to an escape, but it would now have to be a quiet one.

Asher leaped off the roof of the Temple and headed for the Pyramid of Khafre with the trident in both hands. He thought the darkness would let him blend in, but he underestimated how bright and reflective his white wings were.

Shooooooop!

A sharp, black arrow shot straight through the center of Asher's left wing. The pain was so sudden, he almost didn't feel it, and the arrow was so colorless, he almost didn't see it.

"Fuck!"

He pulled a muscle in his bicep from trying to yank out the arrow, but it wouldn't come out. He didn't expect the arrow to be so heavy and dense. His thick, booted feet slammed into the priceless architecture that was the tip of the Pyramid of Khafre. At least it was close to the tip. His flight pattern was quickly altered after losing fantastical blood that was also priceless.

"Shit! Where are you?!" It wasn't the pain that boosted his strength, which allowed him to pull out the enchanted arrow; it was his anger, which would soon be used for his profit. He tucked the arrow away before he heard a few more coming his way. Only this time, he could see them.

"Asher!" Shani screamed in the distance.

He dodged every one of Reymid's arrows as he backed up and over the tip of the steep pyramid. The ones he didn't dodge bounced off the shimmering trident while he tried to find Shani and Logan in the distance. But it was too dark. He could only hope it would strengthen his hearing.

The cracking cement crumbled and tumbled down the peak of the pyramid as Asher made his way to the other side. Wherever he was, Reymid was wasting his arrows, but he was getting closer. Asher could hear the sound of his grunts and fingers sliding against thick string as his arrows released. Asher was running out of time and running out of ideas. He could only duck and cover. The world closed tightly around him.

The air was thin, yet surprisingly windy, however high he was. Asher could still breathe, but could Reymid? His strength overpowered Reymid's. He had been an alchelarcenist longer, right?

Asher slid down the opposite side of the pyramid, but he only made it a few feet before his heel was caught in a deep crevice.

"Ah!"

The snapping sound in his ankle wasn't what worried him; it was the impending tumble that was almost certainly going to punish his already-battered wings. Reymid's arrows were nowhere to be found. There was no trail to follow. Where was Reymid? His footsteps were distant, and his grunts had vanished, but what made Asher's stomach turn was the lack of noise surrounding him. The night was steady. Even the wind calmed down for him. Maybe the air was telling him something was wrong.

The rough cement carved up his clothes and skin, but it was useful. The friction became friendly once it caused him to stop falling. His grip wasn't as strong as he had hoped or expected, but he clung on and didn't let go until he rolled over and had no choice. His wings were all he had, and his faith was probably too high, but at least he had it. His feet thrust against the cement, and he lunged into the air with the trident as his best form of defense.

*****

Lexi wasn't impressed with Moloch's postureless attempt at intimidation. Although his heavy, dark breathing didn't go unnoticed. He didn't blink often, but neither did she. His black jacket shimmered in the dim light almost as much as his eyes and sweaty forehead.

"Is there something that I can help you with?" Lexi asked before she had to hear another one of his deep, groggy breaths.

"Why would you ask that?" Moloch asked.

"You haven't killed me yet, so you must want something. I'm not useful to you anymore. I never was."

Moloch slithered forward, closer to Lexi. Not intimidatingly, but more instinctually. Like a magnet.

"Oh, no," he mumbled, shaking his head, not losing eye contact with her. "That's where you're mistaken."

"Really?"

"Very much so. Something as powerful as you should never go to waste."

Lexi didn't know why, but it wasn't until that point that her stiff exhale was finally released. Her lungs burned, but not for long. Her skin shivered as the air pushed out.

"So, you want to use me?"

"Would you rather I kill you now?"

"I'd rather you explain. That's why we're here."

"Ah, yes." Moloch's teeth were whiter than Lexi had expected. His smile didn't squeeze and tug at her nerves. He was surprisingly normal. "Where are your friends by the way? I'm afraid we won't be able to do this without them."

"You're trying to bribe all of us?"

"Bribe? Alexandra, I am trying to save you."

"I'm pretty sure you're gaslighting me."

"Gaslighting? Are you sure?"

"Nevermind, let me hear what you have to say, and we can talk."

"First," Moloch's hand floated in front of him, holding it out, as if he were surrounded by water. "Come this way."

*****

Shani couldn't hear or see Logan. There was minimal, fluorescent light from the tourist lights outside that bled into the cave from above, but it wasn't enough to see Logan's veins pop out of his neck from distress. Logan wasn't being of any use due to his vocal cords struggling to function through his colossal loss of breath. No matter how hard he tried, he was too scared to move.

"Logan," said Shani. "Don't move."

He couldn't even if he tried. The only spec of light they could see was a sliver of sandy cement peeking out from their hideout a few inches in front of them. The Funerary Temple of Khafre was smothered in shadows, but the unsteady silence didn't make it easy to hide from the tremendous, looming footsteps that were getting too close for comfort.

Shani couldn't take any more of the heavy breathing that vigorously shuddered through Logan's throat. She slapped her hand against his mouth, silencing him to hear the threat growing closer. Only the wind could break the tense silence, or Clement's gargled breathing.

The crackling sand blew in the wind with every step Clement took. They were slow, but steady. His thick boots swiveled in the ground, creating perfect, endless circles. It told Shani only one thing; he didn't know where they were, and they had time. Precious time.

Logan's neck stood stiff. Shani almost pulled a muscle in his neck as she grabbed his chin and forced him to look at her. He could only see her jaw flexing if he squinted, and her lips were hard to read, but when she grabbed his left hand and caught a shadowy glimpse of her pointing to an electric wire, he could only guess it was for the minimal lighting at the scene. Logan suddenly gained control over his body again, primarily in his spine. It shot up straight like a rocket breaking through the ozone layer.

"No!" he whispered before Shani put her hand back over his mouth. He corrected himself and shook his head while mouthing the word, "No" just to please her.

Shani repeatedly shook her finger at the electrical wiring that sat a few feet across from them before slamming her hand into her other hand like a spear.

"Jesus," Logan whispered before covering his own mouth this time. They had to lure Clement into their line of sight. Their best chance was simple. All Logan had to do was lean a little closer to the light to get the shot right. Shani readied her stance. Her feet tucked under her glutes and steadied her fatigued core. Logan reached his right arm slowly and quietly through the dark opening and shot a small lightning bolt at the electrical wiring.

Yes, he silently celebrated. The arch was high and long, but it was a perfect shot. The electrocution was a Christmas tree lighting; flashy before everything went dark. Completely dark. Not a single light remained across the entire campus.

"OH SHIIIIT," said Logan. But no one covered his mouth, which Shani quickly regretted.

Clement's heavy feet bolted across the sandy cement. Shani and Logan could hear and feel the crunch, and this time they knew it was coming toward them. The trap had been set.

"Ready?" Shani whispered.

"No, Shani. I can't see!"

"He's wearing metal. We'll see the shine from the moon's reflection."

"Okay, okay."

Seconds turned into a minute. One long minute that dragged along with his struggling, painful heart rate that poked at his chest. Where was he? Footsteps couldn't be heard, neither could Clement's horse-like mouth breathing.

"Where is he?" Logan asked before the roof of the hideout crumbled before them. Priceless, aging architecture shattered into pieces and trapped them inside their small niche.

"No!" Shani screamed, but Logan caught her attention when part of the roof fell onto Logan's head.

*****

Asher's wing wouldn't stop bleeding, but he refused to look. He wasn't sure why. He could feel the wet, thick liquid pouring down his soft feathers. A few of those mystical feathers flew off as he flew faster than usual over to the Sphinx's head.

"Asher!" Reymid screamed from his gut. Asher's wing couldn't carry him much longer. He could feel the blood soaking into his feathers. It needed to heal faster. He could hear Reymid's footsteps behind him. He was catching up. Asher couldn't resist. He looked back to see Reymid only yards away holding up his bow and arrow, threatening to shoot.

Asher's boots collided with the Sphinx's head. He was wide open, but not for Reymid to take a shot at Asher, but for Asher to take a shot at Reymid.

Come on, Asher thought. He didn't know what it would do. *The trident wasn't in the water. How powerful could it be? It worked for Dimitria, didn't it?*

The anger boiled to a tipping point at the top of his skull. His grip tightened, and he pointed the trident at Reymid. The trident almost ruptured itself. The lightning was like a magnet. A force yearning for its answer. The electricity collided with the tip of the trident and bounced off the shiny edges to reach for Reymid's arrow that stretched in front of his arm.

"Ahh!" Reymid screamed. His electrocution was brighter than Asher was expecting. His reflexes tightened his abdomen together. His elbows bent inwards, but he still stood. His tired feet struggled to fight for him.

"Damn, you're just full of surprises." Asher admired his weapon, holding it high, hoping the connection would never be lost. Unaware of and fascinated by its mysterious powers, he held it close, but Reymid did the same with his own weapon. Reymid's energy sprouted once again, and his threatening posture reformed, with his head even higher than before. He was more powerful than Asher had thought.

Asher caught his jaw before saying, "Oh...no. How...?"

*****

Moloch was a slow walker. Lexi hated slow walkers. She hadn't worked for her entire life to learn how to catch up with long-legged walkers to walk behind someone with longer legs than most human beings and not put them to good use. Nonetheless, he was steady. Every step was on a proper beat. Where was he taking her? How was she going to get out of this? And what was his weakness? Was he still weak?

"In here," said Moloch, gesturing his arm to request her entrance first.

Lexi didn't see a door. She saw a staircase. A downward staircase. It could have led to Moloch's Hell for all she knew, but it wasn't time yet. She did as she was told without saying a word.

The staircase wasn't long, but she still felt as if she was about to wake up from a dream and trip back into reality. And it would be a long, disastrous way down. Every step was a test. For the first time, he was in her presence, and she couldn't see him, but that wasn't what unnerved her. It was the giant, misty room that was bigger than Fenway Park, and if Lexi squinted, she could have sworn it was growing bigger by the second. Or maybe it was contracting like a ribcage before it took a deep breath and expanded once again.

Maybe it's just the magic, Lexi thought. *Or an illusion, but damn.*

Every which way, different energies collided with one another. In one corner was a lightning storm that was smothering a rainbow. The primary colors that drowned the room in sorrow were green and black. But in another, a cobweb. An obscure red and black mist rumbled together around the cobweb as if it were at war with itself. In front of Lexi was what looked like a maze, a maze with clouds hovering over it. Lexi had never seen such black, polluted clouds. A green organism was morphing and planning its deceitful propaganda, calling to Lexi. Asking her to be its next victim. But what she saw the most were black holes. black holes that vacuumed its prey to where it could never be found. There was no pattern. They spread across the room like pimples on skin. It was a carnival. A carnival for the waste of the mystical macrocosm. Only every ride was a haunted house.

"What is this place?" Lexi asked. Something slammed behind her, but when she turned around, there was nothing there. Not even the door.

"It's my own personal sanctuary. Just like the Alliance has theirs, but think of it as more of a nuanced scientific realm. It's essentially the nucleus of Hell. Kali calls it the Green Room."

Lexi turned around to see him standing with his shoulders down and his chin lifted high, admiring the strength manifesting before him. He was more relaxed than before.

"Why are you showing this to me?" Lexi asked.

"Because what you see here is different from what I see. Tell me, Alexandra...what is it that you see?"

Lexi looked around. Every direction held something new, something that was dissolving into another disaster, waiting for its destructive fate. It seemed to be the manifestation of Moloch's brain, if that existed. Or it was as if the stress and sorrow of Moloch's soul squeezed out of him due to having nowhere to go. The mazes that were primarily made up of shadows and what looked like broken glass looked more like entrances to Hell than a game to be played. "I see catastrophe. Disorder. Nature coming to a close, and soon everything will be deranged," Lexi said.

"Are you sure?" Moloch asked.

"Is this man-made?" Lexi asked, dodging the question.

"No, of course not. But if we proceed, it will grow stronger." His raspy voice lengthened, almost as if he'd been waiting to say that.

"You don't know that," Lexi said.

"And how did you come to that prediction?"

"What about this place is predictable? It seems like a manifestation of your soul. Is it?"

"You're not asking the right questions, Alexandra."

"No, I'm just not asking the questions you want me to ask, and I still don't understand why you brought me here."

"To help you understand."

"Understand what? Why you think you're doing the right thing? You think that you're trying to help people, but you're not. Nature isn't supposed to be touched."

"For someone who cares so deeply for a stronger and wealthier environment, you're rather close-minded to the idea that keeping people alive is too drastic to comprehend."

"No, Kali wants to extend human life, you want to extend your own. I can't blame you. It's in your nature."

"Let me ask you something," said Moloch. He intertwined his fingers and pulled them to his sternum. "Why do you think all of these stories that you heard growing up include someone like me? You've heard them all, haven't you? And so many people believe them. People believe they've found the answer. No, they think they *know* they've found the answer. They've latched onto something so unfamiliar with science and their humdrum human lives, yet they think the idea of Hell is inevitable. It's a part of life. Natural."

"And you think because of that, everyone will agree with you?"

Moloch didn't answer. He didn't smile or react. He only stepped closer to Lexi, gently took her left hand, and watched the ticking clock on her palm slowly turn back to where it first was.

"Why did you do that? Why are you helping me?" Lexi asked.

"I need you to listen. I am not the only one who will sustain the energy I need to live. Everyone will live their ordinary lives. Young and healthy, while we will maintain our superior thrones. Right now, yes you age, but slowly. And you have to rely on me for fuel. I am the only one that can keep that meter on your palm where it is. But soon, you won't need anyone. You will live on. Independently, and you won't age. You won't have to worry about anyone. Including yourself."

"You think once I see this room in a different light, then I will help you?"

Moloch's skin almost drained in color the closer he came to Lexi. "No, I think your perspective will change after you come with me."

Lexi hadn't noticed it before, but something was wrong. Her body fought against her commands. Her legs stood stiff as if they were prosthetics, but they were weak at the same time. How much longer would she be able to stand?

She rubbed her head, hoping he didn't see, and asked, "Can I think about this first?"

*****

Brex was going in circles, or so it seemed. The hallways were endless. At least a dead end would give her an answer as to where not to go. Her breathing was faint, and her eyesight blurred every time she blinked. Something about her hand felt fuzzy, but the tingling almost became unbearable. She had to do it. She had to look at her scar.

"Okay," was all she had to say. "Okay." Brex knew if she didn't keep mumbling to herself, she wouldn't be able to let go of the fact that she only had about three notches left until her powers were drained.

She continued her run, but everything started to cramp. Her joints twitched, and her arches couldn't hold her much longer. Not only that, but she was starving. She couldn't remember the last time that she had eaten, but her stomach was diligently working to remind her.

"Okay, okay."

Every breath counted. Every step. Slowly was now the fastest way to get to where she needed to be. Her strongest sense? She needed to listen.

Each drop of water, even if it was minuscule, echoed a powerful laugh. Mocking her elusive state. But the more she listened, the louder the echo was, and the heavier the rain fell. Where was this coming from? She couldn't risk using her powers, but she could follow the beckoning echo.

She didn't know what she was looking for. Maybe it was just an escape, but there had to be an answer. She walked quickly, but kept her guard up, ready to strike at any given moment. But it wasn't needed. After following the echo, she found the location of the sound. It was right under her nose, but something was missing. The darkness shadowed most of her surroundings, but still, she was sure there was not a drop of water in sight. Where could it all be coming from?

The smell was overwhelming, but so far it wasn't helping. The ocean water was a scent that she would never get used to, no matter how long she lived near it. It was a sense of home that could pull Brex in, but from where?

Only three corners blocked her in. There wasn't room for a loud echo, but the longer she stayed silent, the more she could distinguish the sound of bouncing drops of water from the buzzing white noise.

What else? What else? Brex thought. *It has to be coming from something. The running water. Yes. Pipes...or maybe something else...where could they be?*

She reached for the wall. Vibrations. The calming blood rushed to her forearms and bled into the skin of her palms. She closed her eyes even though it was still too dark to see anything, but there was nothing. Careful not to hit her head, she leaned in closer and pressed her ear up against the cold, cement wall, but there was still nothing. But maybe it wasn't her palms that she needed to be listening to.

The floor...

Her boots were thick, but if she kept her feet still and heavy, even her ankles tingled with a steady vibration.

"Alright," she whispered. She wasted no time in dropping face down against the wet floor that was somehow even colder than the wall. But it wasn't difficult to put two and two together. The bitter chill was coming from water. *Ocean* water. The smell was unmistakable, just like Krina said.

"Okay, okay, okay."

Brex needed an opening, but where? Or maybe she could make one of her own. No, it would be too laborious. She would have to look.

"Come on..." It only took a few seconds for patience to be lost and nowhere to be found, but luckily her impatience sharpened her vision, and at the end of the hallway, she found something.

She quietly ran over to something round and flat on the floor. It was still hard to see, but the smooth, reflective texture shimmered brighter than the rest of the floor. Brex almost threw herself down when the outline of the hidden figure turned into a full, detailed canvas. It was a drain.

"Shit," she laughed. She brushed the edges, hoping to see an end. She did. It was removable, but screwed in tight. "Shiiiiiiit."

She didn't have a screw gun, or a wrench, or anything to pry it open, but she took one look at the scar on her palm and knew what she had to do.

"Damn," she whispered. Only a few notches left, but it was enough. Her reflexes stood strong and ignited the flames that smoked from her fingers. All she needed was a little heat. The metal immediately sizzled when the flames made their presence known. Once the metal was nothing but hot liquid, she stuck her slim fingers in the crack and ripped it from the floor. She almost forgot that she still had some of her heightened strength.

She crouched down, still trying not to make too much noise, stuck out her feet, and fell through the dark hole without looking to see what was down there first.

"Geez!" Brex loudly whispered when she realized she had been falling for too long, but luckily, the full foot of water somewhat softened the landing. "Whoa." Somehow there was more light in this new hallway, or maybe it was the reflection from the water, but the light in the reflection didn't appreciate her presence. They began to shake. As if there was an earthquake, but Brex soon realized by the sound coming from the distance that "tsunami" was going to be a more appropriate word.

"Oh no."

*****

Asher's upper body had more blood on it than dirt, but he still stood without feeling like he was about to fall over, having landed on the ground. He checked his scar. His magic was running low. Fighting from the ground was going to have to do. Not to worry just yet. He could last for a few more days, but only for a few at the most...maybe.

"Where are you?" he whispered to Reymid, searching for him in the darkness, but there were no traces of footsteps in the sand.

The temple looked bigger than it was from the ground, but it made a good hiding spot, but hiding wasn't going to be enough. He had to get back to the rest, or would it be better if they were all apart? It would certainly stall Moloch and the rest, but for how long?

The dry Egyptian air puckered his tongue. No air would have been less painful. He wouldn't be of any use dehydrated and immobile.

"Water," he said to himself. What else was there to do?

He waited for the wind to be at its strongest so that whatever noise he made would blend in. He ran around the corner of the temple with the trident in one hand and an arrow in the other. The image of the pyramid in the distance bounced in his mind. It looked like a painting, or maybe a large high-definition screen, but after blinking a few times, he repositioned himself and kept his stance loose but strong. He stayed low with his wings tucked. So far, there was no sign of any arrows coming his way, but if there were, he would have at least a split second to hear them.

Crack!

"There you are." But he spoke too soon. Another arrow landed in his tight grip, "Hot DAMN!" He almost spun in a circle until he realized Reymid was nowhere to be seen. "Nevermind."

Crack!

Reymid missed again, but hit something else. Another cracking sound behind him almost made Asher tumble over, but this time was different. The sharp, clean-cut sound echoed instead with rumbling quakes that made the hairs on Asher's neck stick up. He turned around to see the arrow sticking out of the wall that still stood intact, but something was different.

"What the..." A square dent in the wall surrounded the arrow, perfectly centered. As if someone simply pressed a button. It wasn't until the floor underneath Asher's feet gave out that he realized what the button was for.

"WHOA!"

His back fell first, fighting against a striking wind. After falling several feet, he could see the cement closing back up above him, but he wasn't in total darkness. A green smoke flashed before his eyes. If there were any hallucinogens in him, he would have thought he was falling down the rabbit hole to Wonderland, but that theory was debunked when his wings sprouted just in time for him to safely land on the ground to see nothing but green and black smoke mixing together to create a tornado of chaos. But something was missing.

"Shit, NO!"

He looked around for the trident, but it was nowhere to be seen. He dropped it before he fell.

"No, no, noooooo!"

The rough, sandy floor dug into his palms and knees. He couldn't stand or move until he heard the sound of Lexi's voice saying, "Asher?"

•••••

"Ow, Logan," Shani whispered. "Why don't you walk in front? You keep stepping on my foot."

"My concussion sends its condolences to your foot, but I'll keep my sympathy to myself, thanks. Ow!" Logan hit his shoulder against the wall as he tried to pass her. The only light was from the small specks of moonlight that peeked through the cracks of the ceiling, or whatever it was above them.

"I'm sorry," Shani said after secretly rolling her eyes. "How is it?"

"It's fine. That's honestly not what's worrying me."

"Okay." Shani didn't want to admit it, but she did feel something crawling in between the layers of her skin. But she didn't know what.

"I don't know, I just feel like Clement is still watching us somehow."

Shani reached for his hand. At first, she couldn't find it, but once she did, she hid behind him and dug her nails into his knuckles.

"Shani, I'm sorry. That was probably pointless to say. He's not."

"Why did he trap us in here?" Shani asked.

"What?"

"He could have taken us hostage. Remember, he can't kill us. He needs us. So why down here?"

"Well, if we know, we will know what to look for."

They kept moving, but it took a few more minutes for Shani to let go, and only a few more for Logan to hear a rodent of some sort crawl across their feet and grab onto Shani's forearm.

"Do you want me to give you another concussion?" Shani asked Logan.

"That honestly doesn't sound like the worst thing in the world right now."

They carried on, but whatever pathway they were on didn't end. A few curves drove them left and right, but it all looked the same after their eyes finally adjusted.

"Do you think we should just try to break something down? One of the walls?" Logan asked.

"Maybe, but we need to find the right spot."

"Right, the biggest crack that we can find."

"Even bigger than Asher's mouth," Shani added.

"*Asher's* mouth?" Logan asked, but Shani didn't respond.

They kept low. Shani's knees kept hitting jutting pieces of cement, but she maintained her speed until she noticed a sliver of light coming from the ceiling. It was unusually bright and leaking onto the cemented floor.

"Hey," Shani mumbled. "What if we push through the ceiling?"

The vulnerable ceiling strived to hold its cracks, but they already were trembling in fear. "We might as well try," said Logan.

"We can tuck our fingers through that crack. It might give us some leverage."

Both of them stepped on the pile of stones and clasped onto the ceiling for balance. After they dug their fingers deep into the crack as much as they could, Shani started to count down.

"Okay, breathe. Ready? Three, t—" Her voice trailed off, she wasn't sure why, but a shadow covered the light that guided them to their escape. Her heart didn't skip right away, but once she saw Clement's glowing eyes staring down at them through the sliver, she knew what he was going to do.

"LOGAN!" she screamed. "MOVE!" She pushed him off the perch, and he tumbled backwards, down to the floor before Clement pounded his way through the ceiling.

BOOOOOM!

History quickly repeated itself. Another army of bricks from the broken ceiling tumbled before Shani had a chance to get herself back to Logan.

"SHANI!"

He didn't see her, but what he could make out through the dust and sand that smothered the air before him was Shani dropping her arms like she was jumping into water feet first.

"Shani?"

*****

Brex's fire was useless now. A rush of cold air came before the tsunami clapped her in the face. But once it did, it took her down with each nerve convulsing before falling aloof, but not without the proper preparation. She was now immersed in the cold, rushing water.

"Wah hah?" Brex mumbled under the now ten feet of water surrounding her, but she needed to save her breath.

Brex pushed through the stinging in her lungs when she expanded her abdomen enough for her to stay for however long she needed. She didn't know where Shani was, but she couldn't help but nag herself about how this would have been easier with Shani. Nonetheless, the wave finished its course after tossing itself high over Brex's head. The water was cold, but the salty smell, mixed with a flash of ice soaking into Brex's skin was a refreshing way to jab at her fatigue.

The tackle wrestled her into the water and almost ripped her control away. Bubbles clouded her spacial awareness. She would have hit her head against the floor if she had been any more vicious with her sharp and vigorous movements. But once she could see through the musty water, she drew one arm forward after the other until her feet finally chimed in. She began to swim, and she was fast.

Up ahead was a small speck of light that was pouring in through the ceiling from hopefully another room, but Brex couldn't tell. It was too dark.

She didn't mean to, but it was like a reflex. Her fire was begging to ignite, but it couldn't. Although her heat wasn't completely useless. Her skin was strong and thick after all.

Breathe, she begged her powers, but they didn't need a lot of convincing. She could see the glow even with her eyes closed. The skin on her forearms looked like lava in a children's cartoon. The deep orange color wasn't the guiding lamp she hoped it would be, but it would have to do.

Her hips were the first thing to go numb, then came her feet, followed by her shoulders. She looked back to see that she'd only swum a few feet, but the hallway seemed endless. There was nothing in sight but black, although the pigmentation of the black canvas was growing and her lungs were tightening. Not because of the lack of air, but because the closer she came to whatever black thing was sucking her down, the faster she felt like she was being pulled in. Like a whirlpool. But the longer she thought about the possible threat, the longer she realized it wasn't just potentially problematic. It was happening.

The black whirlpool spiraled out of control, but Brex didn't react. She thought about it, but only for a split second. If she swam away, where would she go? This was her only chance to get air and soon. Even if it was unlikely.

Close your eyes, her conscience told her. She obeyed, but the swirling feeling in her stomach made her soon reopen them until the speed was unbearable. She almost convinced herself she was in a washing machine. Her body was flung in various directions, hitting the walls, ceiling, and floors.

"Ahhhhhh!"

The black hole only sped up. Even when light seeped in through her eyelids.

Wait, she thought. *Light?*

The room kept spinning. She didn't know where to look until the oversized waterslide spat her out onto an almost dry, cement floor. There wasn't a lot of light, but it was still too much for a quick adjustment. She didn't know where she was until she finally took a painful, deep breath in and only choked on a small amount of water that she quickly coughed up. She was alive, and she was on land. She was hopefully safe, and still alone. Until she heard a familiar voice.

"Brex?" Shani said, running up to her with her dry sweater around her waist, and with Asher and Lexi behind her. "Where's Logan?"

20:

"What happens if you leave this place?"

The room was getting hotter, but Lexi, Asher, Brex, and Shani used the sauna to their advantage. Their minds would self-destruct if they didn't stay calm. Lexi disclosed her encounter with Moloch and Kali to the rest, but Brex only listened to half of the story. She needed to find Logan. They quickly got back on their aching feet.

"Look," said Lexi, pointing to a crevice in the wall. "Let's look over there." But after a few uneven steps, Lexi veered away from it. "Nevermind, it looks like a black hole." The black, hypnotizing vacuum stood taller than Shani, but it wasn't the only one this size occupying the room.

"What is this place?" Asher asked for the third time.

"It's what a brain looks like after it has too much cocaine and three seizures and if it was magical. It's a manifestation of unnatural magic," Lexi answered.

"Why is it here?" Shani asked.

"That's a good question," said Lexi. "Maybe if we keep looking, we'll find something. But we have to be careful. Moloch probably left me here to do just that."

"How would we know once we find it?" Asher tried touching something black that swirled like pollution in a whirlpool, but he immediately pulled away before it could touch him back. "I'm getting a headache just by looking at this place."

"Wait," said Shani, "we shouldn't be looking around at anything too much. We don't know what kind of curses infest this place."

"How in the fuck are we supposed to get out of here and get back to Logan and Krina if we can't look around?" Asher asked.

"Ah, there it is..." Lexi whispered under her breath, wondering where their bickering had been hiding. "Guys, let's just keep moving. We need to get back to Logan. Just be careful."

They stayed silent, but the room didn't. The diseased walls spread like a virus around them. The dark green, rough color poisoned the pigmentation in their skin. The only thing leading them was the glow that reflected cacophonously, bouncing from wall to wall.

"Do you hear something?" Asher asked.

"Yeah," Shani snapped, "I hear a lot of your whining. Could you be more specific?"

Asher didn't look at her or respond and instead kept his ears perked and said, "Voices...I think. Or maybe it's...crying." His eyelashes batted uncontrollably, but he let the voices lead him.

"Asher?" Brex asked after he had stood still for longer than she was comfortable with.

"This way," Asher responded, about to run.

"Wait!" Lexi hollered. "We should walk. Keep steady, and your eyes ready."

The four nodded in agreement. Asher finally looked at Shani, knowing he couldn't avoid it for long. She would have a whole speech ready for him if he didn't. And before any more hesitation, Asher inched forward and led the way.

"Over here!" he said as the voice grew louder. "This way!" He changed directions four times before he realized they were going in either a circle or a demented square. But Asher couldn't tell; he was that disoriented.

"Are you sure you hear something?" Shani asked, but her question wasn't answered by Asher; it was answered by someone else.

"Ahhhh..." Shani heard in the distance.

"Wait, I hear it too."

"Hold up," said Asher, once again not looking at her. His jaw loosened as his eyes focused on something peculiar in the distance. "I've seen that before." A few more steps forward, and he was able to make out an old stool that stood in front of a pile of old, random furniture. It had caught his eye a time before, but not here. Not in person. In his dreams.

"Oh, shit," Asher mumbled.

"What?" Brex asked, uncrossing her arms.

"She must be around here somewhere," Asher responded.

"Who?" Shani asked, rushing alongside Asher, wherever he was going.

"That woman that I've been seeing in my dreams." His face sliced the air in every direction, but she was still nowhere to be seen.

"You've been seeing that woman in your dreams still?" Shani's voice raised a notch higher, but not enough to make anyone flinch.

"Did I not tell you that?"

"What? No! Asher!" Then everyone flinched.

"We have to find her, she might know—" But he was cut off.

"Are you looking for me?"

All four hearts skipped a beat, but none as vigorously as Asher's. It was like seeing a movie set in person instead of images on a white cloth from a cheap projector. But the one thing that he had to remind himself of was now the woman with the long brown hair and blue dress could hear him too. Her bones were brittle, and there couldn't have been a drop of water under her skin. Her cheekbones couldn't naturally be that prominent. He wanted to help her.

"Who are you?" Asher asked.

"What he means is, are you alright?" Brex snapped.

Asher only hiccuped a moment before he realized she was right, but it didn't stop him from blushing and biting his lip.

"Yes, I'm sorry," said Asher, running to her. "Are you alright?"

"Yes, I'm fine," said the woman. "Who are you? Why are you here? You shouldn't be here."

"Ma'am, I'm Shani. This is Asher, Lexi, and Brex. We can help you, and you can help us. Do you know a way out?"

"Of course not, but how did you get in?"

"We're not a part of the Alliance," said Brex, "but we're working for them. You're—" She wasn't sure if she should ask, she wasn't sure how, but the words slipped out. "You're not working for Moloch?"

The woman's eyes were so drained, Brex couldn't tell if she was insulted. "I wouldn't be trapped in here if I were."

"Okay. Um...then you should know, there was a mole giving out the whereabouts of the sanctuaries. We were sent to find and relocate all of them," Brex explained.

The woman's eyes and jaw sharpened. "Who sent you?"

"Maya," said Asher, but he might as well have pushed her off a bridge. She jumped back with her arms covering her face and sourly shook her head.

"Did she send you here to hurt me?" the woman asked, leaning on her elbows.

"What? No!" Asher exclaimed.

"She can't be trusted!"

Brex reached out her arms, hoping to be of comfort. "We figured."

"Why are you here?!" the woman asked.

"Because we were lied to," said Shani, about to rip through the green fog falling upon them and condense it all into a trash can. "And maybe if you start telling us who you are and telling us what you know instead of asking us questions, we might be able to get all of us out of here."

The woman nodded and closed her almond eyes.

"Start with your name," said Brex.

"Alright, my name is Bai. I used to live with the witches in Salem. I would help them with their magic. Ancient Chinese medicines were very useful to them. There I adopted a son. His mother died giving birth to him. Magical complications. So, I took him in as my own. His name is—"

"Jethro," Brex softly said.

"Yes, you know him?"

"He helped us."

"Of course, he did," said Bai as she couldn't hold back a shameful, fleeting smile.

"Why do you not trust Maya?" Asher asked. "What happened?"

Bai held a breath for as long as she could until the words had to spill out. "When Moloch came to force the witches to give him the ingredients for his plan, the witches lied to him and told him that he needed the magic of every god of Olympus. He only needed Zeus's."

"So it's true?" Lexi asked. "She really did lie to us."

"How did Moloch not know?" Shani asked.

"Moloch knew there had to be Greek blood. He wouldn't have thought otherwise. However, when he forced the witches to cooperate with him, the people that were soon going to be the Alliance knew he was going to come back. We told everyone his plan. The Greeks were the first to know. We set a trap."

"What kind of trap? What was going to trap him?" Brex asked.

"Something to weaken him, so he wouldn't have the ability to carry through with anything. People got word of what was going to happen. Moloch was bound to return, asking for more. That was when he created the alchelesters. The ability to absorb the powers, so when they were hidden, all he needed to do was find them and build an army. Pigs for slaughter. He didn't need our help. He did it himself, but he needed one more thing. That's where Maya comes in, and her mistake..."

Brex's back stiffened. "What mistake?"

"Moloch knew he was going to need a battery of some sort, something to fuel his work. Something that has no end. He wasn't going to leave without one."

"You?" Lexi asked. Bai nodded.

"Maya knew she would be a much more powerful source of fuel, but she lied in hopes his plan would fail. If there was no brain, such as you see here," she said, gesturing at their surroundings, "the expansion of Hell would eventually fail. He was going to take Maya, but she lied and said I would be a more powerful choice. He believed her. Thinking Maya wanted to save herself. Regardless, I still worked as a source of fuel. He took me instead. I've been fueling this room ever since."

The four of them held themselves tightly together. The light in the room somehow dimmed. It was a room of chaos. A hoarder's dream, but only if that hoarder's soul reflected the darkness that poisoned the room.

"She was just trying to protect people," Lexi boldly claimed. "I understand—"

"No," Bai gently snapped. "I had a son. He needed me."

"You *have* a son," said Shani. "He's fine. Maya took care of him and made sure he grew up to be powerful."

"I'm sorry that happened to you," said Asher, with his arms still crossed. "I knew we shouldn't have trusted Maya."

"Asher," said Brex, trying not to face him. "What would you have done?"

"What would *I* have done?" His palms pounded against his chest. "What would Bai have done, you mean? She didn't get a choice."

"How are you still here?" Lexi asked Bai, trying to calm the ranting.

"I can't die. I'm immortal. That's why I'm a source of energy."

"What happens if you leave this place?" Shani asked.

"I don't know, but I've been here so long. It would probably take decades for this place to weaken."

"So," Asher put his hands on his thighs and crouched down next to Bai, "if you left, Moloch's plan would still go through?"

"For the time being, yes."

"What else do you know?" Brex asked. The way Bai bit her lips told Brex she wasn't done. Maybe she wasn't hiding it, but she wasn't done, and the look lingered until she took another breath.

"There is one more thing," said Bai. She reached down her cleavage to pull out an amulet, a blue amulet that hung tightly on a black string. The sapphire, circular gem sparkled in the little light they had. The green mist mixed into the color to create a wave of oceanic pigmentation. And they all recognized it right away.

"You have the other Stone of Souls?" Shani gasped. Her nerves vibrated at full speed, like being in a subway car that was about to crash.

"How?" Lexi asked.

"The guard at the South African sanctuary. The one that was destroyed and the guard was killed. Yari was his name." She couldn't help but recreate the image in her head, but after years of practice, she was able to wipe it all away with one clean brush. "They took me to use my blood for access. I didn't even know I had it. Not only was Yari guarding the alchelesters that gave Kali, Clement, and Reymid their powers, he was guarding the necklace too. I found it after they killed him and were taking the alchelesters. I suppose I thought it would be safer with me than unguarded on a dead body. But I was mistaken. Kali sensed it immediately. It wasn't easy to hide. It's too powerful.

Just as Maya did, Kali used a protection spell. Therefore, it stays with me at all times. She always knows where it is. Only she can take it from me."

Brex leaned in but kept her voice low. "How are you being fueled?"

"I do eat, but my energy comes from Moloch. It's a science unfamiliar to me, but whenever he comes back, a youthful spirit will return to me, but only for so long."

"No offense," Asher began, keeping his hands out and his eyebrows raised, "like please, don't take this personally or...I mean...has he come yet since he's been back here?"

It was the first time they saw her laugh. Or rather, her version of a laugh. Her mouth and eyes crinkled and her core gently jiggled, but it was a laugh nonetheless. It was almost as if she'd forgotten how to laugh.

"No, he hasn't," she answered, with endearing eyes.

"So he's probably going to come?" Lexi asked. "And soon, right?"

"He has to," said Shani standing up, but keeping her tense eyes fixed on the floor. "She needs more fuel."

"He's going to come through a door of some sort," said Brex, finishing their thoughts.

"We should split up," Asher suggested.

"Shit," Shani ran her fingers through her thick, uncombed hair. "Yeah, you're right."

"Whoa." Asher gasped.

"Shut up," Shani loudly whispered. The four of them jumped up, but they were forgetting one thing. "Wait, we can't just leave you here," Shani said to Bai.

Bai took Shani's sweaty hands, looked up at her, and said, "You have to. You're running out of time." Shani assumed she would elaborate more, but she didn't need to. Shani couldn't waste any more time.

"Guys," said Lexi. "I know we said to be careful, but that's getting really exhausting."

"I agree," Asher. "Let's run. We'll find an exit faster."

And so they did. It wasn't clean. It wasn't a race, but the power being contained in the confined area couldn't compete with the fear exuding from their skin. They dove in every which way, plowing through clouds of gray and black that could have killed them for all they knew, but risk-taking was their only choice.

Brex didn't mind running alone. There was no time to obsess over the repercussions of having no assistance if needed. That could wait for later. Her memory was never sharp, but she tried to memorize her path regardless.

Lightning, fire, black hole, waterfall, mountain, She repeated to herself.

Brex's dehydrated throat gasped for air, but it didn't slow her down. Her legs pounded as they zig-zagged across the uneven, cemented ground. A few feet ahead stood a pile of something dark. Rocks maybe, but she didn't look down before she jumped over it and landed on the other side. She caught herself, but something changed. There was a shift in the light. Something darker. An end, but an end to what?

"There it is."

She didn't know how, but it was an exit. It had to be. It was up a steep pile of dirt maybe twenty feet high, but it was a way out. But what kind of an exit? There was only one way to find out, and she didn't hesitate for a moment to scramble up the dirt pile, her hands and forearms clawing the soil in front of her.

"Ow!" She cut herself on something sharp, but when she looked, there was nothing there. Her knuckle bled down to her wrist. The warm blood mixed into the dirt that was already covering every inch of her skin from her elbows to her nails. Although her cuts were distracting, she continued to climb.

"Come on," Brex whispered to herself. "Guys! Over here!"

The endless black hole was only a few inches away. Most of the adrenaline pumped to her arms. They were holding on. They just needed to stay that way. "Okay, ok—" Her reaction was to let go when a perfectly smooth and clean hand grabbed onto hers out of nowhere. For a moment, she hoped it would be Logan's, but when the muscles in her neck found the strength to lift up her head, she saw the bloody, red scar that resided on Kali's face.

Brex tried to rip away. She didn't care if she fell, but Kali's strength was not only at an advantage, it was overpowering.

"I would let go of me if I were you," Brex loudly whispered over the shattering glass that filled the air in the background. She didn't know where the sound was coming from, but it blended in with the rest of the chaos.

"I can slice your hand off faster than you can burn mine off, so I wouldn't recommend threatening me."

"Fine, kill me then. You know you have no use for me."

The corner of Kali's mouth sparked like an engine. "Come with me."

"No." Brex tried one last time, but it only made her weaker.

"Brex, stop fighting, and come with me." Kali held out her other hand for Brex to take. On her clean left hand was her scar, and apparently it wasn't a secret that Kali's magic was running low. Brex didn't have to think again. She grabbed Kali's hand and pulled herself up.

21:

"Don't talk about her either."

Brex walked behind Kali. She wasn't tall, but her shadow spread across the hallway floor like Slenderman. Kali's shoulders were tucked behind her, and her head floated perfectly level.

It was the silence that made her stomach turn. Their footsteps echoed down the long hallways, but Kali's heels rang at a higher pitch than Brex's. The walls needed a deep dusting. Each brick looked like they were challenged to a game of Jenga, and someone was about to lose. The more she focused and isolated the sound, the more her head pounded. Or maybe it was from something else entirely.

"Ow." She looked at her palm which was going to have more scars on it than it did before. The bleeding had stopped, but the stinging didn't. As far as she could remember, her magic hadn't lowered, but that didn't make her heart stop racing.

"In here," said Kali, clear as a whistle.

Brex was expecting it to be another layer that held some sort of magical manifestation of Moloch's existence, but it was just a room, with couches, a bar, and oil paintings that were begging for new frames. The color red swamped the room. Even the lilies in the corner looked like they were dipped in red paint.

"Is this where you live?" Brex asked.

Kali stepped over to the bar and poured what smelled like whiskey. Brex resented the anxiety now more than ever.

"If you're using the word 'live' in a vague sense, then I suppose," said Kali. "I don't spend all of my time with Moloch, you know? I enjoy being alone."

"And here I thought you were such a people person."

Kali didn't laugh, but her smooth smile was slick and genuine. She handed Brex a glass of whiskey, but Brex shook her head.

"You know poison isn't going to do shit to you, right?" Kali asked.

"I know. I just hate the smell of whiskey."

"Rum, then?"

Brex squinted her eyes. "Sure."

Kali took her time pouring the alcohol. Brex studied her composure. For a brief moment, she wondered how someone who had lived so long could feel so in control. But perhaps her limitless time was how. Practice.

"Rocks?" Kali asked, without looking.

"Please."

One by one, the ice plopped into the drink to make a small splash. It wasn't until Kali slowly walked back to Brex to hand her the drink that her soft trance was broken.

"Why am I here?" Brex asked before she took a sip.

"Funny," Kali commented, pulling one corner of her mouth to her cheekbone. "I thought you would have asked where Logan was first."

How did she know Logan's whereabouts were unknown? The shiver started to crawl up Brex's spine, but she shoved it right back down. Kali would have sensed it if she hadn't.

"Don't get me wrong. I was going to ask that too. Don't get ahead of yourself."

"Let me ask you something first," said Kali, putting down her already empty glass. "Why did you come here?"

"We thought Logan's father was in danger."

"No, you didn't. You knew he wasn't here. Only possibly here, only suspected that he might be here. Only feared. That, and you assumed it was an opportunity to stop me, and to figure out how to do so. You see, Brex. I mean what I say. I don't want anyone to die. That's why I haven't killed you yet."

"Yet?" Brex's facial muscles stiffened.

"That's also another reason. You're refreshingly smart, and aware. You're not entirely useless."

"Why, thank you, but no."

"No?" Kali's eyes perked with a hint of light.

"No, I won't be joining you. I think Moloch already gave Lexi the same speech."

"Oh, I don't need you to join me. You'll have plenty of time to do that once Moloch is done. And believe me. Lexi made it very clear that none of you have any interest in working alongside us. I can't blame you. I'm offering you a deal."

Kali's tone was easy to replicate. Brex's breathing stayed steady and synchronized with Kali's calm vibrations.

"You don't strike me as a 'deal' person," Brex laughed.

"And what do I strike you as?"

"Someone who just takes without asking."

"I'm polite when I want to be."

"Okay," Brex whispered without moving. "Fine, humor me. What kind of a deal?"

"Oh," Kali stretched just an inch taller and lifted her chin. "I seriously doubt this will humor you in the slightest."

"Kali...what kind of deal?"

Kali enjoyed the snapping impatience, especially since the next words that escaped her mouth were, "I can bring your family back."

The words fluttered about in her ears before they reached their destination. They didn't sit right. They didn't sit at all. Instead, they made Brex's clothes begin to finally dry due to the rising temperature wafting from her skin.

"No, you can't. And don't talk about my family."

"Do you know why I am coming to you about this?" Kali asked, leaning in, yet keeping her voice monotone. "I mean, it seems like Logan has learned so much since his mother died. She was a hero after all. Afghanistan is a nasty place, trust me. "

"Don't talk about her either."

"I'm trying to help you here, Brex. You can't possibly tell me that you wouldn't give anything to see them again. Even if it was only for ten minutes. Every single one of them. Not just one of them. All of them." There wasn't an ounce of imbalance to her voice. Brex's anger bounced higher with every word. "People say all the time they would do anything to see someone that they loved again. Trust me, they never mean it, because they know they will never get the chance. Of course, they throw words around like that, as if they were so meaningless. You. You, Brex, are different. Because I don't believe that's true for you at all."

"Why?" Brex snapped, leaning back into her.

"Because you've thought about it. Ever since you found out what was really in this world and what it was capable of, you've thought about that possibility. It's eaten at you. You've lost sleep over it. Brex, they would be alive. Truly alive. They would be themselves. Not some vampire or zombie."

"Kali..." Brex kept her voice quiet. If it was any louder, she might have not been able to stop her voice from cracking. "I just need the man that did this to be stopped. It's been too long. And you're not wrong. I am jealous that Logan is more compassionate, strong, and vulnerable than I will ever be. But I would want my family to come back to the world that they knew. Not one where they have to fight to be able to move on to the next life. Not one where they can't grow old with the people that they love."

"And what was so great about that one? Children suffering from cancer? School shootings? Pandemics? Teachers that don't care about your future? War?"

"You would start a war. A war that may never end because of what you're trying to create. And none of those things will go away. They'll just be on pause. Children's lives won't get better, they just won't get any worse. Suicidal people won't hurt other people, but they'll keep trying and keep torturing their loved ones that they leave behind. That's the worst part. The pain will never go away."

Kali didn't blink. She didn't swallow. The only thing that she did do was pull her eyes inches away from Brex's and say, "But they'll still have a chance."

Brex realized she'd been holding her breath. She released it and asked, "Kali, where is Logan?"

"I don't know," said Kali without thinking twice.

"Don't lie to me."

"I'm telling you the truth...for now." Kali turned her back to Brex, but Brex stood still, not losing sight of Kali's every move.

"Your men are still out there looking for him?"

"We're not going to hurt him. We can't." Kali's words held hollow empathy.

"Then what is it that you're going to do to him?"

"Just a little bit of blood. That's all we need."

Brex's jaw shivered and her fingers crunched together, but the moment quickly passed before she asked, "And how would you define…a little bit?"

"When are you going to understand that I'm not going to kill anyone that I don't need to?"

"Tell that to the families in Miami."

"No," Kali snapped, deepening her voice, but worse, her eyes. "This is what I am trying to tell you, Brex. You are the only ones that can stop more people from dying. Including yourselves. If you stop trying to hunt me, you will remain safe, and you will be happy with more power than you could ever imagine. Never having to rely on Moloch for more fuel. But…if you get in my way…you know I'm going to have no choice."

"Choice…right."

"I was aware early on that there was going to be collateral damage. It wasn't hard to figure that out. I'm not one of those people who doesn't lose an ounce of sleep over the tragedies and propaganda that we implement. Of course, I do."

"Why?" Brex's breath was short, but her temper was shorter.

"Why what?"

"What do you have to gain from this? Where is your family? You've been alive for how long? They're long gone. Aren't they?"

"Don't." The softness in Kali's voice didn't lessen her superiority.

"Why do you care so much?"

Kali's jaw shifted from side to side. Her knuckles turned a shade of white before she said, "Why don't you?"

"I do care. I want my family back more than anything. I mean that." Her throat hurt too much to swallow, and her eyes were too dry to cry.

"But that's just not how it works, right?" Kali brushed the small hairs off her cheeks. "Why don't you want to take advantage of what you are being given? Why don't you enjoy it?"

"I was given this ability against my will. Maya knows how I feel about it."

"Great. Then, I can take it away from you. If that's what you please." Kali nodded her head and leaned against the brick wall.

"No, no. Don't do that."

"Do what?"

"Act like you understand. Stop making it personal. And stop avoiding my question." Brex could smell the heat coming from her fingers and forearms, but she pulled her sleeves over her wrists and steadied her breath. "Why did he pick you? What made you the chosen candidate? You say you care so much, fine. I believe you. People might agree with you even. Besides those two lunks you have working for you. You're a lot smarter than them. Why are you making this so personal? What happened to you?"

Kali's eyes glistened in a sea of mystery.

"You have your version of compassion," Kali articulated. "I have mine. I just have to compromise to make it happen, that's all. Something that I'll have to live with." Kali's enunciation made Brex's shoulders twitch.

"You'll have to live with?" Brex asked. "You won't be living, Kali. You're not living now. Look at this." Brex stomped over to an ugly painting that had so much dust on the top, it almost made her cough. "Just because you drink, hang up fancy shit, decorate your so-called living room, doesn't mean you're living. You're lying to yourself. And everyone around you is lying!"

"You think I don't know that?"

"Kali, where's Logan?"

"Brex..."

"Kali, WHERE THE FUCK IS LOGAN?"

"Logan is not the one you should be worried about."

It was the lack of increasing volume that punched Brex in the gut and stirred it up in a pot of ennui, mixed with a cup of anxiety.

"What is that supposed to mean?" Brex asked, trying to once again match Kali's deceitful eyes.

"You haven't asked about your other friend. What's her name again? Krina? What on Earth made you trust an indigenous shapeshifter?"

Brex didn't know what to ask. Why was Kali asking about Krina? And how did Kali know her name? Brex stuttered to find the right words, but the right question wasn't popping out.

"Wha—?" Brex didn't have to say anything, but now she knew there was going to be a bigger obstacle.

"You remember that herb that Shani used on that TSA agent at the airport?" Kali asked. "Yes, of course I know about that. I managed to get Clement to swipe that from her once I saw that shapeshifter turn into that ugly little fox thing. She can fly, right? And fast? Cause Maya's going to be here pretty soon with the other Stone of Souls if she can."

Brex's chest collapsed, and she couldn't feel her arms.

"Oh, and what else was there?" Kali rubbed her chin. "She'll make a little stop on the way to get Persephone's flower. She's the only one that knows where it is, right?"

Brex's fingertips lit their fire before she could tell them to, but Kali was already prepared. Her shield of fireproof steel materialized in a perfect circle before it rounded about her forearm and blocked the rings of fire that Brex threw her way.

"You're taking this just as personally as I had hoped," said Kali, but Brex ignored her and threw a more dense and heated ball of flame. "This is what I mean, Brex. This control. It's overwhelming, isn't it? That's good, Brex. This is what I wanted for you. This is what you need!"

"STOP IT! BRING KRINA BACK!"

"I can't!" Kali finally lifted her chin to throw a single, thin dagger between Brex's eyes, but Brex dodged it, bending backwards and sliding out of Kali's sight.

"Ahh!" Brex tossed a ball of fire from the floor and came inches away from burning Kali's leg, but only the tip of her knees felt a sliver of heat after Kali jumped onto the coffee table.

"You could live for so much longer, Brex. You can learn. We don't get to live on this planet for long enough. We never have enough time, but now we can. We can be in control."

"No, Moloch can be in control. You can be in control. There's not a moment that you won't be at war. You know that! Kali, just tell me where Logan is."

"I don't know."

"Kali—"

"I DON'T KNOW!"

Kali's anger boiled. Her scar reddened. She couldn't hold the shield anymore. It smashed into the ground almost as if it could feel Brex's fury. The dent in the floor exploded, and small clouds of cement swirled about the elegant metal.

"This won't end well, Brex."

Brex knew that, but she didn't see it ending well in any scenario. Her thundering flames continued to rupture. The dripping lava sparked a small flame in the ravishing red carpet. Between the burning color and the crackling, popping sound of the wool burning, Brex assumed she was already in Hell.

"Telling me where Logan is won't stop you. I just need to know he's safe. Kali, please."

"How many times do I have to tell you that I don't know?"

"I don't believe you!"

Brex's chest expanded, and the back of her shoulders clenched together. The smoke around her wrists left more black than before. Maybe it was the anger, or maybe it was the magic running out.

"Brex," said Kali, trying to prove she wasn't out of breath. "What choice do you have? You're running low on fuel. You have to save yourself. Only you are in control of that. Or you can get out of my way, and I will save you myself."

"You won't be saving anyone."

Brex jumped and pounced forward to push Kali into the cement wall. Kali's superior age was showing. Kali's combative stance was made for motion. More clouds of sand outlined her body and the dent that she made in the wall. Her strength was something Brex would never be able to capture in her photographs. But Kali's head quickly snapped back, unfazed by the pain of blunt force trauma, and immune to being ripped from the solid ground.

Kali's deep echoing scream bounced off the walls and exploded in Brex's ears, but Brex didn't let her eyes close. Not for a second.

"Where's Krina? Tell me!" Brex spat in Kali's face.

"She's already gone. What are you going to do about it anyway?"

Kali sliced thin blades from her knuckles and pulled them above her head. Her reflexes were strong, but Brex's motivation to get back to her friends was stronger. She leaped back and tumbled over the couch, knocking it forward. Kali's face almost matched the color of Brex's skin when her fire was about to erupt. With one smooth motion, Kali lifted the couch and flipped it to an upright position. But her anger quickly shifted to confusion. Brex wasn't there.

"Oh come on," said Kali with a loose twang to her voice, but the silence didn't last long. Brex jumped out from around the corner only to keep the flames lit from her skin high enough to reach the ceiling. It was almost too hot for even Brex to bear. A single drop of sweat dripped from the peak of her forehead, all the way down to her jawline. The flames highlighted the sparkle that Brex displayed. But the only thing that caught Kali's eye was the bottle of whiskey in Brex's hand that flew into the air and smothered itself in lightning-orange flames.

BOOOOOOOM!

Even the rats and mice reacted to the explosion. To Brex, it was another earthquake. Kali's scar trembled and ripened in color before the flames knocked her off her feet and threw her into the wooden bar. The polished tabletop shattered into pieces. Brex couldn't tell if the wood had impaled Kali, but even if she had had time to look, the flames wrapped themselves around the exploded furniture.

Brex had to see for herself. Otherwise, she never would have known. Not an inch of that room was visible. The fire blanketed anything that would let it. The paintings, the couch. But Brex could still see the door, and it pulled her to it like a magnet.

The door ripped open. Maybe it was the melting metal, or maybe the fire ignited her strength more than she thought.

"LOGAN!" she screamed the moment she threw herself out of the doorway. Kali had to have him. She had to know where he was. Kali was probably planning on using him for some sort of leverage.

Four different hallways stood in front of her. Looking at the first one gave her nothing but anxiety. She didn't know why, but the darkness reflecting in her soul trampled her stomach and turned it into one giant knot. Then she stared down the rest of them. None of them gave her the slightest lure to draw her in. They looked exactly the same; dark with a small speck of light that would probably lead her in circles like before, but then the answer was clear. She took one giant breath and went down the first hallway.

"LOGAN!" she screamed again, but all she could hear was her echo. What if he was tied up? What if he was passed out? She wasn't sure if she was going to have enough time, but what choice did she have? Every door needed to be opened and searched.

The first door on her left was empty. The second on her right was the same, but the third one at the end of the hall not only tied a knot in her stomach like before, but this time, the door bounded onto her stomach and trampled it against the floor. Something had to be in there.

"Logan?!" Brex asked as she threw open the door. It wasn't the handsome face that she was expecting to see that was tied to the chair, but instead a different one. "Jethro? What did you do?"

22:

"Why don't you just take my blood right now?"

Maya and Zara sat on the patio outside of Maya's house. It was a quiet evening except for the crickets and the occasional howl. Maya sat with tea and a blanket while Zara fidgeted with her dress and mane that was tucked under her long, curved horns.

"Have you heard from them lately?" Zara asked. She hadn't spoken with Maya in some time. She hadn't had the chance. She was in hiding after her sanctuary was discovered the year before in the White Mountains of New Hampshire.

"No, but Shiva told me Shani made it into his sanctuary alive. He said she hardly seemed distraught or suspicious in any way. 'Strong-headed with too soft of a heart' were his exact words."

"That sounds like him." Zara smiled. "How is Baymour doing? He seems happy." On the back lawn, Baymour was overjoyed to be playing with his new chew toy; a seven-foot-tall stuffed bear that resembled him to the extent that it made Zara laugh into her bubbly tea.

"He is, he needs to leave here soon. He needs to be free. We all do."

Zara gently placed her tea on the side table and rubbed her palms against her thighs. "Maya. May I ask you something?"

"Of course, dear."

"Are you sure they don't know?"

Maya intertwined her fingers and pulled them to her stomach. "I can't think of anyone who would have told them. No one knows except you and me. Besides, they're all too smart to let something like that take them off track. Their determination is too powerful, and their sensibility protects them from harm."

"Would it really hurt for them to know that one of them has the powers of Athena? It might come of use to them."

"No," Maya snapped. She gently set her tea down on the wobbly table. "Each one of their abilities is unique. They are quickly learning and growing stronger by the minute, but getting weaker by the second. Their skills and accuracy are improving, but they will need the energy of Moloch's essence to recharge their power soon. They have to preserve as much power as they can. They have to stay alive. I don't know what would happen if Athena's powers were to manifest. What would happen to her original magic? Would it be smothered and leave her almost defenseless?"

Zara didn't nod. She didn't say anything. She only leaned back and continued to blankly stare into the night sky, hoping the calm night wouldn't be disturbed by the bushes that twitched in the shadows, but to her annoyance, it was. They wouldn't stop. The wind refused to end the riotous harassment.

"Do you hear something?" Zara asked. The cracking sounds of sticks and branches snapping in half weren't breaking the peace. It was swirling her soul into a whirlpool of fear. No one knew where they were, but maybe some*thing* did.

"Ruff!" Baymour heard it too. For the first time all night, he dropped his chew toy and stood guard, paws kneading the ground.

"Yes," said Maya standing up, "but stay silent."

Zara did as she was told. She was tempted to turn on the other outdoor lights, but she didn't know where they were, and Maya would have done that by now if she had thought it wise. The shiny, animated leaves fluttered in the distance and reflected the little light available. Eventually, the snapping faded away. Each moment of silence was longer than the last, until they couldn't hear anything anymore. Not even the crickets.

"I don't know what it is, but something's wrong," Maya whispered. "Into the house." But they couldn't go back into the house. Something was blocking it. A tall, beautiful, white-haired woman stood in front of the doorway. Her eyes were drained of any hope, and her sweaty skin was as red as a rose.

"I'm sorry, Maya."

*****

"Jethro," Brex sighed, trying to untie him. "What did you do? And why haven't you been able to get out of this?" Whatever was leaking from the ceiling dripped onto Brex's dirty cheeks, and Jethro's hair was drenched in it. The walls were made of black and green cement bricks like the rest of the hallways that Brex had already seen, but this room was filled with mold. There had to be something else in there. Brex could smell it, but it was too dark to see. Part of the ceiling was missing. Maybe it was some sort of well, but there was a small beam of moonlight that bounced off Jethro's tired eyes.

"It's some sort of drug that they've given me." Jethro almost lost his breath in that one small sentence, and it was having trouble finding its way back. "I think it's in the rope. Careful. I don't know what it is, but Brex, you have to get out of here. They're going to kill you."

"I know. Why didn't you tell us before?" She threw down the rope and tried to look at him, but he couldn't return the gesture.

"How did you know it was me that told Kali where they were?"

"I didn't until you told me just now."

Suddenly, he found her eyes, but he had a hard time keeping them there. "I'm sorry, Brex. He was going to hurt my mother."

"She would have found out anyway. We can't keep secrets from her. Besides, you weren't the mole. Dimitria was."

"What?"

"She's also dead by the way."

"How?" Jethro's mouth trembled and his eyes watered, but Brex couldn't tell where his pain was coming from.

"Lexi killed her. She was going to kill us."

"Are you sure?"

"Yes, I'm sure." Brex stood, towering above his limp body that still dangled off the metal chair. Her patience created such a wave, the small light that hung from the ceiling almost swung off its hinges."I'm sorry. I know it's hard for you to hear. But Krina is going to get Maya from her home."

"How?"

"Shani's powder. We have to be ready. They'll be back any minute."

"I'm sorry, Brex." Jethro's chest begged for relief. Brex didn't respond, but instead placed a gentle hand on his bloody knee. "Where are the others?" he asked.

"I can't tell you."

His jaw quivered. "Why?"

"I can't trust you. You gave me up to Kali. Don't take it personally. I can't trust anyone right now, but I can help you. I just can't let you be one step ahead of me."

"Okay...okay fine."

The beat-up Nikes slid under his feet, but his knees rallied enough for him to stand up. Slowly.

"What do you need?" Brex asked.

"Nothing."

But Brex wasn't about to take that for an answer. By the amount of blood that mixed in with the water on the floor, she couldn't believe that was true. A sudden thud made the ceiling shake like a gong. Brex wouldn't find the time to argue with him even if she wanted to.

"Come on, just take my arm."

He didn't argue, but the second Brex returned to the black hole that was the endless hallway, she realized none of the directions were calling for her.

"Shit," Brex whispered.

"Brex...Brex," Jethro's stomach was still too bruised to hold himself up and talk at the same time.

"What?"

"To the right."

Brex took the suggestion, with open eyes and head straight forward.

"To the left."

Soon, they were moving fast. She didn't know how they lasted this long, but her eyes were finally fogging. No matter how many times she blinked, they couldn't focus. She checked her palm. Her heart picked up the pace.

"Guys!" she hollered, not caring if Kali heard her.

"Wait, Brex—"

"GUYS!" She knew what he was going to say, but her patience wasn't scarce. It had already ended. Cut into strips, then into a million pieces.

The only thing they could hear were the sounds of faint droplets of water that quickly pricked the corners of the room.

"Jethro," said Brex, quickly gasping for breath. "I need you to walk on your own."

"I know, I know. I can do it."

He let go of her shoulder, but in exchange coughed up blood and spat it on the floor.

"Jesus," said Brex. "What did they give you?"

"I don't know, but I've never been sick before. I didn't even know you could do that. How do you people stay alive?"

"Good question. GUYS!"

Still, nothing was to be heard. If Brex got close enough to the wall, she could hear old pipes creaking as water ran through them. Maybe a few mice, or maybe something bigger.

"GUYS!" Her scratchy throat wasn't going to be able to handle much more. If only she could get more of that whisky. "GUYS! GUYS! HU—"

The hand was icy and wet. It smelled like burnt grass, but Brex couldn't imagine why. It pressed tightly against her mouth. She could still hear Jethro's leg dragging behind him. The hand couldn't belong to him. She could only wonder what Jethro was doing. Why wasn't he stopping this hand? Did he already turn on her? No. How would he benefit from her trust? They already had people for that. But never mind Jethro. If he wasn't coming to help, she could do it by herself, but she did have one last question that stirred in the back of her head. What was this person doing? They were still and trying to shush her. Shush her?

"Shhhh..." the voice said. "It's me."

"Logan." She didn't know if he was injured, but she threw her arms around him anyway. She didn't want to let go, so she didn't. She stayed listening to his beating chest. Same as it was earlier. Deep, with passion manifesting in every beat.

"Come on," he said, sliding his arms down to her hands, unable to fully pull himself away. "We need to find the others."

"Okay, yeah," said Brex.

Logan lifted his eyelids, cleared his throat, and rolled his eyes before he asked, "Jethro, you good?" Only doing so because he didn't want Jethro to hold them back.

"Yes," Jethro swallowed, finally able to stand without wobbling. "I'm great."

Brex led the way. She didn't need Jethro's directions anymore. The only sense of direction she had was the gravitational pull of noise. The only clue. The Green Room was a noisy place that threatened to explode with pressure at any moment. Brex listened for the source of that pressure.

"This way," but she immediately regretted it. It wasn't right. A warning slid into her chest like a knife. She didn't know who put it there or why it was there in the first place, but it slid in deeper with every step she took.

"Wait." She snapped her arm in front of the two men who trailed behind her, but they couldn't see or hear anything. Neither did Brex, but that didn't stop her. She looked between her fingers to steady her focus, but the calm didn't last.

BOOM!

The wall behind them crumbled down in an avalanche that almost swept them off their feet. The small light that shimmered behind the silhouette nearly blinded them, but Brex forced herself to keep her fuzzy eyes open to see what threat Clement had prepared for them.

Clement's hulking body emerged from the clouds. His muscles tightened, and the veins that ran down his biceps and forearms bulged in anger. The cloudy dust that circled around his head mixed with the steam that burned from his skin. His giant, steel-toed boots led him over one boulder that was somehow still intact. Even after he picked it up and tossed it into Logan's stomach, the cylindrical cement stayed in one piece.

"Whoa!" Logan dropped to the wet floor, dodging the mistle before the tire-sized boulder was able to rupture his appendix. It busted through the back wall and rolled out of sight. The pulsing, cemented floor almost bounced Logan back off the floor, and the water that slithered in between the cracks menaced him.

Brex saw the trail of thought leaving his head and into hers. With a simple yet throbbing throw forward, Brex aimed her fire straight for Clement's chest, leaving him nowhere to go but down. His hands slapped the floor, and the moment his skin made the rippling slash, Logan zapped the water with enough watts to light every Christmas tree in London.

"Ahhhhh!" Clement screamed. The light in his dark, yellow eyes sparked once he was able to open them again. But his anger couldn't power him like before. The steam wasn't as hot, and his veins weren't as visible. That didn't stop Brex from pulling Logan and Jethro away from Clement.

"Come on!" she said.

The only hall that was empty didn't carry enough light. But Brex wasn't about to choose between running with light or walking without.

"Don't worry," said Logan, picking up his feet. "I'm right here with you."

They lit the hallway with fire and lightning. The sphere of bolts wrapped itself down Logan's arm. Attached to the other arm was Brex's, both tight and unbreakable.

The hallway was longer than most, but they reached the end, only to throw their tired bodies up against the bricks to find themselves at a dead end.

"So *now* there's a dead end?" Logan shouted.

"Not exactly," said a voice from above. They snapped their heads upwards to see Reymid no more than ten feet above their heads, standing over the lip of an open trapped door. His bow was ready, but by the time they could take another breath, his arrow had already left his shadowed image. They didn't even have time to flinch, except for Jethro. Only Jethro's definition of flinching included a galaxy of stars that shielded everyone's heads and made the arrow bounce off the sparkling force field.

"Whoa," Logan whispered, forgetting to hide his fascination.

"Go!" Jethro screamed. The arrows kept coming, but when Brex and Logan ducked and ran back down the darkened hallway, Reymid jumped down and threw Jethro off his center.

"Ah!" The force field didn't break, but only dispersed. Reymid's boots hit the floor, cracking the cement.

"Jethro!" Brex screamed when she heard the presence of another voice. They couldn't see what was happening behind the shadows, but Reymid couldn't pull out another arrow in time before Brex could throw three balls of fire straight onto his jacket.

"Shit!" He quickly patted the flames off him but not before the heat burned the flesh of his abdomen.

"Go!" Jethro said, once again picking up speed. "I'll block him."

Brex and Logan put their trust in him. They could hear the sound of arrows bouncing off Jethro's force fields, but still diminishing his strength. Reymid was gaining on them. His burns were probably healed by now, but that wasn't the worst of their problems. Clement's probably were too. He could at least stand, and he made that clear when he stomped his way in front of their only exit.

"B—Brex," Logan stuttered, but Brex's jaw was locked tight. She had no plan. None of them did. Brex took one more look at her scar. Only one more notch left. She couldn't risk it, not when Jethro was there.

"Jethro," she said. "Get us out of here."

With heavy breath, he managed to mumble, "There's no way I can—"

"TRY!"

But it was too late. Clement didn't have to use a rock or any weapon to punch the air out of their lungs. Only his clenching fists, which he wrapped around their necks before throwing Logan and Brex to the floor.

Brex tried to burn his skin with the least amount of flame she could ignite, but even if she wanted to ignite any more fire or take one more look at Logan, she lost sight, hearing, and feeling before her arms fell to the floor. Elbows, wrists, then knuckles. But she didn't feel any of it.

•••••

"Brex?" Brex heard before she could open her eyes. "Brex?" she heard again, a little louder. "Brex, come on. You have to get up."

Logan's voice trailed on for a few more minutes before it forced Brex's eyes to open.

"Logan?" Brex wasn't sure if she was talking or making sense. She could hardly feel her lips moving. "Logan, where are we?"

Wherever they were, it was dark, but they had been moved. Was it a dream? Everything was numb. It wasn't until Logan squeezed her bicep that she realized she was propped up on his lap.

"Are you okay?" she asked.

"I'm fine," he said, smiling at her. "But we're not safe."

"Where are we?"

"Don't listen to him," said a familiar voice. "You're safe. Only for now, but you are safe. I'm afraid I can't say the same for Logan, but you already knew that."

"You can kill us, Kali," Brex mumbled, still unable to control her jaw. "Or trap us, or whatever. It won't matter. We aren't helping you."

"I was just being courteous." Kali sat in a creaky old chair. They were in a new room. A bigger one that looked like it hadn't been cleaned in over a hundred years. Maybe that was true, but it had been lived in, but by whom?

"Are you sure you weren't trying to stall?" Logan asked.

"Stall for what, Logan?" Kali's hushed tranquility made her small, with a cracked smile conspicuously prominent. "You've left me no choice at this point, but I must admit I've decided to alter my strategies."

"And how are you going to do that?" Brex spat.

Kali slowly stood up. They'd never seen her so dirty before. The soot under her eyes only made the gold color stand out more. Nonetheless, her poise remained. "Well, I've taken the time to look at your scar, Brex. You can feel the power draining out of you and the fatigue fighting to take its place. You don't have much time left. I can help you."

"I know you can." Brex swallowed her pride and shivered in Logan's arms. "But you're not going to." Brex looked around and noticed something was missing. "Jethro." Her voice suddenly cleared up. "Where's Jethro?"

"Don't mind that now. I wouldn't worry about it. I'm giving you one last chance, Brex. And remember you are in no position to negotiate. Either come with me voluntarily or...well, I don't think you'd be interested in hearing the other option."

Brex's shivering stopped, but her jaw remained tight, and her breathing was still rocky.

"Fine," she said. "Take me. Let Logan go."

"Oh, no, dear." Kali bent down to her level, inches away from Brex's face. "That's the whole idea. I know you say that you're okay with dying, but what about him?" Kali turned to face Logan and locked eyes with him. "And what about her?"

Kali grabbed Brex out of Logan's arms. Logan reached out to stop Kali, but Reymid's arrow was faster. The pain didn't sink in until the first drop of blood leaked from the wound. But he didn't scream, not until he saw Kali holding one of her smooth silver daggers against Brex's throat.

"No!" Logan screeched. He pulled the arrow out of his forearm, but before he could use it, Reymid pulled Logan's arms behind him and wrapped them in a smooth yet stinging rope. Whatever energy he had, whatever happiness he had vanished the moment the material encompassed his skin.

"Don't try to fight it, Logan," Kali resolutely said. "I see the way you look at her. I've seen it many times before, but not with your faith. You look at her like you might never see her face again. Every time. Without fail. Right now is no different. That is something special. So, I'll give you a choice, Logan. Either she dies, or you give yourself up. She's too weak. But you, you're strong. You might have a fighting chance to take me down. So, I'll need your word and cooperation. You decide."

"Why don't you just take my blood right now?" Logan cried. "You have me cornered. I'm bleeding right now, just take it. Please, Kali. Just take it."

"Oh, right." Kali laughed, rolling her eyes. "I forgot to mention." Kali's dagger elongated. It slithered and stretched out to become a circle; a bladed noose. It wrapped itself around Brex's neck, almost choking her, but she froze solid and kept breathing...carefully. "This iron is special. It was simple to make if I'm being honest. You'd be surprised with what Moloch has managed to find over the years." She let go of Brex, but still, Brex remained frozen. "If you don't carry out your responsibilities in the next hour, this will slice Brex's head off. Trust me. No amount of magic will fix that. I need your blood fresh Logan. I can't just store it in a bottle and bring it to the mountains. I also can't take it from you and have you rip it out of my hands once I let Brex go. Your turning wheels aren't hidden very well, Logan."

Logan's heart began to choke him. It was desperately fighting to escape his ribcage, or maybe it was the enchanted rope. He wasn't sure. He couldn't take his eyes off Brex.

"Logan," she whispered. "Don't do it. You have to let me go. It's okay. Just let me go." Tears fell from her glassy eyes.

"Logan," said Kali. "You have ten seconds to decide."

"Logan, don't do it. Don't go with them. You can escape! Leave me behind. It's just me. Everyone else is depending on you."

The longer he looked at her, the closer she seemed. He could describe every detail about her. Her hair had never been so tangled, but it fell delicately over her ears and past her shoulders. Her eyes never lost their twinkle. Her skin never stopped radiating and glowing like the sun. Never.

"You can do it," Brex whispered. "It's okay. Just let me go."

"FIVE SECONDS!" Kali's voice cracked.

Logan let his breath stop for a moment, just a single, yet long perpetual moment. Brex was never going to forgive him, but he had no other choice. Brex's life wasn't negotiable. Not to him.

"I'll go with you," he whispered.

"NO! LOGAN!" Brex fell to the floor. Reymid grabbed Logan by the bicep but kept the rope tied tightly around his upper body. Logan didn't fight. He didn't blink. His eyes never left Brex.

"You're coming with me," Reymid whispered in Logan's ear.

"NO!" Brex couldn't stop screaming. The words vomited from the back of her throat.

"I would advise you to stay quiet, Brex. You should be grateful that he let you live. But since you chose not to join me willingly, I feel no obligation to help you. I'll let your friends do that instead."

Brex's throat couldn't move. Not because the metal was tightening, but because Logan was slowly being pulled away from her. Logan's lost eyes drowned in sorrow but fought to stay on Brex until the door slammed shut.

"I'm going to need you to stay put for a while," Kali whispered with a sense of mocking concern stirring in her voice. "We'll talk later, but right now, come with me." Kali pulled her by her arm, but Brex crumbled to her feet, fighting for her breath and strength. The iron tightened around her neck the harder she fought. "Clement! Carry her." Clement rushed to her assistance and swept Brex off her feet. Her head hung loose off his forearm, but she kept her eyes wide open.

"Where are we going?" Brex mumbled.

"I would save your breath if I were you."

They stumbled along. Down the stairs and to the left before Brex could feel a rush of energy. She couldn't tell if a door opened or not. But something did. Something familiar.

"Gently," said Kali, watching him lower Brex to the cold floor.

"Brex?!" a familiar voice hollered. Brex was back in the green room. Trapped once again. "Brex!" it said again. It was Lexi rushing to Brex's aid. The spectacle of Kali and Clement standing over Brex didn't delay Lexi for a second.

"What did you do to her?" Lexi asked, wiping the tears away and brushing the hair out of Brex's face.

"She had a choice, Lexi. So did Logan, but he made the right one, eventually." Kali crouched down to look into Lexi's eyes. She grabbed a hold of Lexi's wet chin and forced Lexi to look at her. "I know you don't understand. I promise you, you will soon."

Lexi pulled her face away. Kali stood up before she snapped her fingers, and Bai appeared before her.

"No," Bai muttered. Her hair and blue dress blew in the wind as she magically materialized.

"Finally," Kali smiled, not looking at Bai at all, but instead at the radiant, sapphire stone around her neck, before ripping it off. "Thank you for taking such good care of it. You've preserved its power. You are the fuel we needed. You're the only one who could have done it. You should be proud."

"Bai?" Shani shouted, running to her from a hundred feet away. "Bai, NO!" Her long legs pushed faster than she thought they could go. The ground burned from the friction. But the floor turned to a game of dominos when Clement punched the cement ground so vigorously, the stone rippled away from him and knocked Shani off her feet.

"Let's go before the Hermes one arrives," Kali told Clement. "One more thing." Kali put her finger to her mouth. "If you stay put until I get back, I promise no harm will come to you. You'll be great fuel for this place anyway. Brex, once Logan gives me what I need, that iron will be released from your neck. Your head will remain intact. But it won't matter. If you escape, I'll hunt you all, and I won't be alone."

The black hole vanished behind her and Clement. They disappeared into the void while the green mist replaced them.

"Lexi?" Brex mumbled. She shook her fingers, toes, nose, and anything else that she could move. Her gaze slowly crawled its way back to her, but she couldn't manage to sit up yet.

"What happened?" Lexi asked. "Where's Logan?"

The tears returned, or maybe they never left. "He went with them. We have to stop them."

"Brex," said Shani, coming out of nowhere. "What's this around your neck? Brex, how do we get it off?" Shani gently touched the metal that choked Brex. She flinched in even more pain than before.

"He has to go with them, give them as much blood as they ask, or else this will kill me. That fucking idiot."

The others stayed silent. It remained that way until Asher came soaring in, and his wings clapped together.

"Brex?" Asher hollered. "Where did you go?"

"Hello?!" hollered another voice in the distance. "Hello?!" Footsteps bounced against the floor, echoing in the distance. The rest didn't know how to respond, but the echoing grew louder before Jethro appeared from around the corner.

"Oh, God," said Shani, examining his bloody wounds. "What happened to you?"

"J—Jethro?" Bai stuttered. She stood up from a kneeling position with tears in her eyes.

"Mom?" He almost tripped over his own foot, running to her. She caught him in her arms before they melted back to the floor. "I thought I would never see you again."

They stayed silent. But the air pressure increased the longer they stayed still.

"Are you okay?" Asher asked.

"I'm fine," Jethro replied. "Where's Logan?"

"He went with them," said Brex, still sitting on the floor. "They have everything. Everything that they need."

"Are you sure?" Bai asked.

"Yes. We have to go. We have to get out of here." Brex looked around, but they were cornered in the Green Room. A maze of boulders and smoke suddenly surrounded them with no exit out of the corner, let alone the Green Room.

"How?" Asher asked. "I can't even remember how we got in here, and we don't know how to get through the black holes."

"We don't have time to stay here," said Shani, "and where are they even going? If we don't leave right now, we'll lose them." Shani collapsed to the floor, running her fingers through her tangled hair. The rest stayed quiet as they pondered, except for Lexi.

"Why is the nucleus of the spell here?" Lexi asked.

"What?"

"Remember when Kali called Logan and she said that we would know why they wanted us to come to the Pyramids?"

"Because the nucleus and Bai are here," said Shani.

"Yes, but why? Why did they choose a tourist area where they would probably be seen?" The rest knitted their eyebrows and clenched their jaws. "Something's here. Something that needs protection. It's kind of like...this is *their* sanctuary."

Shani released a painful exhale before she said, "Yeah, it's probably this that needs protecting." Her arms flailed about, pointing in every which way.

"What about this place makes it look like it needs protecting?" Lexi kept her chin down but turned to Jethro. "Jethro, would any witch be able to disintegrate this thing, or destroy it in any way?"

"None that I know of. It would take multiple witches, hundreds of potions, and years to make any sort of dent. I don't even know where we would begin. Moloch probably was planning this hundreds of years before the gods were laid to rest."

"Right." Lexi began pacing but kept her focus on the floor. She tied her hair out of her face and cleared her throat. "They're protecting something here. Guarding something."

"Wait," said Shani. "Where did he get all of the energy from before Bai arrived? When he was building it. What did he fuel this place with?"

Lexi snapped her fingers. "Brilliant. Bai?"

"He never told me," she responded, "but it had to come from somewhere. Although, creating something like this isn't easy. He wouldn't be able to create something like this on his own. He must have had help. Whoever it was, they probably contained too much darkness in their soul to live long enough to see it."

Lexi's knuckles cracked against her thighs. "What if they weren't alive at all?" Her voice was soft, but they heard every word.

"What?" Bai asked.

"What if this place was fueled by something dead, but their entity still existed?"

"Are you—?" Shani didn't want to ask, but she managed to let the words slip out. "Do you think it was—?"

"The Moloch that came before him?"

"Lucifer..." Bai gasped. "The leader before Moloch. You think he's here?"

"It's a stretch, but I can't think of anything else."

Brex slowly stood up. "Where are our scars at?" she asked. They all checked with anxiety manifesting in their eyes. Except for Lexi.

"Lexi?" Shani asked.

"Moloch filled me back up," she said, clenching her jaw.

"What? Why?" Shani asked.

"Can we talk about this later?" Asher asked.

"Asher's right," Brex stopped them. "Lexi, you and Jethro should try and find Logan. The rest of us need to look for Lucifer's remains."

"Okay," said Lexi, finally leveling her chin.

"But first," said Shani, raising her voice and gently enunciating her words, "we need to find a way out of here."

No more words needed to be exchanged. Brex led them on the pathway she vaguely remembered before her encounter with Kali.

Lightning, fire, black hole, waterfall, mountain, she repeated this to herself.

"This way!" she hollered to the rest before turning left. Every corner looked the same. They could have been going in circles.

Lightning, fire, black hole, waterfall, mountain.

"Hello?!" they heard coming near them.

"Oh God," Shani mumbled. "Not more..."

"Hello?!" it said again, only this time, no one recognized it.

There was no water around them. No earthly belongings. Defenses were useless, but the voice only got closer.

"Over here!" Asher shouted.

"Asher!" Shani loudly whispered.

"What? Why would an enemy shout for us?"

"Oh come—"

"Hello." Their chests popped like a fire mixing with gasoline. Before them, stood a curvy, young woman with long hair and thick horns wrapped around her head and tucked behind her ears.

"Um, hello?" Asher muttered.

"I'm Zara."

23:

"This is where Lucifer is buried."

"Zara?" Shani asked. "Maya's former apprentice?" She was much smaller than they predicted. Her clothes were skin tight, even her black boots that were knee high and gave her at least an inch in height. The only thing that hung off her was the long, silver and gold jacket that draped over her hips and down to the floor.

"That's right," Zara responded.

"Zara, do you know the way out of here?" Lexi asked.

"Yes, the door is close, but Maya and Krina are already at the Iconic Tower. If we are going to go, we need to go now."

"Where is that?" Shani asked.

"It's not far from here."

"Okay," said Lexi. "Let's go."

The others followed Zara but had trouble keeping up. Her legs were almost invisible when running. She was right; the exit was close to them. But what she failed to mention was that the hidden door had locked behind her when she entered.

"Damn it," said Shani.

"Stand back," Zara gently spoke. They did as they were told, but when Zara punched the door open, hardly touching it, they wished that she had also given a warning to cover their heads.

"Hohhh..." Asher whispered.

"Follow me."

Zara stayed low, but her eyes remained straightforward.

"How do you know where you're going?" Shani asked.

"Dracotaurs, a cross between a human and a dragon, have impeccable vision that can see through most walls and around corners, and...what do you call it in the photography industry?"

"Zoom in and out?" Brex asked.

"Yes, I believe that's correct."

They reached the end of a hallway. Few lights surrounded them, but Zara quickly changed that.

Wooooosh!

A blast of fire raced from her lips. Her breath almost blinded the rest, except for Brex. One by one, the torches lit up all the way down the hall, but right above them was a rusty, dented symbol of freedom.

"I got everyone," said Asher. His wings sprouted once more even though his wings barely fit within the hallway, and the tips scraped off loose pieces of cement. He kicked open the rusty door before he jumped back down ten feet to the floor.

"Waist good?" Asher asked.

"Fine by me," Brex said.

Asher grabbed onto her waist and hoisted her up to the door. Bai was next after Lexi, Shani, and Jethro. But when he offered his hand to Zara, she politely and gently declined with a soft head shake and glided up to the door by herself.

"You can do that without wings?" Asher asked.

"You can't?" she asked, keeping her voice deep and relaxed. "I'm kidding." But she didn't laugh. Not even a curve of the mouth. "I can only jump as high as a kangaroo. Believe me, I wish I could fly as you can."

"Do you?" Asher asked, shaking his amused head before he felt a small nudge from something large and wet behind him. "Whoa, Baymour?"

Baymour was probably happiest to see Asher, but that was only because Asher petted and scratched him under his chin just the way he liked it. Nobody else got it quite right.

"Baymour, what are you doing here?" Brex asked, rubbing her cheek along his soft fur and feeling the wind from his large, wagging tail.

"Believe me," said Zara. "It wasn't easy."

"We need to go," said Brex. "Now. Lexi and Jethro, you good to go with Zara?"

"We're good," Lexi nodded. "Go get Lucifer."

Jethro reached for his mother, hugging her tighter than before.

"Be safe," she whispered to him.

"I will. Don't worry about me."

She leaned back to look at him and brushed his long, blonde hair out of his face, and tucked it behind his ears.

"I'll accompany you to the Tower," said Zara. "You'll need extra hands. Come on, Baymour." He kneeled down and let Asher, Zara, and Brex hop onto him one by one, patiently waiting but building up his excitement for a run of a lifetime.

"Thank you," said Lexi. "Go, you don't have much time."

The seven of them parted ways. Asher hovered above their heads while Shani kept looking over her shoulder until the three others and Baymour were too far out in the distance.

"Shani," said Brex, grabbing her hand as they jogged toward the first Pyramid. "Shani, it's okay."

"I know," said Shani, trusting someone else's instincts for once. "Let's go!"

They ran faster. Even Bai slowly increased her pace. Her painful breath managed to keep up, but luckily, they didn't have far to go.

There it was, the Great Pyramid of Khufu. From where they were standing, the moon sat on the tip of the pyramid. It looked like a lamp from a children's bedroom. The gray and brown silhouette expanded until it smothered the starry night sky until they could finally see the individual bricks that made up the wondrous structure.

"I see an entrance!" Brex screamed. Under a small shadow was an entrance that had to be locked, but Brex didn't know that before she crossed her arms in front of her face and ran straight through it without slowing down.

"Ow, ow, ow." Brex didn't see any blood on herself, but the wood was still sharp.

"Whoa!" said Asher, backing up and almost breaking his flight pattern.

"Brex," said Shani, examining the demolition in front of her. "There's no lock on this door."

"Oh."

They ran up the stairs and into the gallery. Night lights were on, but somehow, no alarm was to be seen anywhere near them. At the other end of the room were two staircases, one going up and the other going down.

"There's got to be some sort of guard," said Asher, finally putting his feet on the ground.

"Yeah, no." Shani shook her head. "They would have a guard keeping watch on this thing at all times, wouldn't they?"

"So that's how we know where it is," said Brex.

"Brex," said Asher, kissing her forehead. "Once we find the guard, we'll find Lucifer. You are a genius. Come on, Bai, you and I will go up, Brex and Shani go down."

"Meet back here immediately if you don't find anything," said Bai. "Then we should check the other two pyramids next."

They all nodded as they clumsily made their way to their respective areas. Brex and Shani bolted down to the lower chamber. They both tried not to fall or go too fast as they hurried down the ramp, but if it hadn't been for Shani's long legs, Brex wouldn't have gotten tangled up in them and caused them both to trip and spiral down the ramp.

"Wait!" said Bai. "I see something up here!"

"Ow," said Brex, sitting up. "Great."

She pulled Shani up by the elbows, and they made their way back up to the other two, who were staring at a map of the entire campus.

"You didn't know there was a cemetery here?" Asher asked.

"No," Bai replied, hastily. "I didn't get a chance to explore the area outside when I first got here. I've been in the Green Room ever since."

Shani jumped over to the map. It was old and needed to be retouched, but they were right. But where would the remains of a creature that was never human be?

"Let's go take a look," said Brex. She led the way, but before she could reach the entrance, she noticed something was different.

"What the—?"

"So, that's the hex..." Shani whispered under her breath.

The door before them wasn't broken. It wasn't even open or unhinged. It was shut, and shiny clean, with a sparkling finish over the wood that made it radiate in beauty against the sandy cement. This time, they knew it was locked without having to try to open it. That didn't stop Shani from running against it faster than Brex had or faster than she had run down the ramp.

"Shani," said Brex.

"Ow!" said Shani as she crashed and caressed her shoulder.

"Don't worry," said Bai. "He didn't build this with me in mind."

Bai brushed her hair out of her face before she stepped forward, but her foot didn't meet the floor. Instead, the scales of a small, white snake slithered against the floor. Her transformation was faster and smoother than anything that they had seen Krina do so far.

Unlike Krina, she didn't speak, but her flashing, bright, red eyes said everything she needed to. She slithered around the rest of the group before her smooth scales slid across the exfoliating cement floor and straight under the enchanted door that should have used a stronger spell.

"Hot damn," said Asher, before he heard a click on the other side of the door. The ugly fluorescent light shone down on Bai's gray and black hair when she opened the door and stepped outside. Somehow the sky was already darker.

"Cemetery?" Brex asked.

"Crypt," Bai responded.

They ran around to the other side of the Pyramid. Shani assumed it wouldn't take as long as it did, but she distracted herself by watching Asher soar around the Pyramid. He looked like a fly, zooming around a human head.

"Is that it?" Brex asked, coming to a halt, stopping at the corner. In the distance, the land before them looked less like a graveyard and more like a battlefield with no more castles standing. A few tourist lights remained lit, but the orange and sandy rectangular tombs lay flat with ancient dents and dusty layers of sand.

"The graveyard?" Shani asked.

The wind's whistle was too loud for Shani to hear her friends running behind her, but she could sense their clenched fists fighting their attempt to stay calm.

"I suppose so," said Bai.

"What do you think is guarding it?" Asher asked.

"Let's hope we find out as soon as we step foot in there."

The four of them shook the ground as they leaped forward. In the distance, they could see the sky turning a dark misty gray. No sun was to be seen, but time ticked next to their ears, and the echo grew louder and faster with every second.

"Let's split up!" said Shani. "Brex, with me. This way!" They steered to the left.

"This way," said Bai, beckoning Asher to the right.

The grid of large, rectangular tombs, mausoleums, ruins, and stone coffins stuck out of the ground and created a game of Jenga. What they were looking for could be anywhere.

"Are we going to open all of these?" Brex asked.

"Only the ones that look like they've been opened in the last few hundred years," said Shani. "I highly doubt anyone's magic is that sophisticated."

Brex tried to focus on finding the hidden cache, but instead, her eyes were obeying her ears' every command. If she heard a single sizzle of noise from behind her, she had no choice. The threat could be anywhere.

"Shani," said Brex. "Do you see anything?" But there was no answer. "Shani?" And no Shani.

"Mmmm!"

Brex heard the mumble coming from the other side of the tomb that she was standing next to. She couldn't see anything until she jumped over it and landed right on top of Shani's barely conscious body, straddling her, one leg over each hip.

"Oh my God, Shani!" Brex screamed, trying to help her stand up. If it wasn't for the metal around her neck, she would have gotten whiplash from how quickly she had wrapped her arms around Shani.

"My head. Shit...my ankle..." Shani mumbled.

"Your ankle? Does it hurt?" Brex didn't know what to do. Could Shani be pulled to her feet or did her ankle need to be tended to first? Brex's hands bounced back and forth before touching anything.

"No, my ankle...something grabbed onto it and—"

Brex quickly understood what she meant when something rough and flexible wrapped around Brex's ankle and swept her off her feet.

"Ow!" The snake-like skin loosened around Brex's ripped jeans, but when she opened her eyes, the snake tail was attached to much more than just a small head.

"What—?" Shani whispered.

Before them stood a tall man with a stronger-than-average build. His threatening posture and demonic facial muscles froze their tongues, and the round horns that wrapped around his ears made their throats twist in knots.

"There are more of Zara?" Brex asked, but Shani straightened her head, popped up to her feet, and pulled Brex by her forearm instead of answering.

"Come on!" Shani screamed. But whoever this man was, whatever kind of dracotaur he was, his tail was longer and stronger than any other creature they had met, and his fire traveled farther.

"Ah!" Shani's jacket caught on fire. She flipped around and ran backwards before she caught sight of a wave of multicolor flames that was so long and bright, it almost melted Shani's corneas.

Brex pushed Shani out of the way and splashed the wave of flames with her own fire and bounced the threat away from them.

"Brex, no!" Shani screamed. She couldn't see Brex's scar, but she didn't need to. Shani could see the power draining from Brex. Her eyes darkened with deep shadows, almost as if the day were turning to dusk. "Brex, stop!" But she wouldn't listen.

"Shani, go!"

"No!"

"Shani, go look for Lucifer!"

There was no water. Not a drop in sight. She had nothing to command, no power, no weapon. Shani was powerless, and Brex was right. Shani took one last glance at Brex. Her skin had never looked so pale and dry, despite the sweat dripping from her forehead. But Shani skated across the graveyard anyway.

Brex held her stance and clenched her shoulders with so much tension, her muscles almost ripped open like a zipper. Her eyes swelled the longer her fire blazed, or maybe this dracotaur's fire was a few hundred degrees hotter than hers. But she couldn't dwell on it. Her sight was failing, and worse, the skin on her hands was starting to tingle. For the first time in almost a year, the heat was starting to bother her.

"Brex! Duck!" Asher yelled from above. She couldn't see where he was, but she could feel him getting closer.

Duck? Brex thought. *Duck from what?* But she did as she was told.

The wall that bound the two clashing force fields of fire stayed strong when Brex jolted her head down, so Asher could rip the dracotaur off the ground, letting his lethal fire spiral out of control.

"Fuck!"

It wasn't the fire that threw Brex off balance and rolled her over and into a tomb. It was the rush of wind that struck her in the face and wiped away any strength she had left.

For the first time that day, she was still, but the sound of Asher struggling to not be strangled by a thirty-foot-long tail, which was denser and stronger than a python, forced her to dig her elbows into the ground and fight to stand up again.

She didn't have a plan, but it was two against one. Asher's knuckles were already dripping with blood, but the claws and punches only increased. The dracotaur had his tail, but Asher had his wings. A mixture of blood and dirt dimmed the bright white color of his feathers. Sand clouded Brex's ability to see the dracotaur strangling Asher while Asher was trying to rip the dracotaur's wrists out of their sockets. Brex could hear a buzz, but it only pulled her towards the menacing danger, until something else was pulled in faster.

Hissssss...

Where was it coming from? The layer of noise piled on top of the buzzing sound already ringing in Brex's ear, but it was growing more powerful and vibrant. A few feet away from the dracotaur that was slowly pulling the life out of Asher, Brex saw, through her foggy eyes, a sliver of white jump up to the dracotaur's neck and pierce his skin so deeply, his dark red blood exploded and smothered his blue and gray coat.

"Asher!" Brex couldn't miss the bright white wings that were now splattered with blood falling to the ground as Bai transformed back into her womanly body to catch the dying body of the dracotaur.

"It's you..." said Bai. Her brows furrowed and her face drained of any happiness.

"What have you done with her?" the dracotaur gurgled.

"More than you ever did. It is my honor to be the last face you'll ever see."

The dracotaur inhaled one last shallow breath before his head turned to the side, and his eyes stayed open as the last bit of life drifted out of his body.

Brex crouched down and picked up Asher before he rubbed his neck and sat up by himself.

"Asher!" said Shani, running over to them. She slid across the sand before gracefully stopping just fast enough to accidentally brush against Asher's sore arm. "Are you okay?"

"I'm fine, I just might need a neck brace," he replied. "What happened with this guy?"

"One of the few things that can kill them," said Bai. "My venom is rare."

"Who is he?" Shani asked.

"Zara's father."

"I didn't know there were more of them," said Brex.

"You will soon enough," Bai said.

"Okay, well, Asher, get up," said Shani. "I found something."

Asher grabbed Brex's forearm to pull his bloody body up. He hopped on one leg until the pain was ignorable.

"What is it?" Brex asked, running and following Shani's zig-zag.

"Right here," Shani responded, pointing to a barren patch of dirt no bigger than the size of a king mattress. The sun was finally rising, but they still couldn't see what Shani could be pointing to.

"What are we looking at?" Asher asked, bending over and dramatically squinting.

"The shoe prints," said Shani. She was right. Not an inch of the small area of barren sand wasn't smothered in the dracotaur's footprints. They only knew the footprints belonged to the dracotaur because of their immense size and the pointed-toe prints.

"This is where Lucifer is buried," said Brex. "Why else would the dracotaur be standing here all day long?"

"Shani," said Asher, "you're amazing. But where exactly do you mean?"

Before them was a small tomb that didn't look as if it were big enough to hold a human-sized body, but they examined the stone coffin nonetheless.

"This looks kind of small, don't you think?" Shani asked.

"Could it be a different one of these tombs?" Asher asked.

"Wait," said Lexi, noticing something odd about the crevice that separated the tomb from the sandy ground. "I think he's underneath."

"Alright," said Asher. "Push on three?"

Shani nodded before she recited, "One, two—"

BOOM!

Bai took care of it for them. Her jaw tightened as she flipped the tomb up and over and her long, elegant robe blew in the shock wave.

"Cool," Asher enunciated.

Below the tomb was a wooden cache that was enmeshed with chains, snakes, and insects. The chipped wood sagged into the earth, and in between the cracks was a faint green light that was so close, they could almost feel the power seeping back into their scars.

*****

Baymour's back was getting boney, but Lexi held on tight anyway. Jethro sat behind her while Zara sat in front, guiding them to the Tower, now only a few yards away.

"Right up here," said Zara. "The lightning is dispersing. The stronger it is, the easier the transition will be. We have to hurry."

Lexi and Jethro slid off Baymour's back and ran to the locked glass entrance while Zara caressed Baymour's face and said, "Be on the lookout, alright, Baymour?" He grunted with his staggered, black smile and grimy teeth.

"Hold up," said Jethro, slicing open the glass with his bare, glowing hands. "After you." And Lexi stepped through the cracked hole.

The building was so tall from the ground, it looked like it was about to fall over. Lexi couldn't help but imagine the chaos that could follow the destruction of Moloch's plan. But the second the three of them stepped into the elevator, she wiped her head clean of anything but the destruction of Moloch himself.

"Come on, come on," Jethro mumbled. His hands were still bloody, and Lexi could barely see his lips move, but she held onto his bloody hand anyway. She didn't need to say anything, but Jethro could only hope Lexi felt the protection embalmed in her that he did.

The elevator door opened to the rooftop. They stepped out as Zara whipped her hair out of her face and said, "Let's go."

*****

"Stay calm," said Kali, gently wiping the sweat from Logan's forehead as his back was to the ground with his hands tied behind him. "It'll be over before you know it. It won't feel any worse than a good, old-fashioned paper cut."

"Who's going to pour the lemon juice?" Logan asked. "You or Moloch?"

"If you sit still, lemon juice will be the worst you'll have to face."

Moloch looked over the Tower. That one, 360-degree, stunning view was only a small fraction of the world that he was going to be able to stay in forever. No one would be able to make him leave. It was all his. Every rush of wind, every drop of the ocean.

"How much longer?" Reymid asked, looking over to Moloch.

"Soon," Clement responded. "Don't disturb him."

"Ready?" Kali asked Logan, still wrapped up in his tight, enchanted rope.

"Whatever you say, Kali. It won't last."

"I can leave you in this rope for as long as I need to, so I wouldn't be too sure about that, Logan."

Kali's nerves shivered as the blade slithered out of her wrist. It was like she was discovering her ability all over again, or as if she were manifesting her powers for the last time. The blade slowly made its way down to Logan's cold, shivering forearm. The blade was colder, but Kali was interrupted before she could pierce through his rough skin.

BOOOOM!

The sound of the door blasting open echoed throughout the sky. Zara was the first one to jump out onto the roof with Lexi and Jethro on either side of her. Reymid wasted no time in firing arrow after arrow straight at their foreheads, but he didn't hit a single one. Staying still, Jethro held a force field so smooth and clear, it could have been easily mistaken for glass.

"I wouldn't bother if I were you," said Zara. "Logan, don't move a muscle."

24:

"Quiet."

On top of the Tower, the night sky stood like a blank canvas with bright white paint splattered onto the already breathtaking artwork. There wasn't much to see from Lexi's point of view. It was almost calm, but Lexi refused to be fooled. There might have only been a few people standing in the way of her and the peace of the universe, but instead of putting up a shield, she used it to her advantage.

"Zara," Moloch whispered, showing his bright, white teeth. "I remember you."

"You should feel lucky," she replied.

"Guys, no," said Logan, still tied up and staying as stiff as a doorknob. "Please, no. They'll kill her. They'll kill Brex!"

"Then stay still," said Lexi.

Logan lay there as still as a rock that gently vibrated against the pavement when a car drove by.

"Is she safe?" he asked with glossy eyes and a clenched jaw.

"Yes, of course."

Logan couldn't see them, but behind him was an unconscious Krina with her hands tied behind her back and duct tape over her eyes. She lay there in the middle of the kiddie-sized pool that Kali had made with her glossy and polished metal. The outer edges stood in a perfect circle that kept the water at a cool temperature even though two unconscious bodies lay there next to Logan. Accompanying Krina in the pool was Maya. Also tied up, but with less restraint than Krina. She didn't need it. Not with Clement standing over them, pouring every last teardrop of Persephone's flower into the pool of Hell.

"K—Krina?" Jethro stuttered. "Krina?" His chest collapsed. His knees almost did too, but he caught his breath before he was completely ripped apart.

"I would advise against this," said Moloch, crunching the dirt underneath his feet with every step he took towards her. "Your people are powerful."

"You'd be surprised how many have turned on you. I know not everyone is salvageable, but that doesn't mean we can't stop you," said Zara.

"Maybe." His posture remained pure and strong. "But that would only be true if you weren't too late."

In the center of the rooftop stood the trident with one stone hanging in the middle. The other was still wrapped around Maya's neck. It stood in the center of the pool. Once Lexi stepped closer to the pool, she could see the bubbling green lava that smelled worse than the first time she stood near it. It was the liquid from the Underworld of Hades.

No, Lexi thought. How was she going to pull them out? This substance called to the mystical congregation. How could she fight against it?

Clement stood next to the pool, ready to stir the blood with the long, unbreakable staff of Moses. Lexi stood with more false confidence than before. She was a quarter of his size.

"Go," Zara whispered.

Jethro let down his shield and let the energy explode like a bomb. Lexi's cut vine wrapped around her arms before she bolted to Reymid and pulled his feet out from under him. His head slapped against the edge of the railing. Lexi used all of her strength to pull him in. He rolled in towards her, and she grabbed onto his bow only to throw it over the railing and off the Iconic Tower.

"No!" He grabbed onto Lexi's ankle, but Lexi's reflexes were faster. She grabbed him by the neck and immediately cut off his circulation and air.

"If you ever touch Asher ever again, I'll throw more than just your bow off the roof. Then again, I might just do it anyway. We'll just have to wait and see." She reached for one of his few remaining arrows, broke it in half, and stabbed him on either side of his torso.

"Ahhhhh!" His clothes were too dark to see the blood creating a pool in the creased leather, but once she pushed him over onto his side to push the arrows deeper into his skin, she could feel the blood lotioning her sweating hands.

Jethro sprang towards Krina. Clement waited for him, behind his own shield of protection that bounced Jethro off, almost cracking his head open.

"No! Krina!"

Her head began to subtly move from side to side. With all the commotion, Clement didn't notice. He stood there, still with potential energy that was waiting to explode.

Zara jumped over to Moloch to tackle him to the ground, but her strength was too much for the old, metal rail that was supposed to keep them from falling over the ledge.

Crack!

The rail snapped off the edge, and the two beings fell to the earth, increasing their speed with every second.

Lexi kicked Reymid to the side only to have Kali ready her knife behind Lexi, thinking she wasn't going to see it coming. Kali's quick instincts told her the aim was perfect. Just a few feet away. That's all she needed. The minimal lighting was perfect, but it still wasn't enough. Lexi was faster.

"Huuh!" Lexi didn't duck, she barely flinched. The strongest part of her now-aging vine whipped the spinning blade back into the hands of Kali. Lexi still wasn't in possession of a weapon that matched the peril of a sharp edge that could puncture a stone at the right angle, but she didn't care. Her ridged boots dug into the cement floor before she threw herself against Kali's guarded body.

Kali held her dagger straight in front, ready to strike again, but Lexi could see the pattern forming faster than Kali herself did. Lexi grabbed Kali's forearm and twisted it out of its socket.

"Ahh!" Kali screamed, but Lexi head-butted her before she could scream again.

"Hold on!" Jethro screamed to Maya and Krina. Maya's eyes were faintly awakening, but the sound of Jethro banging on the shield wasn't making her wake up any faster.

"Jeth—" Krina mumbled. But she quickly stopped when she caught a glimpse of Clement's back.

"Krina!" Jethro could see how red his fists were getting, even under the misty sky, but he wasn't slowing down no matter how devious Clement's eyes were. The force field was too strong, even for Jethro, but the tall shadow creeping up behind Clement was something stronger.

"Ah!" When Krina jumped from the pool, she was her normal, tall, white-haired self, but when her jagged teeth plunged into Clement's arms, she was an untamed lioness that hadn't eaten in days.

"Bitch!"

As blood seeped down his white shirt, the spell finally broke. Lexi whipped her vine against the melting force field. Krina pulled Maya out of the pool just in time to see Kali pull herself up with only a few drops of blood running down her bumpy face.

"I'm disappointed, Jethro," said Kali, walking up to him with two long, serrated swords, one in each hand. "You need others to fight your battles? Aren't you tired of that? Your skills aren't living up to your reputation. I can change that."

"No you can't," he snapped, pulling out two basketball-sized force fields that circled around his wrists, sprinkling sparks of light around the colorful sphere.

"Don't do this, Jethro." Kali's voice deepened, deadly calm. Jethro didn't answer. His chest raged with fiery angst that smothered his face in red. His force fields expanded as well as his speed. The dry surface underneath his feet gripped his leathery shoes as he ran to Kali, head first. His right arm pulled back, ready to strike, but Kali was one step ahead of him. Her blade sliced through Jethro's wrist before her other sword plunged straight into his neck.

"NOOOOOOO!" Krina felt something pop in her throat, but the pain only spread to the rest of her body and soul. Jethro was dead before he fell into Krina's arms. "No, Jethro. Please, no." The tips of her white hair gently brushed against his soft cheek. She pulled him in tight. Naturally, his eyes closed, but she begged to see them one last time.

"I gave him a chance," said Kali, standing over them. "I gave him multiple chances."

Krina's tears mixed with Jethro's blood. She only wished she could have been the last face that he'd seen instead of Kali's, or that she could hear him say one last thing before he was given, as Kali put it, his last chance.

"I'm so sorry." She gently kissed his forehead before she turned to Kali with blood rushing through her veins and said, "You're going to die."

"No," said Kali, crouching down and grabbing onto Krina's forearm. "That's what I'm trying to get through your thick fucking skulls. He didn't have to die, and neither will you. I will save you! I'm saving every last hopeless, pathetic child that doesn't deserve what I'm doing for them. Just shut up, so we can finish!"

Krina was too close to see Kali coax a small blade into her grip and pull Krina in just enough to slice the blade into the back of her shoulder.

"Ahhh!" The pain wasn't what Krina thought. Her scream didn't compare to her scream seconds before. The longer the minor pain lasted, the more it distracted her.

Lexi's eyes were dry from her empty stare. There was hate in Lexi's heart that she didn't recognize. It held still in her soul like a rock as she saw the blood continue to drain from Jethro's body. The adrenaline was already pounding through her. It was just enough for Lexi to push Clement off her with enough time to snap her vines around Kali's neck, but Kali quickly sliced them off. That didn't stop Krina from ripping the blade from her flesh and thrusting Kali to the edge where they could see Moloch and Zara fighting hand to hand. Blusterous wind and scorching heat bounced between them. Zara rounded up a ring of fire before Moloch smothered it with his hands.

"Your father would be proud to see what you've grown into," said Moloch. "I don't want to take that away from him, so I'm not going to. But I promise you, once this is finished. We will leave you be. You'll be no threat to us anymore."

"You are not Hades," said Zara. "You don't have the authority to control that. It's not your decision." She clapped her hands together to create a wave of pressure that threw him back, but only by a few feet. "We will stop you. One way or another."

"I don't think you understand how close we are to finishing this." Moloch lunged forward to light a circle of thirty-foot flames with Zara as the centerpiece. She was trapped in the only fire that was poisonous to her.

"I meant what I said," said Moloch, with his hands still smoking. "After this transformation is complete, we will leave you be. No harm will come to you or the others, but if you try to interfere any further, I would be more worried about my army than me."

"So, even after this is done, you're saying there is a way to reverse this?"

"Not without the sacrifice you won't be willing to make." Moloch's crooked smile wrinkled his dark skin. "We'll talk later." Moloch jumped back up the Tower to fly along the side of the building. Zara followed his inflamed coat, soaring above her head. She patiently waited for the fire to die down, just by a few inches to jump out. Moloch's fire was the only fire that could ever harm her.

Come on, come on! Zara thought to herself.

Woooooosh! She couldn't wait. She blew the fire away, but it was thick and fighting against her.

Woooooosh!

"Quiet," she told herself. "Quiet." She listened. Her breath was calm, and before her eyes, a storm spiraled.

Woooooosh!

A few inches of space opened, and she leaped out to tumble across the pavement, but with no rest in between, she jumped on the side of the Tower, metal digging into her palms, and began to climb faster than she knew she could. The more she climbed the more screeching voices she could hear blending together, coming from the edge of the Tower's roof.

"Like I said, Kali," Krina whispered, close to Kali's face, with a tight grip around her neck. "You're going to die. I wish I could promise that

I'm going to be the one to kill you, but I guess that not knowing makes it all more exciting."

Kali subtly squirmed enough to hoist one leg up and kick her sandy boots into Krina's stomach, but Krina didn't go far. She jumped back, landing on her feet, ignoring the blood dripping down her back.

"What is it that you want, Krina?" Kali asked. "Name it, and it can be arranged." Kali whipped out another blade, but it was longer this time. "I don't want to have to hurt another one of you. So, I will give you what you want if you stand down."

Krina's breath deepened. She couldn't tell if it was from anger, or the loss of blood, but she couldn't answer even if she wanted to. That didn't stop her from leaping forward, kicking the dirt behind her, ready for Kali's blades. But instead of gripping Kali by her throat, Krina's blood-soaked palms landed on the metal edge of the tower. Kali had dodged her attack. Then, Krina heard the sound of a tightening vine pulling someone off their feet.

"Ah!" Kali almost hit her head as Lexi lassoed her, but she was strong. The vines quickly loosened. Krina fought to move, scream, react, anything, but she didn't need to. Lexi's knee jolted into Kali's stomach.

"Get off me!" Kali shouted, trying to push Lexi off her, but Lexi's anger overpowered anything Kali could feel.

Lexi's fists gripped Kali's wrists. If there wasn't so much iron boiling in her blood, Kali's hands might have turned purple.

"Stop fighting me!" Kali screamed. Her arms trembled, but her heart pumped faster. With every beat was an inch of gain on Lexi. The veins in Kali's arms were visible even through her tight, black sleeves. Lexi's adrenaline was strong, but Kali had a hundred years on her.

Lexi didn't see Kali's arm escape from her grip, but Lexi blinked before Kali's arm circled down to Lexi's stomach and stabbed Lexi on the side of her abdomen.

"Ahhh!" Lexi screamed. It was just a flesh wound. Lexi wasn't sure how she could tell, but she could. That didn't help the pain, and the cut was deep. It wouldn't be easy to heal without Asher's blue blood.

"I told you to stop fighting me, Alexandra."

"You won't win," said Lexi, pressing as hard as she could into her wound.

"Then Jethro died for nothing."

A clap of thunder erupted. Lexi pulled back just enough for Kali to strike her in the stomach with her boot. Lexi tumbled to the ground, but didn't go far.

"Clement!" Kali screamed. "Open it!"

His slow nod led to his fist punching through the shield protecting the pool. It quickly dissolved and crumbled to the ground before Clement threw the staff to Kali.

Her aching hands wrapped around the smooth wood while the other hand pulled out one more blade to complete the night.

"Stay still," Kali whispered in Logan's ear. "Moloch!"

Lexi thought her heart would beat out of her chest, but after a moment, she couldn't feel it. She couldn't feel anything.

Moloch returned to the roof and stepped back over the edge. He reached his long and strong arm up to the sky, keeping his eye on his golden treasures. Lexi looked to the starry night to see a navy blue light pulsing with pressure. Something was about to erupt.

"Thank you, Logan," Kali whispered once again.

Lexi charged forward, but the second her hips left the cold rooftop floor, Kali sliced open Logan's arm to watch the blood pour out faster than a faucet.

"Ahhhh!" Logan screamed. It was only a few spoonfuls of blood, but no matter how hard he tried, he couldn't fight.

The moment the blood made its first drip into the pool, Moloch's bolt of lightning met the tip of Poseidon's trident. Finishing climbing the tower, Zara pulled herself onto the roof as she was blinded by the bright, flashing light.

"No!" Zara screamed as she held herself on the side of the building with a kaleidoscope of colors bouncing off each other in the echoing night sky.

*****

"Ah!" Brex sliced her hand open, pulling at the bolted chains, opening the sandy coffin.

"Let me try," said Bai. It wasn't as easy as lifting the tomb, but after a few pulls, the chains snapped. Asher jumped to break open the aging wood. Whatever was under there was covered in so much dust he wasn't sure it was a body, but the green light grew stronger and brighter the closer they got.

"It's him...Lucifer," said Bai. She violently brushed him off. His facial hair was still intact. His arms wrapped across his chest.

"Do you think we have to touch him to recharge?" Brex asked.

Brex, Shani, and Asher leaned in to touch him. They didn't expect so much pressure to plow through their arms and into their chests, but when they retrieved and checked, their scars had circled all the way back to the middle finger, recharging their magic fully.

"Perfect. We'll be okay. Now we just have to get to the other—" But Brex was interrupted. A clicking sound hovered over the back of her neck. The enchanted iron that Kali wrapped around Brex's neck dropped to the floor and slowly bounced. Brex grabbed her neck with one hand and her pulsing heart with the other. "It's done."

Epilogue:

June 30th, 2018

"Breaking news. We come to you live now. It's been almost three weeks since we've started getting reports about biological clocks coming to an end. Many farmers have reported zero chickens have been hatching eggs. Yes, you heard that right. There's no exaggeration there. No decrease in eggs, just flat out zero..."

"A woman in Dallas, Texas was due to have her baby son almost three weeks ago. Two weeks ago, her water broke, but nothing seems to have changed. No more increase in her dilation, but luckily she is in no pain. All she wants is to bring her baby boy into the world..."

"Three weeks ago, a seventy-nine-year-old man was supposed to be cut off life support after he was declared brain dead, but by a miracle, the moment he was taken off his support, his heart kept beating. Now he isn't awake, and doctors don't predict he will wake up, but his family isn't certain what they should do..."

"Greenhouses haven't been able to grow their produce. Plants apparently all over the world have stopped growing. Scientists have guessed that the only reasonable explanation is another pandemic, similar to the 1918 flu. But this still wouldn't explain other events around the globe..."

Acknowledgments:

Two down...one to go! Are you ready? I'm certainly not, but enough about me. *The Stones of Souls* is one of my proudest works of art. I hope you are enjoying the ride so far. Soon it will be over, but that is the best time to go back and read it all again.

I need to start by thanking you, as always. You have good taste. You know that? I want to remind you that finishing a book like this is a TASK. So you are incredible just for finishing it. Welcome to my brain. Good luck getting out.

Next, I'd like to thank my dad for editing my, now, fifth book. Can't wait for you to retire so I can boss you around even more. Thanks to my stepdad, Dan for designing another cover for me. Can't wait for the third. Thanks to my sister, Taryn for maybe picking up another one of my books in the distant future, but who knows? And thanks to the rest of my family for bragging about me to strangers. I'll send you checks in the mail later.

And finally, thanks, once again, to my babies. Lexi, Logan, Asher, Shani, and Brex. You will always be my children. Especially because you're not real so you will stay forever young. I can't wait to close this chapter with all five of you next year when we wrap up this trilogy. Strap in. It's gonna be a wild ride.

www.ingramcontent.com/pod-product-compliance
Lightning Source LLC
LaVergne TN
LVHW091106080826
845145LV00008B/1831